COLD
FEAR

Toni Anderson

Cold Fear
Copyright © 2015 Toni Anderson
Cover design by Syd Gill / Syd Gill Designs

Print ISBN-13: 978-0-9939089-7-2
Digital ISBN-13: 978-0-9939089-6-5

For more information on Toni Anderson's books, sign up for the newsletter on her website: http://www.toniandersonauthor.com

Also by Toni Anderson

COLD JUSTICE SERIES
Cold Fear (Book #4)
Cold Justice Series Box Set. Volume 1 (Books 1-3)
Cold Light of Day (Book #3)
Cold Pursuit (Book #2)
A Cold Dark Place (Book #1)

THE BARKLEY SOUND SERIES
Dark Waters (Book #2)
Dangerous Waters (Book #1)

STAND-ALONE TITLES
The Killing Game
Edge of Survival
Storm Warning
Sea of Suspicion

'HER' ROMANTIC SUSPENSE SERIES
Her~ Romantic Suspense Box Set. (Books 1-3)
Her Risk To Take (Novella ~ Book #3)
Her Last Chance (Book #2)
Her Sanctuary (Book #1)

For Mom,
My inspiration.

CHAPTER ONE

Helena Cromwell allowed herself to be dragged toward the top of the tallest dune that edged the northern tip of Crane Island.

"Where are we going?" she demanded.

"You'll see. Come on, scaredy cat." Jesse Tyson, high school quarterback and her crush of the last six months, had to shout to be heard over the noise of the storm.

"It's too dark to *see* anything." That was a lie. It was pitch black, but her eyes had adjusted to the night and the full moon provided short blasts of silvery light that lit up the world whenever the clouds parted for more than a few seconds.

A shadow moved in the periphery of her vision, and she whipped her head around, jerking to a stop.

"Did you see something?" she yelled.

Jesse tried to pull her forward, but she dug in her heels. Was someone out there? A shiver tip-tapped down her spine. She peered hard into the night, but when the moon reappeared there was only blowing sand and violently lashing grass.

"There's no one there. Come on, Helena," Jesse insisted.

Of course there was no one there. It must have been a trick of the light, or the storm making her nerves dance like Mexican jumping beans. She let Jesse drag her another few steps. No one else would be crazy enough to be out here in this weather, especially on New Year's Eve—she rolled her eyes. This was a stupid idea, and if her dad found out she was here, or that she'd lied about being at Kit's tonight, he'd kill her.

"Where's your sense of adventure?" Jesse taunted.

"Same place yours is gonna be if our parents find out where we are and what we're doing," she grumbled.

"We haven't done anything, yet." Jesse's dark eyes glistened in the darkness.

Her heart gave a little flutter, and she swallowed hard. *Oh, my*. And that was why she was out on the dunes even though she knew better.

The fact they'd both been drinking alcohol wouldn't go over well, either. Not that her dad was ever going to find out. He'd ground her for a year, and it wasn't just because she'd lied about where she was going, or was out with a boy. No one was supposed to be on the dunes at Parson's Point. Her dad worked for Land Management at the Department of Natural Resources and took this kind of trespassing very seriously. The area was part of a stabilization experiment they were conducting to try and protect the Outer Banks from further erosion.

She knew the spiel by heart. If he found out it wouldn't matter that she was his daughter, in fact, that would make the punishment worse.

The hand that pulled her along was confident and strong, not allowing her to balk or change her mind. She started to slip backward in the loose sand, but Jesse grasped her tighter and hauled her with him. She couldn't help but be impressed by all those gorgeous muscles.

Together they staggered over the top of the beach ridge and slid down the other side, sand flying in every direction. She squealed with fright when they stumbled to their knees in the valley between dunes. Then she started giggling hysterically.

"Idiot." She shoved his arm.

Jesse took both her hands in his, and she could feel him staring at her in the darkness. For a moment she thought he was going to kiss her but instead he flashed her a grin—the one that had all the girls in high school swooning—and pulled her to her feet. They climbed up the next, shorter dune and landed near the top, lying side-by-side in the sand. Something dug into her thigh, and she shifted away from it, closer to Jesse.

The wind howled, and she shivered.

"You cold?"

It was now officially January and blowing a frickin' gale. "A little."

Jesse shrugged out of his down jacket and wrapped it around her shoulders.

"What about you?" she asked, even though she was grateful for the body heat still trapped inside the fabric.

"I'm fine." Wide shoulders brushed hers as he shrugged. Eighteen years old and a star athlete, he wore a red plaid shirt over a bright white t-shirt and jeans. "I dragged you out here. I don't want you to die of exposure before I even steal a kiss."

Helena shot him a sideways look. Over the last few months she'd caught him staring at her a few times, but he'd been dating someone from the mainland. The girl had finally broken it off with him on social media—*be-otch*—and just before Christmas, he'd asked Helena to go with him to the New Year's Eve party his friend was hosting. She'd been both thrilled and nervous the entire Christmas break. Now she was here. Squeezed up tight against him and him talking about kisses. Her cheeks bloomed with heat, and she wanted to fan herself, but didn't dare lest he think she was a total dork.

She was a total dork.

Jesse reached out in front of them and parted the sharp blades of grass that blocked their view, revealing an endless swath of beach, and miles and miles of crashing waves.

God, it was beautiful. And so was he.

The ocean merged with the sky in a black abyss. The occasional flash of a lighthouse beacon cut through the otherwise impenetrable gloom. Jesse wrapped his right arm across her back, his hand hooking her waist and pulling her closer. Helena's mouth went as dry as the sand she lay in. Attraction mixed with the two tequila shots she'd downed at the party before he'd dragged her out here. Her nerves sizzled. All she could think of was his hand on her waist, his hard body pressed snug against hers.

Would he try to kiss her? Would she let him? How far would she let him go? She squeezed her thighs together, a little shocked that she was even thinking about making out with Jesse Tyson.

She'd never had a boyfriend, unless you counted holding hands in third grade. She wasn't one of the "popular" girls in school. Jesse made her nervous because she liked him and didn't want to look like an idiot for going out with the best looking guy in school.

Why had he asked her out? Was it a dare? She wasn't that pretty. Her best friend Kit was way prettier than she was, and smarter. Did Jesse think she was easy? Is that why he'd brought her out here? She frowned.

She pushed the uncertainty away. Kit kept telling her she was beautiful and to relax and enjoy herself, to have a little faith. Maybe she should actually listen to her friend for a change.

Helena's breath caught as a twenty-foot wave smashed onto the beach, and made the gulls cry out stridently as they fled to safety. Storms made her nervous. She'd grown up with them, but feared the sea was going to wash away her house and drown them all in their sleep. That's what happened when your dad spouted environmental doom and gloom at every mealtime.

They'd been lucky this time. The storm had skirted the Carolinas and was headed toward Maine and Newfoundland. There was another one on the horizon, but it was that time of year. Jesse's warm hand slipped a little lower on her waist and found the place where her t-shirt met her jeans. His fingers played beneath her waistband as if looking for bare skin.

How had this happened? *Her.* On a date with the high school quarterback?

"What do you think?" He had to shout to be heard over the howling gale and the fierce roar of the ocean. Hardly romantic, but his laughter was so infectious it took a moment to realize he was talking about the storm, not being with him.

"It's terrifying," she admitted with a grin. "But," she watched another wave pile-drive the shore. "It's also thrilling—exhilarating. There's an energy to it…"

"I know, right?" The arm tightened on her waist. "It's as if there's electricity sparking through the air. The sea is so rough you know if it caught you you'd never get out alive."

"And that excites you?" Maybe the guy was nuts. Maybe that's why he asked her out.

"The power of it." He looked at her then. Leaned closer so their lips were only an inch apart. "You know what really excites me?"

She raised an unimpressed brow that he probably couldn't see in the dark. If he gave her a cheesy line she was out of here.

"Kite boarding." His warm breath brushed against her lips—then he kissed her.

The wind wailed spookily above them, but she didn't notice the weather anymore. Her heart banged her ribs like a hollow drum. Jesse turned her so they were facing one another and took her face gently between his hands. Then he kissed her again, not overly confident, but his lips were firm, warm, not wet or sloppy, feeling their way over her mouth, searching for something.

He tasted very slightly of beer, but also of mint. Curious, tempted, she opened up to him and he took the kiss deeper. Then his tongue touched hers and she jumped.

"Sorry." She grinned as she pulled back.

A weird huffing noise had her turning. She let out a strangled gasp as a dark figure loomed behind them. Terror squeezed her heart so hard, pain spasmed along her arm.

"What the hell?" Jesse yelled.

Before her frozen limbs could react, the figure lifted something over his head and brought it down with ferocious force. It made a horrific sound as it connected with Jesse's head.

"Jesse!" she screamed. She grabbed him by the shirt, but he lay there, heavy and limp. She tried to shove at the attacker's legs, but he was so much bigger than she was. *Run*! She scrambled down the dune, trying to scream for aid, but the man swung the object he held sideways, like an axe, and the flat end of it caught her on the side of the head.

A scream rent the air and she realized, almost surreally, that she was the one screaming. Agony exploded through her brain as she flew to the ground, landing facedown. She heard more strikes—oh God, the man was hitting Jesse over and over, even though he just lay there not moving.

She struggled to her feet and faced their attacker. "Leave him alone!"

The figure turned and looked toward her. Oh, hell. Ignoring the splitting pain and disorientation that made her brain feel disconnected from her feet, she took off running, back the way they'd come. She was lithe and nimble. People underestimated her because she was small, but she was fast. The sand shifted and made progress difficult as she clawed her way up the dune, and it suddenly seemed fifty feet tall. She pounded her feet against the slope, clutching at the sharp grass that sliced her fingers. Then a hand manacled her ankle and she fell flat on her face as she was dragged backwards down the incline. She tried to cry out, but sand got in her eyes and mouth. She was suffocating, spluttering, trying to force away particles from her nose, and just breathe.

Blackness whirled in her brain as the need for oxygen eliminated every other concern. The attacker flipped her on her back, and she lay there hacking and choking. By the time she finally cleared the grit out of her eyes and mouth, the man had dragged Jesse down the bank, too, and was rifling through his pockets. Was this a robbery? Was Jesse breathing? Or was he pretending to be unconscious so he could take this animal by surprise and save them both?

She tried to climb to her feet and froze when the assailant turned back toward her. He stood, easily over six feet. She couldn't see his face, but his silhouette looked vaguely familiar. It was dark and he wore a hat pulled low. He dropped to his knees beside her. Put one gloved hand on her throat and squeezed. She grabbed his forearm and fought for breath. His grip tightened. After a few moments of panicked flailing she froze and he eased off the pressure.

A message.

She swallowed uneasily. Nodded.

Okay.

His other hand went to her belt, and he undid the buckle and jerked open the front of her jeans. Terror made her heart beat faster than she'd ever imagined possible. She lay there in the frigid sand, the storm raging overhead, Jesse lying unconscious, bleeding, maybe even dead, just a few feet away. Her limbs shook. She knew what was going to happen even though her mind screamed 'no'. Her teeth chattered as the man dragged tight denim down her legs. She wanted to struggle, wanted to fight, but instead she lay absolutely frozen as he lifted her hips to remove her clothes. She didn't put up a fight. If she didn't fight, if she lay here, maybe he'd do what he was going to do and then let her go. Because she was a coward. She was weak and scared.

The freezing cold sand hit her bare bottom and thighs, abrading her skin. She'd never been so exposed in her entire life. Never felt so helpless. This is what her parents had been warning her about her entire life—don't go off alone...but she hadn't been alone. Her eyes drifted to where Jesse lay bleeding.

Please don't die.

Finally the cold began to make her feel numb and she welcomed it. Large fingers touched her. Pressing. Probing. Doing whatever they wanted as he made little grunting noises that made her throat muscles gag.

The moon came out and she found herself staring up into a face she knew. Her mouth opened in surprise, but his fingers encircled her throat and squeezed until all sound stopped coming out. She started to slip into unconsciousness.

"What do you see?" he asked, releasing the bruising pressure.

Horror and revulsion filled her until she blocked it all out. She couldn't think about what was happening. About Jesse. About this man. Or the fact he was touching her like this. She wanted to live through it. She wanted to survive.

He kept asking what she could see, but her mind floated away. Her fingers inched through the sand and found Jesse's leg. He was still warm, but she didn't think he was alive. Tears filled her eyes, and she made herself think of running on the beach hand-in-hand with the boy she'd been secretly in love with for months. She dreamed about them sneaking innocent kisses and worrying about what their parents might say.

Her vision began to gray and tunnel as the monster peered right into her eyes as if looking for her very soul. All those years being warned about not talking to strangers, about being careful, about being safe...and all along they'd had a monster in their midst.

CHAPTER TWO

Izzy Campbell threw the ball for her flat-coat retriever and watched it bounce along the hard-packed sand as he raced to catch it. The tide was out. The gusting wind caught the ball and propelled it even faster along the mile long stretch of beach. Barney gave chase at full speed, tongue out, legs straining, breath streaming behind him like smoke. He caught the ball mid-bounce, then without missing a beat, turned and brought it right back to where she stood, silvery strings of drool wrapping around his muzzle.

"Lovely," she said with a grin.

He dropped the thing at her feet and crouched back, ready to play again.

She kicked the ball this time and he was off, thrilled to be outside, uncaring of the ferocious wind or damp spray that whipped off the wild sea. She watched him catch the ball and then lie down in the surf to cool off. As sad as it might be, Barney was her best friend in the world. Who needed a man when they had a dog?

Izzy yawned widely. Meeting a man was the least of her worries. She had a seventeen-year-old to get through high school and into college. As a former captain in the Army she'd learned to take life one Herculean task at a time, while trying to anticipate any of the things that could possibly go wrong. Having a man in her life would complicate an already complicated situation. Not everyone found true love or the perfect happily-ever-after.

That thought had her turning to look at the

undulating dunes at the top of the shore. A wave of regret stole over her. Memories from long ago flashed through her mind like a lightning storm, reminding her of a heartbreaking night of torment and terror. She'd experienced many more since then, too many to dwell on, but this was different. This had been the defining moment of her life, and the only person who'd known about it was dead.

Why did she feel compelled to come back to this strip of coast, time and time again? Punishment? Self-flagellation? Her mouth tightened. Maybe. Or were these islands really home?

They didn't feel like it. She felt like an outsider here. An interloper. A goddamned dingbatter.

What she'd done all those years ago was unforgivable, but at the time she hadn't felt as if she'd had a choice. Age had brought a little wisdom, but her mistakes weren't something she could put right with an apology or a twelve-step program. She'd messed up, and she didn't know how to make it right without ruining more lives, her own included. She turned away. It was ancient history. No one would ever know.

The wind whipped her hair past her cheeks, blinding her for a moment. She faced the sea and gathered the strands together in a long twist, stuffing it back under her hat. She pulled the hat down tight, ignoring the short, sharp tug on her scalp.

Last night while she'd been working, a big Nor'easter had brushed its fingers against the flanks of the Outer Banks but thankfully hadn't delivered a flat-out punch. Another storm was brewing in the Atlantic and promised even more fun, depending on which direction it decided to take.

Storms and hurricanes were a constant danger to these barrier islands. Locals only worried when they had to and, frankly, right now, she was too tired. She'd been up all night, working the graveyard shift at the local hospital. Once Barney had a good walk she'd crash for a few hours before heading back to the hospital for a split shift that evening. She was covering for a few colleagues who'd gone to visit family over the holidays. She hoped her sister remembered not to make too much noise when she got home from Helena's house later, but she wouldn't put money on it.

She whistled to her wet, sandy dog and headed toward the boardwalk that led through the cordoned-off dune system. Up on the road, a Department of Natural Resources vehicle had pulled up behind a burgundy sedan that had been parked there when she arrived earlier. God help the poor soul when Duncan Cromwell got hold of them. The guy was fanatical in his protection of those dunes. Her SUV was another hundred yards south, near the lighthouse. Barney arrived at her side, complete with rancid ball, and she clipped his leash to his collar and strode along the path.

Barney started to whine a few seconds before she heard the sirens.

"It's okay, boy." She rubbed his neck and opened the trunk of her SUV, letting the dog hop in before she turned to see what was going on. An ambulance screeched to a stop behind the DNR rig.

Damn.

As tired as she was, she couldn't ignore the potential that someone might need her help. She got into her car and drove up to the other vehicles.

Parking behind the ambulance, leaving plenty of room for a stretcher.

"Stay, boy." She got out and clambered through the thin wire fence, following the route the EMTs had taken. Dread skated along her nerves when she realized exactly where she was heading. *Too bad, Izzy.* Her muscles burned as she climbed the steep foredune, but she didn't slow down. When she got to the top, the scene below made her flinch. Bile hit her throat but she swallowed it. Slipping her way down the bank, she shouted, "What's the situation?"

Duncan Cromwell had draped his coat over his daughter, Helena, who lay unmoving in the sand at his side. He was attempting mouth-to-mouth.

Izzy pushed him out of the way and probed the girl's neck for a pulse. Helena's skin felt like ice. Her eyes were cloudy, her body slightly stiff, but no sign of lividity. Izzy took a clean tissue from her pocket and brushed it across Helena's cornea. The girl didn't blink. No corneal reflex. Izzy placed her hands over Helena's eyes and held them there for long seconds. When she removed them Helena's pupils showed no reaction to the light.

Dammit.

"Do something!" Cromwell grabbed her upper arm so hard she winced. She twisted out of his grip.

"She's gone, Duncan." Cold fear raced through her mind as she looked at the dead girl. Her sister had been staying with the Cromwells last night. Frantically, she scanned the surrounding area. "Where's Kit?"

"I was going to ask you the same question," Duncan said grimly. "Help me do CPR."

Izzy forced away the tears that wanted to form

and found her professional armor. "Helena's gone, Duncan. There's nothing you can do."

"No." He brushed her away and started once again to try to resuscitate his daughter. She met the gaze of the EMT who she recognized from the hospital, and silent communication passed between them. The guy had lost it and who could blame him. She moved to assess the other victim on the ground, a young man she recognized as Jesse Tyson, the police chief's son. Blood matted his scalp, and his nose looked like it had been smashed. Unlike Helena, he was fully clothed. Beneath the trickles of blood, his skin was the blinding white of alabaster. She touched his neck but couldn't find a pulse. His skin was soft, no sign of rigor. She frowned and pulled back his eyelids. His pupils were clear and responsive. She checked his airway, ripped open his shirt and palpated his chest. No penetrating injuries or bruising. Without proper equipment it was difficult to check for pneumothorax and haemothorax, but she did what she could. She undid his jeans and pressed her fingers into his groin, searching for a femoral pulse. All the time, she watched his chest for any sign that he was breathing.

Did it move? Or was that the wind tugging his shirt?

It was so cold out here, even she was shivering. Then his chest did move, just a fraction, evenly on both sides, she was certain of it. And the faintest pulse of blood stirred against her fingertips. She signaled the EMTs to bring over a stretcher. "He's alive. Make sure his spine is stabilized before you move him. Cover him with all the blankets you've got in the rig." Her brain buzzed as she recalled procedure and treatments for severe hypothermia. "Move him *very* gently because you can induce cardiac dysrhythmia if you jar him—go the long way around the dune." She checked for fractures, but with this level of hypothermia the most important thing was getting the patient to the hospital as quickly and smoothly as possible. She dialed the ER. It was a fifteen-minute drive to the hospital. "You need to prepare for a patient with low GCS, apparent head injuries, and severe hypothermia." They'd treat with warm mattresses, hot air blankets, heated IV fluids—but they had to take things slowly in a highly controlled environment. "He'll need a full CT scan and general blood work. Call Chief Tyson to meet us at the hospital." She hung up.

"What about Helena?" Duncan called out angrily from his knees.

Izzy stared at the guy. Tremors shook his body as he tried to rein in everything he was feeling. His eyes were frantic, skin pulled tight over his features as desperation drove him. Who could blame him?

His daughter was her sister's best friend. Responsibility weighed as heavy as a block of cement around her shoulders. What if she was wrong? What if Helena *could* be saved? She'd heard of miracles happening before, especially when severe hypothermia was involved. People weren't dead until they were warm and dead.

"Let's take her, too." She put her hand on his arm. "But, Duncan, don't get your hopes up."

"Hope is all I've got left." He flung off her touch and snarled before he ran to fetch another stretcher.

She took out her phone and dialed her sister,

each unanswered ring feeding her fear like wind stoking a wildfire. The joints in her fingers ached from her tight grip on the phone. Her jaw felt as if someone had wired the bones together.

"S'up?" Kit answered groggily.

The iron fist on Izzy's throat released, and she sucked in a proper breath. "Oh my God. Are you okay?"

"Yeah. Why?" Kit sounded tired, grumpy, but not upset. She obviously had no idea about Helena.

"Where are you?" she asked.

"Home. I changed my mind and came back here last night. Why?"

She hadn't checked her sister's room when she picked up Barney earlier, but hadn't seen her car. She'd assumed Kit was still out. "I wanted to make sure you were okay." She couldn't tell Kit about Helena over the phone. "Look, I have something to tell you. You need to get dressed. I'll pick you up in ten minutes."

"What? Why?" The grogginess was replaced with wariness.

Izzy couldn't face an argument. "Just do it. I love you." She hung up. She was going to ground her sister until she was eighteen, and possibly for the rest of her life just to keep her safe. Duncan came back over the ridge and began slipping down the banks of his beloved dunes. She shielded her eyes against the spraying sand as he raced toward her. Together they very gently moved Helena onto the stretcher but Izzy didn't hold out much hope for the girl. Her heart wanted to break but she compartmentalized the feeling so she could do her job. They worked their way slowly around the biggest hill. Even though Helena was tiny, Izzy struggled to hold up her end of the stretcher.

"We need to call the cops," she shouted over the blustery wind. Her stomach churned at the thought of what they might find, but Helena's death needed to be investigated. Her attacker had to be found.

"I already called them," said Cromwell.

She nodded, and wished she didn't want to run and hide. She was a coward. She'd always been a damn coward. The coat covering Helena slipped and Izzy saw the girl's naked body. There was blood on her thighs and any thoughts Izzy had about her own problems were obliterated. Then her eyes latched onto a piece of jewelry on Helena's slender wrist. The fine hairs on her arms rose as gooseflesh prickled her skin. "I didn't know Helena wore a medical alert bracelet."

"It isn't hers." Duncan's voice was low and guttural. "She was wearing it when I found her."

Dazed, Izzy marched onward as fast as she could. It couldn't be the same bracelet. It couldn't. But deep inside, Izzy knew it was. Even though it was impossible, someone knew her secret. A killer knew her secret.

***

Lincoln Frazer sat at his desk reading yet another request for assistance, this one regarding a series of rapes occurring in Portland, Oregon. He scanned the details and emailed Darsh Singh to take a look at the case file in time for next Monday's team meeting. It was January 1, but as head of BAU-4, which investigated crimes against adults, there was no time to take a break. A week ago, he'd helped exonerate an innocent man convicted of treason, but between high-level vigilante groups, presidential requests, international terrorism, assassins, agency spies, and miscarriages of justice, he was behind on the day job.

Christmas had been a blur. He hadn't seen his condo in days. He showered and ate at the academy, grateful for the peace and quiet of an almost empty building. With the turn of the New Year he hoped life would return to normal, and he could go back to his nice orderly world tracking down serial offenders.

His landline rang. "Frazer."

"How'd I know you'd be in the office?" Agent Mallory Rooney's voice held a touch of sarcasm.

"It's that razor-sharp intelligence of yours." That and the fact Alex Parker had probably tracked his cell phone. "No wonder I plucked you from obscurity to work for me."

"Sure, boss, *you* plucked me from obscurity." The eye roll that accompanied her droll statement came through loud and clear. He grinned because she couldn't see him.

"Did Parker finish running those background checks on Madeleine Florentine?" Frazer asked before she could speak. The Governor of California was President Hague's first choice as replacement VP, and the man was growing impatient for answers.

"Yep, he finished last night. Florentine checks out"—*Thank, God*—"But that's not why I'm calling. Look," she continued, cutting him off as he opened his mouth to ask why it had taken them this long to contact him. "I got a phone call from an old friend of mine, Agent Lucas Randall out of

Charlotte. He was in charge of the Meacher case?" Frazer checked personnel files online as she spoke. He remembered the guy. "He's been called in on a case along the Outer Banks. Wanted me to go down there to help him out."

Frazer searched the Internet for news stories coming out of that region. "A single victim homicide?" He had a stack of unsolved cases on his desk more than a foot high, not to mention trying to help a certain spook surreptitiously track down the assassin who'd murdered the Vice President last month. All of which required a few more skills than investigating a small-town homicide. "The locals can handle it." He winced at the callousness of his tone. That's what happened when reports of unbelievable depravity crossed your desk every single day.

Rooney ignored him. "Two teens making out on the beach last night were subject to a vicious assault. Both were left for dead, but one miraculously survived. But that's *not* why Randall called me."

Frazer's spine tingled, and he knew he wasn't going to like whatever she said next.

"The female victim was wearing a medical alert bracelet."

"And?" Tension coiled inside him.

"It wasn't hers." He heard the murmur of voices, probably Alex Parker telling Mallory to get off the phone and take a break on a federal holiday. "It belonged to a woman called Beverley Sandal."

"Why do I recognize that name?" He typed it into the Internet. "Damn."

"Yeah. Exactly."

His brain catalogued some of the factors in

play. "Ferris Denker is due to be executed this month."

"I know."

"It could be a copycat trying to get him a last minute reprieve."

"I know."

"This was Hanrahan's first big case—did you know that?" He squeezed his eyes shut. Of course she did. Rooney was as big a workaholic as he was. Goddammit. The conviction was solid. Denker had been transporting the body of a young woman he'd killed when the cops pulled him over on a traffic violation. He'd confessed to a series of murders, though some of the bodies had never been recovered. The conviction was good, but the last thing he or Rooney or Parker needed was investigators digging into his former boss's cases. "I need you to get down there ASAP—"

"I can't."

His spine stiffened. Something was wrong.

Another voice came on the line. "What she failed to mention was she's in the hospital." Alex Parker had taken the phone from Rooney. "She, hmm…" He cleared his throat. "Mal had some minor bleeding last night, and the docs want to keep her in and run more tests. Maybe put her on bed rest for a couple of weeks. You're going to have to do this without us."

Fear jackknifed through Frazer. Rooney was in the first trimester of her pregnancy with the couple's baby. Frazer was usually more cautious with his affection, but his friendship with the rookie agent and damaged assassin had begun under extraordinary circumstances. The connection was strong as tungsten steel, the only thing that would break it was death—a real possibility if anyone discovered their secrets. "Is she all right?" he asked carefully.

"She will be."

Mallory Rooney was the best of them. If anyone could keep her safe it would be Alex Parker, but not even Parker could control a medical emergency. Frazer knew the thoughts going through the man's head. Guilt. Fear, that this was somehow *his* fault. Desperation and panic that he couldn't fix it no matter how badly he wanted to.

Frazer understood because he was feeling them, too. He let out a long breath. "Tell her to take all the time she needs."

"I already did," Parker said tightly.

"Yeah, but tell her *I* said so. She listens to me." He shut down his desktop computer. "I want her fit and healthy for work, even if she has to spend the next nine months in bed. I have some personal leave she can use." And there'd be other agents who'd do the same for a colleague going through a tough time. The FBI was a family. They took care of their own.

Frazer put his arm through his jacket sleeve, closed his laptop, and put it in its case. The thought of Rooney and Parker losing the baby put a rock in his throat and reminded him why it was always best to keep his distance. Too late now. "You should name him after me, you know, considering the circumstances." Circumstances that traced back to a remote woods in the heart of West Virginia and facing down another serial killer.

"Mal wants to name him after my grandfather if he's a boy and after my mother if she's a girl." The controlled tension in Parker's voice told him the guy was terrified.

Frazer felt that lump in his throat grow bigger. Shit. "Keep her safe, Alex. I'll take care of the situation in North Carolina."

"Call me if you need anything. I can work the case from here." Amongst other things, Parker was an expert in cyber security and could run traces in his sleep.

"I intend to."

"Happy New Year, Linc."

"Not yet it isn't."

"No shit." Parker sounded pissed off.

"This is my fault, you know. For wishing things would get back to normal."

"You were hankering after serial killers?"

"Yeah. I must be as aberrant as they are."

"Nah," Parker drawled. "You're way crazier than those fuckers."

A reluctant smile tugged Frazer's lips. "Take care of her for us, Alex." Then he hung up and strode out of his office.

Happy New Year.

***

Ferris Denker watched the cockroach idle its way across the floor. He planted one of his feet and the bug switched direction. He did it again and the roach tried to burrow under the rubber heel of his canvas shoe. Poor misunderstood creature. He picked it up and let it run over his hands. The creature's legs felt sturdy but brittle, its feet grasping the whorls and ridges of his palm.

He turned his hand over and the bug fell to the floor, its thin carapace making a dull clicking noise as it hit. The bug popped back up, and they started their game over. Handel's *Concerti Grossi Op. 6* played on his sound system—a pleasant change from the constant din of Christmas carols that had bounced around the Death Row facility over the last few weeks. He tried not to complain. The guys needed a little enjoyment in this sinkhole of despair.

"Hey, Ferris." A familiar voice hissed from the next cell. Billy Painter. The guy had raped and murdered a young woman and then done the same to her eighty-year-old grandmother.

How the jury had wept.

The kid had been here for the last five years and was on his second appeal.

Ferris walked over to the door. The top half was made of steel bars. "What is it, Billy?"

"You heard from your lawyer yet?"

Billy would have seen if Ferris had received any news, but the fact he asked the question was grounds for his new appeal. Billy's IQ and shoe size were almost exactly the same. The guy might have big feet, but he was still dumb as a rock.

"Nothing yet, Billy." The warrant for his execution sat on his poor excuse for a desk. The warden had served it on Christmas Eve, which he'd thought was a nice touch for a closet sadist. Despite having had years to prepare, knowing he was scheduled to die on January 25 made his knees shake—not that he'd ever admit it. They'd transfer him to Columbia for the execution itself, but the last thing he wanted was to make that final hundred mile journey.

"I'm sorry, man." Billy slouched, leaning on the bars. His expression was pained. "I thought you'd-a heard something by now."

"Thanks, man." Ferris twisted his lips. He had brought this day on himself. He'd confessed too much before his lawyer had turned up. Bragging like a child before he'd gotten a signed deal. The woman in the trunk wasn't even cold when he'd been pulled over for a lousy broken taillight, which he could have talked his way out of if he hadn't been high as a kite. No, the cops had caught him fair and square, and he'd sung like a fucking canary.

But he wasn't planning on dying yet.

Living on Death Row was a miserable existence. Even those who deserved to die didn't deserve to be tortured this way. He'd treated his victims better than the state treated inmates. Sure they begged and screamed for a few hours, but after that he'd put his victims out of their misery fast. He might have delivered cruel and unusual punishment, but it had been swift, unlike the justice system.

Justice?

This was *justice*?

He looked around the unit. Vets suffering PTSD. Men who'd been little more than children when committing crimes. Goaded into it by bad influences and life circumstances. All of them victims in their own right. Men like Billy who barely knew right from wrong and didn't stand a chance if you added drugs or alcohol into the mix.

Death penalty laws were flawed in every which way—the cost, the fact it wasn't a deterrent, the fact innocent men were still being exonerated from Death Rows across the country as old evidence was reexamined.

No.

It was a stupid system. And Ferris detested stupid.

He'd never claimed he was innocent, and he had no chance of pleading a low IQ because last time he'd tested he'd measured one-forty. But he didn't want to die, and he didn't want to spend the rest of his life in this miserable hellhole. "Pray for me, Billy."

The younger man nodded furiously. "We had one miracle this year. I can pray for another."

Ferris grinned. He'd always been faintly amused by the camaraderie of the men inside this unit and yet he felt it too. Ferris felt like he was accepted for who he truly was, not for whom people expected him to be.

That was a gift. He'd had it once before, and he was hoping the power of that relationship held true now.

One of the guards entered the cellblock, probably to take someone out for their hour of fresh air and exercise. Ferris sneered. From one cage to another, and yet every one of them looked forward to getting out of their damned cells. He took a step back and heard a crunch, looked down at the black and green smear of dead cockroach on the concrete floor. Dammit.

He bent over and used a tissue to wipe up the mess. Then he tipped the jar and pulled out another roach. The game was just starting.

CHAPTER THREE

A lighthouse perched on the headland, sea oats whipping the air at its base. White sand met the gunmetal sea with a serrated edge of angry surf. A wooden fence ran parallel to the road, theoretically keeping people out but doing a piss-poor job of it. Frazer easily climbed over the obstacle. This area was cordoned off because National Parks Service, in conjunction with Department of Natural Resources, were trying to stabilize the area with mitigation strategies, but considering they were up against the Atlantic Ocean, they had their work cut out for them.

A bit like trying to stem the tide of evil that crept through humanity with only a few dedicated law enforcement professionals.

A cheery thought.

Frazer took in the barren landscape of this remote barrier island as he climbed the dunes to the crime scene. He'd taken a commercial flight to Norfolk and managed to get a chopper to Elizabeth City and hired a car from there. It was getting late now. Less than a couple of hours left until sunset.

He topped the ridge and scanned the area. It was the perfect location for those who needed privacy to feed a twisted appetite—especially at night during a storm. Screams would be swallowed by the wind; shouts for help snatched away and consumed by the landscape.

It was the perfect place to kill. The perfect place to get rid of a body.

This region was generally considered safe. Low

crime rate. Low density of permanent residents over the winter months. Was it a local? He didn't know yet. People imagined a killer would stick out, but they rarely did, unless they were psychotic. Then they were usually easy to track from the wild eyes and blood trails.

He raised the collar of his FBI windbreaker but it did little to keep out the icy breeze. His navy-blue, fine wool three-piece suit might be sufficient for the office but it wasn't designed for facing down a winter squall. When he'd awoken this morning the last thing he'd expected was a road trip to a windswept island.

Life was full of surprises.

The scene below was textbook how-not-to-preserve-a-crime scene, and he didn't bother disguising a sigh. From what he understood, they didn't even have photographs. At eight AM that morning an officer from the Department of Natural Resources had seen a car parked illegally on the side of the road and gone to investigate. The guy had found the naked body of his own seventeen-year-old daughter and that of a badly beaten young man. He'd tried unsuccessfully to revive his kid. When EMTs arrived they'd rushed both victims to the ER hoping they could be saved. Miraculously, the young man had been. The girl was DOA.

Frazer pushed away his compassion for the man. What was done was done, and nothing he could say would ease his burden. Doing his job might, but that job included viewing the father as a potential suspect.

The father, the EMTs, the cops, and not to mention the weather, had degraded the integrity of the scene, making his job infinitely more difficult.

What remained was churned up sand, a pair of jeans turned inside out, underwear, a t-shirt, socks, a wallet lying open, a down jacket, and a spade. The items had likely been shifted from their original position, but they all needed to be catalogued and entered into the chain of evidence so they could at least be analyzed by forensics and used in court should it come to that.

Frazer's job was to make sure it came to that.

A pewter sky stretched overhead, ominous clouds boiling with suppressed energy. Rain might destroy even more evidence, and they had precious little to start with. Crime scene techs were photographing the area inch by inch. The clothing and the autopsy would hopefully reveal who'd done this to the teens, but it was certainly not Ferris Denker. He sat rotting on Death Row in Ridgeville, South Carolina, four hundred miles away.

Maybe, when Jesse Tyson woke up, he'd name the attacker or attackers, and fast-forward the investigation, getting the perpetrator off the streets before anyone else was hurt. Assuming the kid wasn't in a coma or brain damaged.

Even without seeing the bodies, Frazer could imagine the sort of harrowing experience the teenagers had probably endured. He eyed the girl's clothes. He'd been told there were indications she'd been raped, but he'd know more later, after the autopsy. The kids had been treated like garbage, vessels for the unsub's personal gratification and pleasure. The elements should have killed them, and the bastard had known it.

People called these perpetrators monsters, but they were just humans, humans who did inhuman things. Psychopaths who knew better, and did it anyway.

What would having a live victim do to this unsub?

Frazer narrowed his eyes. They'd need security on the boy until they figured out exactly how, but they could use that. He needed to talk to the teen as soon as he woke up. The attack would leave a mark. What kind of mark depended on the young man himself. At the age of fifteen, Frazer's own world had shattered when his parents had been murdered during a home invasion. He'd never gone back to being the boy he'd been before the incident. If Jesse Tyson were anything like Frazer, the events of last night would shape the entire course of his life.

Was that destiny?

If so, destiny sucked. Frazer relished his job, but he'd swap it in a heartbeat to change the past. He thrust the thoughts away. He rarely thought about his parents' murder. He honored their memory by remembering how they lived not how they died, by catching killers and making sure they couldn't hurt anyone else again.

The sight of the CSU tech picking up a young woman's panties scratched at something small and scarred inside his mind. He pushed it away. Sentiment didn't solve crimes. Logic and meticulous investigation did. The fact dangerous predators often operated in the same passionless state as he did, wasn't lost on him. It wasn't that he didn't feel the emotions; he just tucked them off to one side while he did his job—and did his best never to revisit them.

Emotional objectivity was something he tried to drum into the other agents who worked in his unit, especially his friend, fellow agent Jed Brennan who'd helped him catch his first serial killer amongst the chaos of war in Afghanistan. Bottom line was if they got emotionally involved in all their cases, they'd have to swap their suit jackets for something in white with much longer sleeves.

The faces of victims already kept him awake at night. It was a short trip to burnout and he didn't intend to take that road. He could live with nightmares, he just couldn't deal with heartache.

The cry of a gull jerked him back to the present. Isolated beach. Outer Banks. Day One of a murder investigation. Check.

Another agent approached and Frazer went down to meet him.

FBI Agent Lucas Randall was based out of the Charlotte Field Office and Frazer had met him during the Meacher case. He was ex-military, eyes both sharp and weary. If he was surprised to see the head of BAU-4 standing here he hid it well.

"ASAC Frazer." Randall held out his hand. "Glad you could make it."

"Agent Randall." Frazer nodded as they shook. "Is the bracelet genuine?" The bracelet was the game changer. The reason he was here.

"Looks it." Randall pulled the bag from his pocket and handed it over.

Frazer examined the chain through the clear plastic. Thick stainless steel links and a solid looking tag with a phone number stamped on it. A list of alerts. Sand was encrusted in some of the overlapping links, the hint of rust and decay discoloring the metal. It looked as if it had been in the sand for a long time, but the girl had been killed less than twelve hours ago.

Convicted serial killer Ferris Denker had confessed to murdering Beverley Sandal seventeen years ago. So how the hell had her bracelet ended up on a fresh corpse?

"It was the only thing the victim, Helena Cromwell, had on when they found her. Her father knew it wasn't hers, and the local Chief of Police bagged it. But his son is the kid in intensive care, so he had uniforms secure the scene and CSU work it, then he called me. Girl's body is in the morgue of the local hospital awaiting transportation to the nearest Medical Examiner's Office. "

"You know the chief personally?"

Randall squinted against the slicing wind. "We served together in the Army years ago and stayed in touch." Randall had a reputation for being good at his job and being easy to work with. Whatever people said about Frazer, it wouldn't be that he was easy to work with.

But with Randall's involvement and his connection to Rooney, they'd caught a break in keeping a lid on this situation. Frazer intended to use it.

"I want the ME to come here to conduct the preliminary exam." He frowned. "Actually, tell them I want Simon Pearl to do this personally. Call them. Persuade them. He can call me if he wants to. Also I want blood and tissue taken from the vic, ASAP. Toxicology can look for date rape drugs and alcohol levels."

Randall's brows rose in surprise.

If it weren't for the bracelet, he'd be thinking Helena had probably been killed by someone she knew, or during some sort of drunken gang rape gone horribly wrong—not that gang rape ever went

36

right. He pinched the bridge of his nose trying to relieve the tension headache building. Gang rape would make his life easier compared to the alternative, and that realization made him shut down his feelings and concentrate on the facts. It was twisted. Deal with it. "Any evidence suggesting Ferris Denker ever made it out this way?"

Randall shook his head. "Not as far as I can tell."

At Frazer's questioning look he added. "I asked a friend who works in Columbia to send me a copy of Denker's files. I told him I had a personal interest in the case. The agents working it always assumed Denker never left the mainland."

Assumptions were dangerous. "I'll need a copy of that file." He could go through official channels, hell, he could probably ask Hanrahan for his personal notes on the case, but he wasn't ready to take that step yet. Denker had a date with a hypodermic, and Frazer was going to do everything in his power to get him there on time. "Did you mention Sandal or Denker to the police chief?"

Randall shook his head. "As soon as I ran the numbers on the bracelet I recognized the name and significance. I called Rooney because I knew the BAU would want to be involved."

"You talk to your own boss, yet?"

Randall shook his head, eyes narrowing. "Nope, but I'll have to tell her something soon."

SSA Petra Danbridge was easy on the eyes and hard on everything else. "You opened a case file?"

Randall shook his head. BAU only consulted on cases. They didn't run the show, which put Frazer in a difficult position.

"Hold off as long as you can. Afterward you can tell Danbridge I pulled rank."

Randall's lips twisted. "Isn't that what you're doing?"

"Yes." He stared hard at the other man to see if he had an issue with that.

"Okay, then." Randall nodded and looked relieved. Maybe he had a better idea what was going on than Frazer gave him credit for. Controlling the flow of information and, therefore, controlling the press was vital in this investigation. Randall continued, "Chief Tyson's only been on the Outer Banks for a few years so he wouldn't know if Denker was ever rumored to be here or not. Former chief retired to Roanoke."

"We need to talk to that retired police chief. We need to know if anyone ever reported sightings of Ferris Denker in the Outer Banks."

"What are you thinking?" Randall asked.

Frazer swept his gaze over the area. Remote. Quiet. Undisturbed. The perfect dumping ground. "Denker confessed to killing Beverley Sandal, but her body was never found."

"You think he buried her around here?"

Frazer shrugged. "It might account for her bracelet being found on a fresh victim."

"So where's Beverley's body?" Randall's eyes scanned the dunes, as did Frazer's. Frazer knew where he'd hide a body he didn't want found.

Randall shoved his hands deeper into his jacket pockets and swore. "Someone might have discovered Denker's souvenirs and decided to mess with law enforcement. Denker could be orchestrating this from the inside. Maybe hoping to get the execution stayed while casting doubt on his conviction?"

Frazer nodded. He had no doubt the sadistic psychopath was involved. "But the fact remains, Denker is in prison and a young woman is dead, so regardless of motive, we have a new killer to catch." And not an inexperienced one. Taking two victims at once? Both young and fit? That was not the work of a novice just finding his feet.

The myriad of indentations in the sand, the snaking trails of footprints trampled in every direction meant the chances of finding anything useful out here was unlikely. Except for maybe the shovel. Yellow insulation tape was wrapped around part of the handle in a distinctive pattern. Someone might recognize it, or it might yield DNA or trace.

Frazer started working the case out loud. "Whoever put the bracelet on the girl committed the same sort of murder Denker was convicted of, blitz assault, probably rape, followed by strangulation. But he—or she—left the bodies for us to find, whereas Denker always tried to conceal his victims." It wasn't all Denker had done to the victims.

"Maybe he was interrupted?"

"Maybe," Frazer agreed reluctantly. "Regardless, this unsub wanted to send a message and that message involves Beverley Sandal and Ferris Denker. The timing is too precise to be a coincidence. The crimes are too similar." Frazer handed the evidence back to Randall. "Send this and that shovel to Quantico to be analyzed ASAP. Put my name on the request and tell them it's urgent."

Frazer took photographs of the spade with his cell phone.

"You don't think Denker is innocent, do you?" asked Randall.

"That guy is guiltier than sin."

"You think he had a partner?" Randall's gaze sharpened.

"Or a disciple. We'll know more after the autopsy." Seventeen years ago, Ferris Denker had been convicted of murdering seven young prostitutes and three other young women who hadn't been in high-risk professions. Frazer had no doubt the man had concealed the full extent of his crimes and, having exhausted every appeal, was now orchestrating a game of show-and-tell to eke out more time on this planet. Frazer did not intend to let the man weasel out of his punishment.

His old mentor, SSA Hanrahan, had written the profile that had nailed Denker to the wall, getting details right from his being the eldest child, down to the small size of his boots. Frazer had no doubt the conviction was solid but, after what happened in the West Virginia woods at the beginning of December, the last thing he needed was anyone looking too deeply at Hanrahan's cases.

His former boss had made the mistake of feeding information to a powerful vigilante organization called The Gateway Project that tracked and eliminated pedophiles and serial killers before they entered the justice system. Hanrahan's complicity had been revealed in the presence of a vicious serial killer who'd threatened to bring down not only the vigilante group, but also the BAU. Frazer had killed the man, saving the FBI's reputation, the lives of those involved in The Gateway Project and, not to mention, millions of dollars of taxpayers' money. Since then, he,

Rooney, and Alex Parker, had worked rigorously to make sure The Gateway Project was truly finished, but there was one last loose thread remaining.

Frazer had become a federal agent to protect those who couldn't protect themselves. Legally, what he'd done was wrong—ethically he had few qualms. The serial killer he'd shot dead had stolen a nine-year-old girl from her bedroom and kept her captive for nearly eighteen years. When she'd died, the killer had gone on a murder spree, looking for the perfect replacement. Frazer still saw those women's battered faces in his dreams.

Killing that man had done the world a favor. Under the circumstances Frazer had had no real choice, but the price had been a dark stain on his soul, and the knowledge he wasn't as righteous as he'd once thought. The justice system wasn't always "just." Maybe that's why Hanrahan had fallen off the path of right and wrong, but he'd placed Frazer in an untenable situation.

Art Hanrahan was the reason Frazer had joined the FBI in the first place. To say the older man had disappointed him was an understatement.

With Denker's execution only a few weeks away, the window for this new killer to make an impact was narrow. If this murderer went on a spree to cast doubt on Denker's conviction, then there would be more victims. Frazer pushed it out of his mind. He'd deal with this one victim at a time until he had something solid to work with.

Crime scene investigators were bagging the clothes. He and Randall shielded their eyes from the sand that caught on the wind. Trace evidence was going to be impossible. If the young man in the hospital didn't know anything, their best bet was contact DNA, blood, or semen. Maybe a stray fingerprint on the shovel or the girl's body—assuming they could match a sample.

The sand-sharpened breeze grazed his skin. "Rooney told me you guys were friends as kids. You must be disappointed to see me here instead of her."

"The politically correct answer to that is 'no, sir' 'it's an honor to work with you, sir'." Randall's eyes assessed Frazer's ability to handle the truth. "But honestly, I've known Rooney a long time, and we worked well together in Charlotte. She's a damn good agent." He scanned the horizon. A fishing boat out in Pamlico Sound rode the rocky waters. "I haven't spoken to her in a few weeks. Parker's keeping her on a short leash nowadays."

"Leash?" Frazer queried sharply.

Randall grunted.

Despite supposedly being friends, the guy didn't know she was in the hospital, and it wasn't Frazer's secret to spill. "We've been pretty busy," Frazer's mouth twisted wryly. Serial killers, terrorists, Russian spies. Rooney and Parker had earned their Christmas vacation but being in the hospital didn't seem to count. Worry for his agent curled through him like secondhand cigarette smoke. "I thought you were friends with Alex Parker, too?" He tucked his face into his collar.

Randall checked his watch as if he had somewhere else to be. Definitely not comfortable with the turn the conversation had taken. "We served together in the Army, and I ask for his assistance on cybercrime issues. Guy's a frickin' genius, but you already know that or you wouldn't have seconded him to your unit."

The true circumstances under which Frazer had transferred the former assassin to his unit were known to only a handful of people, none of whom would be sharing. A gull landed close by and eyed him like a mark. "It sounds like you have issues with the guy," Frazer said carefully.

Randall shrugged and turned in a circle, maybe trying to keep the chill out by moving. Or maybe avoiding the question.

"What happened?" Frazer pressed.

Randall eyed him like he wanted to tell him to mind his own business. "Agent Rooney is like a sister to me."

"You don't think he's good enough for her?" Oddly, despite everything he knew about Alex Parker, Frazer thought they were perfectly suited.

"She went through hell." Randall let out a ragged sigh. "Parker's got money but…"

"She's not interested in his money." Frazer peered at the other man. "You sure your interest isn't a little less *brotherly*?"

"What? Hell, no." Randall shook his head in denial. He paused for a moment and shrugged. "I guess their relationship took me by surprise. Rooney and I were partners for over a year. A month after she leaves Charlotte she's desperately in love and living with a man she barely knows? A guy I introduced her to?"

"They're a solid team." Alex would die to keep her safe, and sacrifice his soul if she asked him to. "You don't have anything to worry about…" He'd been about to say he'd never seen two people more in love but over the last two months there had been an outbreak of romance in Frazer's unit. The condition seemed contagious and potentially terminal, but so far not deadly.

Frazer had no intention of catching it. Been there, had the divorce papers to prove it.

He eyed a figure on top of a dune about three hundred yards away taking photographs with a zoom lens. He shook his head in disgust and signaled the uniform to get rid of him. Vultures.

"Did the kids bring the shovel, or does it belong to the unsub? If the unsub brought it, was it a weapon or a tool? Was this attack premeditated or were they victims of opportunity?" Frazer asked the question that had been bothering him since he first arrived. "Is this the work of a single killer—or not?" The scene showed conflicting evidence. "Could the bracelet be an attempt to throw us off the real reason for the rape and murder of Helena Cromwell?"

He couldn't afford to ignore any avenues of investigation.

Randall remained silent. Letting him think it out.

Frazer glanced over the vast expanse of the dunes. "Something tells me the unsub came out here to dig for something, hence the shovel." Which suggested an organized offender.

Randall's pupils flared. The obvious clue was Beverley Sandal's bracelet, which meant maybe Beverley Sandal herself was out here somewhere.

"I think we need to expand our crime scene," said Frazer. "Maybe the unsub was disturbed, or maybe he spotted the teens when he was finished digging, and started watching them. Then his lust or lack of control got the better of him and he couldn't stop himself from taking what he wanted." Helena Cromwell.

44

"Which could suggest a disorganized offender," said Randall.

Frazer frowned. "Maybe, but he knew enough to take out the biggest threat first"—Jesse—"mixed signals, which is common in most murders." But his gut was telling him they were dealing with an experienced sexual psychopath who was highly skilled and organized when it came to murder.

"So what now?" asked Randall.

"We investigate. Quietly." Frazer softened the order. "I don't want the media connecting this thing to Denker. We'll let the local Police Department take the lead and organize a search through the dune system, looking for recently disturbed sites, and any evidence at all. If there's nothing obvious to the eye I'll call in ground penetrating radar."

"Looking for bodies?"

Frazer stared at the soft valley between the dunes where a young woman had met her death. "Yes."

Randall swore under his breath.

"Local cops know the area, they know the people. I want them invested and involved in the case. I want you to track the victims' final few hours." Detailed victimology was the cornerstone of writing a useful profile. The feeling like they didn't have much time sat on his shoulders like the devil. This killer was one step ahead of them, and Frazer needed desperately to catch him before anyone else died.

CHAPTER FOUR

They started walking back toward the road. Frazer didn't want dozens of FBI agents or State Police digging into this case. Not yet. First, he wanted to know more about this crime, maybe even solve it before the press got a whiff of the juicy story involving a new murder and a condemned serial killer. He needed to see the girl's body and talk to the ME, contact Hanrahan, maybe interview Denker, talk to Jesse as soon as the kid woke up, speak to the father who'd been the one to find the intact crime scene.

That was going to be fun.

Especially as he wasn't yet ready to rule him out as a suspect. The vast majority of murders were committed by friends or family. Frazer should probably be glad he didn't have many, although he'd made enough enemies to fill the void.

A silver SUV pulled up behind the squad car on the main road. A woman got out, wearing tall boots, black jeans, and a shearling jacket over a chambray shirt. Tall. Caucasian. Early thirties. The breeze played with long strawberry-blonde hair that was tucked beneath a gray woolen knit cap. She came around the hood and opened the passenger door, bent inside to get something. He caught Randall checking out the woman's ass and refrained from rolling his eyes. She straightened with a cup holder containing four hot beverages, and then he started to salivate.

He'd kill for a coffee.

They walked over to the uniform officer who

was talking to the newcomer. The guy handed them each a cup.

"I appreciate it. Thank you." Frazer raised his drink to the woman. She nodded, but her gaze didn't quite meet his.

"This here is Izzy Campbell. Her sister is—" Officer Wright cleared his throat, "—Er, *was* best friends with the female victim."

The woman flinched. She had ivory-pale skin and a patch of freckles across her nose. High cheekbones, wide mouth. Her eyes were a soft dark sage, the same color as the sea oats that covered the dunes. The wind had drawn a flush to her cheeks, but her lips were bloodless, a fact emphasized by a mole that sat above the left side of her mouth.

The beauty mark took him by surprise. He didn't know why. It was one of those so-called imperfections that enhanced rather than detracted.

She stood stiffly, holding firm against a buffeting wind that was strong enough to knock him back on his heels.

Randall shook her hand and Frazer reached out to do the same as they introduced themselves. Her fingers were warm, her grip firm. Her gaze finally met his with a mask of cool detachment that mirrored his own. From the tightening of her lips she knew he was assessing her and didn't like it. People rarely did.

She raised a pair of fine pale brows at him because he hadn't let go of her hand. She didn't jerk it away, but he felt the muscles in her fingers flex as if she wanted to. "I'll need to interview your sister, Ms. Campbell." He watched her closely, but she didn't react with anything except a nod.

"*Doctor* Campbell," the police officer

corrected.

Frazer let go of her hand.

"Izzy works part time at the local hospital. In fact, she was out here walking her dog this morning and helped save young Jesse."

Her mouth formed an unhappy line. "The ambulance crew was already here and the ER did the rest. I was glad to help."

The police officer had a distinctive brogue where the 'I' sound was rounded and stretched. She didn't.

Something about her drew his interest. It wasn't her looks per se. She had an ethereal quality that usually made him shift into reverse gear fast, but she didn't look fragile or delicate. Her standoffish body language combined with the Scandinavian bone structure, rigid posture and slightly annoyed expression intrigued him, made him pay closer attention. She wore zero make-up and had dark smudges beneath each eye. She made no effort to attract male interest, but she captured it anyway. Both the patrolman and Randall were fascinated by way more than her eyewitness account.

"What's your specialty?" asked Frazer.

"I help out in the ER when they need an extra pair of hands."

"Dr. Campbell was an Emergency Physician with the US Army Medical Corps. Served in all the world's hot spots." The officer grinned widely. "We're all very proud of our Izzy."

The guy was more than proud, he was infatuated, and the two did seem pretty tight if she was bringing him coffee.

"Where'd you serve?" asked Randall.

"I was stationed mainly in Texas, Fort Hood, but did tours in Germany and Afghanistan."

"Landstuhl?" asked Randall.

She nodded.

"I spent six unhappy months in Ramstein Air Base back in 2000," said Randall.

"I thought you served in the Army?" Frazer asked.

"Exactly," said Randall.

"Bagram?" Frazer asked the woman.

She gave him a curt nod.

"I'm sure you've seen some pretty interesting things in your career, Dr. Campbell," said Frazer.

"Ditto, Agent Frazer." Her expression was impassive, but there was a tiny flicker in her green eyes that said the passivity was a lie.

He nodded. She hadn't directly answered the question. "What can you tell me about the events of last night?"

Her coolness evaporated and she huddled into her coat. "I've been covering nightshifts over the Christmas period and was working again last night. My sister told me she was spending the night with Helena—that's the girl who d-died." Isadora Campbell's voice caught, but she swallowed the emotion that had leaked through. She must have a defense system akin to his own, a way of disassociating from her emotions, otherwise she'd never be able to do her job. Some people mistook that for arrogance or aloofness. For him it was a survival mechanism. She banded one arm across her stomach as she sipped her coffee with the other. "Helena told her parents she was staying with Kit—that's my sister. Instead, they apparently went to a party I didn't know about." Her expression

49

screamed parental guilt. Was she her sister's guardian?

The girls had exhibited typical teen behavior. Not something that should have gotten them killed.

"Party was at the Cirencester's hotel. Local family," Officer Wright cut in. He straightened up from where he slumped against the hood of his cruiser. "Parents were off island and didn't know anything about it. A lot of young folk were there. Parents are on their way home now. Something tells me young Franky is about to get grounded for a year."

"Any idea what Jesse Tyson and Helena Cromwell were doing out here during the storm?" Randall asked.

The officer rubbed the back of his neck. "According to Franky, who is Jesse's best friend, Jesse wanted to watch the storm and asked Helena to go with him because he's sweet on her. They're good kids, but they'd had a couple of drinks…"

A girl was dead. Frazer didn't care about the party unless it was tied directly to Helena Cromwell's death.

"I need all available law enforcement personnel running a grid search through the dunes ASAP— three hundred yards either side of where the victims were found," Frazer instructed. They were wasting time. "Spreading out another hundred feet either side if the first search yields nothing."

The officer eyed the darkening sky. "What're we looking for?"

"Everything. Anything." He wouldn't voice his suspicions. "Signs of recent disturbance, clothes, litter, condoms."

Dr. Campbell's face paled.

The officer glanced at the sky. "I'll organize it. Not sure we'll get sorted before dark though. Probably better to organize it for first light tomorrow."

Even though Frazer was frustrated, he nodded. They couldn't afford to miss anything due to poor light conditions. They'd have to pray the rain held off. "Sounds like a plan. We need the area guarded overnight. Can you arrange that too?" asked Frazer.

The officer nodded.

"Does Kit lie to you often?" Frazer turned and asked the doctor. A blitz attack was the best way of getting a genuine reaction.

A flicker of emotion rippled over her features. The micro-expression was gone in an instant, but Frazer knew whatever came out of her mouth next was going to be a lie.

"Kit's a good kid." She took a step away from him. "I need to go be with her. She was pretty upset when I spoke to her on the phone—"

"You haven't seen her, yet?"

"Earlier." Another strand of hair slipped free from her hat. Inexplicably, his fingers itched to touch it. That was another kind of investigation entirely and not one he'd conduct while in the middle of a murder case. "After we found Jesse and Helena, I dropped my dog home, and Kit came with me to the hospital. Once Helena was declared DOA, Kit became very upset and went home. I had to stay with Jesse until a specialist from the mainland arrived. When I grabbed coffee on the way home I figured anyone on duty might appreciate one, too. Now I need to get home and check on Kit before I head back into work again."

Kindness? Or a way of insinuating herself into

the investigation?

"How's Jesse doing?" Officer Wright asked.

"His temperature is back up to normal, but he hadn't woken when I left. They were about to do a head CT."

"Why don't we come with you now to question your sister? Get it over with," Randall suggested.

Frazer checked his watch. It was late afternoon and he'd seen what he needed here for today. "Is there a place either of you can recommend where we can get a bed for the night?"

"What about your beach house?" The police officer suggested to the doctor. "You're always complaining no one stays there in the winter."

Dr. Campbell's mouth opened and closed, clearly not happy with the idea.

Why? Did they make her uncomfortable, or was she just tired? "It'll take me an hour or so to make up the beds."

"You could do that while I speak to your sister. Agent Randall is going to go question the other teens who went to the party last night." Randall shot him a narrow-eyed look that lacked appreciation. "For starters, he'll need an address for the Cirencester hotel?" Frazer said to Officer Wright.

"You don't suspect Kit of anything, do you?" The muscles around Dr. Campbell's eyes tightened.

"We wouldn't be doing our job if we didn't question the people who knew the victim best and who saw them last."

"Izzy, we need to know what happened last night. Kit wouldn't have hurt Helena." The officer went to put his hand on her arm, but she shifted away just enough to avoid contact. Not lovers then.

Friends. Interesting. "And we all know kids are more likely to talk freely if their parents—or guardians—aren't there. You remember how it is at seventeen."

She huffed out an unamused laugh. "I hated seventeen. Does she need a lawyer?"

"Relax, Izzy. She doesn't need a lawyer." Officer Wright put his hands on his hips and smiled gallantly. "Look on the bright side, at least you can charge these guys premium rates." He was clearly trying to help, and Frazer appreciated it, but his humor failed to hit the mark with the doc.

"This place have two bedrooms?" Randall asked. Frazer didn't miss the plea in his voice.

Dr. Campbell nodded as she backed toward her car. "We're the first two houses you come to on the right along the highway." She pointed north along Route 12. "I live in the blue house next door to the cottage. Come find me when you're finished here. I'll make sure everything is ready for your stay."

"Don't go to too much trouble. I doubt we'll be spending a lot of time there." Randall's smile was full of boyish charm.

The police officer scowled.

Frazer didn't think the man realized he had competition for the woman's affection until that moment. Thankfully the good doctor wasn't his type. Perfect on the outside. Glued together by pure mulish determination on the inside. He recognized the sort. He saw it in the mirror every day.

***

As Izzy drove Route 12, the horror of what happened to Helena finally began to sink in, along with another unwelcome sensation—relief. Relief that it wasn't her little sister raped and murdered in those dunes, that her kid sister wasn't lying dead on a slab in the morgue.

Her throat ached from battling emotion. She'd been able to keep it together earlier because she'd had no choice, but Helena had been a sweet person who'd been kind to everyone, who worked hard at school. She'd been a stabilizing influence on Kit at a time her sister desperately needed it. Izzy pressed a hand to her sternum, willing herself not to throw up. She couldn't afford to lose it now.

That a murderer was on the loose was bad enough, that he might know what she'd done…

Maybe someone had found the bracelet on the beach? Maybe Helena herself had found it in the sand and put it on before she died—like some cursed charm. Izzy put her foot on the accelerator and fought the wind that threatened to shove her off the road. She needed to get to Kit, to pull her sister into her arms and squeeze tight to reassure herself that she was really okay.

It was another mile to their property, which sat on the edge of Rosetown. She usually liked the tranquility of the islands in winter, the abandoned shorelines and pounding waves, the peace, the isolation, the lack of tourists. Right now the emptiness felt oppressive and reinforced her decision that as soon as Kit graduated high school, Izzy was selling up and moving on. Bad memories outweighed the good. Guilt was eating her alive.

The houses came into view. The rental cottage was slightly closer to the sea than their own home. Both houses stood on stilts and were painted pretty shades of blue and green with wraparound porches.

She'd freshened the white trim herself this last summer, though she hadn't told Kit why. Like everyone on the Outer Banks, she worried about erosion. She worried the properties might lose their value as the sea encroached, but right now they were in good shape, and she intended to capitalize on that. Sell the houses, send Kit to college, and figure out what to do with the rest of her life.

Sounded like a plan.

Izzy pulled up outside their home and grabbed her bag. Got out and ran up the steps to the back porch. The door was unlocked, and it was dark inside, the storm shutters still covering the windows. Barney greeted her with a lick and a waggy tail. She gave him a hug and kissed his whiskers.

"Kit?" she called, dropping her bag beside the door. No one answered. A bolt of fear shot through her. "Kit!"

"What?" The girl erupted from the couch.

Her racing pulse eased and Izzy flicked on the overhead lights. She went over to her sister and pulled her into her arms. Squeezed her tight enough to hurt. She was so angry and yet Kit had only lied about going to a party, something most teens did at some point.

She choked back a sob. Cruel reality had finally caught up to Kit, and there was no protecting her this time.

"The FBI is on the way here to question you about what happened last night."

Kit pulled away from her grasp. The blood drained from her cheeks, and her waterlogged blue eyes grew huge. "What?"

Izzy should probably feel guilty for delivering

the information so bluntly, but the events of the day on top of a sleepless night left her too tired for subtlety. If she didn't get some sleep soon, she was going to be more liability than help, but the hospital was short-staffed and they needed her.

"I dropped off some coffee with Hank on my way home. He was still at the beach. Met two FBI agents there."

Kit sobbed and Izzy pulled her back against her chest, rubbing her hand up and down her sister's spine. She'd gone to the beach hoping Hank would tell her that they'd caught the attacker, and they could all sleep safe in their beds tonight. That would have been too easy.

"One of them was going to follow me back here to talk to you about Helena." The good-looking blond one, who'd looked at her like she had something to hide. "He'll be here any minute." She shivered. He'd scared her a little with those sharp eyes that searched every dark corner of her soul.

"It's all my fault, Izzy." Kit's words ran together. "If I hadn't lied to you about where we were going last night Helena would still be alive."

Her sister broke down again, tears dripping off her cheeks and her chin. Izzy's heart cracked wide open. She stroked baby-fine hair and wished she could take away this burden too. "I wish you hadn't lied to me about where you were going last night, but that is not why Helena is dead."

She was dead because some animal had brutally killed her. A monster who'd cared nothing for the sanctity of human life or the wishes of another human being. Izzy fought for people's lives almost every day. Her vocation was the only reason she could live with her past. Her stomach turned as she remembered Helena's naked body. The bruises around her slender throat. The blood on her thighs.

How many monsters were in this world? How did you fight them?

The memory of the FBI agents standing resolute on the beach in their dark flak jackets flashed through her mind. They fought them. It was their job. She released a pent up breath. No wonder the agent's eyes were cold. He must have ice in his veins to do that job.

"Why is the FBI coming here?" Kit whispered. "I thought they only dealt with big cases?"

Good question, and Izzy had no idea. She had a horrible feeling it was related to that bracelet Helena was wearing, and that thought made her stomach roil.

"They want to ask you what happened last night. Maybe who was at the party. What time Helena left."

"You think someone from the party killed her?" Kit started crying again, and Izzy tried to comfort the young woman who sometimes felt like a stranger, and other times felt closer than a sister. When their mom had died last year, Izzy had resigned her commission and moved home so Kit could finish high school without disruption, but things hadn't exactly gone smoothly. Once Kit graduated, Izzy was moving on. Maybe she'd reenlist. Maybe she'd get a job in a busy city hospital where she could use more of her skills to help people. There was another option. One that ate constantly at the back of her mind.

Kit's crying jag ended and she wiped her eyes. She was so pretty and so smart. Izzy had loved and protected her from the womb and wished she could wrap her up and keep her safe forever. But the more you tried to protect people the more they rebelled. The world wasn't safe. Her sister needed to open her eyes and understand the very real danger that existed out there. Losing your best friend to a killer was a hell of a wakeup call.

"Having federal agents looking into Helena's murder is a good thing. Hopefully it means they'll find this person before he strikes again." She pushed aside the fear that would drive her crazy. She wasn't some defenseless teen. "The Feds are renting the cottage while they're here so I need to go get it ready before I head back to work."

"What?" Kit sounded horrified.

"Hank suggested it." Izzy pulled a face. Hank Wright was a good friend of her uncle's. "Trust me, we might need the money, but I wish he hadn't opened his big mouth."

"Do you *have* to go to work?" Kit asked. Her eyes were big and pleading.

"They're short-staffed until tomorrow." She couldn't leave them with no Attending. "Then I'm off and we'll spend some time together. It's only a few more hours. You should go to bed and get some sleep after the FBI leaves. Where did you go last night after the party?"

"Here."

Her sister must have heard her unspoken question. *Without Helena?* She went to kiss her on the forehead, but Kit pulled away.

So much for that.

Izzy blew out a big breath and headed to the cupboard where she kept the linens for the vacation cottage. "I need to go get the place ready. Want to keep me company?"

Kit hugged a cushion and shook her head. Shocker. "I don't want to talk to them. I don't want to talk to anyone. I can't believe Helena's dead. She's my best friend—how could I have let her go off without me?"

The thought that Kit could have been killed too...

Izzy grabbed sheets, towels and comforters, battling with the towering pile as she headed toward the door. The sound of Kit's sobs drove nails of grief through her heart but she kept moving. Izzy was used to stressful situations and coped with disaster by keeping busy. Maybe that's why she'd gravitated toward emergency medicine. Maximum chaos, minimum time to think.

She grabbed the keys off the rack next to the door. "If the Feds can help catch Helena's killer this has to be a good thing. Tell them everything you know."

"But I don't know anything," Kit wailed.

With one exception Izzy was a big believer in following the rules, which had made her a damn good Army officer. She opened the door and there stood the federal agent, Frazer.

He was one of those individuals who was so ridiculously handsome you could barely look at him. Worse, he knew it.

"Kit," she shouted. "The FBI is here, baby."

Barney came to meet the newcomer. Izzy expected the man to be too self-important to greet the dog but he went down on his haunches and gave Barney a good scratch on the neck. After a few moments of mutual adoration the guy stood. The blue of his tie matched the ocean in his eyes.

"What's his name?"

"Barney—or barmy, depending on the day." She held his gaze, and he took it for the challenge it was. "You can talk to Kit alone, but if she decides she doesn't want to speak to you anymore she doesn't have to." She called over her shoulder. "Did you hear that, Kit? I'll be at the cottage. If you get uncomfortable with Agent—" She turned back to the guy. "Sorry, what was your name again?"

"ASAC Frazer." His eyes glinted, obviously not used to women forgetting details. Or maybe knowing she'd lied about the fact to give herself a little power when she felt so powerless.

"If you don't want to talk to ASAC Frazer, come over to the cottage and get me, okay?"

Kit mumbled something that could have been anything from "bitch" to "sure." It certainly wasn't "thank you" or "I love you."

Her sister's lack of appreciation and general sense of entitlement was staggering and Izzy swallowed the hurt and the resentment. Their mother had spoiled the younger girl, and Kit's lack of consideration for others drove Izzy crazy. Another reason she'd spent so much time away from home.

The sharp-eyed Fed didn't miss her momentary loss of composure. She buried her reaction, something she'd always been good at, but the military had honed the skill into a mask no one could penetrate. It made for a hell of a game of poker. "Upset her and you'll find out where I conceal my weapon."

His eyes creased at the corners, but he didn't fool her for a moment. "Left shoulder holster, so you're right-handed. Looks like a Glock-17, but tricky to say for sure without getting a better look." The guy's gaze slid over her chest with glacial indifference, but suddenly she knew that was an act too. A wall. His own defense mechanism.

His eyes landed on her mouth, on the mole that sat just above the left side of her upper lip. She resisted the urge to touch her face self-consciously. Warmth filled her, and she knew she was blushing. As a physician and a former soldier, blushing was not in her repertoire. She moved past him, heart beating frantically as she went out the door.

Emotions were high, that was all. She was not attracted to this guy. She'd rather date Hank, and he'd given up asking her months ago. Her dog stayed behind, and she left them to it. She wanted ASAC Frazer to find the killer and leave them alone. She had enough problems in her life without adding a tall good-looking federal agent into the mix.

CHAPTER FIVE

Izzy headed down the path between the two houses. She rounded a corner and almost screamed when she bumped into someone. "For Pete's sake, Uncle Ted. You scared the crap out of me."

Her mother's brother gave her a repentant smile. "Sorry, I figured I'd come by, see how you were holding up. Heard about Helena. Reckon Kit would be pretty shook up."

Izzy indicated she needed to get past him with her armful of linens. "She is, but she's busy right now, and I need to go make up beds."

"You've got guests?"

She heard his tread heavy on the steps behind her. "Two FBI agents while they investigate the murder. Hank suggested they stay here." She rolled her eyes even though her uncle couldn't see her.

"FBI? Jeez." Ted blew out a breath. "That's Hank for you, though. Always thinking about the bottom line. He doesn't realize you have enough on your plate."

She got to the top of the stairs and put the linens on the heavy wooden bench that sat on the deck. Working quickly, she pulled back the storm shutters and Ted helped her by opening up the other windows.

She gathered up the linen and put the key in the lock but paused to find the door was already unlocked. *Kit*.

Inside, she was hit by the distinct odor of weed. Dammit, this was why her sister had looked freaked at the idea of the Feds staying here. She must have come back here when she'd left the party without Helena—and Izzy doubted she'd been alone.

Ted cautiously sniffed the air. "When was the last time you were in here?"

"Over a month ago." Bitterness leaked into her tone. "If the FBI weren't here I'd kill her myself." She flinched at her poor choice of words.

Ted chuckled and started opening the windows.

It was going to take a hell of a lot of air freshener to mask this odor. "If she has a boyfriend and is having sex in this cottage…" Izzy's fingers clenched with frustration at all the things she couldn't control.

"She's seventeen, Iz-biz. Didn't you have a boyfriend when you were seventeen?"

The comment was like a knife to her flesh. Her eyes flashed to his, but he was unrepentant. "And look how that ended." Shane had been seventeen when he'd wrapped his car around a telephone pole—driving drunk and going way too fast. Another painful memory she'd unsuccessfully tried to outrun.

She shook it off. It had happened a long time ago. She was tired and angry and miserable. She dumped the linens on the couch and dug under the kitchen sink for rubber gloves and a spray bottle of cleaner. Other people had it far worse than she did, she reminded herself.

Her mind flashed to Duncan Cromwell's futile attempts to raise Helena from the dead. Dear God. Her heart lurched. Her sister sneaking off to parties and apparently smoking weed, and acting out, weren't so bad when you stacked them up against that. But they were issues Izzy would have to deal with. And right now she didn't have the energy, or the expertise.

She sprayed all the counters and began wiping them down.

"Need any help?" asked Ted.

"I can manage."

"I'll just stand here and watch you then." He tucked his hands in his jacket pockets and slouched against the living room wall.

She grunted, then found another pair of gloves under the sink and tossed them at him. "Fine, start in the bathroom. There's disinfectant under the vanity."

Ted grinned. "Was that so hard?"

Asking for help didn't come easy. Delegating stuff at work was different. Everyone had a role to play there. Everyone had a responsibility they were trained and got paid for. She checked her watch. "Look, I'm back on duty in a little over ninety minutes. I need the smell of pot out of the air, beds made and the place clean enough for two FBI agents to move in shortly thereafter. Pitch in or leave me alone. I don't have time for chitchat."

Ted chuckled as he headed to the back of the house. "You always were a sweet-talker, Isadora Campbell. It's a wonder men aren't queuing up around the block to take you out on a date."

She straightened up to hurl an insult at him, but snapped her lips closed. He was right, so why bother arguing. She didn't do sweet-talk. She was a realist. A pragmatist. She didn't stroke egos or waste her time gossiping. She didn't angle for information unless it pertained to her job or her sister, and apparently she was even crap at that because she knew very little about Kit's life.

In the military Izzy had easily blended into the

system and become an integral part of the machine. In the civilian world she intimidated people, especially men. Or she wasn't attracted to the ones who were brave enough to ask her out. Hank, for example. And she wasn't the type to be worn down by repeated asking. She was built stubborn, and that was a good thing.

She was fine on her own.

She frowned, trying to remember the last time she'd actually gone on a date. While she was in the Army, that was for sure. Well over a year ago. And as for sex...she snorted as she wiped under the toaster. If it were up to her, *homo sapiens* would be well on their way to extinction. She'd been in a few relationships over the years, and sex was a good way to relieve stress, which was important when the world was going to hell and wanted to take you with it. But the military's way of moving people around and strict rules on fraternization had killed most of her relationships.

Didn't mean she didn't get lonely sometimes.

She pushed away the image of the FBI agent who was currently next-door in her home. He looked arrogant and aloof, but there was no denying the guy was hot. She smiled to herself, trying to imagine him in her home with the feminine sofas and laid-back beachy atmosphere. She couldn't do it. He didn't fit. She *could* imagine him naked in the shower, and her detailed knowledge of anatomy pushed her brain into overdrive. Wet hair slicked back, eyelashes spiked, hard muscles defined beneath warm skin beaded with water droplets. A fine sprinkling of golden hair arrowing down to... Hah! She eyed her yellow gloves and shook her head. Who was she kidding?

Even if she were interested in someone like that, he wouldn't look twice at a woman like her. He was made for black silk and satin lingerie. She was rubber gloves and white cotton. He was expensive brandy, she was *Lysol*. He was law enforcement—a lump formed in her throat—she wasn't.

She thrust the image of him away. She couldn't afford to let down her guard, not even in her daydreams.

Ted started whistling in the other room and she jolted. She'd almost forgotten she wasn't alone. Ted and Kit were all the family she had left. Kit might be running a bit wild, but it was nothing Izzy hadn't done when she was seventeen. She'd deal with it. Talk to Kit. Steer her back on track to finish high school and get into a good college.

She tried not to think about Jesse Tyson lying unconscious in the hospital. She definitely didn't want to think about poor Helena or her heartbroken family. She put the cleaning cloths in the kitchen sink and pulled out the mop. Murder left an indelible stain on people that couldn't be washed away. The sooner these Feds caught this bastard the better, even if it meant she ended up in jail.

***

Frazer stood in the middle of a shuttered room with Kit Campbell, a younger, less uptight version of her sister, who sat hunched up on the couch. She shared the strawberry-blonde hair and effortless beauty of the doc. He'd bet she had the boys at school jumping through hoops to get her attention and probably didn't even notice.

The wariness in her gaze was from youth, not

experience.. Her hands formed fists. Her jaw was clenched. She looked scared and defensive, which didn't work well when trying to gain information from interviewees. If her sister hadn't been so overprotective he would have suggested hypnosis, but he'd save that for another day.

Maybe he could work the charm he was famous for in some circles. "How about you put on a coat and we go walk the dog on the beach?"

Kit frowned in sudden confusion and sniffed loudly. "I thought you wanted to talk about Helena."

"I wouldn't mind stretching my legs and, yes, I'd like to know more about your friend, Helena. It's an important part of catching the person who did this to her."

Huge, grief-stricken blue eyes latched on to his—as if she'd finally realized this wasn't about her. She nodded and stood, then disappeared down the hall, presumably to put on some extra layers of clothes.

The dog nudged his hand insistently. Frazer had always been a sucker for animals. His ex had taken their dog, saying he spent too much time at work to take proper care of him. To forget the rest of what she'd done he gave the hound a good rub. He didn't have time for a pet in his life because his hours were insane, but he missed the uncomplicated affection.

He looked up, wondering where the teen was. The gloom of the room was depressing. He walked across to the French doors, went outside and pushed back the storm shutters, latching them on the outside. He came back inside and closed the door to keep out the freezing wind. Even though the sun was going down, the natural sunlight helped relieve the shadows. Barney wagged his tail in approval.

He used the alone time to snoop. The floors were hardwood with brightly colored area rugs strewn throughout. A medium-sized fake Christmas tree stood in the corner, but the lights weren't turned on. There was a pale blue sofa dotted with lacy white and flowery cushions, a pure white armchair which seemed risky considering Barney who was following him around like his new best friend, waiting for him to do something interesting. A pink poinsettia sat on the dining room table, pots painted in pastel colors lined the windowsills. And plants everywhere. Lots of healthy looking plants.

His ex had once said not even a houseplant could survive his neglect. Now he had an office full. Not that he was bitter.

He'd always known exactly what he was going to do with his life, something his ex had failed to understand even though he'd told her from the very beginning. Law enforcement sounded a lot more glamorous than it was. The majority of marriages didn't survive the pressure—another shitty statistic from a job that took as much as it gave. But he wouldn't swap it for the world. He'd been offered far better paying positions and turned them down without a single regret. He was meant to hunt killers.

The house was soft, warm, soothing even. A very feminine setting at odds with Dr. Campbell's aloof persona—not that he didn't see her as female, she was definitely female, but... He stared harder, trying to put a finger on what was bothering him about the juxtaposition. Had he expected military sparseness? Possibly.

The woman was an attractive enigma and he was a sucker for puzzles. But now he was thinking about a woman when he should have been thinking about a murdered teen.

He checked out the photographs on the mantel. Lots of pictures of Kit in various stages of development. A few with an older woman with almost identical features to the other two women— their mother? Probably. A photo of Isadora Campbell in her military uniform caught his attention. Hair smoothed tight against her skull. That damned beauty spot drawing his attention to her lips. She looked spick and span and bright as a new penny, but her eyes were shadowed. She was hiding something, he just didn't know what it was or if he should care.

People who dedicated themselves to the service of their country always earned his respect, but it didn't mean he trusted them implicitly. He needed to check her alibi and look at her service record. See what Parker could dig up. He glanced at his watch—five PM—and decided to call Parker later. He and Rooney had bigger things on their minds right now and Frazer wasn't even sure why he was interested in Dr. Campbell. She wasn't a likely suspect for the murder and, on a personal level, he'd be gone in a couple of days. Dr. Isadora Campbell would probably never cross his mind again.

He quietly laughed at himself. So much for not being his type. Attractive and temporary were *exactly* his type. But he had work to do. No need to complicate things here.

He scanned the photographs, looking for more

clues about the two sisters. Tucked in almost as an afterthought at the back of the mantel was a photograph of the mother and a dark-haired man in wedding garb.

"That's my dad." Kit had come silently back into the room and watched him cautiously. She'd pulled on another pair of gray sweats and a fleece lined hoodie. "He died before I was born."

"I'm sorry to hear that."

She shrugged. "I never knew him so it's not a big deal." Which probably wasn't true. "Mom died last May. Izzy left the Army to look after me."

"It's tough losing both parents when you're so young." He knew from experience. "You're lucky to have your sister looking out for you."

The girl shrugged as if it was no big deal. Her sister had given up what was presumably a successful career to take care of her, but the teen took it as her right. She had no idea how fortunate she was.

"I'm ready if you still want to go for that walk." Impatience leaked into her tone.

He raised his brows, but she didn't seem to notice. He bet the good doctor would have preferred another tour of duty to raising a seventeen-year-old. Respect for the woman went up another notch.

Kit headed for the French doors without bothering with a leash or a key. She let the dog out and then went outside onto the deck, leaving the place wide open.

"You might want to start locking up around here," he suggested, trying to keep his own tone mild.

Her eyes popped wide as they swung to his.

"You don't think the killer is still around, do you?"

No one ever wanted to believe a killer was a member of their community, or someone they knew. Stranger danger was a lot easier to live with and in reality accounted for a very small proportion of murder cases. "Until the cops have him in custody I'd err on the side of caution."

She still didn't bother to lock the door. At his pointed look she pulled a face. "Izzy's just next door." Then she headed down the wooden steps.

He frowned. "So the killer gets to attack her first?"

The girl gave a rude laugh. "The guy would be an idiot to go after Izzy. She'd kick his ass."

Was she really that dumb, or this callous? "I'm sure Jesse Tyson felt the same way."

Her lower jaw dropped at his words and then her mouth worked soundlessly for a moment. Frazer waved her ahead, trying to mask his impatience. The dog ran on, sniffing the grass. The tide was way out and birds poked and prodded the sand for worms with their sharp thin beaks as dusk began to settle.

"What can you tell me about last night?" he asked.

Kit's gaze went beyond him to the beach house.

Frazer glanced over his shoulder, but no one was visible. He frowned. "I'm only interested in finding the person who killed Helena. I'm not going to tell your sister anything you confide." He remembered his time at high school. All he'd cared about was getting the best grades and not getting kicked out so he could get a scholarship to go to college. Nothing else had mattered.

Somehow he didn't think that was Kit's version of high school.

"What do you want to know?" The girl huffed and strode away from the cottage. With the tide out they could walk around to the next beach without getting their feet wet.

"You told your sister you were staying at Helena's house last night?" he pressed. He'd had an easier time interviewing psychopaths.

The girl nodded and finally started talking. "Helena wanted to go to Franky Cirencester's party. Jesse had asked her out—which was huge for Helena because she's been crushing on him for months." She covered her face with her hands and started crying. "I can't believe what happened. I keep expecting her to call me and tell me about her date. It's like something out of a horror movie."

Except Helena wouldn't stand up at the end of the scene. She'd never take another breath. She was dead. No acting. No retakes.

"This was their first date?"

She nodded.

"Jesse is popular in high school?"

Kit nodded again.

"Helena wasn't?" His use of the past tense brought more tears.

"Please, God, let this be an awful mistake." She gulped and started to hyperventilate.

Her pain made his stomach twist. A small part of him knew he should comfort her, but that wasn't the way he operated. Distance was his thing. For good reason. It helped him see the whole picture. "Put your cupped hands over your mouth and try to breathe slowly," he instructed. If her sister collapsed, Isadora Campbell would probably string

72

him up by his balls.

Kit got herself back under control with a few slow deep breaths. "Helena wasn't one of the popular kids. She was smart and pretty and too damn nice to be one of the bitchfest crowd."

His eyes narrowed. Was that self-reproach in her tone? "What about you? You part of the popular crew?"

Her eyes flashed and she snorted out a bitter laugh. "Am I a bitch, do you mean?" She nodded. "Yep, I can be. Helena was the nicest thing about me." Shadows haunted the depths of her eyes. "I think that's why Jesse asked her out. She's the sweetest person I know. Is Jesse going to be okay?" Her voice hitched with concern. Kit seemed less of a bitch and more of a thoughtless teen.

"He's alive, probably due to your sister's expertise." The young man hadn't regained consciousness yet, but it was early days. He'd suffered severe head trauma. Brain damage was a possibility. They wouldn't know anything until the kid woke up and opened his mouth. "You went to the party. What happened there?"

She crossed her arms and looked away from him. "The place was packed. We all hung out for a while. Danced. Ate—everyone was supposed to bring something." She glowered at her feet. "Then they started playing some dumb games." She looked angry. "I got pissed off and went to the hotel pool."

"What time?"

"Just after midnight."

While Frazer and her sister had been at work, trying to save the world. He didn't want to see mirrors in his and Isadora's personalities, but they were impossible to miss.

"You went swimming alone?"

She pressed her lips together and shook her head. Tears refilled her eyes.

Impatience lit through him. "Who were you with?"

She rubbed her hands up and down her arms. "A guy."

He waited.

"He's new to the school. Name is Damien Ridgeway. I, um, went swimming with him."

Frazer didn't ask if clothing was optional. She wasn't his sister. "Did you see Helena leave with Jesse?"

Kit nodded. "She came and asked if I wanted to come with them to the beach. I laughed at her." Her eyes were blotchy and swollen as she dabbed them with a wet tissue. "That was the last time I saw her. I laughed at her and gave her a look like she was stupid. No way would Jesse want me tagging along with the two of them." She caught the sleeve of his jacket. "If I'd gone with her she'd still be alive, wouldn't she? No one would've attacked three people."

"It's unlikely someone would have confronted three individuals unless they were carrying a weapon. But murder isn't an exact science so it's possible he'd have killed you, too."

A shudder wracked her body. "She was such a good person." She stood in front of him, looking up from under her bangs with fierce blue eyes. "Was she raped?"

He held her gaze. "We don't know for sure and anything I say now is spoken in confidence. This isn't schoolroom gossip." It was a risk to speculate but he'd worked enough cases to know he was probably right. He needed Kit Campbell to trust him because he needed to know what was going on in every level of Helena's life, and that included high school. "She was probably raped." Frazer had to catch Kit as her knees buckled. Her pain and anguish rang out on the thin breeze. Barney rushed over to see what was wrong, but Kit quieted and her screams turned to sobs and she clung to him, tears soaking into his shirt.

"It's not fair. It's not fucking *fair*! Helena was saving herself for someone special, and he stole that from her!" She slammed the bottom of her fist against his chest. "He stole it like he had the right."

He held onto her elbows, trying to steady her and wishing he'd given Randall this assignment. Teen drama was not his thing, although maybe he was being a little unsympathetic. She'd just lost her best friend. "She was a virgin?"

"I don't even know if she'd kissed anyone properly." Her eyes were so red they looked like they were bleeding. "She was the nicest person I ever knew. How can I live knowing what happened to her?"

She threw herself into his embrace, and Frazer found himself wrapping an arm around the girl to keep upright. He swallowed tightly. There'd been a time when he'd wondered how he could go on living when his parents had died, but he'd found his vocation. It was up to Kit to find hers. He looked toward the cottage and there was Isadora Campbell watching them from the deck of the cottage with an unreadable expression on her face.

He had no personal experience with siblings but understood the dynamics from a psychological perspective. Older siblings tended to be more responsible than younger ones. They were caretakers, not risk-takers.

Kit finally pushed away from him, and he happily let her go.

"Did anyone else leave the party around the same time as Helena and Jesse?" he asked.

"I don't remember." Her voice was bleak now. "I stayed in the pool. I drank more beer and made out with Damien. *That's* what I did while my best friend was being raped and murdered at Parson's Point." She wiped the cuffs of her hoodie over her blotchy face.

"Where did you go afterwards?"

Her pupils widened. "What do you mean?"

"You told your sister you were staying at Helena's home. She told her parents she was staying here. Where did you go? What did you do?"

"I came home." She folded her arms and refused to meet his gaze. "I'm cold. I want to go back now."

Frazer stared at her for a long moment. She was hiding something. Over the years, after thousands of investigations coming across his desk, sometimes it was the weirdest fact or fluke that solved a case. Good police work involved asking the questions no one wanted to answer. Frazer understood the need for secrecy and discretion— and that's why he always looked in the shadows. Deciding not to shine a light there yet, he nodded and they started walking back to the cottage. Barney followed.

"Do you know anyone who might have wanted to hurt Helena or Jesse?"

She shook her head. "No. Never. Helena was below everyone's radar and everyone loved Jesse…" Then her mouth went wide. "Except Jesse's ex-girlfriend. I saw what she wrote about him online last night when he posted a picture of him and Helena at the party. She called Helena a whore." Tears filled her eyes. "I want to punch her in the face for that." She turned toward him. "You don't think she had anything to do with this, do you?"

Because of the bracelet factor, together with the rape and the fact two victims had been handled at the same time, Frazer doubted a jealous teenager had committed last night's murder. "I'm not willing to rule out anything at this stage." Except Ferris Denker who sat in his cell waiting for execution. "We'll follow all leads, but if the girl was involved *I'll* be the one to make sure she's held responsible. No punching anyone in the face, okay?" Not that he hadn't done far worse in the pursuit of justice.

She nodded reluctantly, then her eyes cut to his. "Promise me you'll find out who did this."

He glanced up at Isadora as she watched them from the deck, and thought of the innocent young woman who'd had her future stolen from her. He didn't make promises he couldn't keep. "I'll do everything in my power to catch the person who did this, Kit. But you have to promise to tell me everything you know, and anything that you hear from your schoolmates. You don't need to tell anyone you're talking to me, but I want to know all the rumor and gossip. Deal?"

He held her gaze until she reluctantly nodded. "Deal."

CHAPTER SIX

The lights he'd strung around the window blinked as he sat back with his beer and a bag of chips to watch the evening news. "First homicide of the year," was the opening title of the piece. That made him sit up a little straighter in his chair. He hadn't thought of that, but he supposed it was one for the record books.

The reporter was one of those pert blondes with narrow bright red lips and nonexistent tits who thought she was something special. She wasn't. They showed a shot in the background of the Outer Banks but it was a picture of Cape Hatteras, not the Lighthouse on Crane Island.

What the fuck? They couldn't even be bothered to send a news team down to get fresh footage? They'd just recycled old film from reporting on the storm the day before.

Unknown assailant. One victim dead. Another miraculously surviving. *Blah*. His lips twisted. That jock asshole should be dead. He'd pounded the fucker hard enough to pancake his brains, but obviously not hard enough.

He smirked. He'd taken what the boy had wanted, and it had been magnificent. The kid couldn't identify him; he hadn't had a fucking clue. He'd probably wake up a vegetable, drinking food through a straw. That would distract the chief and local cops who were all a bunch of fucking morons anyway. He sipped his beer. Would the FBI be any smarter? *Nah*. He knew how to cover his tracks, and he'd been getting away with it for longer than most of them had been on the job.

He relived the moment when the moon had come out and he'd stared deep into Helena's eyes. It had sent a sharp thrill through him when she'd recognized him. The memory made his cock swell. It had felt good for someone to finally know what he was and how he had fooled them all.

Cops were conducting a wider search tomorrow. He rolled his eyes. About damn time. What did they need, an engraved invitation? Someone was in for an ugly surprise. A few someones, come to think about it.

The newscaster moved onto a spate of burglaries of houses that were empty for the holidays.

He sat up. What the fuck?

That was *it*?

Nothing else?

He shoved the beer on the table and stared at the screen, waiting for more. But the newscast finished without another word about the murder of Helena Cromwell or Beverley Sandal. He sat there stunned.

That was all the airtime he'd earned? And they said he was callous. Excitement died as anger grew. What about the bracelet? They needed to report on the bracelet, dammit, but maybe they hadn't figured out the connection yet. Surely they couldn't be that dense?

Denker was sitting on death row pissing his pants as his final day neared. Turned out the pussy was scared of dying. Funny when he thought about it. All those bitches begging for mercy years ago and getting none? He wasn't a big believer in karma, but he found the thought pretty damn amusing. But Denker was his friend. Probably his only true friend because he understood him and his needs and wasn't a pansy about it.

They'd gone to school together. Committed their first murder together. Some girl who'd been hitchhiking alone along a dark road at night like a gift. She'd practically fallen into their laps. They'd stopped, given her a ride, and without even discussing it, the two of them had dragged her into secluded woods, and she'd screamed her fucking head off until he'd hit her so hard he'd cracked her skull.

She'd never been found.

Sometimes they'd killed together. Other times they'd acted alone. Both had different needs and hungers, but there were plenty of women to be found if you knew where to look. Prostitutes and runaways were almost invisible. Drug addicts almost expected to turn up dead. He and Denker had made them disappear.

Ferris had been a good friend. They'd learned a lot from one another. Experimented. Swapped notes on the best way to avoid getting caught by the cops. When life had taken them in separate directions they'd lost touch. When Denker had been pulled over with a dead taillight and a body in the trunk, he'd mourned the loss of his friend's freedom but also laughed his ass off. Ferris had always assumed he was the clever one. Oh, the irony.

Ferris's confession had gotten the cops off his back, but it burned when he'd claimed so many victims as his own. A short time ago, Ferris had smuggled out a letter and asked for help. They'd figured out a couple of twists to throw the cops and delay the inevitable.

He wasn't scared of dying—he was looking forward to it, but the idea of being found out...he didn't like that none.

The plan was easy enough, and he didn't mind giving the guy a little hope, especially as he got to take back what was his. Screwing with the authorities was fun, too, but he didn't want to get caught.

He walked into his spare bedroom and opened the closet. Stared at the rows of shoes he had stored there. Red high heels mixed with sandals and ballet flats. He picked up one of the tiny sneakers he'd taken last night—brushed a little sand from the toes and felt his dick go rock hard.

He'd been high on adrenaline by the time he'd left the beach. Satisfied with his night's work, and the intense pleasure of something he'd been denying himself for too long. He always took his hunger to the mainland, controlled himself on the islands. The community was too insular here, especially in winter and he didn't want anyone asking too many questions or putting anything together.

He cupped the small shoe in his big hands, rubbed his thumb over the hard rubber heel. It felt so good.

For the first time in months he'd felt really alive. Challenged. Victorious. Sated.

He'd had a good idea where Beverley had been buried, but it had still taken over an hour with a metal detector to dig out the bracelet. His original plan had been to go over to the mainland today and find a suitable offering to leave for the cops to find in exactly the right place, but the teenagers had turned up at the dunes and it had seemed like too good an opportunity to resist.

The shovel…*shit*.

His skin went clammy as he realized his mistake. He'd left it behind…He'd worn gloves when doing the digging. But he'd removed the gloves to do the girl. To touch her skin. To absorb the softness of her flesh. She'd been so perfect. So stunningly acquiescent. A shame he'd had to kill her so quickly. He'd always liked her.

Afterward he'd rushed away, worried more teens might show up looking for the first two. Rash, he realized. He should have taken a few more minutes to make sure he hadn't left anything behind. He didn't think they'd tie the shovel to him directly. He'd planned to put it back afterward, and he hadn't worn gloves when he'd taken it. But would it be recognized?

Fuck.

His mood soured.

Of course Izzy would recognize it. And the cops would investigate and dust for prints, and he'd be sitting in a cell like Denker. It had been dumb to take it, he just couldn't resist the symbolism.

He looked outside into the blustery dusk. Dammit, he hadn't wanted to go out again tonight. He'd wanted to stay home and have a few beers. He deserved them after all his hard work and sleepless night.

Memories came crashing in and his hands shook. The rush of blood. The crazy high that made him feel invincible. He lay on the bed and pulled out his phone, looking at the pictures he'd taken. He held the sneaker against his chest. He remembered the fear, the pain. The girl had been a virgin and he wished he could do it again. She'd died too easy, hadn't told him a damn thing he wanted to know. The intense pleasure the memories aroused had him catching his breath and closing his eyes as he touched himself.

He felt sorry for Ferris—denied real pleasure all these years. Had he seen the news? Was he jealous? He groaned as he remembered every detail. Every gasp. Every flinch. Her pretty brown eyes. Long silky hair.

How did a man live without that? *He* wouldn't be able to. And that's why he had to fix his one small mistake before anyone figured it out. He put it out of his mind for now. He'd do it later when it was full dark. And maybe he wouldn't wait so long next time. Or maybe he'd keep them alive for longer and give himself time to enjoy the thrill. But that was risky. He just needed somewhere quiet to play for a few hours. Somewhere where no one would interrupt the things he needed to do.

***

"Five foot two inches tall. Weight, ninety-nine pounds, three ounces." Medical Examiner Simon Pearl looked up from his notes. "There's nothing to her. She's tiny."

Frazer nodded. Seventeen-year-old Helena Cromwell lay naked, contained in a plastic sheet atop a large stainless steel table. She was slightly built. Fragile bones. Elegant fingers. Small breasts. Narrow feet. Her skin was white, except where blood had pooled. She'd been little more than a girl, but her age hadn't mattered to the man who'd wrapped his hands around her throat and squeezed.

It wasn't lost on him that she'd have never wanted a stranger to see her like this. An autopsy was an invasion of privacy on a grand scale.

Shame welled up inside Frazer. When Rooney had first called him about a single victim homicide he'd considered it beneath his notice. The fact he'd thought the assassination of a powerful old man was more important than the destruction of such innocence made him sick inside. Helena's sweetness, her potential for good, versus the evil of a twisted politician who'd wielded power as a weapon, uncaring of those who got in his way, was infinitely more worthy of his time. His effort.

This was his forte. This was where he belonged. Not talking to presidents, but picking apart crimes. Finding the bad guys before they hurt more innocents. But his job was full of politics, and if he didn't play the game someone would play it for him.

As much as he tried to keep his emotional distance, viewing dead bodies slammed home his responsibilities. Crime scene photos didn't do that. But dead naked seventeen-year-old girls like the one in front of him, did—she belonged to him now, and he'd do everything in his power to find the person who'd snatched her life away. Then he'd return the favor.

"Clothes and evidence have been bagged, yes?" asked Simon Pearl.

"She was found naked. Evidence was bagged and sent to Quantico." But he had the horrible feeling he'd missed something important and needed to review the list of evidence as soon as he got the chance.

The ME pursed his lips, his eyes dark and

angry. "What exactly do you want me to look for? Why not send her straight to Raleigh for a full post?" The ME was a fifty-year-old veteran, and they'd worked together before. More specifically, the guy had worked on Denker's victims. Frazer wanted his unbiased eyes on this case. He crossed his arms over his chest. Said nothing.

The ME let out a deep breath. "You know I'm married, right? I actually have a wife at home waiting for me? One who gets pissed when I'm not on vacation when I promised her I would be? Maybe if *you* took a break occasionally—"

"It's important," Frazer said simply.

Simon grunted and continued to stare at him for another long moment. Frazer had spent years collecting favors. He'd been calling them all in steadily over the last few months and had the feeling he wasn't done yet.

Simon finally shook off his annoyance and clipped the microphone back on, speaking into a digital recorder. He noted age, height, weight, sex, hair, and eye color. Helena's state of nutrition. Scars—she had a small one on her clavicle that looked like a procedure from a broken collarbone. No tattoos. The ME looked at her teeth—she'd had a textbook perfect smile. The fact she'd never smile again made Frazer want to hit someone but he shoved it down and forced the thoughts away. He didn't get angry. He got justice.

Simon took photographs as he went. Contusion on the right side of her scalp where she'd been hit with something unyielding. Frazer's bet was the shovel. DNA would help verify that.

Red marks and dark bruises mottled her throat. The ME stretched her eyelids apart. "Petechial hemorrhaging suggesting she died of asphyxia. Looks like manual strangulation. I won't know for sure until I open her up." He noted a few other marks and abrasions. "There are no obvious defense wounds. Once the attacker got hold of her, I think she was completely overwhelmed by the man's strength and probably her own fear."

"No indications she was drugged or bound or Tasered?" The man who'd killed Mallory Rooney's sister had used a stun gun on his victims before dragging them away to his lair. Frazer was glad the serial killer was dead, but he still wasn't happy that he'd been the one to put a bullet in the bastard's brain.

The ME shook his head. "I collected tissue samples for analysis, and don't see any obvious Taser marks." He moved on and Frazer forced himself not to react as the man moved the young woman's legs apart and photographed the blood on her thighs. "There are indications of sexual activity. I can smell a rubber." He moved away to grab a swab kit. When he came back, "What the...?" The man's voice stumbled and trailed off.

Frazer tensed.

The ME leaned closer to the victim, picked up a pair of forceps, and grabbed hold of something that was inside the girl's body. Slowly he removed the item. It was a clam shell.

For a moment, the thudding of blood through his ears was the only thing Frazer could hear in the cold basement. He met the ME's wide-eyed stare.

"Are you fucking kidding me?" The man's voice vibrated with anger. "Does Ferris Denker have a copycat?"

"Or a partner we never caught." Frazer

unfolded his arms and moved closer to the ME. The fact Denker had always placed something in his victim's vagina was not information that had been released, either to the press or during trial proceedings. This meant the killer was closely associated with Denker—close enough to know intimate details about the killer's MO. Denker had also liked to spend a little more playtime with his victims, time to maximize their fear, and maximize his own pleasure at feeding off the victim's pain. Frazer didn't know if this unsub shared Denker's proclivities for torture or not. Helena hadn't been mutilated but her murder felt rushed. As if she were a victim of opportunity rather than planned. The means to deliver a message while slaking a vicious hunger. But Frazer wasn't sure if he was seeing this new unsub distinct from Denker.

What was his signature? What made him tick?

Frazer spoke quietly. He didn't want anyone overhearing them. "We found a medical alert bracelet for a woman named Beverley Sandal on this girl's wrist." He nodded to Helena. "Beverley Sandal was one of the women Denker admitted to killing when he was convicted, but her body was never found." They held each other's gaze for a moment. Both pissed, but Simon's eyes held a measure of forgiveness and understanding. Now he knew why Frazer had requested him personally. He knew why he'd dragged him out of his nice warm home and away from his family.

Frazer wished he'd been wrong. Wished for some crazy coincidence, although the bracelet had been a distinct calling card. A gauntlet thrown down to the authorities.

"You can take her back to Raleigh now and

finish the post." He held out an evidence bag for the shell, and Pearl slipped it inside. Frazer had what he needed although he was far from happy about the development. "I'm sending this to Quantico for analysis. We might get lucky. He might have left prints or hair or something."

They both turned to look at the victim lying on the table. Death never got any easier, but it was always worse when the victim was young. "This information can't get out."

"Press would have a field day," Simon agreed. "I'm not going to tell anyone. I want that bastard to reap what he sowed and scream all the way to hell."

Frazer's cell buzzed in his pocket, and he checked the screen and pressed his lips together. "Looks like we have good news and bad news. Jesse Tyson woke up and is talking. Bad news is, he's asking for Helena."

***

It was after ten PM. The ER was quiet, and Izzy only had a few more minutes before she could go home and sleep for a week. The last time she'd felt this drained had been in a field hospital in Afghanistan after an invitation to a tribal meeting had turned out to be a trap. They'd lost two soldiers that day, and another young man had lost both legs below the knees. The fact those men and women went to war to help protect her freedom was humbling, especially if the authorities knew what she'd done seventeen years ago they'd take hers away. But using her skills to help people was a way of giving back and had to be better than twiddling her thumbs in prison—that's what she told herself.

Was today's murder related to what had happened all those years ago? Izzy closed her eyes and kneaded her temples. She didn't know. How could it be? It was impossible, but doubts slid through her mind like shards of broken glass. And tomorrow they were going to search the beach. Her hand shook as she filled out patient notes. She needed to be ready. She needed to brace herself for whatever they found.

The knowledge that a young woman had been violated, the thought that it could have been Kit, hell, it could have been her, made her feel sick. Killing for pleasure was the antithesis of all she believed in. She'd do anything in her power to help catch the guy, but she also prayed he was long gone, and they'd never hear from him again.

She finished updating patient notes at the nurses' desk, and turned. She jumped as she realized someone was standing right next to her.

"Sorry. Didn't mean to startle you."

"Chief Tyson." She held on to the desk to keep her balance and tried to remember the last time she'd eaten. It had been a while.

The man's face was haggard. Deep grooves cut into his forehead, and his eyes were reddened and puffy from fatigue. Normally he was a good-looking guy, but the events of the day had taken their toll. She doubted she looked much better. "How's Jesse?" she asked.

"He woke up and is talking. Knows who we are and who he is," said Tyson.

"No dizziness or pain?"

Tyson shook his head.

A thousand pound weight lifted from her shoulders. "That's great news. I'm so glad."

Lee Tyson scrubbed his face. "I feel like I should be out there, investigating this thing, finding whoever attacked them." The tortured expression on his face tore at her usual reserve.

"The FBI is here. They'll find who did this," she said. "You need to look after your son."

He nodded. "I guess. Dr. Bengali thinks he's gonna pull through. I needed a break, and I wanted to thank you for what you did this morning."

Uncomfortable with gratitude, she brushed it off. "I was just doing my job, Chief. Same as you do yours every day. I'm glad he's recovering. Did he say anything about the attack?"

Tyson shook his head. "He doesn't remember anything about last night—short term memory loss is what the doc says."

Dissociative amnesia was common after a traumatic incident like this, especially those that involved head injury. She'd seen it a lot in combat troops. "It might come back." Or not. She grimaced. Poor kid.

He checked his shoulder. "ASAC Frazer suggested we might try hypnosis on Jesse in the morning, see if he can pull any memories that way—assuming there's no issues with Jesse's medical condition."

Izzy's eyes widened. "Hypnotism?" Frazer didn't look the type. "Well, I suppose it can't hurt. Except…"

Tyson's eyes went bleak. "Except for when my son finds out Helena was murdered on their first date."

Hell.

"ASAC Frazer is one of the Bureau's top criminal behavioral analysts. I'm gonna have to assume he knows what he's doing."

Izzy wasn't surprised. Frazer had analyzed her from the get go. The guy didn't miss a thing and was sharp as a number ten scalpel blade.

Tyson rested his hands on his hips. "I'm spending the night here, but now we know Jesse's going to be okay I want Charlene to go home and be with Ricky, our youngest. Her mother is staying at the house." He paused, watching her intently. "I could get one of the patrolmen to run her home, but they're either on duty or need to be up at the butt-crack of dawn to conduct the search of the beach. One of the nurses mentioned you were about to go off duty." He cleared his throat.

She finally understood what he was asking.

"You want me to drop Charlene home?" she asked. The Tysons lived at the other end of Rosetown so she literally passed their door. "No problem." She checked her watch. "I'm done as of one minute ago. Let me sign out, grab my coat, and I'll come down to Jesse's room and pick up Charlene before I leave."

"I appreciate it."

It was the least she could do. Ten minutes later she found herself outside Jesse's room. His vitals were good from what she could see on the monitors. The worry now was coning—when sneaky intracranial bleeds caused blood to accumulate, and the brainstem to swell and press down on the spinal cord. Izzy figured if he made it through the night he'd be fine. Compared to how she'd found him that morning, what she was seeing right now was a miracle. She leaned against the doorjamb to keep out of the way. Jesse's bandaged head rested against the pillows, but his skin color was good, and he was actually smiling at something his father said. Would he be still able to smile when he remembered what happened last night? It was important they try and shield him for as long as possible, but the police needed answers.

Frazer, the good-looking Fed with arctic eyes, stood behind the police chief, taking everything in. The image of him holding Kit in his arms on the beach earlier made her chest hurt. She wanted to be there for Kit but didn't know if she'd be able to give her sister the support she needed. Frazer glanced her way and, for one long uncomfortable moment, they stared at one another. Something unexpected passed between them. A sharp ache that she could tell from the look in his eyes he didn't want to explore any more than she did, but they both had to acknowledge.

Her skin felt tight, and she held her breath.

Charlene Tyson diffused the tension by scraping back her chair to stand. She kissed her son on the forehead. "You're sure you don't want me to stay, too?"

Her husband stood and took her hands in his and kissed her fingers. "He's gonna be fine, love, but the staff will only allow one person to stay overnight and that's gonna be me."

The chief's hand rested momentarily on his weapon. Izzy's gaze shot to Frazer's. He was watching her, almost waiting to see if she caught on. The killer hadn't meant for Jesse to survive. His dad was staying partly as a parent, but also as a bodyguard.

Apprehension rippled through her blood and her pulse jumped. The threat was still out there. The danger very real. She straightened away from the wall. She needed to get home and make sure Kit was all right.

The chief and his wife headed out of the room, and ASAC Frazer followed them.

"Can I speak with you for a moment?" Frazer said to her.

His hand landed on her lower back as he went to draw her away from the others. She jumped when he touched her. His pupils widened, and his mouth tightened for a fraction of a second before he let her go.

Good to know she wasn't the only one affected.

"Your sister wasn't big on home security."

She didn't know what she'd expected him to say, but it wasn't this. "I don't think she even knows how to lock a door."

"Teach her." Those bright blue eyes burned with intensity.

"You think the killer is still out there, don't you?" A wave of ice encrusted her spine. She'd lived with fear of one sort or another for years— fear for her mother, fear someone would discover their secret, fear for her patients, fear of what the next war might bring. This felt different. It was visceral and life-threatening.

His expression shut down. "You need to start locking your doors."

She nodded. "Okay. I'll tell her." And pray she listened.

Charlene Tyson had her coat on and turned to wait for her near the nurses' desk.

"I have to go."

"One more thing," said Frazer.

She waited silently.

"I'd like all the spare keys to the beach house."

She kept her expression neutral. "You don't trust me?"

"Why would I?" His voice was honey smooth and raised gooseflesh on her arms.

She huffed out a little laugh. "Good point. So how do you know I won't hold back a key?"

"Because if you did and I caught you, I'd arrest you for interfering with a federal investigation."

She eyed him with amusement. But she wanted him to do his job and catch the killer. Nothing else mattered. "I'll get them to you tonight. What time will you be back?"

"The morning will be fine. You're obviously exhausted."

Because she looked like crap. She grinned. Nice. "There might be time to get them to you tonight, depending when you get there. I don't want you worrying that I might come snooping when you're asleep. I need to eat and unwind for a few hours anyway."

The light in his eyes changed from detached interest at the idea of her snooping, to hunger—not the sexual kind. "What are you eating?"

"Chinese takeout. I called in an order before I came down here."

He checked his watch. "Call them and triple the order. I'll be another fifteen minutes talking to Chief Tyson, then I'm picking up Randall from the police station, and we're heading back for a few hours' sleep before the search starts at first light."

She raised an expectant brow.

He cleared his throat. "Please?" he added, looking suddenly uncomfortable as if he'd just remembered she didn't actually work for him.

She was used to alpha personalities, but she'd

been a captain in the Army, a physician, and owned a certain amount of alpha herself. Still, the request was practical and Izzy was the queen of practical. "Fine. What's your buddy up to?"

Frazer looked amused at her use of the term "buddy." "He's knee deep in teen angst."

She gave a mock shudder and held up her hand, palm out. "Give me the ER any day. See you back at the cottage. I'll add the total to your bill."

She went to turn away, but he caught her wrist, pulled her close. Her heart pounded so fast she felt like a rabbit trapped in a snare. He spoke softly into her ear, and she knew he'd be able to hypnotize the pants off anyone if he set his mind to it.

"I know you carry a gun," he said very quietly, "but be careful anyway."

She shook herself out of her surprise. She couldn't afford to let him unsettle her. His concern wasn't personal. He was just doing his job. And maybe he knew she had something to hide. She walked away with his eyes on her back, but refused to turn around to acknowledge his stare. She got to the end of the corridor and smiled at Charlene Tyson, who stood waiting patiently.

"Sorry that took a while. Are you okay?" she asked gently. The woman nodded, though she looked more drained than Izzy felt. She glanced over her shoulder and caught Frazer's gaze still on her. He grinned slowly and, dammit, he looked hot.

Heat rose in her cheeks for the second time that day. Just because she was attracted did not mean she was going anywhere near the guy. The aesthetics were fine, but the guy himself? Bossy and authoritative. No freaking way. He was way too smart to tangle with, even though she had a horrible suspicion the tangling would be amazing. But she'd been with other guys who looked good on the outside and who'd known as much about pleasing a woman as a fish knew about riding a bicycle.

And she had something in common with the fish on the bike—they could both get off without any help. No handsome FBI agent required.

CHAPTER SEVEN

Frazer looked up as Lucas Randall opened the door, balancing his overnight bag on one arm, bag of takeout in the other. He sniffed the air. "You've been smoking pot?"

"Yep, that was me." Frazer stretched out his shoulders until the bones clicked.

Randall came inside. "Reminds me of my college dorm."

Pine scented cleaner competed with cannabis in a not unpleasant combination. Frazer had opened all the windows and turned up the heat. Fresh air cleared away the cobwebs in his brain, and failing a drug test because of secondhand inhalation wasn't something he intended to let happen. "I suspect Dr. Campbell's sister had her own party here last night, which explains why she didn't miss her friend this morning and wasn't forthcoming about her activities after she left the party."

"How old is she exactly?" Randall tossed a bunch of spare keys on a shelf beside the door.

"Seventeen," Frazer replied, looking at the keys and hoping that was all of them.

The other agent dumped the bag of takeout on the big glass coffee table. Then went through and ditched his pack in the second bedroom. The smell of the Chinese food made Frazer's mouth water.

"Kids at the party said she left with a kid named Damien Ridgeway at around two. You think she came back here?"

Frazer nodded. "Looks that way. You talk to Ridgeway?"

"Nope. Not yet. What's the deal with Izzy and her sister? Where are the parents?" Randall was asking in a professional capacity, but the guy couldn't mask the personal interest. The shot of desire that had hit Frazer when he'd touched Isadora Campbell at the hospital earlier was enough to make him back the hell off. Which was why he'd sent Randall for the food.

"The mother died last May of pancreatic cancer. Captain Campbell resigned her commission from the Army Medical Corps and came home to take care of her sister. Kit told me her father died before she was born but I haven't checked into it." Frazer looked through the offerings and pulled out a carton of beef and black bean sauce. He dug in using the chopsticks provided, starving because he hadn't eaten in well over twenty-four hours and had forgotten the fact until Isadora mentioned food.

Isadora. Ridiculously beautiful name. He'd always been a sucker for pretty names and beauty spots.

"Big age gap between siblings," Randall commented from the open-plan kitchen.

"Seventeen years—the doc is exactly twice Kit's age. Makes me wonder if maybe they have different fathers. Or even if Isadora could be Kit's mother."

"Why'd they hide it?" asked Randall.

Frazer shrugged. It was a little Victorian, but he was just playing with ideas.

Randall had taken off his tie and suit jacket and grabbed one of the other takeout cartons. "Accidents happen, even in happy marriages." He spoke around a mouthful of food. "I'm a lot younger than my eldest sister and was definitely not planned. Dad blamed me on a good bottle of gin."

"Nice." Frazer found it hard not to like the guy. And since Alex Parker had called a few minutes ago, the terrible tension inside him had finally eased up a notch. The medical situation had stabilized, but the doctors were insisting on keeping Rooney in for a few days. Rooney and the baby were both doing okay. Parker was staying there, too. It would take a SEAL Team to get the former CIA operative to leave Rooney's side. Frazer wasn't foolish enough to try, nor did he want to.

He respected love and devotion as much as the next man, even though it hadn't worked out for him.

He and his ex had both been obdurately independent.

Frazer found the thought of spending every hour of every day with another human being cloying and claustrophobic. Constant company made his brain ache. Regular sex might make up for some of it, but Frazer liked his space, mental and physical. Now he was thinking about sex, after trying not to think about it ever since Isadora Campbell had turned back to look at him and blushed so prettily when he'd caught her.

The good news was she didn't want to be interested in him any more than he wanted to be interested in her. Or maybe that was the bad news, considering they both seemed to be losing the fight against basic physical attraction.

Thankfully he was an expert at ignoring not only his own wants and needs, but also the wants and needs of others.

He nodded to the murder board he'd borrowed

from the police department and set against the dining room wall. On it he'd put pictures of Helena, Jesse, the dunes, Helena's father, the shovel, and the bracelet, which represented all sorts of complications he didn't want to write down but had to. "What did you learn from the other teens at the party?"

Randall coughed up a noodle. "Let's just say I don't remember things being that...advanced...when I was in high school. Or maybe I was a lot more innocent than I realized."

"Drugs?" asked Frazer.

"Drugs, sex, and rock 'n roll. A couple of the kids admitted there were uppers flying around the party, but nothing 'major'." He placed air quotes around the word and went back to inhaling his food. He chewed for another moment. "The alcohol was flowing and the Cirencester kid is going to be lucky not to get strung up if his parents lose their liquor license over this." He pointed chopsticks at Frazer. "What really blew me away—pun intended—is a game they played where the guys all threw their cell phones into a bowl and whoever got picked out won a blowjob from one of the girls."

"Happy New Year," Frazer said wryly. "Who won?"

"Damien Ridgeway."

He winced. "Was Kit the one delivering the prize?"

Randall gave a shrug. "Apparently. They disappeared together."

"To the pool?"

Randall nodded.

Frazer had told Kit he wouldn't tell her sister her secrets, but that didn't mean others would keep quiet. It wasn't his problem, but he couldn't help feeling sorry for Isadora, and pissed that her sister was running wild. A lot of people might blame the guardian, but if he could take control of his life at fifteen, there was no excuse at seventeen.

Not his business. "What was the general feeling toward Helena?"

"Nice kid—maybe a little too nice. Not into drugs or screwing around. Top student, hard worker. A dancer. Overprotective parents, especially the father."

Frazer thought of her narrow feet and long toes. It seemed to fit that she'd been a dancer.

The "overprotective parents" raised red flags, but parents were suspects in every murder investigation. "I'll need to interview the family tomorrow. Chief Tyson told me both parents had to be sedated, and he had a female officer staying with them in the house tonight. She's a family friend." Which was useful as long as her loyalty lay with discovering the truth. "What about Jesse? What was the general feeling about him?"

"Didn't find anyone with a bad thing to say about the young man. Ace student, captain of the football team, but not an asshole. Girls wanted to date him. Guys wanted to hang out with him." Randall shrugged. "What's the next move? My boss wants a report. I can't stall her forever."

Frazer pinched the bridge of his nose. Petra Danbridge was competitive and she was pissed with the BAU for hiring Rooney instead of her. Thankfully she didn't know the reasons behind the choice, although in retrospect he'd much rather deal with Rooney on a daily basis than the SSA from Charlotte. Hanrahan had made a damn good choice for all the wrong reasons. Frazer wasn't a case agent but he did outrank her, and he knew all the right people. He didn't want to pull too many strings and draw attention to what was going on down here until he had to.

"I need another twenty-four hours if I can get it." Even that wouldn't be enough. Danbridge would either pull Randall because a single victim homicide wasn't a federal case, or she'd put more investigators on it and figure out the Denker connection.

"I'll do my best but if I get a letter of censure in my file—" Randall didn't look convinced.

"I'll deal with it." Frazer promised. "The ME found a seashell placed inside the victim's vagina."

Randall froze in the act of eating and put down his food. The fact Denker liked to put objects inside the victims was in the case files. Randall knew what it meant. "So the guy is either an old associate or a new friend of Denker's. Either way they must have communicated."

Frazer nodded. "I have a call in to the warden to try and access copies of his mail and tapes of any phone calls. She hasn't gotten back to me yet. I'm betting he'll make a move soon and I want to be ready for him." He'd also asked Parker to find out as much as he could without going through official channels. Having a cyber security expert on his team had made him rethink all electronic methods of communication. There were no secrets in cyberspace, unless you were the king of code and data manipulation.

"You think Denker's going to suddenly plead innocent? Claim that his confession was forced?"

"I doubt it—I mean the victim was in the trunk

of his car and the condom he used when he raped her was in a trash bag with her clothes. Not only that but the guy would lose face and his ego wouldn't be able to cope if he suddenly claimed he wasn't really the big nasty serial killer, but some poor asshole too stupid to plead innocent. All he can really hope for is that his sentence is commuted to life in prison with no chance of parole."

"I'd rather get a bullet."

"Yeah, but you're not the one facing imminent death, and Denker's in love with himself. He'll do anything he can to stay out of the death chamber." And Frazer didn't intend to let him.

He looked back at the murder board. He'd drawn an arrow from the bracelet to the name "Beverley—1998." Christ, that was the year Helena Cromwell had been born. Above that another box with the initials "FD" sat. He didn't want someone snooping and leaking Ferris Denker's name to the media.

Beverley had gone missing in February. Denker had been arrested later that summer. Frazer needed to determine the connection to the Outer Banks.

"How do we figure out if this new killer is an old associate or a copycat?"

Frazer finished his food and put the carton on the table. He'd worked thousands of crimes over the years and he always started the same way. "Look at the victim, the evidence. Work up a profile using inductive and deductive methods. Assume as little as possible until we can prove it. Right now we don't even know for sure the attacker was a single male. We need those forensic results back ASAP. The Denker angle is just another aspect. Don't get distracted by it."

Randall nodded but looked unconvinced.

"Do you have the evidence list?" Frazer asked.

Randall retrieved his notes and passed over the information. Frazer went through it twice before he finally figured out what he'd been missing. "What the hell happened to Helena's shoes?"

***

Izzy lay in bed staring at the pale shadows on her bedroom ceiling as she listened to the rhythmic beat of waves in the background. A flash of an image played inside her mind—a little girl running in and out of the surf, her father shadowing every step and making sure she wasn't dragged away as she giggled crazily and let him sweep her up into his arms.

Her throat ached. It had been a long time since she'd remembered anything good about her childhood without it being overwhelmed by other memories. She shifted restlessly under the covers, unable to get comfortable as thoughts of past and present collided.

Should she confess?

Damn. The whole point of leaving the Army and coming home was to make sure Kit didn't have to go into foster care. Confessing would mean that sacrifice would go to waste. Her sister would find out the truth—on top of losing her best friend she'd have to face everything alone, then end up in the system and probably drop out and have to repeat the last year of high school. Considering the path she was already on, Izzy didn't think it would be a good idea.

She only had to wait until Kit graduated. After all this time what did it really matter?

The sound of the wind rattling the shutters was both creepy and comfortably familiar. The cadence of the ocean soothed her and usually sent her straight to sleep, but not tonight. The sea was the only thing she'd missed when she'd been away all those years—not her mom, not her kid sister. She saw them regularly, if infrequently, but she didn't miss them. Not the way she should have. They were a unit and she felt like an outsider.

It had added another layer of guilt when her mom died. She hadn't been a very good daughter. Another reason to step up and do what needed to be done. But living back here in the town where she'd grown up wasn't easy.

It was claustrophobic living in a community where people thought they knew you inside out just because they knew your relatives. Her family's dirty secrets would make them shudder, and her and Kit would be outcasts. She pushed the thoughts away. Kit must never know—perhaps ignorance was the only real gift she could give her sister.

She rolled over in frustration. She'd been so tired when she'd gotten home, barely able to keep her eyes open. Now thoughts were whirling inside her head so fast they spun. A floorboard creaked and she froze, before realizing it was Barney moving from one spot to another.

When she'd gotten home, after putting the Chinese food in the oven to keep warm, she'd searched the house, weapon drawn, looking in every linen closet, in the showers, under every bed. No monsters. Not today. Kit had been asleep in her room with her headphones and the TV on.

Just as Izzy had relaxed, Agent Randall had knocked on the front door and nearly given her a heart attack. She'd handed over the food and spare keys with the firm warning that if anything was damaged at the beach house she'd be talking to his boss. He'd winked and promised to be good. Openly flirting and not shy about it.

Lucas Randall was exactly the sort of guy a woman like her should have smiled back at. He was good-looking, intelligent, funny, and approachable. He had a cute name, cute face, body that looked like it would be worth exploring under the G-man suit.

But when she closed her eyes it wasn't him she saw.

She punched her pillow.

The faint sound of metal grinding against metal had her shooting bolt upright in bed. What the hell was that? She threw back the covers, went to the window and looked out. Her room faced south with a view of sea oats, sand, and ocean. She pulled on a pair of sweats beneath the oversized olive "go-army" t-shirt she wore to bed. She palmed the Glock-17 off her nightstand and checked that there was a bullet in the chamber. She kept it pointed at the floor, but away from her ever-present excitable dog, who was always game for a new adventure. Through the north-facing window in the living room she could see the cottage dimly lit as if someone was in the sitting room or had left a light on. It looked quiet, peaceful.

It was doubtful the noise came from her paying guests. Another faint grinding noise had her listening harder, trying to pinpoint the exact source. It sounded like it was coming from *under* the deck.

Raccoons? Ponies? Her father's ghost?

"Dammit." She slipped into a pair of flip-flops by the French doors, hesitated with her hand on the door knob. She could let Barney out to chase away whatever it was, but if he got bitten or kicked by a wild animal, a five-minute excursion would turn into an all-night adventure to the vet's office. But what if it was the man who killed Helena last night? He'd have no compunction about hurting her dog.

Why would he be under your deck, dummy?

But what if he was? She shuddered.

The gun rested against her thigh with solid reassurance. She was armed and not afraid of going head-to-head with anyone, especially not with the FBI billeted next door. She wasn't a fragile seventeen-year-old. Truth was, she never had been. If it was the man who'd killed Helena this thing would be over. The FBI would leave the Outer Banks and her secrets would remain exactly that.

She grabbed the flashlight she kept behind the curtain on the windowsill. "Stay," she told Barney as she eased open the door, closing it on him before he could race off into the night. If it was a wild animal it'd run away as soon as she showed her face. If it was a person, she was armed and dangerous, and the FBI was right next door. She could shoot, she could defend herself, and she sure as hell could scream for help. She paused on the deck and looked across to the beach house. No movement there.

If it was a raccoon she had no desire to be spotted out here with her weapon. She didn't need to be anyone's comic relief.

It was dark, but the night sky clear. Suddenly

she became aware of her heartbeat pounding through her ears, deafening in intensity. Distracting as all get out.

Come on, Izzy, where's your backbone? Where's your training? She searched for her courage as she eased down the stairs, caught between wanting to scare whatever it was away, and wanting to catch anyone who was up to no good. Her hands tightened on the grip of her pistol. Finger off the trigger.

At the bottom of the steps, she flicked on the flashlight only to discover she'd made a critical error. The switch clicked uselessly and nothing happened. A frisson of alarm crackled through the air and a wave of gooseflesh swept over her bare arms. The feeling of menace grew as the silence stretched. Thick shadows saturated the space beneath the house and fear lodged in her throat. She shook the flashlight and banged it against her thigh as if that would help. It rattled uselessly. Shit.

"Who's there?" She felt like an idiot, talking to shadows, but she made her voice as commanding as possible. Nothing moved except the sea behind her and the wind rustling through the dune grass with the hiss of snakes.

A sudden screech made her shriek out loud and take a half-step back. Her finger wrapped around the trigger as a large tomcat dashed past her and leapt toward the other cottage. *Oh, my God.* Her heart pounded. She exhaled and lowered the gun, sagging against the railing as she turned to watch the animal run away. A cat. She'd nearly shot a damn cat.

The next moment her head was slammed into the railing and light burst behind her eyes, cascading along her nerves through her entire body as agony exploded. Aiming the Glock at the sand, she pulled the trigger as she dropped to her knees. The gunshot reverberated through the night, echoing off the water with a powerful punch. She heard a muttered curse, then the sound of running feet as she struggled to rise. Nausea rolled in her stomach, blood dripped from a scalp wound.

A few seconds later a door banged and more footsteps thumped down the wooden steps next-door.

"Dr. Campbell? Are you okay?" ASAC Frazer.

Was she ever glad to see him. He took her Glock from her fingers and she didn't object.

Agent Randall appeared next, running out of the cottage. He was still struggling to get a t-shirt over an impressive looking chest when he arrived.

She smiled unsteadily. Not hurt enough to be unable to appreciate some six-pack abs apparently. That was a good sign. "Someone was under my house and smashed my head into the railing when I confronted them." Her voice was a croak, but she hauled herself up the post, counting to ten to find her balance. "I got a shot off into the sand and he ran away."

"Which way did he go?" Frazer asked, looking as if he wanted to take off after them, but was forced to stay with her.

"Toward the road. Go. I'm fine." The sound of a small engine roaring to life filled the air—a dirt bike most likely. Randall took off running. Frazer stood staring at her like he thought she was nuts. "Exactly what happened?" he asked.

She touched her temple gingerly. Right now, she wanted to close her eyes and get the dizziness to stop. She braced both hands on her thighs, breathing through the pain, wishing she'd called the cops in the first place. Stubborn didn't even begin to cover it. "I heard a noise down here. Decided to investigate." She cleared her throat. "A cat ran out and I turned to watch it run away, assuming it was the culprit. I let my guard down." She pinched her lips together, pissed. "Someone hit me from behind."

"Did you see anything? A face?"

"White lights and tweety birds." She didn't bother to see if he appreciated her humor. She gritted her teeth and made herself stand upright, wobbling only slightly as her vision blurred. "I didn't see anything that could identify someone. It was a man, but that's all I've got."

"What makes you say it was a man?"

Izzy frowned. "The size and feel of his hand on my head felt like a man. He was bigger than me and I'm not exactly petite." She squinted. "Maybe I saw a pair of black work boots?"

Frazer flicked on his flashlight and swung it under the deck. The door to her little tool shed swung open.

"What the hell?" She went to take a step forward, but he put an arm around her shoulders, holding her in place. Maybe he knew how close to falling over she really was. "Why would anyone break into my tool shed?"

"Wait." Frazer narrowed his eyes as he surveyed the scene. Izzy hated how conscious she was of the strength of his arm, the heat of his fingers touching her. "Can you tell me if anything has been stolen?"

She went to step forward again, but he gripped

her tighter, forcing her to stay exactly where she was. She looked up. "From here?"

He nodded.

She hung onto him then, less steady on her feet than she'd realized. She turned her attention back to her tool shed and tried to blink the blurred vision out of her eyes. Lawn mower, weed whacker, hammer, shears, screwdriver. Some dried bulbs. Empty plant containers. Trowel. A half bag of soil. "Everything looks like it's there."

"Are you sure?"

The intensity of the question made her look again. Okay, shit. *Pay closer attention.* It all looked right... Her eyes caught on an empty wall bracket. A sense of dread sliced between her ribs and made it difficult to breathe. "The shovel. The shovel's missing." Izzy thought her knees might collapse, but Frazer's hold kept her upright.

If he noticed her distress he didn't comment. He pulled out his cell phone, one-handedly flicked through some images and then held the screen in front of her nose. "Is this your shovel?"

Her eyes bugged as she recognized the scene from yesterday morning. The dunes where Helena had died. A shovel lying in the sand. *Her* shovel—identifiable from the yellow insulation tape her mother had wrapped around the handle, years ago. She hadn't paid it any attention at the time, she'd been more concerned about the teens. But that was her shovel, and it had been used to bash Jesse over the head.

"Yes." She swayed, a buzzing sound roaring in her ears. She must have staggered because suddenly he pulled her tight against him. Holding onto him, she laid her cheek on the smooth planes of his chest and closed her eyes, just for a moment, to try and stop the world from spinning so wildly.

He smelled like warm linen with the faint scent of aftershave.

He wrapped both arms around her, and she gripped the material of his shirt and held on tight. When was the last time she'd leaned on someone? She didn't know. Couldn't remember. She took a few deep breaths to make her pulse slow, to try and get herself back under control. After a moment she realized she was inhaling his scent and pressing her body flush against his from knee to chest.

Crap.

She pushed away unsteadily. "I'm okay, thanks. I need to sit down."

"Don't touch anything," he warned. His blue eyes radiated cold authority rather than warm comfort, which was exactly the reminder she needed about who he was and what he did. She nodded and then slowly walked down to the beach and collapsed heavily in the dry sand. Her body shook. The man who'd killed Helena had been here tonight, underneath her house. He'd stolen *her* shovel and used it to beat Jesse. Then he'd come back—why? Was she a target? Kit? It didn't make sense—and yet, it made a terrible kind of sense.

Every muscle in her body tensed. This couldn't be a coincidence. He knew what she'd done and was torturing her with the knowledge.

She staggered to her feet. She should tell the FBI everything she knew, but then they'd arrest her and no way was she leaving her sister unprotected. Her hands clenched into tight fists. She could almost hear her mother's hysterical screams reverberating around her head.

She'd do anything she had to, but she wasn't letting this sick sonofabitch get anywhere near Kit, even if that meant lying through her teeth to the FBI, including the guy who made her insides melt every time she saw him. Worse, he made her feel safe and protected, but she knew he'd turn on her in an instant if he ever discovered the truth. She wasn't about to let that happen.

CHAPTER EIGHT

Lincoln Frazer was pissed, and he rarely got pissed.

What had the woman been thinking, investigating alone in the dark, one night after a brutal rape and murder had been committed a few miles down the road?

Except what was she supposed to do, call the cops every time she heard a strange noise? That would get old fast. Isadora Campbell had been a soldier. She was armed. She wasn't some simpering idiot, but he was still pissed. He wasn't a sexist asshole. He believed everyone should be prepared to protect themselves because cops couldn't be everywhere at once. Men and women should both learn self-defense. Kids should know how to fight back. So what the hell was his problem?

The image of Isadora Campbell wearing a toe tag was his fucking problem.

She'd refused to go to the hospital so Frazer had insisted she go to bed instead. Doctors really did make the worst patients. She'd looked tired and wrung out and he didn't need the distraction. The fact she was becoming a distraction was another reason he was pissed off.

When she'd clung to him earlier, molding her soft curves and long limbs against his, he'd held her not to give comfort but because she'd felt good in his arms.

He flexed his fingers into fists. Other people crossed lines. He drew them.

When he'd seen her heading outside earlier

tonight, he'd deliberately turned away. He'd decided she was probably letting her dog out, and hadn't trusted himself to follow her out onto a moonlit beach.

Instead she'd walked straight into the arms of Helena Cromwell's killer and his "feelings" could have gotten her killed. The fact the killer had been so close was both frustrating and curious. Frazer watched the CSU tech dusting the tool shed and its contents for prints. Randall had another evidence tech photographing tire impressions from whatever motorbike the unsub had used to get away.

Izzy had positively identified the shovel used in last night's attack, which told him a couple of things.

The killer was probably local. And he'd made some sort of mistake.

Had the unsub stolen the Campbell women's shovel simply because their house was on the edge of town, and the shed was easy to break into? Maybe the killer had known the doc was on duty at the hospital on New Year's and wouldn't be around. Frazer had a suspicion the unsub hadn't meant to leave the shovel behind at the crime scene yesterday so it might yield something useful.

The guy had made a miscalculation coming back here tonight. Frazer wanted to capitalize on that error. Could one of the Campbell women be involved? They both had alibis, neither had motive and neither were strong enough to simultaneously overpower both victims.

But Kit's new boyfriend was an unknown factor...

Frazer needed to pin down an exact timeline of Kit and Ridgeway's activities because they'd ended up getting stoned right next door. Ridgeway might have had the means and opportunity to commit the crime. Even if Ridgeway wasn't the killer, he or Kit might have seen something useful. They needed to talk to the kid ASAP and run thorough background checks on all three of them.

Presumably the killer had returned here because he worried someone might recognize the shovel and had come back to wipe away any potential evidence he'd left—which pointed away from Kit and Izzy. It was their shovel, their shed. No need to pretend they hadn't touched it.

The tech stood back. "There's blood on the railing behind you," she noted.

Frazer glanced behind him. "Dr. Campbell's, but you should sample it anyway." She'd hit her head pretty hard, patched herself up with butterfly sutures and declared herself "fine."

Stubborn.

He moved out of the CSU's way. He still had Isadora's Glock in his pocket. If she hadn't been armed, there was a good chance she'd be dead. The thought of what might have happened only yards from where he sat, trying not to think about her, was beyond disturbing. This was why he didn't get involved. It took away his focus from the killer while he worried about the prey—but wasn't that why he did what he did in the first place? Because he worried about the prey?

"I'm finished." The crime scene tech packed up her kit and he nodded his thanks as she headed back to her car. Hopefully she'd find something that would nail the guy. Finish this thing.

The good news was, Frazer now had a lot of information to digest to build a profile—it wasn't an easy process and it wasn't magic. Getting it right wasn't about guessing correctly. He used some inductive reasoning, drawing on years of research and data. The problem with inductive profiling was it relied on the subsample of criminals who'd been caught, which immediately produced bias in the data. It also assumed behavioral consistency—that an offender behaved in the same way over a period of time even while committing different crimes— and the homology assumption—the assumption of similarity between different offenders who commit similar crimes.

Neither were proven.

But Frazer was pretty sure he could conclude that the killer's ego would be huge. Fantasy would play a large role in how he committed and refined his murders. The killer would have average to above-average intelligence. Be sexually competent. Probably be an older or only child.

Deductive reasoning was more accurate but took much longer to build into useable information. Common sense also played a part—the offender was likely to be strong enough to hike through the dunes, wield a shovel, and ride a dirt bike, which narrowed the suspect pool a little.

Now that he'd realized Helena's shoes were missing, he'd started running ViCAP searches to see if any links to other crimes could be found. Then he'd get Felicia Barton working on a geographical profile and the theory of distance decay—and see if they could figure out where this unsub was most likely to live.

Intuition and instinct from years of hands-on experience played a much more intangible role in his profiling methods. Frazer didn't think this killer would be easy to catch. He had the horrible feeling this particular killer had been flying under the radar for years.

What did Ferris Denker have to do with this case? If they were compatriots, it put the age of the killer in the upper part of the range—forties to sixties—old for a serial killer who'd never been caught. But if the unsub was a disciple all bets were off, although he was likely to be younger and more easily influenced.

Frazer didn't like guesswork. He liked facts and needed to concentrate on what he actually knew.

Frazer shoved his hand in his pocket and touched the doc's pistol. Better give it back to her before he called it a night. He headed up the wooden steps of her deck and let himself in through the French doors. The lamp in the corner blazed. Barney came over and he gave the dog a scratch. The rustling of blankets drew his eyes to the couch as someone sat up. Isadora.

"Where's Kit?" he asked quietly. He'd assumed the younger woman would be here too. A chaperone of sorts, a barrier.

"She was wearing earphones and didn't wake up. I let her sleep."

His lips tightened. The younger woman needed to understand what was happening and indulging her wasn't going to do that. Sheltering the girl was dangerous for both of them. He'd talk to her himself tomorrow.

"Did you find anything useful?" A yawn took her mouth as she stretched her arms wide. "Sorry," she said as she covered her lips.

"Samples have gone to the lab. You and Kit

will both need to give fingerprint and DNA samples so we can rule them out."

She nodded. "What's next?"

She sounded pensive and he looked at her, really looked. There were dark circles under her eyes. Despite the thrust of her jaw she looked fragile. When was the last time she'd slept? She'd worked the night shift the previous night and hadn't even had time for a catnap today. "You should rest," he told her.

She started to shake her head, so he took her hand, dragged her to her feet, ignoring the fact she tried to resist.

"Bed."

She gave a husky laugh, false and designed to deflect his attention away from the fact she obviously didn't want to go to sleep. "You're a little fast for me, Agent Frazer."

The fact she kept demoting him was interesting too. She understood rank and the associated levels of power. Was she trying to annoy him? If so she'd be disappointed. Rank meant nothing beyond the ability to give orders—which he took full advantage of. The most important thing for him was getting the job done. Being the best was important too, but not because of his ego. It was because of his promise to the victims and the people of this country. He rarely gave a thought to anything else.

Her laugh bothered him more. The deep sound of it grazing over his flesh like fingernails just biting the skin.

Get over it.

He propelled her in front of him, trying not to look at the curve of her hips or her ass. He usually kept his thoughts locked up tight—including the occasional flares of attraction he experienced on the job. Good thing Parker wasn't here, he realized. He'd get the wrong idea. Frazer's reputation was one of ice, not fire. It was ironic he was attracted to someone exactly like him. Not someone who broke down and cried in the face of adversity, but someone who straightened their backbone, looked you in the eye, and told you it didn't hurt.

There was definitely fire beneath Isadora Campbell's aloof exterior.

Damn.

He hated that he saw that in her. He knew why he kept people at a distance. What was her excuse? And what would it be like if they both let go of their armor for just one night?

He didn't need this. She didn't need it either. He was one night stand material and she was part of a case. Neither had time for anything but getting this killer off the streets.

The door to her bedroom stood wide open. He handed her the weapon, then the bullet clip, and urged her inside. He pointed to the bed. "Get some sleep. I'll lock up when I leave."

She put the Glock and ammunition in the drawer of her nightstand, tugged the baggy sweatpants down, hooking them up into her hands to fold them neatly and put them on a chair beside the bed. He didn't think she'd undressed in front of him to seduce, it was more the act of someone who was used to getting changed in the company of others and was completely unselfconscious about her body.

But olive drab had never looked that good before. The t-shirt came halfway down her thighs and revealed a long stretch of pale slender legs. He'd managed to keep his eyes on her face earlier. Now, as she tugged the hem of her shirt, it molded the material over her breasts and her nipples stood out like beacons.

Was it cold, or was she thinking what he was thinking?

He dragged his eyes from what looked like a perfect body as she slipped beneath the covers. Sexual awareness sizzled through the air.

She cleared her throat and looked anywhere but at him. "Thanks for dealing with the crime scene people."

"It's my job."

She flinched at his harsh tone.

Damn. He'd made her uncomfortable. He turned to leave.

"Was that the person who killed Helena, hiding under my deck tonight?"

He hesitated. The air held a different kind of tension now. "Probably."

"Why did he steal my shovel?" Her eyes pierced him, but he had no answer. "Are Kit and I in danger? Will he be back?" Her eyes drifted toward the Glock's hiding place.

"It pays to be vigilant." Christ. He sounded like the cold-hearted prick he really was.

She sucked in a noisy breath and then clutched her arms around her bent knees. "Most of these killers have a specific type, don't they?"

Frazer turned to face her again. "I don't know enough about this killer to say." Yet.

She nodded and winced. Touched the bump on her head. "Hopefully you catch him before he attacks anyone else."

A reminder he hadn't done his job properly. "We were right next door—why didn't you pick up the phone?" And maybe that was why he was pissed off. She'd heard a noise, but rather than reach out for his help she'd investigated on her own and gotten hurt in the process.

"I didn't want to look like a fool if it was just a raccoon."

"You'd rather keep your dignity than your life?" He took a step back into the room.

She laughed. "Not my dignity…"

"Independence? I'm an FBI agent."

"And I was a soldier," she said sharply.

"That doesn't mean you have to do everything yourself." He sat heavily on the side of her bed, reached out a hand and eased her hair aside to check out the gash there. Her hair was soft and the color of spun sunshine in the lamplight. The breath he blew out contained all his frustration.

She held his gaze. "Don't pretend you're any different from me."

Shock moved through him that she'd recognized him the way he'd recognized her. He shut it down.

"Next time, call me." He put one of his cards on her bedside table.

Her chin lifted, but she nodded. Then she swallowed nervously. The action rippled down her throat, and he couldn't stop his eyes following the movement all the way down. She had the prettiest neck and collarbones. If they'd met under any other circumstances, he'd be doing his damnedest to taste her there.

He raised his gaze to her face. He didn't think he'd ever seen anyone with that soft shade of green eyes before. Warm, deep green, unadulterated by any trace of brown or hazel. A heavy silence fell between them. One that pulsed with unspoken questions and messages. What did she taste like? What sound would she make if he kissed her?

He eased up onto his feet. This was dangerous and couldn't go anywhere. "Did you take anything for the headache?"

She licked her lips, and he felt a corresponding reaction in his dick.

"I don't like taking painkillers."

"Of course you don't," he said dryly.

"What does that mean?" Her eyes flashed up at him.

He took another step back, disconcerted he wanted to pick a fight with her to gain a little distance. Distance was usually a given. "Nothing. Get some sleep. I'll see you in the morning." He closed the door on her pissed off expression and blew out a sigh of relief that he'd survived the encounter without doing anything stupid.

Not his usual MO.

He didn't even fully trust Dr. Isadora Campbell, and he certainly didn't intend to act on the attraction between them. He locked the French doors from the inside, lifted a key from the rack by the front door, and slipped outside. Waves washed against the beach. He didn't like tonight's developments on any level, personal or professional.

And worse than dealing with Isadora Campbell was the fact he could no longer put off calling his old boss.

Former SSA Art Hanrahan had retired from the BAU before Christmas, and they'd parted on bad terms. Frazer pressed his lips together. He'd have to suck it up because Hanrahan was the expert on Ferris Denker and his crimes. Hanrahan would know if the guy had ever taken the victim's shoes. He'd know the most likely candidates for an accomplice.

The moon was already setting and he had to be at Parson's Point at dawn. He may as well work for another hour. He had reports to read and emails from his team to address. He didn't want to be stuck out here longer than he had to when there were so many things going on back in Virginia...

The image of Helena Cromwell's pale corpse flashed through his mind—one of hundreds, maybe thousands. He already knew she was going to be one of the victims that stayed with him. Maybe it was the fact she'd been on the cusp of adulthood and had had it so brutally stolen away from her. Maybe it was the fact she looked like his mother.

He clenched his jaw. As satisfying as it was to catch a killer, he wished it didn't come with the knowledge that they were always too late for the first victim. He'd give it all up to save just one person. His throat went dry as he thought about his parents, but he pushed the memories away. Suddenly, thinking about all the things he'd like to do to a naked Isadora Campbell didn't seem like such a bad way to spend his time. Sure as hell beat reminiscing about his shattered childhood.

***

A few hours later, Lincoln Frazer stood looking over the dunes that guarded Parson's Point. His work was too ugly for poetry, but there were rare moments when he could appreciate the charm of a situation. Moments when he paused in his hunt for predators long enough to acknowledge beauty. Sometimes it was something intangible, an emotion, a feeling—like the love he'd seen grow between Rooney and Parker. Or the belief in an ideal—like Scarlett Stone's absolute faith in her father, a man the world had abandoned long ago. Sometimes it was physical—Isadora Campbell came to mind, and that damned beauty spot of hers.

Right now, it was a swathe of land that lay half-submerged in the ocean. The bright yellow of the sun picking out the honey and gold of the beach. Peach and pink bleeding from the sunrise into the ocean. The wind had dropped and the air felt warm.

The islands held a fragile beauty that could be swept away with one angry stroke of the ocean, but their strength lay in their fluid adaptability.

Maybe the people who lived here were on to something. The sand in his shoes spoke of family vacations and laid back atmosphere. Of barefoot children playing in the shallows, wild horses prancing. He looked across the sand dunes. It was unfortunate his world had crashed into this one, bringing with it the ugliness that made up his life's work. He had a horrible feeling it would get worse before it got better.

He stood in line between two other men on a boardwalk that ran between two sections of protected dunes, waiting for the search to begin. A shout went up and everyone began moving slowly forward. About twenty officers ranging either side of him. Officer Wright stood on the highest dune nearest the road, running the show. For now, Frazer was happy to let him. He walked steadily through the sand, systematically scanning the ground in front of his feet.

He'd sent Randall to interview the Ridgeway kid. Having talked to the other teens, he was most likely to pick up any detail that didn't fit. But Frazer had done a little background check on the new kid in town. In trouble at his old school with disciplinary issues, raised by a single mother, who was devoutly religious if her monthly donations were anything to go by. Ridgeway was definitely worth a deeper look.

A shout went up to his right and they all stopped. A crime scene tech ran over to photograph and collect whatever had been found. Anything and everything. They started forward again. What had been a straight line of police offices was now broken up by the landscape. Some law enforcement officers on top of dunes, others hidden from sight in the valleys.

Periodically a shout went up and they all stopped for the evidence to be tagged and bagged. He doubted these scraps caught in the grass would mean much or be admissible in court, but he didn't want to tip his hand about exactly what he expected to find today.

The sun's dawn rays produced long shadows in the sand. They reached the area where Helena and Jesse had been attacked. Empty now, except for the indentations that dappled every inch. Maybe the shoes were out here somewhere. His mind flashed to Helena's delicate features and cloudy eyes. The bruises on her neck. Tension entered his jaw and he forced it away. Don't think about Helena. Think about her killer instead.

What were you doing here?
I think I know.

He climbed another dune, through a section of interlocking sand ridges, and then over another rise until he finally saw what he was looking for. He stilled. He held up his hand and crouched down, examining the ground in front of him. A shout went up and everyone waited. A crime scene unit technician ran over. The same woman he'd met last night.

"We need to stop meeting like this." Her breath was hoarse from all the running she'd been doing. He gave her a smile but knew it didn't reach his eyes. She glanced nervously away.

"Can you photograph that area for me?" He pointed ahead.

"Sure." She got down on her knees beside him and took the photographs.

"Can I see them?" he asked.

She passed him the camera and he checked the shots. They confirmed what his eye had seen. A grave-sized hollow in the sand, almost indiscernible unless you were looking for it. He called over Officer Wright.

"I want this dune area cordoned off, but carry on the search around it." He pointed out the ridge lines. "And I want every crime scene tech you can spare in this space."

Wright jammed his hands on the equipment belt on his waist. Then he scratched the back of his neck. "Doing what?"

The CSU climbed to her feet and looked up with a tight expression on her face. "Dig. We're going to dig."

She'd spotted the same thing he had.

Frazer nodded.

Wright whipped his hat off his head and wiped the sweat off his brow. "Jesus."

Frazer checked his watch. "You guys get started. The ME's office is on standby with a helicopter if you find anything that looks human."

"Where are you going?" asked Officer Wright, looking pissed.

"Call me if you find anything." He was going to hypnotize Jesse, and to interview the man who had found the body—figure out if a father might have raped and murdered his own daughter. Some days the fun never stopped.

CHAPTER NINE

By the time Izzy dragged herself out of bed, Kit was long gone. Izzy had called and left a message on her cell, telling her to be careful because the Feds thought Helena's killer was still on the island. Izzy would fill her in with the details about last night as soon as she saw her.

Rather than relaxing, Izzy had busied herself by going to the store and stocking up on everything they'd run out of while she'd been working. She'd written a shopping list and asked Kit to do it, but she may as well have been speaking lower German. Somehow Izzy needed to figure out where she was going wrong with her kid sister. She sure as heck hadn't gotten away with not doing chores or not respecting her elders.

Izzy put her groceries in the back of her SUV then heard a tapping noise. She looked around and there was Uncle Ted in the diner next door, sitting with his cronies in their favorite booth. He tapped on the window again and she swore without moving her lips. The noise got louder and more insistent. She sighed as she closed the trunk.

She headed into the diner, unzipping her jacket as a rush of heat and the smell of bacon assaulted her senses. Kit worked here a couple of shifts a week. It was retro style with black and white checked tables and red vinyl bench seats, and it was Izzy's favorite place to eat in winter. In summer, you could barely get in the door.

"How are you doing, Izzy?" asked Mary Neville, the waitress. She had a younger sister who'd been in Izzy's class at school. It reminded her she had roots in this area that went back decades. But maybe roots didn't count for much on a sand island.

"Just a coffee, please, Mary."

"Come and join us!" Pastor Rice waved her over to her uncle's booth. He was a thin man, with sandy hair just beginning to turn gray. He was a good-looking guy, reminding her a little of Kevin Costner.

She plastered a friendly smile on her face, squared her shoulders and went over, pulling a chair to the end of the table.

"Ted was telling us it was your sister's best friend who was murdered." The pastor's smile faltered. "I'm so sorry. Please pass on my condolences and if she feels the need to talk I'm always available to listen."

"Recruiting again?" Seth Grundy sat against the window, opposite. He was the local mechanic and always gave them a good deal on any work that needed done. He was bald-headed with thick black brows and brown eyes that missed nothing.

"Spreading the word of Jesus is what I do, Grundy. It wouldn't hurt any of you to turn up to church occasionally."

"I'm a former Catholic," Seth retorted. "I eat guilt for breakfast."

"Hey, I go to church," complained Mr. Kent, who'd been her science teacher in junior high. Hank Wright was the fifth member of their motley crew, but he was busy today. With the exception of Hank, her uncle's friends were all in their early-fifties or older. They usually hung out at the diner on a Saturday morning rather than a Friday, but as today was a holiday they were obviously making an exception. On a Saturday night they went to Bert's, the bar on Main Street, and there was a weekly poker game that rotated between their houses. If you believed their complaints, none of them ever seemed to win.

Mary brought Izzy her coffee and filled up the empty mugs around the table. She collected the empty plates and went on her way. Izzy noticed Mr. Kent eyeing Mary's behind as she left and the pastor nudged his elbow and made him spill his coffee.

"What?" Mr. Kent protested. Even though it had been years since she'd been in his classroom, she couldn't think of him as anything except Mr. Kent.

"You know what," said the minister.

Her old science teacher shrugged. "No harm in looking."

"Why don't you ask her out," the pastor suggested. "'Stead of just looking?"

"Don't be ridiculous."

"Why is it ridiculous?" Ted asked.

Sweat formed on Mr. Kent's forehead as he snatched a glance at Izzy. "She was one of my students."

"A lifetime ago," Pastor Rice shook his head. "And she just got divorced," he hissed, leaning low over the table.

"Feels wrong." Mr. Kent looked down at his coffee.

"You don't do it, someone else might," Seth goaded.

Mr. Kent sent him a quelling look. "Keep your hands off, Grundy."

"Just sayin'." Seth grinned. According to her Uncle Ted, Seth had a reputation with the ladies.

Mr. Kent sent him a glare and then slowly got up and walked across to where Mary was cleaning tables on the other side of the diner. There were a couple high school students giggling over their phones. A retired couple she recognized from her walks with Barney, and a sports physio she knew from working at the hospital.

Mary looked up as Mr. Kent approached and a moment later she was blushing. Izzy turned away to give them some privacy.

"I hear there was a disturbance at your place last night." Ted nailed her with the same direct gaze her mother had had. The resemblance always unnerved her. Probably because she'd never gotten away with a damn thing with her mother.

"Why didn't you call me?" he asked.

It had never even crossed her mind. "Someone broke into the shed." She shrugged. "Kids, probably. The FBI was right next door." Her loose hair and the woolen hat she wore today hid the healing scab on her head. She didn't need anyone fussing over her. Her Glock was snug under her jacket, and she didn't intend to go anywhere without it for the foreseeable future.

"What did they think they'd find in your potting shed?" Ted asked with a frown.

"Pot?" Seth snorted.

Izzy looked at him sharply. Did he know Kit smoked marijuana, or was that a wisecrack? "I have no idea." She sipped her coffee. The Feds wouldn't want the news about her shovel being used in the attack on Jesse and Helena to be general knowledge. She wasn't an idiot.

"Kids will steal anything that's not nailed down," Mr. Kent said, returning to the table, and putting a piece of paper in his jacket pocket. He always wore a sport's coat and looked like a teacher even during the school holidays.

"Success?" the pastor asked with raised eyebrows.

Mr. Kent tried to hide a smile, but the gleam in his eye didn't lie. "I'm taking her out to dinner tomorrow night."

"Better not mess up else we'll all pay for it." Seth smoothed a hand over his slightly rounded belly.

"Your gut would thank me."

"My gut is perfectly content, thank you very much."

"We'll know how well he's doing if he gets any extra bacon," Ted chimed in softly.

"As long as he doesn't get extra sausage," the pastor said sternly and then they all started laughing.

It was like dining with schoolboys. Izzy drank her coffee, wishing it wasn't quite so scalding so she could escape sooner.

Ted turned his attention back to her. "Did they steal anything?"

"No." She avoided those sharp eyes of his and shrugged. "It was nothing. Kids messing around. Come check for yourself if you don't believe me."

She didn't miss the exchange of glances around the table.

"Did you have your gun on you?" Ted asked.

She did not like the fact they were all glued to her words like dogs waiting for a treat. "Yeah."

"Did you scare the shit out of them?" he

pushed. She could feel his concern for both her and Kit.

"Probably." She forced a smile. In reality it was the other way around. The assailant had scared her to death. "But I try not to shoot people on my days off. It's too much work patching them up again, and my boss frowns on conflicts of interest."

The men laughed because they knew she was a doctor, and the atmosphere lightened. Would she miss this sense of community when she left? A little, but not enough to stay. When they started talking about Helena's murder again, she was reminded of all the reasons she needed to leave.

"I can't believe someone would do something like that to a young woman," the pastor muttered under his breath. "And attacking the police chief's son?"

"Took some balls," Seth agreed, slurping his coffee.

"The FBI say anything about who they think did it?" Pastor Rice asked her.

She eyed him in amusement. "You seriously think the FBI confides in me?"

"Well, you're a doctor, and they're staying at your place."

"They're renting the cottage next door, not bunking down on the sitting room floor."

"Maybe you can get a peek at the evidence when you clean the place." Her former science teacher suggested with his eyes sparkling.

And *that* was why Frazer had asked for all the keys.

"I don't think so." Izzy doubted the FBI would be there that long. These men were worse gossips than a thousand raw recruits. "If you guys are so interested in the murder, why aren't you helping out with the search?" Her hands shook as she raised her cup to her lips again. Poor Helena.

"They didn't want our help," Seth said and then pushed his bottom lip out.

So they had volunteered. Figured.

"Said it was law enforcement personnel only." Mr. Kent played with the packets of sugar in the dispenser.

The thought of what they might find today twisted her gut, which was why she needed to stay busy. Her mind played the usual game of hide and go seek with her conscience.

"How's Kit holding up?" Ted asked.

And the reason for her continued silence reared up and bit her on the ass. Forget about dropping out of high school, her sister would be vulnerable to a killer. Not only that, Kit would find out the truth about her parents. Izzy couldn't do that to her. It hurt too much. "Not well," she admitted. "She can't stop crying."

"Poor kid," the pastor's pale blue eyes were alight with inner fervor. She had no doubt he'd be around to offer spiritual comfort.

"Think this will keep the tourists away?" Ted asked.

"This? You mean the brutal slaying of an innocent young woman?" Izzy clenched her jaw. Local people were nothing if not pragmatic.

"I just meant—"

"Hey. There's Hank," Mr. Kent interrupted.

Officer Wright walked in the door, spoke quietly to Mary, handed her a thermos and then came over and sat heavily on the edge of the bench seat beside Mr. Kent.

"I've only got ten minutes. Taking some hot drinks back out to the guys at the beach." Hank laid his arm along the table, sitting awkwardly. His face was pale.

"Find anything?" Mr. Kent asked, stirring another sugar into his coffee.

A little clutch of panic dug into Izzy's heart muscles.

"Got forensics excavating what looks like a shallow grave."

Bile poured into Izzy's mouth, but she forced it back down and washed away the taste with coffee. Don't react. Don't react.

The pastor's mouth dropped open. "They think someone else has been murdered out there?"

"No one else has been declared missing." Hank picked at his teeth with his little finger and shrugged. "But FBI wants to bring in ground penetrating radar."

Abruptly Izzy stood.

"You're leaving?" Ted asked. He looked disappointed and so did Hank, but she couldn't sit here listening to this conversation without throwing up.

"I need to get the groceries back home before they defrost."

"This is your first day off in weeks and that's your plan for excitement?" Ted clenched his hands where they rested on the table.

"You think it'd be more exciting if I sat around all day gossiping with you guys?" She raised a brow and then tried to take away the sting. "I'm gonna walk Barney. Go for a run. Maybe do yoga, and then take down the Christmas decorations. They don't feel appropriate anymore."

Ted's expression became downcast. "You're right. I'm sorry. I just wanted to try and cheer you up a bit, Iz-biz."

Izzy looked at Hank's bleak face and felt the weight in her chest grow heavy as a neutron star. With Helena dead and the FBI digging up that beach there was nothing in this world that was going to cheer her up today. Which reminded her she still had to tell Kit about last night and confront her about smoking pot. Her plans for the day took a nosedive, but she may as well get it all over with so the worst was done and they could figure out a way forward. She'd talk to the school counselor, get Kit an appointment.

She thought back to all the hope and promise the New Year had held just thirty-six short hours ago. So far, January sucked.

***

Helena's Cromwell's mother, Lannie, sat opposite her husband in a ladder-back chair. She had long straight hair, and big brown eyes that had probably been pretty before her world had shattered. She reminded him of his own mother with a wholesome natural beauty that was both simple and ageless. The knowledge of how quickly beauty faded in death hit him sideways. He turned his attention to the surroundings so the mother couldn't read his thoughts.

The family home was warm and comfortable, with a dated kitchen and a big calendar on the wall filled out in bold colorful print. A large fluffy cat wound itself around the table legs. Its food bowl was empty. Someone had forgotten to feed it. A loud meow broke the silence, but no one paid any attention to the poor creature.

"What was she doing on the dunes?" Helena's father, Duncan, asked suddenly. "She knows how important it is to keep off the dunes. She knows better than anyone not to go running over that area. I *told* her." The man's fingers clenched and unclenched, working himself into a fury. "How many times did I take her with me to make sure no one was trespassing? How many discussions did we have on the importance of protecting the dune systems for the very existence of these islands? I thought she understood. How could she have been so *stupid*?"

"God. What does it matter!" The wife snapped like she hated the man. "No one cares about your stupid *dunes*. Helena's dead and all you care about is work? She's *dead*."

Grief manifested itself in different ways, Frazer never knew what to expect, except the unexpected. He watched closely, needing to see everything. Every nuance. Every interaction.

They were clearly still in shock. The pressures on the relationship would be huge and would only get bigger. Parents of murdered children often struggled to stay together. If there were any cracks in the marriage they became chasms, not least because they were about to be put under the microscope as potential suspects. The Cromwells' other children, aged fourteen and twelve, were in the den watching TV. A terrible age to experience such devastating loss. Old enough to know what was going on, and resent being excluded, especially the teen. The teen wanted to be treated like an adult.

Frazer would have told the kids exactly what was going on, maybe sparing the more gory details. There wasn't always a correlation between age and the ability to handle reality. Children were more resilient than parents gave them credit for, and it was their sister who'd died so brutally. He'd give them enough information to understand the events so they were prepared when other kids said cruel things at school. But Frazer wasn't a parent so what the hell did he know.

"Where were you on New Year's Eve?" he asked.

"In bed by eleven." Duncan Cromwell looked up at him. "We're not exactly party animals."

His wife looked away like she couldn't bear the sight of her husband. "Some years we try to stay up, but when the kids were little we got out of the habit and now..." Now she was searching for meaning in her life.

The silence stretched thin.

She turned back to him. "Was she raped?" Her eyes pleaded with him to tell her no.

But he couldn't lie. "It's probable."

Her eyes welled up with fresh tears. "My poor baby."

"How do you know she didn't have sex with that boy? Jesse Tyson?" Duncan Cromwell spat the words. "How do you know he didn't rape her?" His hatred was palpable. Had he been out on the dunes? Had he seen Jesse and Helena having sex and then attacked them in a rage? It was Frazer's job to figure that out.

"I can't be a hundred percent sure of anything, which is a reason I need to ask you more questions about how you found them. You didn't know

Helena was on a date with Jesse Tyson?"

They both shook their heads. "She never told us." Lannie Cromwell plastered her hand over her mouth.

"She told you she was sleeping over at Kit Campbell's house?"

Duncan's eyes narrowed. "Why wasn't Izzy watching them like she was supposed to be?"

"She was at work and thought Kit was here with Helena." Frazer gave in to the need to defend her.

"She never thought to check?" Duncan asked bitterly.

"Did you?" Frazer queried back.

Duncan's gaze ricocheted off his. "I trusted Helena. She'd never have even thought to lie to me until she started hanging out with Kit Campbell. She'd never have gone off with a boy without that little bitch egging her on."

"You seem very angry at the idea of Helena having a boyfriend," Frazer said carefully.

"She was too young. At that age, young men are after one thing."

"And Helena knew you felt this way?"

Duncan nodded.

"Which is why she lied to us," Lannie snapped.

Duncan ran agitated hands through his thinning hair. "Look, I know I made mistakes, but I wasn't the only one. The most important thing is catching the bastard who hurt Helena." The man's desperate gaze reminded Frazer of broken glass. Parts of him were sharp, parts were splintered. He was falling apart on the inside.

Serial killers often began to unravel at some point. So did grieving parents.

Frazer took charge. "We're in the early stages of this investigation. I'd very much like to talk to you about the scene you came across yesterday morning, Mr. Cromwell. Ideally I'd like to hypnotize you to tap into any subconscious memories."

The man's eyes went round enough to see his whites and his mouth dropped open. He glanced repeatedly at his wife. "I can't." He shook his head. "Not in front of Lannie."

"I want to know everything." Her voice was a guttural growl. "I *need* to know."

Shocked at how she was behaving, she looked toward the glass door where their other children were watching TV. There was no noise from the other room.

"It isn't a bad idea to share what you saw with your wife, Mr. Cromwell. I realize the horror and grief are raw, but the imagination can be worse."

"No. No. Nothing is worse than that. Nothing." Duncan Cromwell pressed the heels of his hands against his eyes, rose to his feet. The cat ran between his legs and the man tripped. "Dammit!"

Frazer held his breath.

Duncan bent down and grabbed the kitty, hugged the creature to him and buried his face in the pure white fur. "I can't get the image of her out of my head, Lannie. Every time I close my eyes I see her lying in the sand like a broken toy. I don't want you to see that. I don't want you to suffer, too." The crack in his voice sounded like heartbreak.

"I'm already suffering, D. I need to hear what happened to Helena. I need to know it all." And weigh exactly how badly she'd let her daughter down. Frazer knew the steps.

The man stared at his wife, defeat written in every crease on his face. Frazer helped him sit back down. "Take a deep breath in. Hold it. Now let it out slowly." Frazer guided him through a few more breathing exercises, noticed Lannie Cromwell was doing them too. Most people did. It couldn't hurt. "Relax," he told the guy, "and close your eyes." He didn't abuse the trust that went with hypnotism, although he'd once tried to trick Rooney into answering a question while supposedly in a trance. She'd caught him even then.

The cat struggled and squirmed to get out of Cromwell's grip. The man let it jump down.

Ideally, Frazer would encourage the man to lie down and get comfortable. Play some new-age music that created a false environment—a safe environment. But they were trappings, not essential. The main thing was calming the mind and getting it to focus on where you wanted it to go.

"Do you always work on a federal holiday?"

His wife snorted.

A sad smile curved Cromwell's mouth. "I never stop working. There's always something to catch up with. Research to check. Reports to write. Data to collect."

"You love your job?"

"It's what I always wanted to do, ever since I was a little boy. Protect the land. Not just talk about it the way some tree-huggers do, but actually make a difference."

"It was a blustery morning. The sea was rough. Why'd you go out to Parson's Point?"

"I got a report of a washed up harbor seal down on the beach at Rodanthe. I went to check it out.

Saw there was a car parked on the side of the road near the lighthouse."

Jesse Tyson's car. It had been taken into evidence.

Cromwell's breathing was settled and deep. "So I stopped to make sure no one was in the dunes."

"What did you see when you first arrived?"

"There were several sets of footprints running through the sand. I remember being angry. People around here are quick to complain about erosion but most of them can't read a no trespass sign no matter how big you make it. I remember I unzipped my jacket because I was so hot with anger."

The same jacket he'd draped over the naked body of his daughter. The same jacket that was now in evidence waiting to be processed, as were the rest of Cromwell's clothes. "What happened next?"

"I came up over the foredune ready to give someone hell. I got to the top and looked down..." He swallowed audibly. "My eyes couldn't make sense of it."

"Can you describe the scene in detail for me? Tell me everything you see."

Frazer thought the guy was going to break out of the dream state, but after a few shallow breaths Cromwell sank heavily back against the wooden chair. "I saw the boy, Jesse, first. He was lying on his back, head lolling off to the side, blood staining the sand. A split-second later I saw the naked body of a young woman—her knees were bent and parted. She was," he breathed slow and deep, "sp-spreadeagled in the sand."

Vagina exposed. Staged for shock value. Degrading the victim even more than they'd

143

already done. The fact the father had found the body might have heightened the thrill for the killer. Awful to witness, important to know.

The mother covered her mouth with her hand. Tears filled her eyes.

"Part of my brain was thinking that I'd interrupted two people who'd had sex but they were so incredibly *still*...it didn't look natural. I kept trying to process it." Duncan Cromwell swayed a little in his seat but his emotions were submerged in this state of altered consciousness. "I realized it was Helena. I felt like someone had hit me with a brick—the force of that knowledge. I ran..." Tears streaked the man's cheeks—common during hypnosis and grief.

"Where were Helena's hands?"

"They were resting on her stomach. That's when I saw the bracelet." The man was growing more agitated. He wasn't deeply under, but the detail was there and Frazer didn't want to push it.

"Was she wearing any other jewelry when she went out?"

The mother nodded vigorously, but Frazer raised his hand to keep her quiet.

"She wore gold stars in her ears. Her mother bought them for her when she'd aced her math test last year."

"Were her eyes open or closed?"

"Open. Wide open. I kept waiting for her to blink. When I got closer I could see they were bloodshot and cloudy. There were marks on her neck, and blood on her thighs." He bit his lip. "I can't believe someone did that to her—to Helena. You wouldn't treat an animal that way."

Helena had gotten off lightly compared to some

victims—especially Denker's victims—and if that wasn't the saddest thought of the day Frazer didn't know what was.

Cromwell continued. "I took off my jacket and covered her. Then I called 911 and started mouth-to-mouth."

Lannie held out her hand to her husband, but he didn't see it. Frazer watched her fingers curl and slowly withdraw back into her lap. "Ambulance arrived and then Izzy Campbell showed up around the same time, but she didn't even try and save Helena." The tone turned malicious.

"Helena was already dead, Mr. Cromwell." The man had subconsciously known that, he'd even said her eyes were cloudy.

"It was freezing, and she didn't even try." Cromwell's rage had transferred, which disturbed Frazer.

"She helped save Jesse Tyson," he said carefully.

"Whoop de fucking do." Acid laced the man's words and he opened his eyes. Frazer held his gaze but let it be. He was hurting. His child was dead and Isadora Campbell was an easy target. Rational wasn't always a choice.

He repeated the deep breathing exercises with the man to calm him down again and moved on. He needed to see the scene clearly. "So Helena lay on her back. Where was Jesse in relation to your daughter?"

"He was at a right angle to her. Boots close to her hips."

Frazer wished he'd seen it first-hand. It sounded like the killer had staged the bodies to look a certain way. "Did the boy look like he'd been moved?"

The father blinked. "Yeah, he'd been moved. There were drag marks down the face of the dune." He frowned, staring at an image in his mind. "But not Helena. I didn't see any drag marks around her body."

There were shades of a disorganized offender here. The explosive violence, lack of restraints, the fact bodies had been left in view where they'd been killed—all traits of a so-called disorganized killer. But to him, the crime scene itself reflected control. The lack of physical evidence—no trace had been found on the victim in terms of hairs or semen or blood. The ME was going to take swabs off her skin in an attempt to find contact DNA. The assailant may have taken the teens by surprise—incapacitated Jesse with the shovel. Then taken his time assaulting Helena, who'd been his true target. She hadn't resisted, hence the lack of defense wounds. The killer had left the bracelet on her tiny wrist to deliver Denker's message. This was assuming Jesse hadn't been part of the attack. There was nothing to suggest that, but Frazer refused to discount anything at this point. The bracelet strongly indicated other factors were in play. He ran the scenario through his mind. If Jesse was in on it, why beat the kid and leave him for dead? No, the pair had both been attacked. Jesse had been the greater threat so take him out first, fast and hard. What would Helena do?

"She ran," said Frazer.

"And he caught her." This from the mother who looked like she wanted to throw up.

"The boy's wallet was lying in the sand next to him. I could see dollar bills in it. Why would someone take the kid's wallet out of his pocket but not steal his money?" Duncan was frowning, as if he was standing on the beach looking down at the scene—exactly what Frazer needed him to do.

"I'll check his credit cards." But Frazer's brain sparked. Had the unsub been searching for something else in that wallet? Something even he carried on the off chance he might one day miraculously have sex. If that was the case, this crime had definitely not been planned because most experienced rapists were savvy enough to carry a condom. "Did you see a shovel at the scene?" Frazer asked.

Duncan closed his eyes again. "Yes. Off to the left as you looked at the sea. I didn't pay it any attention. I kept seeing Helena's clothes strewn around the place and thinking it was so cold last night. She must have been so cold." His shoulders shook as tears ran unheeded down his cheeks.

The mother hugged her stomach with one arm and covered her face with the other.

"Did you know Helena was seeing the Tyson boy?" He was repeating questions from earlier because that's what investigators did.

"She wasn't seeing him." The father's denial had a ring of desperation to it. He didn't want to believe his little girl had lied to him. "That Campbell girl is a bad influence on Helena." Duncan Cromwell's eyes got wide. "Was. *Was* a bad influence." His voice dropped away to nothing. "I don't think I'll ever get used to saying that."

"How long had they been friends?"

"They started hanging out after Kit's mother died last year. Helena gravitates—gravitated— toward people who were suffering."

"She sounds like she had a kind soul."

"She was easily led." Cromwell bit out. "She'd never have gone to that party unless Kit Campbell convinced her to lie to us."

"Did you know she drank alcohol?" Frazer asked. According to the other kids she'd had a couple of tequila shots.

"She would never..." Duncan sputtered to a stop. Then he shook his head. "Obviously I didn't know my daughter very well."

"From everything I heard, she was a great kid. You should be very proud of her."

"She lied to us, had a secret boyfriend, drank, and God knows what else, but you think she was a good kid? I don't recognize this person you're describing as my daughter, ASAC Frazer."

"The girls lied to you because they wanted to go to a party. Teens do that. No one could have foreseen the consequences." Although he could have. Years of seeing murder victims meant if he ever had kids he'd probably keep them under surveillance 24/7. God knew how Alex Parker or Mallory Rooney were going to cope, but he suspected some sort of electronic tracking device might be involved.

"You didn't leave the house at all on the night of Helena's murder?" Frazer kept his eyes on the man.

"No. I wish I had. If I'd been at the dunes I might have been able to stop this." Duncan Cromwell stood and started pacing again. "Where was Kit Campbell when Helena was attacked? They're supposed to be best friends. They were supposed to be together. Where was the little bitch?"

Whoa.

"It wasn't Kit's fault either, Mr. Cromwell." His words didn't seem to penetrate. Grief was an ugly creature.

The cat resumed her begging, and Cromwell strode to the cupboard and pulled out a box of kibble, which he poured into the empty dish. The cat started crunching on the food. He looked up. "This is Helena's cat. She usually feeds him."

They locked eyes and the realization Helena was never coming back to feed her cat hit home with renewed force. It would hit home every day for years to come, usually a few seconds after they opened their eyes.

"When can we bury her?" Lannie asked.

Frazer saw the strength in her gaze. Hoped it was enough to get the family through this.

"It depends on whether a second autopsy is deemed necessary."

The mother looked appalled by the idea. Bad enough to suffer that indignity once, but twice? Or maybe everything paled to insignificance when your baby was murdered. Maybe nothing could ever be worse than that.

"I promise to keep you updated and do my best to get your daughter's body released as soon as possible."

"Thank you." She inclined her head stiffly. She looked both stronger and more fragile than Duncan.

"You own two vehicles?"

"One." Duncan shook his head. "I use a work truck and we have a minivan."

"Any bikes or motorbikes?"

"No. Well," his eyebrows pinched, "that's not true. We have pushbikes in the garage. The kids use

149

theirs." He jerked his chin toward the connecting door. "But me and Lannie haven't biked anywhere since the summer."

"And Helena?"

Duncan's expression soured. "She rode everywhere in Kit Campbell's VW. Hasn't touched her bike in months."

Frazer's phone buzzed in his pocket, but he ignored it. He was pretty sure Duncan Cromwell had told him everything his brain could handle at this point. He wasn't off the hook, but Frazer would wait to see the evidence before he made his next move. This was no ordinary rape-murder, not if Ferris Denker was involved. "The local police might have more questions for you." He hadn't mentioned that officially it wasn't his case, but as he was a senior FBI agent it was unlikely anyone was going to call him on the details.

He went to leave, then hesitated on the threshold of the front door. "I know it's painful, but you should talk to your other children about Helena's murder."

"They're too young to understand." Cromwell shook his head.

He looked the man in the eye. "I'm not saying give them details, but tell them enough that they understand what's going on—because if you don't, the other kids in school will. And they won't be kind about it. They'll be brutal." He slipped a card into Duncan Cromwell's hand. "This is the name of a psychologist I recommend for grief counseling. Do it for your kids' sake. Do it for yourself. But do it."

He walked outside and checked the message on his phone.

The crime scene techs at the beach had uncovered human remains. Parson's Point was officially a dump ground.

CHAPTER TEN

After dropping the groceries at home and taking the Christmas decorations down, Izzy decided it was time to confront Kit. She pulled up outside a small cottage on the north side of Rosetown, right next to St. Olaf's Church. Her mother's old VW Beetle was parked at the curb. It was Kit's car now.

Pastor Rice's house was the other side of the road, facing the church. A small graveyard lay behind the quaint red brick building with its white wooden spire. Her mother was buried there.

Izzy put her hand on the door handle and elbowed it open. Barney watched her attentively from the cargo hold, ears pricked. "Ten minutes." She told him. Because he understood every word and, apparently, knew how to tell time. She left all the windows cracked for him. It was a cool day and she wouldn't be long.

She checked the road before she crossed, but traffic was light. It was January 2. A Friday. Some people had returned to work but many more had taken it as a vacation day and made it an extra-long weekend.

The cottage she was headed for belonged to the church, who rented it out at a reasonable rate to families in need. It had been freshly painted bright white, the shutters a sky blue, and the shingles had been replaced since she'd been here last—the day her mother's headstone had been installed. She knocked on the front door. No sound from within.

She waited, but no one answered. Kit's car was here so Izzy wasn't about to walk away without exerting a little effort. She headed around to the back door and knocked again. The lawn was slightly long but not out of control. Her glance went to the open garage at the end of the drive. A beat-up Chevy van took up most of the space, but a black dirt bike was tucked down one side. A tingle of awareness shot up Izzy's spine. Still no answer from the cottage.

Was Kit avoiding her? That was entirely possible. But so was the chance her sister was in danger. Izzy pulled out her cell and dialed her sister's number again. A snatch of a ring tone floated over the tall fence from the direction of the cemetery. And along with it another sound— voices. Then the voices grew louder. People were arguing and one of those people sounded a lot like Kit.

Izzy reached into her jacket and grasped her Glock and ran back the way she'd come, jogging to the main gate, trying to force herself to relax. Memories of Helena's dead eyes refused to leave her alone and amped up her fear to full-out panic. She increased the pace but then slowed, hugging the wall of the church as she peered around the corner. Some tall lanky guy held onto Kit's arm with one hand, a cigarette dangling from the other. He leaned down and yelled into her face. "It wasn't my fucking idea, and the cops are going to crucify me if they find out."

Whoa.

The young man had straight, ink black hair and pinched narrow features. She didn't recognize him. She held the gun in a two-handed grip, pointing it at the ground but making sure it was visible as she stepped around the corner and approached the teens who stood at the end of a cracked concrete path.

"Get away from her," Izzy gritted out.

Kit's jaw dropped and her expression turned incredulous. "Oh, my God. Go away, Izzy. This has nothing to do with you!"

Izzy kept her expression neutral at her sister's less than happy greeting. Nice.

"I said, get your hands off my sister," Izzy repeated to the creep. The cop comment had her senses on high alert. What had he done that would make them crucify him?

He snorted and said to Kit. "*That's* your sister? You're right, she's a total bitch."

Izzy flinched and her mouth went dry. The young man didn't seem to recognize her, which meant if he was the bad guy, he didn't know anything about her past misdemeanors.

Kit jerked her arm out of the boy's grip. "Shut up, Damien." She turned back to Izzy. "What are you even doing here? Why do you have your frickin' *gun* out?"

"I saw him attacking you."

Damien shook his head and rolled his eyes. Kit looked like she was going to stamp her feet like a two-year-old.

"Dammit, Izzy, we were arguing. If you shoot everyone I shout at, you'd better start with yourself."

Ouch. She ignored the hurt that statement wrought and slid the weapon back into the holster, but she didn't snap it closed.

"So, what were you two arguing about?"

"None of your business," Kit muttered.

Izzy narrowed her gaze at both of them. "Fine. Why don't we add this to the list of potential topics? If you ever do drugs on my property again, you," she pointed to the guy she assumed to be Damien Ridgeway, "will be receiving a visit from the police."

He sneered. "But not your precious sister?"

"For God's sake, grow up. She'll be talking to the cops, all right, but she isn't the one supplying." She held Kit's gaze with narrow eyes. "She'll also be grounded until school finishes."

Kit crossed her arms over her chest. She was wearing a couple of long sleeved t-shirts and jeans so tight Izzy could see the joints in her knees. "You can't ground me, Izzy. You are not my mother."

"Thank God." Izzy smiled her professional smile. "But I'm your legal guardian and I can limit your funds enough you can't even afford to buy gas, let alone cannabis."

"Sal will give me more shifts at the diner." Kit gave her a sly smile. "And, anyway, I don't need to *buy* it. I can get anything I want if I ask nicely enough."

Damien smirked at the ground.

The insinuation in the word "ask" was blatantly sexual.

"Jesus, Kit, you're seventeen. Don't mess up your life when you're just starting out."

Kit shook her head. "Why am I the only high school student getting reamed out for being normal? Everyone does it. Why do you have to be such a hard ass?"

"Helena didn't do drugs," Izzy argued.

Kit's blue eyes glittered. "Helena's dead, Iz. Thanks for reminding me."

"Is this how you honor her memory? By going off the rails?"

Kit's eyes filled, and the tears brimmed over. "What does it matter? She'll never know!"

Izzy knew she was handling this wrong. If someone broke their leg, she was more than capable of repairing that injury. But when it came to messy emotions like love and guilt she could barely cope with her own issues, let alone a hormonal female who'd lost her mother and her best friend within the space of a year. Part of her wanted to wrap Kit in her arms and baby her, the other part wanted to shake some sense into her.

Kit was better than this, although she was doing a damn good job acting like a loser. The government should bring back compulsory National Service and give these youngsters some understanding of hard work, sacrifice, and service. The fact Izzy thought of the teens as youngsters made her feel as ancient as sand.

Damien shifted his feet, drawing her attention back to him.

"Where were you last night, Damien?" Izzy quizzed him.

He remained silent. Was he the one who'd broken into the tool shed? Was he the one who'd stolen her shovel? He was too young to have watched her on the beach all those years ago, but could he have killed Helena? Izzy couldn't read him. "Where's your mother?"

"None of your business."

"I see you have a dirt bike."

His brows jammed together. "So what?"

She turned to Kit because Damien wasn't going to tell her a damned thing, the little weasel. "The night of the party, when you came back to the cottage—did you see anyone outside, near our house?"

Kit's expression changed, and then she shook her head. "I didn't see anything, Izzy. I was so wasted I wouldn't have noticed a thing unless it bit me on the ass."

Damien smiled in a way Izzy did not like. She narrowed her gaze at him and the expression vanished. "What about you? Did you see anything?"

"I was too busy looking at Kit's ass to be looking out the window."

She lunged forward and grabbed the guy, shoving him against the brick wall. His eyes went wide and his skin lost color. "You want me to tell the cops about you supplying a seventeen-year-old with weed?"

Kit started screeching to let him go and Izzy shoved him away from her.

He kept his mouth shut but the anger in his gaze burned. After a tense moment, he took another long drag of his cigarette, dropped the stub, screwing it into the ground with his heel. "I don't think you know your precious sister as well as you think you do, bitch."

She gritted her teeth at the "bitch" insult. Wasn't the first time she'd been called it. Probably wouldn't be the last. As for not knowing Kit very well, tell her something she didn't already know.

"I'll talk to you later, Kit." He turned away, walking down the fence to a gate Izzy hadn't spotted earlier.

Kit gave Izzy an exasperated look and stalked off down the path. "I can't believe you just did that."

"He was hurting you when I arrived."

Kit rubbed her arm. "He was holding onto my arm. Jeez. I'd have decked him if he'd tried anything."

And then he could have knocked the crap out of her, the same way some asshole had done to Jesse and Helena. "Damien could be the killer."

"He's a friend of mine." Kit defended him.

"Didn't look like much of a friend to me."

"That's because you don't have any friends, Izzy. You're too fucking high and mighty for the people around here."

Izzy flinched, but she didn't have time for a pity party, not with a killer on the loose. "Last night someone broke into our toolshed, and smacked me on the head when I went to investigate."

Kit's expression turned to one of total horror. "What time?"

"About two."

"Why didn't you wake me?"

"When my gunshot didn't wake you, I figured you must be exhausted and needed the rest."

"You fucking shot someone?" Her sister's mouth hung open.

Izzy shook her head. "Just into the ground to attract the attention of the FBI next door."

"But you didn't wake me?"

"You had your headphones on…"

"And you wonder why I don't talk to you?" For once Kit looked disappointed in her, rather than the other way around.

A wave of shame rolled over Izzy. Kit was right, she should have woken her, but it was too late to change that now. She was used to doing things on her own. Izzy pushed on because what she had to say was more important than sisterly issues. "The thing is, when ASAC Frazer and I took a look at the shed I realized our shovel was missing, and..." She had to swallow repeatedly to get the words out. "He, ASAC Frazer that is, showed me a picture of the shovel that was used to beat Jesse the other night, and...it was ours." She moved closer so her words didn't carry on the wind. "Whoever broke into the shed last night rode a dirt bike. Is it possible Damien left you at some point in the evening on New Year's—when you were asleep?"

Kit stared at her.

"I guess what I'm asking is, do you think he could have done it? Attacked Helena?" Izzy finished awkwardly.

Kit's lips parted and she shook her head. "I don't think so."

Really? "So why did he say the cops would crucify him if they found out? Found out what?"

Kit turned and walked to their mother's grave. Izzy followed at a distance. Her mother's stone had fresh flowers and a little Christmas tree— presumably left by Kit or Uncle Ted.

"It's not what you think, Iz." Kit picked up her purse, which lay beside the stone. "Damien has been in trouble with the law before. If they find out he was smoking pot, he'll get kicked out of school and he wants to graduate high school and try and get a decent job." She looked up, eyes pleading. "There's no way I'd be with him if I thought he'd hurt Helena."

After a moment Izzy nodded. What else could she do? "Promise me one thing."

Her sister closed her eyes. "What?"

"*If* you have sex—which you shouldn't be

doing, but God knows you wouldn't be the first seventeen-year-old to do it—please, please, use protection." She raised her hands when Kit opened her mouth to argue. "I don't want to hear anything except that promise, right now."

"I'm not an idiot." The expression on her sister's face shut down. "Sure, I promise." Kit knelt beside the grave and pulled away some of the longer grass. She stayed that way for a few minutes while the anger and sorrow of the last few days dissipated. "I wish Mom was buried next to Dad."

A shudder went through Izzy at the idea.

"She always said how much she loved him."

Izzy closed her eyes and clenched her hands into fists to try to contain the emotions that welled up inside her. They'd both idolized him.

"I'm glad she's not here to see this."

Izzy nodded. She was glad, too. For different reasons.

Kit straightened the flowers and then picked up the little Christmas tree before rising to her feet. "Helena put this here before Christmas." She sniffed tearfully, the moody teen shifting into the grief-stricken young woman. "We'd better take it down else we'll have bad luck."

Tears streamed down Kit's cheeks. This time they streamed down Izzy's too.

She sniffed. "I'm sorry I couldn't save her, Kit."

Kit gave her a wobbly smile. "Me, too."

Izzy's phone buzzed and she dried her eyes and checked the screen. A slice of dread cut through her. The police chief needed to see her, urgently.

***

He drove along a highway he hadn't traveled since Ferris Denker had been caught. He whistled along to some classic rock station on the radio, feeling happier than he had in ages. He laughed as he remembered the scare Izzy Campbell had given him last night. Scared him out of his ever-loving mind. First the cat rubbing against his leg as he'd wiped prints off the lock and door, then Izzy coming outside with her fricking gun drawn. Thankfully, she hadn't seen his face.

If she hadn't gotten that shot off, he might have taken her. The idea of having Izzy Campbell at his mercy was tempting. Taking her from beneath the nose of the FBI? Electrifying. Izzy was something else. He admired her. She was smart and pretty. But underneath that cool front, lay deliciously dark secrets. All these years he'd watched the family from the shadows, wondering if the day would ever come when he revealed what she'd done. So it was just as well he hadn't taken her last night because then the show would be over and it was too much fun to rush. He licked his lips. He was getting aroused again and he glanced in the back of the van. He'd taken a whore. Given her some coke and tied her up so tight she'd be in agony if she woke up, but not dead. She wasn't dead. Anticipation was driving him crazy, but he had to do this right, and he wasn't some amateur who couldn't control himself—well, except for Helena and that had worked out fine. His buddy Ferris was relying on him and he loved the fact he was the one outside orchestrating this shit, when Ferris had always considered himself the brains of their little club.

Another thirty minutes and he saw the turn off.

The sign was so weathered and faded he wouldn't have been able to read it unless he'd already known what it said. "St. Joseph's School for Boys."

He turned down the rutted, overgrown road, the suspension rattling and bouncing over the uneven ground. He drove past the decaying red brick building with its central clock tower. The school had been abandoned thirty years ago, but the building had been falling into disrepair long before that. Most of the windows were broken, the ground floor ones boarded up to prevent break-ins. Why they bothered was beyond him. There were bats in the belfry and rats in the cellars, damp and rot on every level in-between. A fire had taken one wing of the building a few years after they'd graduated. It had been the final straw for the school and it had shut its doors forever. Maybe Ferris had set the place alight himself.

He wished he'd thought of it first.

He drove on, past the tennis courts and the overgrown athletics track. His gut churned as he remembered all those boys with their skinny legs and knobby knees. The changing rooms had been burned to the ground years ago. He and Ferris had seen to that, smoking dope and pissing into the flames.

He wished the gym teacher was still alive so he could kill the bastard. His hands shook from the fury of what the man had done to him. Ferris had always said the guy had set them free, allowed them to become who they truly were, but he didn't believe him. He'd been created by one man's twisted lust and what he'd become was payback for no one giving a damn.

It was so clichéd for the abused to become

abusers, but this was a school and it had taught him well.

He drove farther until he hit the edge of a wood. He looked for the path, but it was so overgrown he couldn't see it. Shit. Ferris had told him to display the corpse wearing Beverley's bracelet directly over the spot where they'd buried their first victim, under the noses of their teachers. Obviously, he'd altered that plan when Helena had interrupted him in the dunes, but this would work. In fact, in terms of getting attention, two murders worked far better than one. He parked and got out, parted the brambles where he thought the path should be. Thorns caught at his clothes, but he brushed them aside with his thick work gloves. He pushed through and spotted the hut that had covered the well. There.

He grinned and went back to the van, opened the back, dragged off the tarp.

The whore rolled on her back, twisting against the bonds, dilated pupils telling him she was still high. He grabbed her ankle and dragged her roughly toward him, bending to haul her over his shoulder. She was a prostitute he'd picked up, with a micro skirt, black leather bustier and desperate eyes. The black patent leather heels had shone brightly in the sun, attracting his attention. That's how he'd chosen her. That's how he'd known she was the one.

He tramped through the dense undergrowth with the woman over his shoulders, batting away the briars. Hell. The area was almost totally reclaimed by the forest. Crazy how fast that happened. His heart beat a little faster at the thought of what was to come. His erection strained against his zipper as the woman struggled against him. The coke was wearing off. She was starting to understand this wasn't some drug-fueled hallucination. This was real.

He went past the well. Beyond was a large American oak that had probably been planted before the revolution. He turned right, pushing through the saplings and bushes. There, finally, a large clearing with a series of large stones that formed a circle about ten feet in diameter. He dumped the woman on the ground.

The woman's terrified eyes met his, clearer than they had been when she'd first told him the price and climbed into the cab. She wasn't worth what she'd asked but he hadn't planned on paying her. He took off his gloves and removed a condom from his back pocket and covered himself. The DNA floating around in her pussy should keep the cops busy for a year. Get a few johns some interesting visits from the cops, that was for damned sure. He placed the condom wrapper carefully in his vest pocket and zipped the pocket. He'd shaved his body hair to prevent leaving any behind. There would be no mistakes this time. He put his gloves back on, wishing he could touch her the way he wanted to and knowing it was impossible. She was a token. A cheap gift for Ferris. The hunger was growing stronger, as if by allowing himself to take Helena it had destroyed the control he'd always prided himself on.

It was temporary.

Ferris was in trouble and he'd allowed his monster a little extra freedom to feed. He'd lock it back down soon. Chain it up and beat it into submission so he didn't end up in a cell like

Ferris's.

He leaned down and ripped the duct tape off her mouth.

He didn't care if she made noise. There was no one around for miles.

She screamed and he hit her, his excitement growing as she fought him. Maybe the coke had given her strength but she had more spirit than he'd imagined. The sight of those heels kicking in the dirt pushed him over the edge, making his brain bleed with want.

She fought and fought, but in the end, it didn't take long.

"Do you see it?" he asked her.

But the moment the light began to fade in her eyes was the moment he exploded and he kept going, remembering how good it had felt to die. Remembering the blinding whiteness and the call of angels and wishing he could have stayed there with them.

He finished, breath hoarse in his chest, wishing it didn't have to end, knowing it did. He pushed her hair away from her forehead. She was better off now. He'd done her a favor. He knew there was an afterlife, he'd glimpsed it—a world of such beauty, a white tunnel of light, and the feeling of peace and tranquility and welcome unequaled on this earth.

It was a trade of sorts. By taking what he wanted using brute force, sex became a million times more satisfying. In return he sent them to a better place.

Ferris needed to torture his victims to eke out as much pain as possible; he just wanted to watch them die.

He cleaned up the site. Removed her clothes

and the ropes. The duct tape. He posed her, more out of deference to Ferris than his own inclinations. Although there was no denying he liked to look at the things he owned. Usually he had to hide or disguise the fruits of his labor, never being acknowledged and, more importantly, never being caught, unlike poor old Ferris. It was worth it, but it didn't mean he wouldn't enjoy this short explicit playtime in an effort to help out an old buddy.

He bent down and inserted something inside her body, leaving it visible to anyone who looked. He got a kick out of the act even though it wasn't his craziness he was recreating. Ferris said he couldn't leave them covered in his DNA. He couldn't leave them alive with their memories, so he marked them with something else. Something tangible.

He leaned down and picked up the black patent heels with shaking hands and cradled them gently against his chest. He didn't know why he took them. The gym teacher had always made them remove their shoes at the door—apparently even pedophiles liked a clean floor. For whatever reason, the shoes reminded him of each act of complete domination. All he had to do was touch their shoes, and he could relive each one of them floating away as pleasure filled his body.

It made it real for him, over and over again.

He'd have to get rid of them soon. He knew that, too. And the photographs. They were evidence linking him to murder and he wasn't dumb.

He scanned every inch of ground, checking his pocket for keys and wallet. He'd left his phone in the truck, disabling the battery and SIM card as soon as he left the islands. Taking every precaution.

Satisfied that he had everything, he stood back and admired his handiwork. She hadn't been pretty in life, but now she was beautiful.

"Sleep tight, angel." He smiled.

CHAPTER ELEVEN

Grains of sand scoured the pale dome of the half-buried skull. A seagull cried out overhead, waiting to see whether or not it was going to scavenge an easy meal in what little remained of the corpse.

Not on his watch.

Frazer stood with his arms crossed, overlooking the dig site.

As soon as they'd uncovered the first bone, the ME had been called. Simon Pearl had sent one of his assistants because he was busy finishing the autopsy on Helena Cromwell. Noting the state of deterioration of the body, the assistant had also arranged for a forensic anthropologist to meet them back in the lab. The skeleton had long since been picked clean of flesh by critters that lived in the sand. Little else remained except some tattered pieces of gray material, probably duct tape. The crime scene technicians had worked their way meticulously through layers of loose sand. Sieving every scoop for potential evidence.

Randall approached from the direction of the beach and the two of them moved away from the others.

Frazer was careful to keep his voice down. "I want a lockdown on any information about a possible ID on the victim until we are one hundred percent certain who this is. Let's compare dental records and rush DNA before we inform the family."

The one good thing about finding someone you cared about dead, it beat the hell out of never knowing what happened to them. Just ask Mallory Rooney.

Randall nodded. This was what they'd both feared when they'd recognized the name on the medical alert bracelet. The Denker case was already making headlines as his execution neared. The anti-death penalty lobby was in full battle cry, whining about how unfair it all was to the condemned prisoner. They'd think differently if it was their loved ones murdered, and there had never been any doubt Denker was one hundred percent guilty. But that wasn't Frazer's issue.

Good or bad, the death penalty was on the statute books of some states in the US and he'd do everything he could to make sure the justice system was served. It might be a little hypocritical considering he'd taken the law into his own hands in the past, but when weighing the balance of good and evil, right and wrong, his conscience was clear.

"You talk to Damien Ridgeway yet?" asked Frazer.

Randall shook his head. "I've set up a meeting with him this afternoon along with his mother. Kid was thrown out of his last school for dealing drugs. He does own a dirt bike."

He had opportunity, but there was no clear motive unless he'd latched onto Denker in some way. "He's eighteen?"

Randall nodded.

"Check out his parents and dig deeper into his background before you interview him. Keep it light. Don't tip our hand." He was a definite suspect, but Frazer wasn't ready to cross anyone off that list unless they had an unbreakable alibi.

Isadora Campbell had been with a group of

doctors and nurses who'd brought in the New Year with coffee and brownies, then she'd dealt with a range of cases including a baby with a high fever, a thirty-year-old female with an inflamed appendix, and a reveler who'd celebrated a little too hard and managed to break his ankle going from one bar to another. And that was before two. No way could she have disappeared for forty minutes during that mayhem—not without her absence being noticed.

He watched one of the CSU technicians carefully lift the skull out of the sand and place it in a box lined with sterile plastic bags. This beach wasn't the worst resting place a person could hope for. There was a peacefulness to the ocean that seemed appropriate for someone who'd probably endured horror before they'd died.

Was it Beverley Sandal? No point raising the parents' hopes, only to dash them again with forensic results. She'd been missing for seventeen long years. A few more days wouldn't make any difference. Some killers played sadistic games with the victims' families and he wasn't about to let the man in prison hurt those people any more than he already had.

CSU were gently lifting the rest of the bones and placing them in the lined box.

The ME stood up and stretched out her back, revealing a small baby bump that reminded him of Rooney—who was going to be fine, damn it. He'd spoken to Parker and they'd ruled out pre-eclampsia and a few other serious conditions. The ME was eyeing him like he'd ruined Christmas. He got that a lot.

She slowly walked over to where he stood. She twisted around and stretched out her back. "You're not one of those men who think pregnant women can't do their jobs properly, are you, ASAC Frazer?"

"No, I'm dubious of anyone's skills until they prove me wrong—pregnant or not." He sure as hell didn't like the feeling of responsibility that came with having an unborn child at a crime scene. He was suddenly aware how vulnerable they were—a little person totally dependent on the wellbeing of the woman who carried them. "Anything you can tell me about our vic?" He changed the subject.

One side of her mouth twitched into a smile. "If I had a dollar for every time law enforcement asked me that question I'd be a wealthy woman."

He waited silently.

"I heard you didn't have a sense of humor."

He frowned. "I have a sense of humor."

Randall looked away.

"No." She shook her head. "You don't."

Frazer's eyes narrowed. Maybe she was right. He didn't care.

"We have a female, judging from the general size of the bones and the shape of the pelvis, but my colleague can give us a better assessment back in the lab."

"Any idea how long the body has been buried?"

Her eyebrow rose as if to say "Are you kidding me?" but she remained silent.

"Years rather than months?"

She grunted. "It's hard to say."

Of course it was.

"Certainly months rather than days."

Great. So far she'd given him nothing he couldn't have figured out for himself. "Yet, I'm the one without a sense of humor," he muttered quietly.

There was a shout from the dig site.

"What've you found?" the ME asked as she walked back down the path they'd worn in the sand. Duncan Cromwell was going to have a fit at the destruction they'd wrought, assuming he didn't go mad with grief first.

Frazer and Randall followed the ME. They all stared into the shallow pit, more than a little shocked to see another skull staring up at them.

"Shit." Randall voiced what Frazer was thinking.

Was this a mass grave? A wave of sorrow hit him. Hopefully the second vic's DNA was in the missing person database. If it was another one of Denker's victims, it might provide closure when the family needed it most—before the killer took his secrets to the grave. But if the victim was an unknown...

A new investigation might call for the postponement of Denker's execution and a reopening of the old case. Regardless of the fact Denker was a sadistic killer, and not an innocent man. The judicial system seemed designed to keep those killers alive for as long as possible, regardless of evidence, or the hurt it caused the victims' families—

He cut himself off. It was exactly that sort of flawed thinking that had gotten The Gateway Project started. He'd shut the organization down, and for the most part believed in the justice system, including the death penalty, as flawed as it was. The thoughts reminded him that his friend CIA Intelligence Officer Patrick Killion had called him to say he was following a lead on the assassin who'd killed the Vice President. After seeing Helena Cromwell's delicate corpse it didn't seem so important anymore, especially when they couldn't arrest the assassin anyway. All they could do was make sure she knew The Gateway Project was done and that she was being monitored. They just had to find her first.

But these people, serial killers who tore apart humans for the fun of it? These were the people he wanted to hunt to extinction. These were the people he'd go to his own grave to destroy.

The ME squatted down to peer closer at the second skull. Frazer had an appointment at the hospital, but he was reluctant to leave.

"Looks like it's going to be a long day." She smiled, but there was a tiredness to her eyes. He wanted to tell her to take a break, but knew she'd have his hide if he did.

"You know this was Blackbeard's territory, right?" she said.

Another sadistic serial killer.

Frazer kept his expression stern. "Let me know if you find an eye patch."

She pulled a face and he hid a smile.

His cell rang and he checked the screen. His mouth dried up. "Excuse me, I have to take this." He turned and walked away. He'd been dreading this conversation since Rooney had first called him. "Hanrahan? Thanks for getting back to me. Look, I need your help."

***

"I don't know how I can help, Chief. Hypnosis isn't something I have any experience with." Izzy rubbed her arms. Kit had taken Barney home and offered to walk him. Her sister had actually promised to be more safety conscious and keep the doors locked when she was home in the future. The danger might finally be sinking in, except Kit seemed blind to the idea that Damien Ridgeway could have been involved in Helena's death.

They were in the hospital corridor down from Jesse's ICU room. Chief Tyson leaned closer so he could speak without being overheard. "Dr. Bengali couldn't spare the time from his rounds and he suggested I call you." His eyes were sympathetic, but they held that edge of authority that she reacted to automatically. After years in the military, she found her back straightening, her chin coming up.

"Okay, but you better check it's okay with the Feds first."

"Already did." Tyson nodded over her shoulder.

She turned. ASAC Frazer was striding down the hallway, wearing the fine-wool navy suit with his FBI windbreaker thrown over the top just like yesterday when he'd been out at the beach. She was hit once again by the stone-cold beauty of the man. All lean lines and sharp cheekbones. Blue eyes raked her up and down, and then moved on. Dismissed.

Thank God.

The sexual awareness that had shimmered between them last night was hidden beneath a wall of icy indifference, but she knew it was there now, cruising beneath the surface like a lazy Great White. Izzy reminded herself that just because there were sharks in the ocean didn't mean she had to get bitten.

"How's your son this morning?" Frazer asked the police chief.

"He wants to know what's going on. He wants to see Helena," Tyson told him grimly, keeping his voice low.

"It's time to see if we can bring back his memory. I'm not going to lie—this is going to be a shit time for the kid. It'll seem like it's just happened and that's why having him under medical supervision seems appropriate." The look he threw at Izzy suggested she was the best choice out of a bad lot.

"Usually this is a one-on-one process. Under the circumstances you can both sit in, but I need you to keep silent no matter what you hear. And don't occupy his line of sight, in case he opens his eyes."

The chief nodded and headed into his son's hospital room. Izzy started to follow, but Frazer caught her arm. His fingers accidentally brushed the edge of her breast. She jumped. He moved his grip but kept hold of her arm. A wave of heat spread from the point of contact.

"Whatever Jesse reveals cannot be discussed with anyone."

The fact he disconcerted her so easily, then insulted her so thoroughly, pissed her off. Had it been calculated? The light in his eyes gave nothing away. She jerked away from his grip.

It was obvious he didn't trust her to do her job and that was the one area where she had absolute faith in her abilities. "I understand doctor-patient privilege."

"But this involves your sister. No matter what Jesse says, you cannot reveal what you know, not even to Kit." His blue eyes thawed a degree. "I know this is hard on her and on you, but this is a criminal investigation, and it's Jesse's personal business... His testimony may be needed in court."

She took a step back. "Believe it or not, I'm not an idiot."

"I never thought you were." A smile twitched the corner of his mouth. "The other thing is the statements we release might seem at odds to what actually happens here today. I need you not to contradict anything that's said through official channels."

She frowned. "You want to manipulate the killer?"

He nodded. She shouldn't be so attracted to him, but apparently intelligence and good looks were a turn-on regardless of overbearing personality or potential danger to her freedom.

She bit her lip. "Damien Ridgeway has a dirt bike," she blurted suddenly.

"I know."

"Oh. Okay." She blinked, deflated. "Good." He went to move away, but this time she caught his arm and tried to pretend touching him didn't affect her. "Also, I overheard him arguing with Kit. He said if the cops found out, they'd crucify him."

"Found out what?"

She let go of his arm. "I don't know. He didn't say and Kit wouldn't tell me."

"When did you see him?" Frazer's voice dropped to a low murmur and he moved close enough she could feel his body heat warming the space between them.

"Earlier. I went looking for Kit and she was at his house—well, in the cemetery next door."

One eyebrow quirked.

"Our mother is buried there. Kit spends a lot of time tending her grave. Anyway, I thought I should let you know what I overheard."

"Good." With that monosyllabic reply, he turned and walked into Jesse's room. Izzy rolled her eyes to the ceiling, blew out a breath. She followed slowly, closing the door behind her. She sent Jesse a reassuring smile and checked his monitors to make sure his vitals were stable. Even though he had no dizziness, good pain and nausea control, they'd given him another CT scan— probably because it was a miracle he was unscathed. She read his chart—blood pressure and oxygen levels were good. Heart rate steady. She raised her hand to get ASAC Frazer's attention and pointed to an adjoining door. She wanted to make sure an anesthetist was on-call to assist with a sedative in case things went sideways. Frazer nodded without pausing in his conversation with Jesse. She slipped out, spoke to a friend of hers who gave her a small dose of sedative should Jesse become agitated, and promised to be nearby unless there was an emergency. Izzy used another thirty-seconds to stuff her jacket in her locker and grab her white coat and stethoscope. Professionally armed, she slipped back into the room.

It was dark inside now, except for the glow of monitors. The lights off, blinds lowered and closed. The sound of birdsong and waves washed through the room. It brought her immediately to the beach. She sank down into a chair in the corner of the room, beside the police chief who watched his son like a grizzly mama watched her cub.

Frazer sat in a chair beside the bed. Jesse lay

watching him. Frazer kept his voice a low murmur that seemed to sink inside her bones and warm her from the inside out.

Then he was doing deep breathing exercises with Jesse. He'd taken off the windbreaker and suit jacket, removed his tie and undone the first two buttons of his shirt. Something about his looks totally worked for her, but she suspected he had that effect on most women.

"We're going to do a simple exercise where I count down from five to one and you're going to go back to New Year's Eve." He counted down. "Where are you, Jesse?"

"Franky's place. His mom and dad are away and he's invited pretty much the entire school to a party there. His parents don't know. It's going to be huge."

He sounded so excited Izzy wanted to stop the whole thing right now, let Jesse live on in blissful ignorance. But it couldn't last, and he might harbor some piece of information that could help catch the killer.

"Franky's parents really don't know?"

"We kept it under wraps from all the olds. No way would his parents or my dad let us hold an unsupervised party." Jesse snorted with oblivious boyish charm.

Chief Tyson crossed his legs and Izzy felt the tension flowing off him in waves.

"You sound excited?"

"I invited Helena Cromwell." The excitement in Jesse's voice was like a knife through her chest. She clenched her fists in her lap.

"She pretty?"

Jesse's smile grew wide. "Oh, my God, she's

beautiful. But more importantly she's nice. I've learned to steer clear of the nasty ones, no matter how hot they are."

Her heartstrings started to tug a little.

"My last girlfriend was—well, let's just say she is *not* nice—but Helena is something special. I'm shocked she doesn't already have a boyfriend."

Her heartstrings snapped. Dear God.

"I hear you. My ex-wife was perfect on the outside, but all I had to do to piss her off was not notice she'd had her hair cut or a new manicure and she'd make my life miserable for a week. Life's too short to deal with that crap."

"No kidding," Jesse replied. His voice had grown quieter. Was he remembering?

"Can you tell me what you did when you got to the party?"

"It was fun for a while, but then some of the girls started doing some fucked up shit. They decided to play one of those stupid games where they pulled a guy's cell phone out of a basket and then they pick out a girl to give him a blowjob. But it was a set up to get the new guy in deep shit."

"So the new guy wins a blow job? Who was the lucky female who got to do the honors?"

"Kit Campbell."

Her eyes whipped to Frazer, but he ignored her. This was why he'd warned her to keep her mouth shut. She gritted her teeth on the urge to speak.

"Was Kit in on the joke?"

"Nah. The 'popular' girls don't like her." Jesse's brow wrinkled. "Why do they call them popular when no one likes them?"

"It's a phenomena unique to high school. What did Kit do?"

"She called their bluff and dragged the guy off to the pool with her." Jesse blushed. "But I don't know what happened there. Helena said Kit could handle herself."

Izzy frowned. Helena had just let Kit walk away? Then she thought about her sister—you didn't *let* Kit do anything. She just did it.

"What happened next?" Frazer's smooth calm voice did something to her insides. Soothed her agitation. Eased her heart rate. Maybe he'd hypnotized her too—a terrifying thought.

"I wanted to get out of there. It got noisy. I wanted to watch the storm and I wanted to be alone with Helena. I asked her if she would like to go for a walk." He stopped abruptly as if something had spooked him.

"You took her to the dunes?"

"I know we shouldn't. Mr. Cromwell will kill us if he finds out and my dad will be next in line." The words resonated around the room like a gunshot and Frazer met Izzy's gaze for an instant. Could Helena's father be involved in her murder? Izzy pushed the thought away. He'd been devastated, but she knew from experience that some people were sublime actors.

"It wasn't Helena's idea. It was all me." The kid was taking responsibility for more than he knew. "I don't want her to get into any trouble."

"Did you kiss her?"

A blush crossed Jesse's face. The chief's knuckles turned white in his lap. He had to be aware that if Jesse killed Helena, his son would very likely incriminate himself in the next few moments, possibly destroying his life forever.

"I kissed her."

"Did you have sex?" asked Frazer.

"No," Jesse said the word firmly. "Helena's not like that. She's pretty sheltered. I don't think she'd even been kissed before."

Frazer didn't go where she expected him to go with his next question—obviously she was a linear thinker. "How much cash were you carrying?"

Jesse frowned. "About fifty bucks. I wanted to have some money in case Helena was hungry and wanted to go somewhere to grab something to eat."

"What else is in your wallet?"

"Emergency credit card parents gave me last year and told me never to use." He laughed. "Student ID, driver's license, some old receipts, a condom."

The chief's foot twitched.

"You carried a condom but weren't expecting to have sex?"

Jesse shook his head. "Franky put it in my wallet when I was dating Jessica."

Jesse and Jessica? Ugh.

"He said she'd had sex with her last boyfriend and he didn't want me getting her pregnant or catching something the first time I 'nailed a chick'. Franky's expression, not mine."

"Did you have sex with Jessica?"

Frazer was right. This wasn't anyone's business but Jesse's.

The boy's laugh came out embarrassed. "Jeez, this isn't something I talk about but..." He gave a deep sigh, as if he harbored a terrible secret. "I'm saving myself for someone special. That's why Jessica dumped me."

"Because you wouldn't have sex with her?"

Izzy felt Chief Tyson's tension deflate. She

caught his gaze. His eyes were brimming with tears and she gave his fisted hand a quick squeeze.

Jesse's cheeks burned. "Sounds pretty dumb, right?"

Frazer sat quietly for a moment. "No, actually it seems smart. Sex screws up all sorts of things between people."

That felt like a warning. She held herself perfectly still so he couldn't analyze anything she did.

"You think people should be in love?" There was wistfulness in Jesse's voice.

Frazer's lips thinned. "I think people who have sex should be of legal age, sound mind, honest about what they want and how they want it. No one should feel coerced. Love is important to some people," he conceded.

But not to him.

It made him more appealing rather than less. She understood him. It was difficult to fall in love when you never let anyone close. One day she hoped to find someone to connect with, to be herself with. But the idea of truly opening up was terrifying.

Frazer had obviously tried it once, hence the ex-wife.

She knew he was attracted to her, hard to ignore the way he watched her mouth sometimes, although she knew the mole on her lip was distracting. But it was impossible to misinterpret how he'd checked out her body last night. Was he always so standoffish with women he was attracted to? Or did he behave that way because he was a professional working a case?

"You think people should wait for marriage?"

asked Jesse.

"I don't think marriage is necessary for sex, but I think honesty is." For a short moment his laser-sharp blue eyes met hers and a surge of electricity blasted through her nerves. Had she thought him cold? The guy was not cold. He was just able to control whatever he was feeling, whereas she seemed adrift in an unexpected sea of emotion.

"Who knew you carried a condom in your wallet?" asked Frazer.

"No one. Well, Franky, but I doubt he told anyone. Why would he? I didn't tell my parents. Dad's cool about most stuff, but Mom would freak. She still thinks I'm eleven." Jesse grinned. He clearly didn't realize that his dad was in the room right now. Izzy was shocked at how effectively Frazer's hypnosis tricks were working.

Just when she'd thought she'd figured out all the things she had to be afraid of.

"Could anyone have seen it when you opened your wallet?"

"Sure. I keep it with the bills." He grimaced. "Most of the guys in my grade carry one in their wallets even though most of them have zero chance of getting laid. I guess someone might have spotted it, but it's not a crime, right?"

"No, it's not. It's actually a very smart thing to do. So you kissed Helena. Can you tell me what happened next?" asked Frazer.

The boy grew quiet. "There was a noise." Jesse wet his lips and stared off into space.

Oh, God. Izzy sat on her hands and braced herself. The chief squeezed her shoulder in reassurance—or maybe he was simply holding on. She wasn't sure, but his grip was fierce.

"You're safe, Jesse. I'll keep you safe. I promise." Frazer's voice was low and calm. "Tell me exactly what you heard."

Jesse's heart rate started to speed up on the monitor. Hers was already racing. "The wind was howling and the waves were huge, smashing into the beach with a massive roar. I was kissing Helena, but then there was this rush of sound, like someone running toward us. We broke apart and looked up." Blood pressure was one-twenty over ninety, and rising. He shifted his legs in agitation as if he wanted to get out of bed, to run. "Some guy had a baseball bat or something, up over his head." Izzy heard the gasp of shock in his voice as he remembered. "He hit me. Fuck! Kept hitting me. Why would he do that?"

The chief's fingers tightened almost painfully on her shoulder.

Jesse's heart rate continued to climb and Izzy touched the vial of sedative in her pocket.

"Helena screamed at him to stop, but he didn't. Then she took off running. I tried, but couldn't get up. I think I passed out." He looked confused.

"Did you regain consciousness at all?"

Jesse started to shake his head and then hesitated. "I felt him pull me down the dune. The sand was gritty against my back. And he rifled through my pockets."

"Can you remember anything about the man, at all? Scent? Sight?"

The teen shook his head, dark hair flopping over his brow. "Shadows. I saw shadows." Jesse looked around the room now as if searching for answers. Tears streamed down his face. "Where's Helena? Did she get away?" He started to raise himself into a sitting position, and Izzy climbed to her feet.

When no one answered, he grew more agitated. "She didn't get away, did she? What did he do to her? Please tell me." The boy's voice was stronger now. "Where is she? Is she hurt?"

"You don't remember anything at all after he dragged you through the sand?"

The boy paused for a long moment. "I heard something."

A shiver crawled over Izzy's skin.

"What did you hear?"

"It was like a grunting sound, like someone…doing it." Horror stretched the boy's eyes wide. "…Having sex. And he said something. 'Can you see it?' That's what he said. I think. I must have passed out."

Izzy tried to blink back the tears and wished she could find that professional place inside her where none of this touched her, but she was in too deep. She knew all the players. Knew what tragedy happened at the end of the story.

"Did you recognize his voice?" asked Frazer.

"No. No." There was a long pause. "But…it was familiar somehow. Like I *should* have recognized him."

Frazer murmured something for Jesse's ears only and suddenly the young man was no longer hypnotized.

"Where's Helena?" he asked, fiercely.

"Jesse," his father warned, coming to his feet.

"Tell me, goddamn it!" Jesse yelled. His heart monitor raced, BP one-fifty over one-ten and he looked like he was on the verge of getting out of bed. Izzy was on her feet and at his side. Frazer looked pissed when she withdrew the syringe, but he nodded, pretending it was his decision and not hers.

"Son, the man who attacked you." Chief Tyson cleared his throat repeatedly. "He murdered Helena."

Tyson took his son's hand, and she used the distraction to shoot the sedative into Jesse's IV. Jesse started sobbing. "No. No. That can't be true. I was right there! Oh, my God. He raped her, didn't he?"

Izzy disposed of the needle and put a call into the anesthetist on stand-by, then stood hunched over the nearest counter, waiting until the drugs took Jesse into oblivion. He started to make a wailing keening sound that tore at Izzy's soul and scattered it like bits of confetti. Everything he'd lost. Everything Helena had lost. It was all too much to bear.

After a few more seconds of grief the room went quiet, and Jesse's heart beat calmed down to a strong regular sinus rhythm. His BP was normal, breathing regular.

ASAC Frazer came to stand beside her. "I'm sorry you had to hear that," he said quietly.

"Don't." She held up her hand and wiped away tears she hadn't been aware of crying. She glanced at Jesse but he was out cold and his vitals had returned to resting levels. "I wish he'd seen something useful, but I'm glad he was unconscious when the bastard…"

Frazer nodded and shrugged into his jacket, obviously off to the next part of the investigation.

"Don't mention this to Kit."

She grabbed a tissue and blew her nose. Don't

mention she knew Kit had been auctioned off like a hooker to give a blowjob at a party she wasn't even supposed to attend. Great. Some guardian Izzy was turning out to be. "Damien Ridgeway is eighteen. That might be what he was referring to earlier."

"I have more important issues to worry about than teenagers having sex."

Izzy flinched. Dammit. That was her responsibility.

Chief Tyson joined them. He looked wrung out.

"I want your office to put out a statement that you have a witness helping you with your inquiries."

"Draw the perp out." Tyson nodded. "What if he comes after Jesse? I can't be here 24/7 to protect him."

"I have some people I can contact. People I've used before under these sort of circumstances."

The chief's face was haggard. "Department can't afford personal bodyguards. Budget is already tight."

"The FBI can assist with cost." Frazer stared hard at the man, as if willing him to say yes.

Tyson touched his brow. "Fine. If it'll help catch this sonofabitch and keep my son safe, do it. I'll mortgage my home if I have to."

"You both need to keep quiet as to the extent of Jesse's knowledge."

"Or lack of it," she said. "He's bait."

Frazer didn't deny it. "It's one of the few things we can use right now, and the sooner this person is caught the safer everyone will be."

Izzy nodded. He was right. Of course he was right. But he was also a ruthless operator, prepared to use an injured, vulnerable young man. The killer was worse though. Izzy had to assume Frazer knew what he was doing.

"Thank you for coming in on your day off," he said to her unexpectedly.

How could she have refused? A girl had been murdered. Not some random stranger, but a girl she'd fed, and who'd slept over dozens of times. Her chest felt tight like if she breathed in too deep, her lungs would crack.

"We can set up a time to hypnotize you about what you saw last night—"

"I don't think so." She took a step away from the FBI agent.

"Why not?" His eyes watched her like the proverbial hawk.

"I don't want you inside my head," she told him honestly.

"Scared of what I might discover?"

"Yes." She didn't let him comment. She walked away, wishing she could leave the islands and take Kit with her. Wishing she didn't know things she shouldn't about death and murder. At the door she glanced back. Jesse was asleep and Frazer was deep in conversation with the chief. Part of her wanted him gone from the islands, back to his cubicle in Virginia. Another piece of her knew she'd miss him when he was gone—miss the opportunity to get to know him better. He was complex enough to be interesting and handsome enough that a woman would have to be dead not to be intrigued.

She wasn't dead, but she was smarter than that. She had to be.

CHAPTER TWELVE

Frazer did not handle downtime well and generally used it to either practice at the gun range or go to the gym. Right now, he pounded the sand, sweat pouring down his back despite the cold breeze coming off the Atlantic. This was the worst part of any investigation. The waiting. It helped that he had so many agents and so many cases to keep track of, but most were still on vacation. Darsh Singh was working a series of homicides in DC and Moira Henderson had flown up to Alaska to help examine several bodies that might be the victims of a serial killer who'd died in custody last year. Jed Brennan was playing happy families while recovering from gunshot wounds. Matt Lazlo was taking a couple of weeks to sort out the mess that surrounded the wrongful conviction of former FBI agent Richard Stone, at the same time supporting his new girlfriend and also—if Frazer was any judge—his future mother-in-law. Richard Stone was now receiving the best treatment possible for his cancer. All they could do was pray the man lived long enough to enjoy being exonerated.

The fun never stopped at the BAU.

Rooney was still under observation but signs were good. Alex Parker had sounded more relaxed in their last conversation—less *I-can-kill-you-forty-different-ways-and-still-make-it-look-like-an-accident* and more *I'm-a-millionaire-cyber-security-expert-don't-tell-me-how-to-do-my-job-jackass*.

Considering he and Parker had almost come to

blows when they first met, it still surprised him how quickly they'd become friends. There wasn't anyone he'd rather be working with right now.

Frazer didn't know anything about computers beyond the basics. Parker was running phone records and had hacked into the prison's Internet server to see if he could find any recent communications between Denker and anyone on the Outer Banks. All emails went to the prison, not to individual inmates. Still, there were plenty of ways to communicate if you knew how.

He wanted background checks on all the guards and to find out as much information on the lawyer and the groupies that had attached themselves to the violent predator. Parker was also cross-referencing his ViCAP searches, examining any reports of rapes and/or murders where the victim's shoes were taken and seeing if there were any other factors to link the crimes. The shoe thing was complicated by the fact so many victims were never found, and many who were found were completely naked—so a killer with a shoe fetish or who took shoes as a souvenir to extend the fantasy and relive the crime might not be immediately apparent.

IDs on the two bodies pulled from the sand were the most important pieces of information to tie down. Trace evidence from Helena's body would be next. He shoved the image of her out of his mind—again. Once Frazer had more details he could get more people involved using the geographical profiling angle. Right now he was stuck waiting—hence the sweat on his brow and fire in his lungs.

A news conference was scheduled for

tomorrow morning at nine, but he didn't intend to be there. His face on this case would raise flags. He'd contacted his friend, Robin Greenburg who owned a media conglomerate and had given him an advance statement and requested he have his editors downplay the investigation. Frazer had saved the guy's life years ago and at the time Robin had promised he'd do anything for him. Frazer held the guy to it. The great thing about Robin was he was happy to help manipulate killers so the cops could nail them. And if Frazer or the FBI repaid that cooperation with exclusive interviews or some inside information at the appropriate time, who was to say it wasn't for the greater good?

It worked for Frazer.

After hypnotizing Jesse Tyson he'd tried to catch up on some sleep, but as soon as he closed his eyes the image of Helena Cromwell merged with the images of other victims for whom he'd never found justice.

Jesus. When was the last time he'd seen a naked woman who wasn't dead?

He ran faster until his lungs strained to bursting point. Some days it felt like no matter how hard he worked, no matter how many bad guys were incarcerated or taken out, there were always two more ready to take their place. This case had started out as an operation in damage control, but it had become a reminder of why he did what he did.

To protect people.

To get the bad guys off the streets.

Not to hobnob with presidents or bigwigs.

The fact he was using these powerful people should have made him feel some measure of guilt, but his motives were pure. And he'd saved the lives of some of those same people because he was good at his job. Turnabout was fair play.

But something about Helena's spirit, her goodness and innocence spoke to him, reminded him it wasn't the powerful or rich who needed his help the most. It was the poor and the voiceless.

In addition to the Denker connection he needed to consider all the usual suspects in her murder. Her father's alibi was weak because the rest of the household had been asleep. The unsub had worn a condom, presumably the one stolen from Jesse's wallet—he made a mental note to get Randall to ask Franky Cirencester what brand he'd bought, see if they could match it to residue.

Most serial rapists would carry a condom in their rape kit, so the attack on Helena hadn't been planned. Chief Tyson was running background checks on all the male residents on the islands, looking for arrests for breaking and entering, peeping toms, stalking, sexual assault. Anything that might give them a place to start looking. After another mile, he turned around and started back to the beach house. Randall had checked into Damien Ridgeway. The young man had a history of supplying drugs to classmates at his old school. It would be quite the jump to rape and murder, but not impossible. His alibi for Helena's murder was Kit, who by her own admission had been wasted. But they couldn't find any connection between Damien Ridgeway and Ferris Denker yet, and that was the key to solving this thing.

The agents working the Denker case back in the nineties hadn't thought Ferris had a partner, and maybe that was the most chilling aspect of this case. That some accomplice had been out there killing for the last seventeen years and the authorities had never suspected a thing.

Frazer's breath was rough in his throat. Leg muscles were starting to burn after seven miles.

Randall was creating a list of dirt bike owners on the island. The agent had so far kept his boss at bay, but Frazer would have to deal with her at some point in the next few hours. Maybe he *should* call in the troops? Hanrahan's work had been solid and the conviction was good. The fact was, he didn't want other officers on this case. He didn't want to have to relinquish control and head back to Virginia. He wanted to be in control. He wanted to solve this thing. Find justice for Helena. Maybe, after all he'd been through in the last few months, he needed to prove himself again.

And if that wasn't a God-complex he didn't know what was.

It wasn't just the case taxing his mental energy. His unwanted attraction to Isadora Campbell pissed him off. The only consolation was she looked as disheartened about whatever was going on between them as he felt. She wasn't some romantic fool who dreamt of happily ever after—like he'd ever fall for a woman like that. They were both pragmatists, too busy with their jobs and lives to get too involved. He did not need the distraction. But she intrigued him with the secrets that shadowed her eyes, with her dedication to her country and the ungrateful teen in her care, and that damn beauty spot that kept dragging his attention to her lips when he was supposed to be thinking about serial offenders.

A jangle of metal at his side had him glancing down. Izzy's dog, Barney, had joined him along the homestretch of the beach and kept up with an easy lope. The dog he could handle. The woman was best kept at arm's length. He grinned through the exertion as he neared the edge of Rosetown.

The woman he was trying not to think about sat on the sand on a yoga mat, a small cooler off to one side. Barney went straight in for a wet kiss, making Frazer resent the hell out of the dog. She laughed and pushed the mutt away.

"Yuck." She wiped her mouth.

Frazer stopped a few feet away, braced his hands on his knees and bent over catching his breath. The dog jogged off to drink out of his water bowl. Frazer nodded toward Izzy's water bottle with a questioning brow.

"Go ahead." Her expression was serene, but the look in her eyes carefully guarded. "We're supposed to be getting another storm." She nodded toward the water. "You'd never know it from the slick cam."

"Slick cam?" They both glanced at the flat ocean.

"It's what the locals say for dead calm." Her smile lit up her eyes. "Whole other language they've got out here. Pizer means a porch. Whopperjawed means something isn't straight. And you're what they call a dingbatter."

His heart finally slowed enough for him to say more than a few words. "Do I want to know?" He drank more water and wiped his mouth with the back of his hand.

"A name they use for someone not from around here," she filled in.

"You say 'they' like you don't consider yourself one of them either."

Isadora shrugged her shoulders, emphasizing

the hollows of her collarbones—places he desperately wanted to taste. "I was away for a long time."

And some people never fit in, no matter where they were born or how long they stayed.

"How do you do it?" she asked suddenly.

"Do what?" He finished the water.

"Chase killers?"

The strain of the recent murder was starting to show in the dark circles around her eyes and in the whiteness of her knuckles as she wrapped her arms around her knees.

He shrugged one shoulder. People asked him this question a lot. "I like stopping the bad guys."

"But what makes someone enjoy killing another human being? Are they born evil? Is it genetic?" She buried her face against her knees.

"Latest research suggests there *are* genes associated with being a murderer."

She looked up, horrified.

"Doesn't mean that everyone who has those genes is going to become a killer." He sat down in the sand beside her, settled in, comfortable talking about what might create a murderer—far more than thinking about how pretty Isadora's hair was in the sunshine. "Brain scans of convicted killers show reduced activity in the pre-frontal cortex—"

"The emotional impulse control center."

He smiled because she was smart and he liked smart. "And higher activity in the amygdala—the area that generates emotions."

"So the image of a sociopathic killer not feeling emotion isn't quite accurate?" she asked.

"I'm not sure they've conducted thorough enough studies to clinically diagnose mental health status of all the killers they tested, but no, that study suggests murderers generally are more likely to feel anger and rage, but be much less able to control those emotions." He sat up. "Researchers found a gene that produces an enzyme that regulates neurotransmitters involved in impulse control—if men lack it, or have a low-activity variant, they are predisposed to being violent. It's found in about a third of the male population."

"But a third of the male population are not violent, right?"

He eyed her long legs in those clingy leggings. "The theory is that if males with the gene are the subjects of child abuse, and therefore more likely to suffer brain damage, then the gene is triggered. Mental illness is also a possible factor."

He watched a shudder make its way across her shoulders. She trailed a hand through the dry sand between them.

"So the killers can't help it?" she asked.

He pressed his lips together and stared at the ocean. "Blame genetics or crappy childhoods. They still make the choice to kill others even though they know it's wrong. My job is to stop them, and I'm good at it because when I'm not, people die."

Her gaze caught his. Those soft green eyes full of understanding and empathy. He reached out and touched her hand. She let his fingers curl around hers, and squeezed him back. A jolt of something fundamental shot through him. From the way her eyes darkened she was feeling it too.

And then something struck him about the case. "Know anyone who owns a metal detector?"

***

Izzy handed Frazer a cold beer from the cooler she'd brought down from the house. Today was about relaxing and trying to forget there was a killer out there somewhere. Of course, her pistol was nestled inside her bag within arm's reach.

"Thanks." He chinked his bottle against hers and tipped it back, swallowing large gulps just as he had with the water. It was impossible not to watch his Adam's apple bob up and down the strong column of his throat. Streaks of perspiration darkened his blond hair. His t-shirt and shorts were damp too, and her eyes roved over him hungrily. His body was toned and taut, long legs lightly covered in golden hair. Powerful looking thighs and a flat stomach, which didn't seem to have an ounce of extra flesh. She'd thought it was the fancy suit that made him look so damn perfect, but even dressed down and sweaty, he owned it.

She dropped her gaze and sat cross-legged, sipping her beer even though she wanted to down it in one gulp. "Why do you want to know who has a metal detector around here?"

"Humor me." He'd sprawled his lean length down in the sand beside her.

She passed him a blanket so he didn't freeze to death as he cooled down after his run.

"Well, I haven't done an inventory"—he quirked his brows as if amused—"but there's actually a treasure hunting group or society or some such—I know because I give the members regular tetanus shots when they cut themselves on old coke cans. Pastor Rice fancies himself quite the expert, although he likes to go alone, says people distract him, and he likes to commune with God. Uncle Ted has one that my mom bought him when he retired. She hoped it would give him something to do besides look after her."

"You have an uncle?" He took another long swallow of beer. She tried not to watch a line of sweat roll down his temple into his hair. It shouldn't look sexy, but it did.

"My mother's brother. My parents moved back here in the eighties, but Mom's family lived on the Outer Banks for generations."

"So this really is home for you?"

Izzy pulled a face. "It should be." She checked her shoulder, but Kit wasn't home. The owner of the diner had called and asked her to take a shift. Working might take Kit's mind off her misery so Izzy thought it was a good idea. Or maybe she'd see other friends she could grieve with.

"I never really felt like I belonged here. I always had itchy feet." She looked at him lying so close beside her she could see the flecks of gray in his eyes. That's what made his eyes such a cold blue—that and the fact they saw straight through bullshit. "Actually, that's not quite true."

His gaze sharpened as if she was about to tell him some important secret—no way in hell, but this was personal, more personal than she usually got. "When I was sixteen I had a boyfriend who died in a car accident. After he died I had the overwhelming urge to get away." Izzy drew herself up into a tight ball.

Frazer said nothing. There was nothing to say.

"It was a tough year." And losing Shane had been the lesser of two tragedies.

Frazer leaned closer and she could smell the hot musky scent of him. He stared at her mouth like he wanted to kiss her. The idea made her nipples instantly harden against the fabric of her t-shirt. Hopefully, he'd put it down to the cool wind blowing off the Atlantic.

"Is that why you became a doctor?"

"Part of it, I suppose." A wave of nostalgia hit her as she thought about Shane. He'd been so young—Kit's age, Helena's age. Gone before he'd started living. Stupid. Innocent. "He'd been drinking, ran into a telephone pole. It was his own fault, but it was hours before they could get him out of the wreck." She shied away from the memory because she'd been there holding his hand when he'd died. She'd begged him not to go, not to leave her.

"You couldn't save him so you decided to save the world?"

Basic psychology, but her true reasons were a little more complex. She'd been escaping and atoning for her sins. She shrugged. "What about you?"

"Me?" A small smile curved those perfect lips.

"Yeah, you. What made you want to save the world?"

His blue eyes held an almost icy sheen in this light. That was his defense mechanism, she realized. Being the aloof observer, never really engaging, never letting anyone in. But he didn't look away from her the way she expected him to. Instead, he said quietly, "My parents were murdered."

"Murdered?" she asked sharply.

"Home invasion when I was fifteen."

"Oh, fuck. You were there." She could see it flickering over his features even though he probably thought he revealed nothing.

"Yes."

"You saw it happen." Her throat was so dry she could barely get the words out.

His mouth tightened.

Watching Shane die was bad enough, but she knew how murder felt. It felt like demons and darkness and evil.

And he'd embraced it.

"I became a federal agent so I was the one who got to ask questions. My turn."

Izzy held still. He was going to quiz her about her father. Had they identified the bodies they'd found on the beach? The idea made her want to gag.

How could she lie to the man after what he'd just told her? How could she not?

Her heart hammered. He watched her pulse skipping in the base of her throat. Would he put it down to fear or desire? Both were running rampant through her body.

He leaned a little closer and for a second she thought he was going to kiss her. Then her phone dinged, jerking them both out of the moment. She checked the screen and her mouth dropped open.

An image appeared. A young woman on her knees in front of a guy who sat in an armchair with his legs spread, face aimed at the ceiling. They were fully clothed. No faces were visible. But the suggestive pose said everything that needed to be said. The message that came with it slammed her in the gut.

"Kit Campbell gives head while BFF has hers smashed in. Poor little Helena. Best friend's a slut. KC blows."

Izzy dropped the phone.

She bent to pick it up, but Frazer beat her to it. He looked at the image for a long moment before typing something into her phone and sending it. Then he deleted the message while she watched him, stupefied.

"I'll have someone trace the photograph and whoever sent it to you. I suggest you go find your sister and make sure she hasn't already seen it."

God. This would destroy Kit.

Her cell rang again. This time it was Chief Tyson. Frazer moved so close his shoulder brushed against hers as he tried to listen in—unnerving the crap out of her. After a curt message from Tyson she hung up and climbed to her feet. "Kit's at the police station. She was arrested for assault."

CHAPTER THIRTEEN

Chief Tyson met her at the door of the Rosetown police station.

"Where is she?" The fury in Izzy morphed into something that tasted bitter in her mouth. This man had enough crap to deal with. Helena had been murdered, and his son had almost been beaten to death. This incident was both frustrating and mortifying and underlined how bad she was at being a guardian.

"Come on back. I'll take you to her." He held the top of the counter high enough for her to pass through ahead of him.

"Jesse's okay?" she asked quietly.

"The bodyguards arrived a couple of hours ago. Charlene and Ricky are with Jesse right now anyway." He shot her a look. "I came in to handle this personally. Because I owe you."

"You don't owe me anything." Izzy wanted to curl up with embarrassment but straightened her spine. "But I do appreciate it. Can you tell me what happened?"

"Group of girls sitting in the diner started taunting Kit over some photograph."

"Have you seen it?" she asked.

He pressed his lips together. Nodded.

"Someone texted it to me." Izzy could hardly breathe. "Did you read what it said?"

His lips were bloodless now. He indicated a door with his head. "She's in there. You can go talk to her. I'm about to go talk to the parents of the girl she punched."

"Punched?" Izzy grimaced.

"Broke her nose," Tyson clarified.

"Oh…" *Shit. Fuck. Hell.*

"I'll see if the girl still wants to press charges when she realizes she'll then also be facing charges of spreading child pornography." Chief Tyson didn't say anything else, but the glint in his eye gave Izzy hope.

Suddenly the door behind them burst open and there stood ASAC Frazer, hair damp, the sharp scent of citrus shower gel coming off his skin in waves that made her want to inhale him. His blue suit was back in place, crisp white shirt, red and gray stripy tie—knotted perfectly but slightly askew. How he'd done all that in the time he'd had was beyond her.

"I told you to wait for me." His eyes narrowed, and she was reminded this man was used to being in charge.

She put her hands on her hips. "Looks like you caught up, so what's the problem?"

His blue eyes were frosty with disapproval.

She went to grab the door handle.

"Wait." He touched the tips of his fingers to the top of her arm. Shivers of something dark and sensuous skittered along her nerves. She was disconcerted enough to do as he asked.

To Tyson, Frazer said, "I have someone trying to trace the primary source of the photograph. There will be charges pressed when we find them. Make it clear to everyone involved that this is a criminal matter, I want the kids deleting that image rather than spreading it far and wide."

"Might be too late for that." Tyson nodded. "But I'll make sure the message gets out, then I'm going back to the hospital." He hesitated. "Has this got anything to do with Helena's murder?"

"I don't know," said Frazer. "Honestly? I doubt it."

So what was he doing here? Izzy pushed open the door into the interview room and there sat Kit in a hard plastic chair, glaring at her. Her sister's eyes were red and fresh tears streamed down her face. Izzy doubted she'd stopped crying for more than an hour since she'd found out about Helena.

"Did you see it?" Kit didn't look embarrassed at all. She looked downright furious.

Izzy nodded.

"I suppose you think they're right. That I'm a slut?" The words were a challenge, but there was enough uncertainty in them for Izzy's anger to dissolve.

Izzy shook her head and sat down next to Kit, drawing her into her arms and letting her sister's head rest on her shoulder. "I wish I'd been home that night. I wish I'd checked with the Cromwells about your plans." If she could turn back the clock and do everything differently, she would.

"We'll find out who took the picture and who spread it around social media," said Frazer.

"What does it matter? It's gone viral now." Kit's words were bitter. "I should just quit."

"Quit what?" Izzy asked sharply.

Her sister's young, blue eyes flashed. "School. Life."

"Don't talk like that," Izzy admonished, fear squeezing through her veins.

"My best friend is dead. And who's going to hire me for a real job now? Some dirty old man who thinks I can polish his knob while answering his phone? Everyone's going to see that photo and think I'm a whore. It's going to be around forever."

"And whose fault is that?" Izzy snapped impatiently.

Kit's lip curled. "And there's the truth about how you really feel."

"I think you need to take some responsibility for the photograph. You shouldn't have been doing it in the first place." Izzy's voice rose. She wanted to comfort and rail at her sister all at the same time.

Kit's chin went up. "Now it's my fault?"

"Of course it's your fault!" It was hers too. Dammit. "In today's society where cameras are everywhere? What were you thinking?"

"I wasn't thinking that some asshole was going to post it online saying what they did about Helena," Kit snarled. "They dared me to do it, so I did it. Screw. Them."

"No," Izzy stuffed both hands into her hair. "Screw you, apparently." She stood and paced, wishing she knew what to do for the best. She didn't want to judge, but this wasn't okay. Izzy took a few deep breaths, trying to calm down. Being a guardian of a seventeen-year-old sucked, but then so did losing a mother and best friend— and no one knew that as well as Izzy did. The thought made her racing heart slow. Kit needed her support, not her censure.

Frazer stood near the window and watched the interaction. Dissecting their relationship. Dissecting her.

"I just think you're too young to be doing *that*—especially at a party you didn't even tell me you were going to." Izzy's insides froze as the horrors of what could have happened to her sister

205

flashed through her mind.

Kit sneered as only a teen could. "Maybe if you learned to give good head you wouldn't be stuck home every night like some fucking virgin."

"A fucking virgin. Now there's something I'd like to see." Ted's voice made her whirl around as he slipped into the room. He held his hand out to Frazer. "Ted Brubaker. Izzy and Kit's uncle."

Izzy's cheeks burned with heat, but it wasn't embarrassment—it was fury.

Frazer nodded and introduced himself. "Isadora was telling me about you earlier."

Izzy raised her brow at his tone. Like they'd been sharing confidences.

"How did you know to come down here?" Izzy asked Ted.

His cheeks whitened. "Pastor Rice was sent the photograph in the hopes he could save Kit's immortal soul. He called me about it. I called Hank, and he told me Kit had been arrested."

"So now all your cronies have seen it too?" Kit's eyes widened, and she crossed her arms over her chest. "Oh, my God."

"What did you expect? That you got to choose which guys ogled it?" Izzy smacked her hand forcefully on the table and both Ted and Kit jumped. Not Frazer though. He watched her intently. Then his phone dinged with an incoming text.

"Would you mind waiting outside?" Frazer asked Ted politely. But it wasn't a question.

Ted muttered something about "only wanting to help" and then headed out the way he'd come.

"Who is the guy in the image, Kit?" Frazer asked as he seated himself across the table from her sister.

Kit crossed her arms and glared at him.

"You promised to tell me what was going on. You promised to tell me all the rumors and gossip," he continued.

Kit had made him promises? And neither of them had bothered to tell her? Izzy worked hard to keep her anger contained because even though she felt like she was the one losing control, this wasn't about her.

"Who is it?" he repeated the question.

"Damien Ridgeway." Each syllable was bitten off.

"I'll help you," Frazer told her, "but I think we need to go over the ground rules, one more time." He leaned closer, and his voice was so frigid it made ice crawl up Izzy's spine. "You tell me *all* the rumors, all the high school gossip, and I'll find out who killed Helena. Got it?"

Kit's gaze shifted away from him and flicked over the floor.

"So I'm thinking you should have called me when you first saw this, rather than lashing out," he said, leaning back in his chair.

Kit glared.

"I want the truth about what went down on New Year's Eve. You got drunk?"

She hesitated, then nodded.

"After the party you and Damien went back to the rental cottage and got high on cannabis?"

So Izzy hadn't removed the smell as well as she'd hoped.

Frazer shot her a look that suggested it would take more than a gallon of Lysol to fool him.

Kit nodded again, looking miserable.

"How did you get there?"

Kit slouched farther down in her chair. "On the back of his bike."

Izzy wanted to shake her sister all over again. That's why she hadn't seen Kit's car the next morning.

"Is it possible Damien left the cottage at some point during the evening?"

Kit's mouth compressed into a straight thin line. "I didn't see him leave."

"Is it possible?" Frazer pushed.

Kit's slim shoulders bobbed up and down. "Maybe. I-I don't know." The first sign of uncertainty.

Frazer nodded and leaned back in his chair. "I'm going to trace that photograph, Kit, but to be honest it might be difficult to press charges because, as suggestive as it is, there's no nudity, no intimate body parts on display." He pulled out his cell and eyed the image with his head tilted to one side. "It actually looks staged to me, like something a pissed off seventeen-year-old would orchestrate to get back at the other girls at the party. But the scheme backfired when Helena died."

Kit threw him a look that was both full of gratitude and reluctantly impressed. Because he hadn't fallen for her trick and immediately condemned her the way Izzy had.

Izzy's mouth dropped. "So, you mean you didn't give him a…"

Kit shot out of her chair. "For God's sake, Izzy. You can't even say it. Jesus. Blow job. Fellatio. That's a term you're probably more familiar with as it's Latin."

"You didn't do it." Izzy repeated stupidly. Why

it made her feel better she had no clue.

Kit eyed her archly. "Maybe I did it for real after we got high?"

But she hadn't. Izzy knew she hadn't. "I should have hosed the place down," she said instead.

Kit sneered. "You should try it some time. It's called having fun. I wasn't expecting it to become an Internet sensation, I just wanted those bitches to freak out for a while before I showed them the other photograph. Prove what idiots and bullies they all are." Kit showed them her phone with another photograph taken side-on with Damien's pants clearly zipped and her smiling innocently up at the guy. Same pose, a million times less pornographic. "After Helena was killed I forgot all about the stupid photographs. Then I got pissed about what they wrote. Fucking bitches." Kit wiped her eyes and picked up her coat. "Can I go now?" she asked Frazer.

"Who took the photographs?"

"Franky. Jesse's friend. But I don't think he'd have sent the picture to anyone, not with what happened to Jesse and Helena. He's a good guy."

The guy was in a shitload of trouble already. Izzy doubted he'd admit to another infraction.

"It's a starting place and that's all I need." Frazer looked like he'd solved the whole problem. He texted something on his phone then checked his messages. "Chief Tyson got the girl you hit to drop the charges. You *will* need to apologize."

"Like hell."

He looked at Kit for a moment as if he was trying to figure out why she didn't operate under the rules of normal logic.

Welcome to my world.

"Do it for Helena. You get tonight to think about it, otherwise you'll be back here tomorrow, and Miranda's parents will press charges for assault."

Kit's narrow-eyed glare could blister paint. "Fine. Whatever. I'll apologize to the bitch, but the whole time I do it I'll be staring at her squinty eyes and stupid fricking nose."

* * *

Kit stalked out, heading to the waiting room, which was thankfully empty except for Ted. Izzy followed close behind.

Ted stood when he saw them. "How about I take you home, Kit-kat?"

"I'll take her," insisted Izzy.

"I'm not a child. I can drive myself." Kit was close to flouncing off like some pissed off debutante.

Izzy took another deep breath, searching for her elusive inner Zen. "I don't want you driving when you're this upset."

"Why? Scared I'll embarrass you?"

"No, I'm scared you'll run off the road, or hit another car because you're too upset to concentrate properly."

"I don't care," Kit spat.

Izzy opened her mouth to argue, but Frazer beat her to it. "Go with your uncle, Kit. I'll arrange for your car to be driven home." He held open his palm for her keys.

"Fine. I'll go with Ted." Kit slapped the keys into Frazer's hand, treating him with the same disdain she treated everyone else.

Izzy should have been embarrassed, but she was too numb from the events of the last few days. She trailed outside the police station, and a feeling of complete and utter failure settled around her shoulders as Kit stalked off toward Ted's truck without a backward glance.

She folded her arms over her chest. "She hates me."

"She's hurting."

"And I made her furious. Rather than supporting her I acted judgmental."

"She's acting like a brat and is old enough to know better," Frazer said grimly. "Any guardian seeing their underage charge apparently performing oral sex is allowed to get a little upset. I'd be worried if you didn't."

"Why did she let me think the worst of her?" Izzy didn't get it.

"I'm guessing it was a way of punishing herself for what she sees as failing Helena."

Izzy turned horrified eyes on him. "And rather than talking about her feelings, she let everyone think she was screwing around with Damien when Helena was killed?"

"She *was* screwing around with Damien when Helena was killed—doesn't mean it was her fault. But she needed them to think the worst of her because that's how she feels about herself. And she wanted the excuse to lash out at people, including you, when she proved them wrong."

"How did you know she was lying?"

One side of his lips curled up, and there was a glint in his eyes that made her breath catch. "Let's just say I had a little help from a guy who's good with technology."

She watched Ted and Kit drive away. Kit didn't even look at her. Izzy wanted to hide her eyes with her hands and make it all go away, but that was weak and pathetic and not something Izzy would give in to. "Do you have kids?" she asked instead.

He shook his head and stared out at Pamlico Sound, which ran about a hundred yards behind the red-bricked building. "No kids. No one."

"Not even a dog?" He loved dogs. She didn't know what she would do without Barney.

His eyes hardened. "My ex took my dog. After a week or so, he escaped her yard and was hit by a car." His shoulders were rigid, his face a series of stern lines.

"Do you think she did it on purpose?" Izzy asked. She'd heard the bitterness in his voice when he'd spoken about his ex to Jesse earlier.

"Let's just say I had no problem signing the divorce papers after that."

A lump formed in Izzy's throat. He didn't say more, but she knew it had hurt. "I'm sorry about your dog."

His gaze remained impassive. "It was a long time ago. Your uncle has always lived on the island?"

She nodded and they started walking towards her car. "He was mayor for about fifteen years. He retired when my mom took sick. Helped to look after her. She had cancer."

"You didn't nurse her?"

Tension radiated along her spine. "I was deployed." And grateful to be deployed. "Made it back just before she passed. Ted watched Kit when I bought out my commission."

"Why did you enlist?"

"At first it was expediency. They paid for medical school, which I couldn't have afforded otherwise." The sea breeze tangled her hair. "But I was honored to serve my country." They weren't just words. It had been a privilege to give back, to support troops who needed her. "And the Army suited me. I enjoyed not having to make decisions about what to do with my life."

His brows rose. "That's a pretty honest assessment though you don't seem like someone who has difficulty making decisions."

"It isn't the easy stuff I struggle with—like what to make for dinner, or whether or not I should workout. And I know what I'm doing when it comes to patient care." Her gaze cut to his and then quickly away. "But figuring out where I can be the most effective? Where I'm needed most? Someone forcing me to take a vacation? The Army makes those things easy."

"You don't strike me as someone who likes being told what to do."

"I don't, except in certain situations." And suddenly her mind was in the gutter and for the third time in fewer days a fierce blush heated her cheeks. "I'm not talking about in the bedroom." Because whether he was interested or not, she wasn't about to have that misunderstanding between them. The day someone started tying her to the bedposts was the day she broke their jaw. "But I like rules, I like structure, organization, standard operating procedures. All the things teenagers hate."

As silence stretched between them Izzy remembered the words Kit had thrown at her.

Maybe if you learned to give good head you wouldn't be stuck home every night like some fucking virgin.

Dammit. She wasn't going to care about what her messed up little sister thought of her. "What about you?"

"Me?"

"The FBI must be chock full of rules."

He laughed and his whole demeanor changed. For a moment he lost his stiffness and looked younger, the curve of his mouth pulling her in and seducing her with its fullness. "The FBI does love rules." He shrugged. "It's an advantage of being an ASAC—I have less people ordering me around. But taking orders doesn't come naturally to me. You might have noticed, I'm pretty damned bossy." The gleam in his eye said "in and out of the bedroom." But maybe that was her imagination working overtime.

The wind ruffled his damp hair. "You're pretty senior to be down here working a case."

He shrugged and straightened his slightly crooked tie. "The agent who should have been here is pregnant and there were complications with the pregnancy. I came in her place."

"Is she okay?" Was that why he'd looked so tense and angry when he'd first arrived?

"Yes. She's going to be okay." From his expression she realized this woman meant something to him. He'd said there was no one in his life but that didn't mean—

"It isn't mine."

"Pardon?"

"The baby. I can read your thoughts from the look on your face. You're thinking Agent Rooney is having my baby. But trust me, I might care about her but not like that." He muttered under his breath. "I value my life too much."

If he could read her mind that easily, she was screwed. She took a step back and found herself brought up short by her car. "It's none of my business."

He took a step closer. She watched him, mesmerized by the intensity of his gaze.

"I meant it when I said there's no one in my life. No commitments. No obligations."

The air in her lungs vanished as she read the offer in those blue eyes.

"But my priority is the case." He tilted his head to one side as he regarded her. He obviously knew she was attracted to him, and that she was wary. Unfortunately it was his job that scared her to death—and those acute observational skills.

She found herself sucking in air as her heart went wild.

He straightened to his full height, a good five or six inches above her 5'6" frame. Not so tall she couldn't lean up and kiss him if she wanted to. She held herself firmly in place even as her fingers curled with the effort of not reaching for his lapels and pulling him down to her lips.

"You should get back to Kit."

His words snapped her back to reality and she fumbled her keys. She shouldn't be thinking about kissing the guy. She had a teenager to ground. She cleared her throat and asked, "Do you really think you can get control of that photograph?"

"Not me, but a friend of mine."

With her car door unlocked, she faced him again. "I don't know how to thank you, but I am grateful."

"Earlier you mentioned food." He grinned at her surprised expression and she caught another glimpse of the man beneath the badge. "I don't have time to get to the store. Anything edible in the cottage would be all the thanks I need—even a loaf of bread and a pint of milk."

He opened the door for her, standing close enough to feel the heat of him jump across the space that divided them. His gaze shifted to her lips. She stared back, heart skipping as she imagined what it might be like if one of them crossed the line and took the other one with them. Then the shutters came down as if he realized his thoughts were showing on his face.

His expression grew serious. "Keep an eye on your sister. You might want to keep her off social media tonight. It's going to be a rough ride for a while. The good news is Kit has a thick skin, but combined with Helena's death?"

"I'll watch her." The genuine caring in his voice warmed something deep inside. She got into the car and he closed her door, and then strode quickly away without looking back.

She needed to keep her distance, she reminded herself. Even though she was attracted to the guy, she couldn't get sucked in. ASAC Frazer had just found the remains of two bodies out at Parson's Point. Bodies she'd helped bury seventeen years ago.

***

It was almost seven o'clock when Izzy carried the pot of chicken curry in both hands and a plastic bag filled with some basics hooked on her arm. She almost went flying down the steps when Barney rushed past her out onto the beach to chase a seagull who'd landed too close to his water bowl. She steadied herself and took a deep breath. The bird flew off and Barney gave her an *I'm-so-clever* grin.

"Doofus." She laughed softly.

The dog followed her up the steps next-door and sat beside her as she put the pot down to knock at the door. She tried to tell herself the thought of seeing Frazer didn't make her pulse skip, but she was lying.

The door opened almost immediately, to a harried looking Special Agent Randall who had his phone pressed to his ear. He held his finger up to ask her to wait for a moment, but Barney went right inside and made himself at home. Izzy felt a bit stupid standing there with a pot of curry, but she'd promised food, and it seemed the least she could do after all the help he'd given her with Kit.

Randall hung up and ran his hand through his hair, making it stand up on end. "Sorry, that was a friend of mine. One of Frazer's BAU agents. I discovered she's been in the hospital for the last few days, and he didn't even tell me."

From the clenched jaw and glitter in his eyes this was a bad thing. Randall pulled it together and forced a smile. "What've you got there?"

"I went on a cooking spree and made enough to fill the freezer. I told ASAC Frazer I'd drop off something for you two for supper, and some milk, eggs and butter, because I know you guys are busy." She handed the pot over, potholders and all.

"Smells great. Thanks." He shook his head as if

clearing out his earlier mood. "You wanna come in and share?"

"No thanks. I already ate with Kit." She dug her hand into her pocket and pulled out a small bag of rice. She tucked it into his suit jacket pocket because his hands were full. She and Kit were getting on for a change and she planned to take full advantage.

"I take it ASAC Frazer"—*God, I don't know the guy's first name*—"should have told you about your friend?" It must be the agent he'd told her about earlier.

Randall grimaced. "I guess he's keeping a confidence, but she's the one who called me in on this—I've known her for years. You'd think he'd…" He shook his head again. "Doesn't matter. I'm whining."

"He must have his reasons. Maybe your friend asked him to keep it to himself?" Lucas Randall seemed like a heck of a nice guy—exactly the sort of man she should be dating if she ever really wanted to find herself a man to have a relationship with. Why couldn't his eyes intrigue her, his smile?

She glanced behind him and saw a large white board set up against one wall. She couldn't see what was on it, but the reality of what these men were doing here hit home. She took a step back. "Anyway, I better get home to Kit. She's hit the eating phase of depression, so I put her to work making cookie dough."

"Thanks for the food. Oh, hang on—" He grabbed some keys off the sideboard. "Kit's car is parked around the side of the cottage. Frazer won't be back for hours tonight, if at all, but I'll leave him some food—the bastard." He grinned to soften the insult.

The three small throwaway words "if at all" caused a twinge of panic to surge inside her. It reminded her their time here was temporary. Very temporary. Izzy wanted to ask where Frazer was, but it was none of her business.

"Do me a favor and keep those doors and windows tightly locked tonight." Randall's dark brown eyes ran over the bulge of her gun she wore beneath her jacket. "Keep that thing close."

His words brought on a fresh wave of unease. "Is there something you haven't told me?" she asked.

He shook his head, but she suddenly didn't believe him. It seemed that not telling people everything they needed to know was an FBI habit—although she couldn't exactly claim innocence in that department. She said goodbye and headed home.

How long would it be before someone came to her door and told her they'd found her father's body buried at Parson's Point? Not long enough, that was for damn sure.

CHAPTER FOURTEEN

For the millionth time he looked at the photograph on his cell phone and wondered why it affected him so much.

He'd seen hundreds if not thousands more graphic images. Usually the woman was naked. Pussy and tits on full display as she bent over, sucking off some guy's cock. This image was tame by comparison. The girl wore a short skirt, but no underwear or skin was visible. There were no shoes on her stocking-clad feet. Her hair was tied up into a loose ponytail on top of her head.

The image was almost innocent if you discounted the look of bliss on the strained mouth of the lucky bastard getting blown.

Despite knowing who the girl was, the photo made him as hard as stone every time he looked at the damn thing and that was despite jacking off so often his dick was sore. He shifted uncomfortably in the seat of the white van.

He slunk lower in his seat as the girl he was after finally came out of her house. She lived on Roanoke. She had dark hair and finely plucked brows. She began jogging and he started the engine and drove past her, about half a mile to the parking lot of a green space where, according to her social media posts, she ran early in the morning on a regular basis.

It was a Saturday, but it was quiet.

He waited until he saw her approaching in the side mirror. He got out and opened the side door of the van. A little dog shot out, trailing a lead behind him.

"Topper. Dammit, Topper!" he cried at the dog.

The girl smiled and grabbed the end of the leash as the ball of fur ran around her legs excitedly. She picked up the dog in her arms and came towards him, holding out the mutt.

"He's adorable." She laughed and closed her eyes as the dog licked her face.

He slammed her full force in the face, his fist catching her jaw and knocking her to the ground like a wrecking ball. Her hands flew wide, and she dropped the terrier who scampered away, yipping. He scooped up the girl and threw her inside the van, climbing in behind her and slamming the door shut. He knelt on her back and stuffed a gag in her mouth, pulling it tight. She tried to buck him off, but he outweighed her by a good hundred pounds. He pulled both hands behind her back and bound them with duct tape. Then he grabbed one ankle, then the other, hogtied her until her feet and hands almost met in the middle of her back.

She rolled around, but she couldn't go anywhere. Her face was distorted in fear and agony, snot and blood smeared over her cheeks.

She wasn't looking so tough now. Little bitch.

He took her phone off a clip at her belt. Removed the battery. He had plans for this one. Intended to take his time with her. Get a little payback. She deserved it for messing with someone he cared about. He climbed over the front seat and started the van, reversing out of the space. The little dog he'd found wandering around the streets earlier that morning ran into the park with the leash dragging behind him. It had all gone down without a hitch. Piece of cake.

CHAPTER FIFTEEN

Frazer and Hanrahan surrendered their weapons and submitted to a thorough search before they walked through the first in a series of metal doors and sally ports. When Frazer had visited a Supermax facility in Colorado on Christmas Eve, he hadn't expected to be back behind bars again quite so soon. They followed the guard who'd been assigned to take them to the interview room. This place was older than the Supermax facility, smaller, dirtier, and noisier. It stank of unwashed bodies and blocked drains. Of hundreds of men locked up in a confined space. It had less sophisticated security than the Supermax, but no one was escaping without a full-scale military assault on the complex—or a cunning plan.

Protesters both for and against the death penalty were already gathering not far from the main entrance, carrying placards and banners. It happened whenever there was an execution but the warden would be watching for any hint of trouble.

Frazer had gotten the phone call he'd been expecting after he'd spoken to Isadora in the parking lot of the police station. Ferris Denker had requested an interview with Hanrahan. Just as well—Frazer had been within an inch of doing something stupid with the sexy doctor next-door. Instead, he'd put some distance between them and had driven from the Outer Banks overnight, catching a couple hours sleep in a motel before picking up Hanrahan at Columbia Metropolitan Airport en route. The reunion had been stilted, and

Hanrahan had been quiet on the drive down, rereading his notes on the case, deep in thought.

Now he asked, "Who takes the lead?"

"You do. I'll jump in when I need to," said Frazer. Hanrahan didn't need any pointers. Frazer had learned everything he knew about interviewing serial killers from this man. Memories from that West Virginian wood tried to crowd into his mind, bringing with it the familiar sense of betrayal but this time Frazer ignored it. They'd both made mistakes. He didn't excuse what Hanrahan had done, the same way he didn't excuse his own actions. But he wasn't about to reveal his own sins and end up on death row like these predators—more importantly he wasn't about to expose people he cared about, or destroy an institution he believed in. They kept their silence out of loyalty to one another and the BAU—and the knowledge that when they did their jobs right, they saved innocent lives.

Being angry with Hanrahan was hypocritical, and served no purpose.

"I want him to feel important, important enough to warrant one of the best BAU personnel coming out of retirement to talk to him."

Hanrahan flinched.

"You were the best, Art." Frazer spoke quietly. He paused. Now was the time to let it go. "What you did went against every ideal you'd taught me, but it's done now. Over." It wasn't an apology, but the other man seemed to understand it was a truce of sorts.

Hanrahan sent him a look that spoke volumes. "I made you compromise yourself and I know what that costs."

"I made my own choices. I always do," Frazer said bluntly. He strove for perfection and that's what he demanded in others.

Hanrahan stopped their forward progress. "I've helped put away some evil human beings, Linc, but the greatest achievement of my life was pulling you out of that room in Ohio—not just because I rescued a kid, but because of all the good you've done in your career. All the people *you've* saved."

The memory of that long ago night was locked up tight inside Frazer's brain. It didn't get out much. "Your second greatest achievement was putting a bullet in the man who killed my parents." And who'd held him captive for five long days. "If you hadn't, I'd have ended up in a place like this because I would have hunted him down and I *would* have killed him. Make of that what you will." Remnants of the rage-filled fifteen-year-old wanted to leak through but he held him tightly in check. He always did.

"It makes you human."

"Not good enough," Frazer snapped.

"I made you…" Hanrahan's voice caught. The words could never be uttered out loud. "I know I screwed up last year. If I could go back and fix it, I would. But you made the right choice."

"There was no *choice*." The anger escaped briefly. Frazer indicated the other man move ahead of him. "But I don't lose sleep over it. I don't lose sleep over any of the monsters who are gone from this earth, so let's make sure Denker joins their ranks. And let's see if we can get his partner before anyone else has to die."

They reached a room with another steel door. The guard opened it and waved them inside.

Hanrahan went first. Frazer followed, giving an uncertain smile to the man sitting chained behind a table that was bolted to the floor. Frazer scraped his chair back as he sat and made a big show of arranging the file folders he'd brought with him as if he were unsure where he'd put everything he needed.

"Agent Hanrahan. Good to see you. I'd shake your hand, but I'm a little tied up." Denker's smile creased the skin around his eyes as he raised his shackled arms. "You're looking well. Retirement must suit you."

So the guy followed the news—most serial killers did if it pertained to their cases or their lives.

"Retirement does suit me. I earned it." Hanrahan dropped heavily into his seat and leaned back in his chair with a deep sigh. "I hear you've been doing well, Ferris. Warden told me you earned your theology degree?"

Ferris nodded. "Decided I better find out more about Heaven and Hell if I was going to be visiting soon." *Heaven*? He had to be kidding. "Do you believe in the power of repentance, Art?"

"Well." Hanrahan ran his tongue slowly around his teeth before answering. "It's easy for someone to say they repent, Ferris. I think you actually have to believe it to make it count."

A tight grin slashed Denker's lips across his face. Hanrahan had testified in court that Denker was incapable of experiencing human emotions such as empathy or regret. He saw his victims, all things really, as means to his personal gratification. "So you don't think my repentance will mean much to a Christian God? You think I'm going to Hell?"

"I think we're all going to Hell, Ferris,"

Hanrahan said with a tired grimace.

Denker's eyes narrowed. "Some sooner than others."

Frazer could only hope.

"So what did you want to talk to me about?" Hanrahan ran his eyes around the room as if bored. *Stop wasting my time. Tell me something interesting.*

Denker ignored Hanrahan and turned his attention to Frazer. "Who's this kid?"

Frazer was well aware he looked a good decade younger than he actually was. He used it to an advantage. He held out his hand awkwardly across the table, forcing himself to grasp the man's clammy fingers even though he was chained. "Lincoln Frazer." He wasn't about to admit being higher up the totem pole than Hanrahan. He wanted to stay in the background and observe, for now.

Denker squinted as if searching through memories. "Name sounds familiar."

Frazer smiled, pretending to be pleased the guy had heard of him. "I took over from SSA Hanrahan when he retired. I'm glad that you agreed to meet with us before you, er…hmm." Frazer coughed. As if they'd been the one to request this meeting, not the other way around. "I was, er, hoping to ask you a few questions to use in my criminal psychology lectures."

Denker looked both flattered and irritated. He ignored Frazer—because as egotistical as Denker was, he was on a mission and that mission was saving his own ass. He didn't think Frazer could get him what he needed. His mistake.

"Talk to the governor, Art. Get the death penalty quashed and I'll even mark assignments for aspiring Feds." He nodded toward Frazer like he was a mook. As if they needed him to be experts on aberrant behavior when the guy was a textbook predator: narcissistic, calculating, manipulative. No empathy, no remorse, no conscience.

Frazer already knew what made Ferris Denker tick. Having women helpless and at his mercy. Causing pain until he ejaculated from the pure sadistic thrill of it. Denker thought that the fact he tortured and killed to classical music made him a more sophisticated killer. Frazer didn't care about the soundtrack, he just wanted justice for the victims, and maybe a little payback.

Hanrahan shook his head sadly. "You know I don't have that sort of power, Ferris." He opened his hands wide. "The judge made the decision and the appeals process is finished. Time to pay your dues."

Denker's gaze shifted between them before finally settling on his own fingers which he stroked over one another in a way that made the hair on Frazer's neck stand taut. "What if there were other crimes?"

Hanrahan shook his head and shifted to lean forward over the wide desk. "You had your chance to come clean. It's over."

"What if I tell you where the bodies are buried?" Denker asked sharply. "You only found five. I confessed to ten."

Frazer tilted his head. "We've found your dump site, Mr. Denker."

Ferris's eyes flashed with anger. Something about his little scheme hadn't gone entirely to plan. Interesting. "You found *one* of them," he said tightly.

"Do you know who we found?" Frazer asked curiously. What would the guy admit to? Could his aim be getting involved in a conspiracy to murder charge, where they had to keep him alive to catch and convict the other killer? Was that Denker's game? If so, would he give up the other player? And did the other player realize this?

Frazer's first priority was getting killers off the street.

"I know where you were looking. I watch the news." Again Denker dismissed him and concentrated on Hanrahan.

Maybe he wasn't ready to give up his accomplice yet. Maybe there really was honor between serial killers; or maybe Ferris Denker didn't know a damned thing.

"How many more are there?" Hanrahan demanded.

Denker's eyes flicked high left. "At least three sites." He was telling the truth.

Frazer hid his revulsion. If Denker saw it, he'd use it.

"How many more victims are buried out there, Ferris? Where are they buried?" Hanrahan asked.

Denker shrugged a bony shoulder. It was difficult to imagine this man being strong enough to overpower all those women, but he had been. Had he worked alone? Was this current killer an old associate? A new disciple? He needed Parker to work his magic and figure out how the two were communicating.

"We'll need more to go on than the vague indication that more bodies are out there," said Hanrahan impatiently. "Neither the state's attorney nor the governor will roll over for vague promises.

They're not idiots and South Carolina doesn't grant stays of execution unless there's a miracle—you know that."

"Fine." Denker sat up straighter in his chair, scenting his prize. "Bring me a map. I'll show you where one of them is buried—as a show of good faith."

"Not sure bartering the bodies of women you murdered for extra time on this Earth will get you through the gates of Heaven," Hanrahan muttered.

"A map of where?" Frazer asked, ignoring Hanrahan's comment.

"North Carolina. There are woods out near Maysville."

Frazer nodded to the guard who left to fetch a map. Another guard stood at the door.

"How often did you visit the Outer Banks, Mr. Denker?"

The guy was smiling because he thought he was getting what he wanted. "Quite a few times. It's a pretty area."

"Did you drive Route 6 all the way to Ocracoke?"

Denker nodded, chains jingling.

Ocracoke was only accessible by ferry. Alarm bells started to beep inside Frazer's head, but getting a few geographical questions wrong wasn't proof of anything. He wanted to probe more but couldn't risk showing his hand. "You have any friends out there?"

Denker's eyes sharpened on Frazer. "There was a time when I had a lot of friends."

Denker had been a popular guy. Lots of female friends. Lots of drinking buddies. They'd all been shocked when his crimes had been revealed.

"Any of them ever visit you in here?" Frazer asked.

Denker reared back in his chair and sneered. "I can see why this guy got the job, Hanrahan. He figured out people actually visit guys like me in jail. Hell, he should read my fan mail. I've had two proposals since I've been in the joint. I thought about accepting one of them, but no conjugal visits so...what's the point?" The smirk returned. "But you already know all that, don't you?"

Frazer unleashed a little of his own predator in his return smile. "Don't you miss it, Ferris? Doesn't it piss you off knowing there are other men like you, only smarter and more successful because they never got pulled over for something as dumb as a broken taillight? Doesn't it burn your gut they're still out there enjoying themselves while you're stuck in here, jacking off with all the other losers?"

Denker's eyes went hard, black. Little orbs of evil.

Evil didn't scare Frazer. He enjoyed cuffing it and locking it in prison to rot or die. Death was easier than living in a hellhole like this for some of them, and he was fine with that, too.

"I've got some happy memories to sustain me." Denker shrugged.

"Vivid fantasies too, huh? Must bite that you can't act them out."

A tic worked in Denker's jaw, revealing his growing agitation. The guard came back with a map and spread it out on the table before them. The look Denker threw him said he'd finally figured out Frazer wasn't the weak link in this chain. "I'll need to be released from my shackles." He indicated his bound hands.

Frazer nodded to the guard.

Frazer watched him carefully, but the guy wasn't a threat to them. He might be able to get a punch in, but Frazer was bigger and not afraid to fight back. Denker liked victims he could control and dominate. Submissive women he could torture without fear of reprisal. On top of that, he wouldn't risk attacking federal agents or a guard because that could interfere with any appeal or request for clemency. Goading the sonofabitch into a mistake was the least Frazer could do.

Denker shook out his wrists like they hurt and picked up the marker the guard had provided.

"You never admitted to being abused as a child. You could have used it in your defense," Frazer suggested.

Hanrahan sent him a warning look but Denker was sentenced to die in twenty-two days and time was running out. For him.

"I wasn't abused. I was born this way," Denker muttered.

"I don't believe you."

Denker's eyes glittered. "What would you know about it? Were you some poor little boy whose daddy couldn't keep his hands off his ass at night?"

Frazer kept his expression mildly amused. "I know it wasn't your father because he died when you were very young. I mean it could have been him but—"

"My father was a good man!"

Frazer raised his brows. "Maybe an uncle, then? Scout leader? Teacher?"

The man's eyes reacted almost imperceptibly

to the last word.

Teacher. "Is that where you met your friend? Your killing buddy who was smart enough to keep his car in good repair?"

Denker's smile turned ugly, clearly enjoying knowing something Frazer didn't. Playing mind games, but all he said was, "I'm obviously not the only one good at fantasy."

Frazer leaned over the table. Denker stared intently at the map, as if trying to pinpoint the exact spot he was talking about.

"If you give up your partner, I'll talk to the governor," Frazer said quietly.

"I don't have a partner." Denker still didn't look up.

"Why are you so keen to protect him? Is it your abuser? You don't have to be scared of him any longer, Ferris."

When Denker finally reacted, his eyes burned with rage. *Interesting.* "I'm not scared of anyone."

"Well, it can't be for love or friendship—you're a psychopath, you don't know what love is, and your idea of friendship is probably not sadistically torturing someone to death."

Hanrahan tensed beside him.

Denker stilled, then smiled a cold reptilian smile. "You'd be surprised." He stabbed his finger on the map. "There. I don't remember her name. She was my first and I made a lot of mistakes. She didn't die easy, but she sure as hell was a lot of fun. Consider her a freebie." His lips grew tight with regret. "Tell the governor I'll reveal where all the bodies are of everyone I killed if I get my sentence commuted to life."

Frazer dragged the map across the table. "If I

find anything there I'll make an appointment to see the governor—but you know how busy these people can be."

A grin spread over Denker's face that made Frazer's gut clench. "I'd suggest sooner rather than later."

***

Izzy had just got out of the shower after taking Barney for a run on the beach when Kit walked into her bedroom unannounced. Izzy's wet hair was wrapped in a towel, which kept threatening to topple off her head as she pulled on her jeans. Her heart bounced painfully against her ribs in fright at the intrusion. At least she didn't lunge for her gun.

"*After* I apologize to that bitch *Miranda*," Kit's voice reeked of venom, "I want to go see Jesse in the hospital. Then I'm going to work my shift at the diner."

"You sure you want to work today?" Izzy asked, surprised.

Kit's face was stern. Whatever vulnerability she'd shown last night had vanished. "I've been thinking about Helena, a lot. I figure this is what she'd want me to do. Talk to Jesse. Keep my chin high. Ignore the bullshit princesses. Graduate high school and get the fuck off this island, the same way you did. I never understood why you left before. Now I do."

Izzy hoped Kit never discovered the whole truth.

"I'll drive you to the police station and the hospital and drop you off at the diner. You finish at ten, right?" Izzy spoke quickly. "I'll pick you up after work. I want to know you're safe."

"I thought that's why you put the tracker app on my phone?"

Izzy grimaced. Busted.

"Look," Kit said patiently. "I appreciate the thought, but I'm seventeen and I have to start looking out for myself. I'll park in front of the diner, and I'll make sure Sal walks me out."

Sal owned the diner.

"What if Sal's the killer?" Izzy hated to bring it up, but why ignore the possibility?

"If he is then he has all afternoon and evening to do his worst. Plus, I'll tell him I told the FBI he was walking me to my car. Short of having a protection detail it's the best I can do."

Izzy opened her mouth to argue.

"You can't trail me around forever," Kit pointed out. "I can't follow you around either and despite that gun," her gaze touched the Glock on Izzy's nightstand. "You're not invincible."

It irritated her that her sister was right. "Fine, but I'm driving you to the cops and to the hospital. You call me when you're leaving the diner." Izzy braced herself. "What about the photograph?"

"Damien posted the cleaner version on his social media accounts and wrote about how we'd planned to do a feature on online bullying for our social studies class about truth and perception, but the 'bitches' beat us to it. I guess he had the most to lose." Kit shrugged a shoulder.

Izzy hid her surprise. She still didn't trust the guy.

"I haven't seen anyone sharing the X-rated version around today and everyone I know has taken it down. Anyway, what am I gonna do? Hide away for a year? I don't think so. I don't care what anyone thinks—except Jesse. I need him to know the whole truth. If I have any more trouble I'll tell the cops." She looked at her watch impatiently. "How long are you gonna be?"

Izzy scrubbed the towel over her wet hair. "Five minutes."

"Why don't I drive myself to the police station and you can—"

"No," Izzy said firmly. "I'm coming with you to the cops and to see Jesse. He might not want to see you and I don't want you pissing off anyone if that's the case."

Kit grinned at her unexpectedly. "Determined to keep me out of trouble, Iz? Mom would be proud."

Izzy looked away and turned on the hairdryer full blast. A lump of emotion knotted inside her throat and she choked down the words that wanted to escape—that Izzy had stopped caring what their mother thought years ago when her mom had stabbed her husband with a screwdriver and forced Izzy to bury the body by threatening the life of her unborn child.

That was not something Kit ever needed to know. Her mother had put Izzy in the position she now found herself in and, frankly, she hated her for it.

CHAPTER SIXTEEN

An hour later they walked out of the police station. Hank Wright had been there and had shown both Miranda Hutchens and her parents the second photograph, along with the message about the dangers of online bullying. Turned out Kit hadn't been the only one having to apologize.

Kit had left her car at the diner and caught a ride with Izzy. Although she wanted to baby her, Izzy knew it was impractical and probably unnecessary. It was difficult to imagine a murderer would attack anyone now that they were all on high alert. Kit had promised to call Izzy when she was leaving work and come straight home with no stops along the way.

They headed inside the hospital and Izzy was surprised to see Agent Randall talking animatedly to Chief Tyson outside Jesse's room like they were old friends.

They both looked up when she and Kit approached.

"Kit would like to talk to Jesse for a few minutes," Izzy asked Chief Tyson. "But only if that would be okay with you?"

Both men frowned and then looked at one another. Randall shrugged. The chief licked his lips and then nodded. He addressed Kit. "Don't talk to him about the assault. Don't ask him any questions about that night. He doesn't remember much after he was hit on the head and is still in a lot of pain whenever the meds wear off." His eyes turned flat. "If you upset him, I'll haul your ass off to jail, got it?"

Kit nodded meekly. "I don't want to upset him. I thought he might want to talk about Helena with someone who knew and loved her." Tears gathered in her eyes, but she blinked them back. She seemed to have finally realized that this wasn't about her.

The chief opened the door and let her in. Jesse's mother came out with a worried expression on her face.

"Want me to go in with them?" Izzy volunteered even though she didn't really want to.

"No," Tyson said. "Jesse's starting to chafe at the restrictions. It'll be good for them to spend a little time together. Get the grieving process started."

"I need to go home. My mom has a church meeting at four." Charlene Tyson checked her watch. Izzy had discovered the other night that Charlene was an epileptic and wasn't allowed to drive.

"I'd give you a ride, but I need to drop Kit back at the diner around five."

"You sure that's a good idea?" asked Chief Tyson.

Izzy held her hands wide to say it wasn't her choice, but she understood the need to bury herself in work. "She wants to try and carry on life as normal. It seems like a reasonable thing to do."

"I'll take her to the diner," Tyson said. "That way people will be reminded I'm not happy about the whole photo saga."

She glanced at Agent Randall. "Did they figure out who sent that awful message yet?"

He nodded. "Yes and no. A friend of mine tracked it and deleted it from most sites. It originated from Franky Cirencester's phone, but he said it he didn't send it to anyone. He thinks someone must have picked up the phone when he put it down somewhere at the party. He was pretty drunk from all accounts."

"So who was it sent to?" she asked.

Randall eyed her cautiously, judging how much he could reveal. "Jesse's ex-girlfriend, Jessica Tuttle. She's the one who spread it around the next day with that message. Her email address was on about half the original texts and she posted it on social media. She wasn't exactly difficult to track down."

Izzy shook her head. Charlene's mouth hung open.

"Thank goodness she's an ex-girlfriend," the chief stated with a grimace. "I'm assuming there are charges that can be brought?"

Randall nodded. "Frazer said to leave it with him. He was going to talk to a few people and figure out the best approach."

Tyson nodded. "I want to be kept in the loop." He put his hands on his hips. "What she wrote about Kit and Helena was plain wrong."

A strong sense of gratitude hit Izzy out of nowhere. The fact she didn't have to handle this alone was a huge relief. "Thank you," she told the Tysons and Randall. "Thank you so much for your help with this."

The chief sent her a wry smile. "You've got your work cut out with that one."

Charlene's eyes filled with tears, which she quickly blinked away. "None of us are exactly winning parenting awards."

Chief Tyson put his arm around his wife's

shoulders. "Hey, they went to a party and didn't tell us about it." His face grew sad. "We did the same sort of stuff at their age. It's normal. No one should have died."

"So why do I feel like such a failure?" Izzy blew out a long, audible breath.

"Because you have a teenager to raise." Charlene smiled tightly. "And we're the lucky ones."

On that sobering thought Izzy and Charlene headed out. Izzy wondered where ASAC Frazer was and was proud of herself for not angling for information. She didn't think he'd returned to the cottage last night. Maybe he was gone for good? The idea brought with it a mixture of relief and anxiety.

They walked back to her car in silence. The weight of everything that had happened was exhausting. She didn't know how cops handled it. She kept wondering if they'd IDed the two bodies they'd found on the beach yesterday. The fact she could have told them the identity meant she was wasting their time, time that could be spent hunting the killer. Although they'd have to run the DNA through databases anyway, she realized. They wouldn't just take her word for it.

"Is that your car, Izzy?" Charlene caught her by the arm.

Izzy jerked out of her thoughts and glanced up. *Oh, shit*. Every window in her SUV had been smashed. Thank heavens Barney was at home.

Dammit. Hurt and fear competed in her brain—hurt won. Why would someone do this? She drew in a deep breath, trying to calm down before she spoke. "I guess you're gonna need another ride home, Charlene." She checked her watch. "I'll call the garage for a tow."

"And I'll call Lee." Her husband. "He needs to see this."

Izzy shook her head. "He's got more important things to worry—"

Charlene's fingers bit into her arm. "What if it's related? What if it's the same person who attacked Jesse and Helena?"

Everything inside Izzy froze as terror rose up inside. It was crazy, but at the same time the Outer Banks was a low crime area. These things simply didn't happen here.

"You're right, of course, you're right. Call him." Because someone was targeting her and until the bastard showed his face, she was running blind.

***

"Denker knows exactly what's going on," Frazer said grimly as they left the prison. He looked at the map. "He's manipulating our every move and someone's helping him. Now we have to involve more people in this circus."

He and Hanrahan climbed into the rental car and he plugged the location Denker had said was a dumpsite into his GPS. Frazer clipped the Bluetooth device to his ear so he could talk and drive at the same time. Then he pulled out his cell to call the SAC of the Charlotte division of the FBI in North Carolina to organize the search for human remains and a shallow grave. His cell rang before he could dial. Randall.

"Any progress?" asked Frazer. The guy had been pissed with him earlier because he hadn't told him Rooney was in the hospital. It was her business.

"I just got a call. Another body. On the mainland this time. Prostitute reported missing from Greenville yesterday. Body dumped an hour south of there on the grounds of an abandoned school."

"Who found her?"

"Couple of kids messing around in the woods with their dog this morning."

That would have been a grisly discovery. "How do we know this is related?" The murder of a prostitute would normally fly pretty low on the radar.

"Easy. They found my business card with my direct phone number on her." There was a pause. "*In* her."

Jesus. "I don't suppose you know who you gave that particular card to?"

"Nope." Randall's voice held a trace of excitement. "But I got a new batch printed because my extension number changed. I've only handed out this particular card during the Helena Cromwell investigation."

So the killer lived on the island. Frazer had already suspected it.

"Send me the address of the murder scene. I'll go there next. We have anything back on the skeletal remains yet? Or DNA from Helena or the shovel?"

"Quantico is still running DNA against the databases and the ME's office hasn't called yet. Did your visit to Denker shake anything loose?"

"It rattled him, but I wouldn't say it shook him. He gave us a dumpsite in North Carolina. Now I have to call your SAC from Charlotte and bring him up to speed. You can call Danbridge and fill her in if you want before he does—that'll buy you some brownie points. Thanks for holding off on that." The words felt weird on his lips. "Thank yous" always did.

"Where is the dump site Denker gave you in North Carolina?" asked Randall.

"Near a place called Maysville."

Randall released a heavy sigh. "Guess where the latest murder vic was found?"

"Maysville." Frazer gritted his teeth.

"Yep. On the grounds of St. Joseph's School for Boys." Randall reeled off the address.

"Something tells me these guys have got more games of show-and-tell planned. Ask the local police on the island to warn people to take extra precautions until we catch this guy." Frazer was about to hang up but found himself saying, "And keep your eye on the Campbell women until I get back."

"You think they're suspects?" Randall asked carefully.

"No. I think the killer stole their shovel because he's familiar with them, their home and belongings. I think there's a connection there."

"The doctor had her windshield and car windows smashed in this afternoon. Someone took a baseball bat to it, right in the hospital parking lot."

"No cameras or witnesses?" asked Frazer, trying not to react. Why hadn't she called him? Why would she call him?

"No one saw a damn thing. Cameras don't cover that part of the hospital grounds."

Why was she being targeted? "Is she okay?"

"She wasn't there at the time. Thankfully, she was talking to me and Tyson because Kit wanted to get in to see Jesse. So she's fine, but a bit shaken up." A calculating edge entered Randall's voice. "You coming back to Rosetown tonight?"

The guy was going to use the opportunity of Frazer's absence to make a move on Dr. Isadora Campbell. Jealousy rushed through him in an ugly wave. But why? He had no intention of letting anything happen between them, at least not during the investigation.

What about afterwards?

What if she met someone else first, someone good-looking and charming like Lucas-fucking-Randall? Someone who wasn't a manipulative, controlling bastard who'd use any tool or any*body* to break a case.

What about it? He didn't need a woman in his life.

"I'll be there, but it'll be late." He needed to contact his media connections. The discovery of four bodies and the excavation of another possible gravesite wasn't something he could keep quiet any longer. Frazer should give the case to someone else from his unit and get back to doing his job as supervisor. The Denker connection was about to get blown wide open, if not by them then by the asshole's lawyer. But he didn't want to let go. He wanted to find Helena's killer. He wanted to see Isadora Campbell one last time.

"I have to make some calls. What are you doing now?" Frazer asked.

"I'm on my way to interview the retired police chief in Roanoke, and also see if I can get a lead on obtaining surveillance footage for anyone leaving the island yesterday morning, a couple of hours before the prostitute disappeared. Cross-reference the information with traffic cams on the roads between here and Greenville."

"Good idea." That should keep him occupied for a few hours. "Let me know what you find out." He hung up and dialed Parker. "How's Rooney?"

Hanrahan's ears perked up at that. He'd been the one to bring Mallory Rooney into the BAU for reasons that had been unclear at the time. Now they were crystal.

"No placenta previa indicated and everything else seems normal so she's being released from the hospital tomorrow as long as she behaves herself." Parker's voice grew stern, and he was obviously talking to the woman herself.

Relief expanded inside Frazer at the news. "Good. That's good. I know it's the weekend but things are moving fast down here. They found a murdered prostitute in Maysville wearing a business card that Lucas Randall knows he handed out on the Outer Banks. And, in a nice twist, Ferris Denker just revealed the location of one of his victims to Hanrahan and me. Same probable dump location."

"You're looking for how Denker communicates with his partner?"

"Yes, but I think they think they're too smart to leave an obvious trace. Randall's going to check CCTV footage and Automatic License Plate Reader databases to see who left and returned to the island yesterday around the time of the latest murder, but it's multi-jurisdictional so it might take some time to untangle the red tape and get everyone onboard."

"You want me to investigate the staff, the warden?"

"Everyone," Frazer said. "Including all visitors to the prison. I know it's another big ask when Rooney's stuck in bed—"

"What? No. It's fine. Gives her something to do besides driving me and the nursing staff crazy."

Frazer heard a rude comment from Rooney, but it was obvious things were much better with the pregnancy if Parker was teasing her and letting her work.

Fingers crossed.

Frazer smiled to himself that he still subconsciously used his mother's old Christian superstitions.

"Denker only has twenty-two days left on this earth. He wants the sentence commuted to life. And is prepared to barter the locations of his victims for that. He asked me to talk to the governor," said Frazer.

"And this new killer will make people start to ask questions about a partner or copycat—maybe make them doubt the conviction. The victims' families are gonna want closure before he takes that information with him to the grave," said Parker. "The governor might have no choice but to postpone if only for a short time."

Frazer and Parker had both seen the extremes Mallory Rooney's family had gone to in order to find her missing sister. It followed that other families would be just as desperate.

"I tried to keep this out of the press, but with this second murder and the discovery of human remains—"

"Followed by another dig? Press is going to be

all over this like a coonhound scenting blood."

And the pressure would be on.

"The idea Denker could escape his death sentence makes me furious," Frazer admitted.

"Preaching to the choir, dude. But life in prison wouldn't be so bad if he tells us where he buried the bodies."

"He'll never reveal them all."

"Let's squeeze what we can get out of him and hope he fries."

Frazer felt a reluctant smile tugging his lips. "I'm going to concentrate on finding this other killer so Denker has one less card up his sleeve." And so no one else had to die. Frazer said goodbye and hung up.

"You and Alex Parker seem pretty pally, under the circumstances," Hanrahan noted quietly.

Frazer said nothing.

"Why are you going back to the Outer Banks?" asked Hanrahan.

"That's where the killer is."

"Are you sure?"

He shot his former mentor a look. "He was there on New Year's Eve. He stole the shovel from a local family and injured another woman when he went back the night after to clean up any evidence he might have left behind."

"If he really was local he'd have used his own shovel," Hanrahan countered. "Don't they all carry them in their trunks for when they drive on the beach?"

"We think he rode a dirt bike to the murder on New Year's." But suddenly Frazer wasn't so sure about his theories—what if the real reason he wanted to go back to the Outer Banks was because of the strawberry-blonde with the sage green eyes? The idea shook him. Nothing ever came between him and the job. Then he remembered something else that let him breathe easier. "The killer placed Special Agent Randall's business card on the latest victim—cards he only handed out during Helena Cromwell's murder investigation. The guy's a local, or at least staying in the area. I'm running down a list of people who own dirt bikes on the island."

"Won't you need to stay in Maysville?" Hanrahan pushed.

"Maysville is important. Denker says this is the site of his first kill. I need to bring in someone familiar with the case to liaise with local police. Someone I can trust."

Hanrahan snorted. "What makes you think I'll take it?"

"I know you'll take it."

Hanrahan grunted. "I thought you weren't done punishing me yet?"

"I'm not." Frazer knew his smile was thin as he glanced at an incoming text. "Petra Danbridge is meeting us there."

"Sweet Mary and Joseph."

"Apt. The name of the school where the latest victim was found is St. Joseph's School for Boys."

Hanrahan's brown eyes widened, forehead crinkling. "That's where Denker went to school."

Frazer's hands tightened on the steering wheel. "We need to check out the school records. See who his friends were."

But Hanrahan was shaking his head. "All destroyed in a fire, years ago."

"Did you talk to any of the staff? Anyone who

might remember Denker and who he hung around with back then?"

"I never had a reason to track any of them down. The evidence was irrefutable and we never suspected a partner."

"Then that's priority number one." Building a deductive profile was time consuming and this case was going at warp speed with clues from the past and the present colliding. He needed to see this new victim, he needed to check into Denker's connection with St. Joseph's. His phone rang again. Randall. He answered, trying to think where he could find a helicopter and pilot at short notice.

"We have another missing girl." Randall didn't bother with pleasantries.

Shit. Frazer switched him to speakerphone because Hanrahan needed to hear this.

"Jessica Tuttle went jogging this morning around six AM. Didn't return home."

"This is Jessica Tuttle as in Jesse Tyson's ex-girlfriend?" Frazer clarified. "The girl who spread the picture of Kit Campbell far and wide on the Internet?"

"One and the same."

"Where was Kit at the time Jessica disappeared?"

"Lucky for Kit, I saw her taking Barney for a walk on the beach at about 6:20 AM. No way she could make it to Roanoke and back in that time."

Frazer crushed the insidious idea that Randall might have spent the night with Isadora Campbell to make that convenient observation.

Who she spent her time with was none of his business—but it could be. He knew it could be, if one of them ever got the nerve to make the first move. He'd never been accused of lacking nerve before.

He concentrated on the road ahead, and the case, not the woman he wanted to get naked and plunder. "Any history of the girl taking off without telling her parents?"

"She's not the most reliable of teenagers, which is why her parents track her phone. It went dead at pretty much the exact moment Jessica is believed to have disappeared. Police officers and sheriff's deputies are organizing search parties and door-to-door even though it hasn't been twenty-four hours yet. Helena's murder has everyone spooked."

With good reason. Dammit. "I'll call you when I get closer to OBX. Meet you at the police department unless they've already found her."

"What about Maysville?" asked Randall.

"I'll go there for a quick look-see but Art Hanrahan is coming back onboard for this investigation, and he's going to be our FBI liaison at Maysville. We're about to have a lot more warm bodies working on this."

"We need them."

"Yeah. Keep me apprised of the search for Jessica Tuttle." Frazer hung up. With a teenage girl missing this case was about to explode. And if this case went viral what would that mean for the photograph of Kit Campbell and Damien Ridgeway? Despite Kit's bravado he didn't want to see her destroyed when the national and international media got hold of this thing. He called Parker again. "I need another favor, several favors. In fact, I'm gonna need your whole cyber security team working on this, and we don't have much time."

***

The cops had dusted the door handles of her SUV for prints and then Seth Grundy had towed the vehicle to his garage up in Whalebone. Agent Randall didn't know if this was the work of the same person who killed Helena or some random act of violence. No one had seen anything and she had no idea why anyone would target her this way. Even if someone knew what she'd done seventeen years ago, it made zero sense to trash her car unless they were just trying to piss her off. In which case, it was working.

Ted had told her countless times she could use his truck without asking permission should she ever need it. For reasons known only to himself, he had three working vehicles. Izzy decided to walk over to his house rather than ask him to bring it over. Barney needed the exercise and she needed to cool off. It was late afternoon and Ted lived a few miles north of Rosetown in the small cottage where he and her mother had grown up on the southwest edge of Bodie Island. She put Barney on his leash to walk through Rosetown and over the Bonner Bridge, which linked the islands. Officially, pedestrians were not allowed on the bridge, but it was quiet and Izzy figured the cops had better things to do than give her a ticket. The sea was calm in the Oregon Inlet below.

On the other side of the bridge she moved off the road and onto the track that ran through the marshes, up into the shrub thickets. It wasn't rental cottage country, nor were there any towns or hotels close by. It was isolated and quiet and Izzy had often wondered what it had felt like to grow up in such a lonely place. After a while small trees began to appear, live oak, black cherry, buckthorn, and holly. She usually liked this part of the island, but the dense shadows under the canopy put her on edge. Suddenly every tree trunk and bush seemed to conceal possible danger.

She stumbled over a stone and cursed. The biggest thing she had to fear was fear itself. It stopped people thinking and acting rationally. She had a gun and a dog and she was fit and not too proud to run for her life if she needed to.

Really, what were the chances some bogeyman was stalking her through the forest when she hadn't told anyone her plans?

A noise off to her right had her jolting and whirling around to face the threat. Heart hammering, she tried to see through the gloom, but short of going into the bush to investigate she couldn't see anything. She eased Barney's leash into her left hand so her right hand was free to reach her weapon. Barney whined and normally she'd have let him go. He knew the way to Ted's house and in the winter this area was generally deserted. Today, she held him tight.

The wind was getting up and on top of everything else going on in the world, another big Nor'easter was sitting out in the Atlantic stirring things up, trying to decide if it wanted to go north or over the top of the Carolinas.

Storms were a fact of life here, but a really big storm, like Hurricane Irene in 2011, could destroy the bridges between the island chain and cut them off from the rest of the world for weeks, if not months. The idea of being trapped here with a killer made her stomach cramp.

She lengthened her stride, sweat blooming across her shoulders as another rustle came from deep within the woods. Dammit. It was probably a frickin' squirrel, but by the time she saw Ted's home amongst the trees, she and Barney were almost running. They burst out of the trees like lunatics.

The house sat in an open space with a large raised vegetable garden and a barn that was almost the same size as the house. All the trees close to the property had been felled because of the danger from frequent storms. The two-story house was painted a pale gray with white trim, and had a wraparound porch. The storm shutters on the windows on the top floor were still closed. It didn't look like Ted had bothered to open them since the last storm had battered them the night Helena was killed. Ted tended to be economical with his labors and considering his bedroom was downstairs and with this new storm hovering, Izzy could understand why he hadn't bothered taking them down. Barney barked excitedly and she let him off leash, knowing he wouldn't go far from the main house. She hurried up the steps onto the porch and knocked on the door.

When no one answered she turned the knob, expecting it to be open, but her shoulder crashed against the wood. Locked.

"Well, hell," she said. Even Ted must be spooked.

She headed back down the porch steps and peered inside his truck. There were no keys in the ignition or under the sun visor. Damn.

His SUV was parked beside the barn that doubled as a garage so she walked over and opened the door of the four-wheel drive, leaning inside to check for keys.

"How's it going, Iz-biz?"

She jumped so hard she cracked her head on the doorframe. "For the love of God, Ted!" She rubbed the knot she now sported on the back of her head. "Stop creeping up on me. I could have shot you."

"You're the one stealing my car," he pointed out, giving her a wry smile.

"I was going to borrow your truck—the way you've told me a million times to do and 'not to ask'—but the house was locked and the keys weren't in it. Is this you finally being security conscious after sixty-plus years of pretending the rest of the world doesn't exist?"

He dug into his hip pocket and pulled out a set of keys and dropped them into her palm. "I figured if someone could hurt a nice girl like Helena then who knows what they'll do to an old goat like me. Dingbatters everywhere. Place is going to hell. Talking of dingbatters, how is the FBI getting on finding Helena's killer?"

"I have no idea. They don't confide in me." She clasped the keys, which were still warm from his body heat. She looked at him properly. "You look very smart. New jacket?" She reached out and touched the lightweight but sturdy material of his black jacket.

He shrugged and stuffed his hands in his pockets. "There was a sale on in Manteo. We all bought one." He looked a bit embarrassed by that.

"You, Seth, the pastor, Hank, and Mr. Kent?

What, are you like a gang now?" she joked.

He snorted and shook his head. "We thought it'd look cool if we went bowling or whatever—Seth's idea."

"Are you off to the bar?" She checked her watch. He met his buddies there almost every Saturday night, but it was a bit early yet.

"Nah, not tonight. Carl's taking Mary out on that date so I figured I'd go to the movies in Corolla. Wanna come with me?"

"Who's going?"

"Me and Kenny. Seth and Hank are both working." Lines creased his forehead and fanned out from the corners of his eyes as he frowned. "Where's your car?"

She was surprised the grapevine hadn't been quite so efficient this time around. "Someone smashed all my windows when it was parked outside the hospital. It's at Seth's place getting fixed."

"I guess that's why he's busy tonight. He never mentioned it, though."

"It's not exactly big news..." She trailed away. It still pissed her off.

Ted's lips mashed together. "Why's it happening, Izzy? We don't normally get this sort of trouble around here."

"Hell if I know." She huddled into her jacket, wishing she had answers and could feel safe again. With the theft of her shovel, then being smacked on the head and now this, all in the wake of Helena's murder, it was starting to feel personal. "Seth said he'd get the glass tonight and it'll be ready by morning. Mind if I keep the truck until then?"

"Sure. Actually you'll be doing me a favor.

Leave it at Seth's place when you pick up your car because it needs a service. If I do it in winter he gives me a special discount."

"Cheapskate." She kissed his sandpapery cheek. "Thanks." She whistled to Barney who came crashing out of the woods like a thing possessed. She opened the door and the dog jumped into the cab as if he rode in the front every day.

"You be careful. Keep that gun loaded and your doors locked." Ted put his hands in his pockets and stared off into the bush. "Something doesn't feel right around here."

"I'll be careful." She looked into his tired eyes, the ones that reminded her so much of her mother's.

"Storm's coming," he warned.

She could feel it.

Ted stood back as she reversed the truck in a wide half circle. Out of the open window she called, "You be careful, too, Uncle Ted. I worry about you out here alone."

"Don't you worry about me, Iz-biz. Just take care of yourself and your sister. You're all that really matters."

CHAPTER SEVENTEEN

Lincoln Frazer didn't remember the last time he'd slept for more than two hours straight, and he was beginning to think the zombie apocalypse wouldn't be such a bad thing—he'd fit right in. He was in the rental car, heading west on Interstate 40 toward Beaufort, North Carolina.

At Maysville, he'd had to smooth over Petra Danbridge's ruffled feathers and bring her up to speed on the investigations. Officially, the Charlotte Division was now running the show on the mainland, but Chief Tyson was conducting his own part of the investigation on the islands—and Frazer was consulting for him, alongside Lucas Randall.

After Frazer had spent forty minutes reassuring SSA Danbridge that he wasn't a backstabbing blue-flamer who was trying to steal all the glory for himself, he'd then had to persuade local cops that once they'd finished processing the current crime scene they needed to bring in cadaver dogs and start searching for more bodies—all on the word of a condemned serial killer.

He needed a stiff drink, but consoled himself with a bottle of water and some headache pills. By the time he'd finished at Maysville it had been too late to drive to the morgue before they closed for the day, and Simon Pearl hadn't returned his calls. Frazer didn't know if that meant good or bad news.

The old abandoned school had been a fitting place to find a dead body. It looked like the classic haunted asylum, complete with eerie mist that had clung to the crooked peak at the top of the central clock tower like wisps of smoke from that long ago fire. Boarded-up windows had stared sullenly out at the world in blind despair. Frazer was surprised it hadn't been bulldozed years ago. The Catholic Church owned the land. Maybe it was appropriate it was now a burial ground.

Dense thickets surrounded the clearing in the woods where Elaine Patterson's body had been found. He had the suspicion that Denker, or his accomplice, had hoped the FBI themselves would be the ones to stumble upon the dead woman. She'd been displayed in a demeaning way, designed to maximize shock value. The track marks on her arms confirmed she was a drug user in addition to being a well-known sex trade worker in the Greenville, North Carolina, area. The killer had considered her trash, something to be used and discarded, with a total disregard for the sanctity of human life.

Her shoes were missing, but then so were all her clothes and belongings. Were shoes this killer's thing? Were they paraphilia, or trophies? Or both?

Was there another body buried around here, or was Denker jerking them around for fun?

Ground penetrating radar could be used in the clearing itself, but the whole school property would now need to be searched by dogs, which was going to take days of meticulous police work. Hanrahan was working his magic at the scene and impressing the hell out of everyone in attendance with his legendary reputation. As long as he got the job done, Frazer didn't care. Frazer didn't allow anyone to sit on their laurels or ride past glory. Not even himself.

Alex Parker and his cyber security team could not find any trace of Jessica Tuttle's cell phone. This was very bad news as the girl was still missing. The good news was they'd removed the image of Kit and Damien from every server it had been saved on, and from every cell phone it had been sent to. That wasn't to say someone couldn't have saved it separately on their hard drive or on a flash drive and it could resurface at any time. But between them they'd done everything they could to minimize the damage to a couple of vulnerable young teens.

It was a small victory in a morass of losses.

Damien Ridgeway was still on his list of suspects, and he intended to grill the young man tomorrow morning. Right now, he was on his way to the home of one Mildred Houch, former secretary at St Joseph's School for Boys. Parker had tracked her down for him. He didn't call ahead and hoped to God she was home and he wasn't wasting his time.

The clock was ticking for Jessica Tuttle, though it was possible she was dead before they even knew she was missing.

He drove past Beaufort city limits and the GPS system told him to hook a right down toward the water. He eyed the giant mansions lit up with glittering arrays of Christmas lights and wondered why anyone with less than a dozen children would choose to live in rambling mausoleums. He hung another right and then immediately another. The houses on this row were smaller, but had big yards separating the properties. He pulled up outside number nineteen, noticing the lights were on and a TV was flickering inside. He climbed out of the car and dialed Mildred Houch's phone number.

As he listened to it ring, he saw the silhouette of a person crossing the drapes. A woman answered and repeated the number back to him.

"My name is Assistant Special Agent in Charge Frazer of the FBI. Am I speaking to Mrs. Mildred Houch?"

"That is correct." She sounded elderly and fragile and intrigued.

"I'm hoping you can help me with my inquiries. Are you available?"

"Oh, I'm not sure how I can help the FBI—"

"It will only take a moment of your time, Mrs. Houch."

"Oh," she repeated. "Well, I suppose I could...when would be a good time?"

Frazer knocked on her front door. "Now would be perfect, ma'am."

A shocked gasp came through his cell and then silence as she hung up. She opened the door with a security chain on. He held his creds up to the light. "Sorry to bother you so late, ma'am."

The door was shut in his face and for a moment he feared she wasn't going to talk to him after all. Then he heard the slide of the chain and she opened the door and motioned him inside. "You'd better come in."

She was tall and graying. Her bent posture reminded him of a crane. She peered at him through thick glasses. "Can I get you a warm drink, Agent Frazer? It's freezing out tonight."

"No, thank you, ma'am. I need your help regarding St. Joseph's School for Boys."

Enlightenment moved over her features. "This is about Ferris Denker." She wrapped her cardigan tight around her tall, thin frame and moved back into the lounge. She sat in a chair that was pulled close to a gas fireplace. She picked up the TV remote and turned it off. The sudden silence had weight.

"I'm curious what you remember about him?"

An amused smile curved her lips. "It's a bit late, isn't it? Unless you're writing his obituary."

This was true. "I take it you weren't close to him?"

She pursed her lips and regarded him curiously. "He was no worse than some of the others."

Frazer frowned. "It seems like an odd way to phrase it."

"St. Joseph's School for Boys was a boarding school for troubled youth, Agent Frazer," she said primly. "The boys who came to us might have sung in the choir, but they were not choirboys."

"Any idea why Denker ended up there?"

She regarded him quizzically as if wondering why he was asking this now. She was right. This work should have been done years ago. "He'd been upsetting the neighbors. Rumor had it he was tinkering with the little girl next door."

"Tinkering?" his voice grew quiet.

She shrugged. "I don't think there was ever any evidence. No one pressed charges. But he was sent to us and from what I understand the neighbors moved away soon afterwards." She eyed him over her specs. "It happened a lot more than you might think. Not everyone wants to get the police involved when their children misbehave."

He knew it, but it turned his stomach that there were so many voiceless victims out there.

"Did he cause trouble at school?"

"Like I say, he wasn't particularly disruptive. He got good grades. Was talented at music. Not very good at sports." She opened her mouth and closed it again.

"What?" He pressed.

Her eyes shifted nervously. "I don't know if it was true or not, but a couple of the boys claimed they'd been sexually assaulted by one of the teachers around the time Ferris Denker attended our school." Her chin ducked into her chest. "The gym teacher. Mr. McManus." Her cheeks went crimson. "I overheard some of the boys calling him some very inappropriate names."

"Was Denker one of the pupils who claimed to have been assaulted?"

"No." She flapped her hand at him as if the idea was absurd.

Frazer frowned. "Were any charges ever brought?"

She shook her head. "There was probably nothing to the accusations. Gerry McManus categorically denied ever doing anything wrong. He was a nice man with a wife and children."

Many pedophiles were. "Were any of the boys who claimed to be abused examined by a doctor?"

Now her ears turned pink. "Of course, we had a doctor on staff. He said there were no bruises or physical signs of abuse." Her voice lowered as if sharing a confidence. "Dr. Rabon suggested some of the boys might have been engaging in sexual relations with one another, which was against school rules, obviously." Her lips primped. "He suggested some of the older boys *might* have been interfering with some of the younger boys." She looked away. "It was an all-boy boarding school."

She shrugged a gnarled shoulder. "These things happened."

A thin thread of rage ran through his veins. He'd gone to an all-boys boarding school. His mother had been a teacher at the school before she'd been murdered. If a kid had gone to her claiming abuse, she'd have kicked ass and taken names to get to the truth. It was the school's job to protect the weaker children from those ready to abuse them.

His school had kept him on as a pupil after his parents' death. He'd inherited a little money, but could never have afforded to stay on there without the school's charity. They'd provided tuition, room and board, and he'd known how lucky he was to get the opportunity. He'd worked his ass off, needing to be the best at everything he did, to make his parents proud and to pay back the school for their generosity. Ever since he'd been rescued, he'd known exactly what he was going to do with his life. And to do it, he'd first needed a degree and a scholarship.

Fifteen years old and he'd known exactly what he was going to do with the rest of his life—and here he was doing it, listening to weak people repeat the excuses they'd fed themselves that enabled monsters to flourish. He couldn't afford to show his disdain or his contempt, but it didn't mean he didn't feel it. "Do you remember Denker having particular friends?"

Two lines appeared between crinkled iron-gray brows. "There were two other boys he spent most of his time with. I don't remember their names."

"The school records?"

Her face went white. "Everything was

destroyed in a fire in 1985. The school closed down. I decided to take early retirement."

Damn. "Is the gym teacher still alive?" That was one thread he could chase up and tie off.

"No. Gerry died of a heart attack on the football field—in front of all the kids actually. It was horrible. It was the second death at the school that year."

If the accusations were true, Frazer suspected some of those kids would be been dancing for joy on the sidelines.

"The other death?"

"Some of the boys went swimming in the pond even though they weren't supposed to. One boy drowned. Another was revived with CPR, but it was a close thing."

"Can you remember the names?"

She frowned, starting to look agitated.

This was getting him nowhere. "I'll leave you my card. Please call me if you remember anything. Anything at all. Do you know where any of the other teachers are?"

She shook her head, her eyes widening behind the lenses of those thick glasses. "No, I'm sorry." Her hands clutched one another in agitation. "I thought they might question us back when they arrested Ferris for those awful crimes, but no one ever came."

Maybe they could figure out who worked there by tracking old tax information and social security numbers, but it would be a laborious and longwinded process. He paced and glanced around the room. There was a framed photograph of a much younger and prettier Mrs. Houch sitting on the steps of an old red-bricked building.

It was the school, he realized. He picked it up. She'd been very pretty. "You must have caused quite the stir in an all-boys school."

Her hand went to her chest and she laughed. "Oh, I had my moments, Agent Frazer. But I was married to a wonderful man who worked for an insurance company. He died young, but I never found anyone to replace him." She pointed to the wedding portrait that hung on the wall. Her advanced age was obvious in the crepe skin of the hands she used to adjust a framed photograph's position on the sideboard, but not in the eyes that twinkled with happy memories.

"I still think of myself as the woman in that photograph," she said sadly. "It's a reminder life's short even when you live to a ripe old age like me." Her eyes turned sad. "I can see now that I didn't do the right thing by those boys who accused Gerry McManus of abusing them." Her mouth firmed. "I was a rule follower. I never thought to step out of line. I expected those in charge to take care of everything the way it should be taken care of." She frowned at her array of framed pictures. "I haven't been much help, have I?" Her forehead furrowed. "But I do have a big box of loose photographs, some will be from the school. Would you—"

"Yes."

She smiled at his abruptness. "I do respect a man who knows what he wants and goes after it. My Harry was like that—and he would have done the right thing." Her cheeks plumped into little apples. "Come on, you'll have to help me get the box from the bottom of my wardrobe." She set off, chuckling to herself, but he stood rooted to the spot because he hadn't gone after what he wanted. Not when it came to anything except his job. He wanted Isadora Campbell. In his bed. He wanted her hair tangled in his fists and the taste of her skin on his lips as he came inside her.

Shaking his head at himself, he followed Mildred Houch down the hall. He was tired. Cranky. Not thinking straight. He was not taking advice on his sex life from a woman in her eighties—although she'd been young and beautiful once, so why the hell not?

He forgot about everything else as he pulled out a large box from the old lady's wardrobe. He suppressed a groan because it was going to take hours to sort through this mess.

Then he got a text, and he knew time was up.

***

The image made Ferris go as hard as stone. He stared at the pale limbs open and splayed. The vivid red secret center of a woman. The long dark hair that draped over milky white breasts, tipped with tight cherry-pink nipples he wanted to bite. The sense of longing was so vicious inside him he wanted to smash everything in his tiny cell into smithereens. What he wouldn't do to touch her warm flesh. To smell the essence of her, the stench of her fear. To hear her scream and beg as she gave him what he wanted.

He stared at the precious image with a delicious hunger that both hated and loved the person who'd sent it. He needed to do this again. Needed to feed his inner animal. Tomorrow he'd talk to his lawyer. Try and find a way out of this awful place where his humanity was as worthless as the women he'd killed.

He turned off the cell and removed the SIM card and battery, and slipped it into the hole he'd made in the mattress.

His erection throbbed in the sweaty cotton pants he wore to bed and he touched himself, knowing it wouldn't be satisfying, but it was better than nothing. He picked through his memories for someone who looked like the dark-haired girl in the image. Remembered a woman he'd grabbed from a hiking trail over in Tennessee. He closed his eyes, mentally took out his knife and went to work.

***

Frazer stood and looked down at the waves that extended within a few inches of Jessica Tuttle's toes. The water crept closer, as if the sea wanted to claim her, wash her clean and embrace her in its depths.

He'd managed to get a pilot of a small plane to fly him from Beaufort to the First Flight Airstrip—where the Wright brothers had flown the very first airplane. His modern-day pilot had been skillful but certifiable because he'd been quite happy to land on the strip in the dark even though it didn't have any lights. Chief Tyson had used patrol cars to light up the landing zone. Frazer had survived. Jessica Tuttle hadn't.

Yesterday he'd been angry with this young woman. Today she became another one of his victims.

She lay naked across what looked like beach but, he'd been informed, was apparently Route 12 on this part of Currituck. She was displayed like

Helena and Elaine had been, but this time her cell phone was stuck in her mouth and, unlike the others, she'd been severely beaten.

There was something a lot more personal about this murder. Rage was evident. The killer had enjoyed himself and taken his time because bruises had already started to form, different shades of red and blue. She'd been raped, sodomized. This was a very personal kind of murder.

Frazer was struck suddenly by his powerlessness to protect people. Maybe the idea he made a difference was just his own ego and lunacy competing for attention. Giving himself an atta-boy pat on the back to make working the long hours and witnessing the endless suffering seem worth it. He'd been working this case from the very start and women kept dying. Jessica's pale corpse taunted him like so many before her. He closed his eyes for a moment and there was Helena, and Elaine. Other women, murdered or missing, flashed through his brain in quick bursts that made him open his eyes again. Shit.

Alex Parker had been the first one to figure out Jessica Tuttle was dead—aside from her killer, of course. Parker had been monitoring her social media accounts and had noticed immediately when several obscene images were posted from her cell phone. The first one was with the message "JT blows". The last was of her dead body displayed here on the sand with the caption "Not good enough though, Bitch".

Horrifying. Graphic images. Meant to scare and intimidate. Shame and demean. Meant to taunt police and cause the public to lose faith. To incite panic.

Parker had immediately blocked all access to the accounts and tried to track the cell phone, but the killer had been savvy enough to remove the location metadata from the images. And after the photos had been uploaded to Jessica's accounts, the killer had deactivated the SIM card and removed the battery. Parker had gotten the general vicinity of the cell phone tower but no closer than that.

Chief Tyson stood beside him with his hand resting on his equipment belt. "We looking at a serial killer, Linc?"

Frazer nodded. "The press is going to start arriving soon. In droves." Compounding a difficult situation and turning it into a damn circus. His influence only went so far, and it was officially tapped out.

"We're going to need klieg lights and a tent." Frazer glanced at the sky. There were no choppers yet but in a few hours the spotlight would literally be on them and he didn't want Jessica Tuttle's parents seeing their daughter this way. She'd made mistakes—what kid didn't? But she didn't deserve this.

The image of blood pooling around his mother's body seeped into his head and he turned away. He pulled out his cell and dialed Simon Pearl again. If the ME didn't answer this time he was going to send the HRT team to the guy's house.

"I was about to call you with the results from the forensic anthropologist," Pearl said, answering with a tired-sounding voice.

Frazer glanced at his watch. Midnight. "You're still at the morgue?"

Pearl laughed, but it was an unhappy sound. "My wife asked me the same thing. If she didn't know how much I love her, she'd think I was having an affair."

What would it be like to have someone you loved waiting for you? Not a wife who berated you for not being home for dinner, but a partner who cared? His parents had had that sort of marriage. Solid. Strong. Supportive. It was something he'd assumed he'd have too. He'd been wrong.

And now he was obviously delusional from lack of sleep to even be thinking about the M-word.

"What do you have for me?"

"I finished the post on Helena Cromwell and some test results are in. She had very low levels of alcohol in her system. She wasn't on any birth control and no drugs were found in her system. There was evidence of sexual intercourse. Impossible to say whether or not it was consensual as there were no abrasions or cuts. She didn't fight. No DNA beneath her fingernails. Condom matched the brand Jesse Tyson said he had in his wallet. She died of asphyxia due to repeated manual strangulation."

"Repeated?"

"I found bruises in different places on her neck. I think he took her to the edge of death several times before he finished her off."

Frazer eased closer to Jessica Tuttle's body and shone his flashlight at the victim's neck. The bruising was widespread. "I think he did it again. We have another victim."

Pearl swore. "Fuck. I only just finished with Elaine Patterson. Same MO, but she had coke in her system."

So maybe he'd gained control of the prostitute with drugs before incapacitating her. It was likely he'd killed before—people didn't turn into killers overnight. It was a progression—first the fantasy, maybe hurting animals or children, a little voyeurism, perhaps an assault, rape, maybe a fumbled attempted murder. Then, finally going all the way. Prostitutes and runaways had likely been victims of this killer before. There was no direct evidence, but they were easy pickings and a great place for serial killer work experience.

Pearl gave a world-weary sigh. "One of my assistants is on his way. This guy is escalating way too fast."

One dead girl every day for the last three days. Definitely way too fast.

No one was getting any sleep, but they had to stop him before anyone else died.

"Denker doesn't have long to get whatever the hell it is he wants." Sentence commuted to life? Was that really worth the lives of all these poor women? To the killer it probably was. These sexual predators were notorious for believing their victims were worth less than nothing. Frazer wished someone had put a bullet in the guy when they'd caught him, but that would have been too easy. "What did you discover from the bones?"

"Two skeletons. One male, one female."

"Male?" said Frazer.

"Yes. And the forensic anthropologist is pretty sure the male had been stabbed."

Frazer frowned. It could have been a similar situation to the attack on Jesse and Helena and the guy had just got in the way. "Any ID?"

"Dental records turned up nothing. We're running DNA."

"Any ID on the female?"

"Beverley Sandal. As you suspected."

The result felt a little hollow. It was a relief in some ways. The end of a mystery as to where she'd ended up. Art Hanrahan would want to talk to the family. He'd known them for a long time.

Frazer thanked the ME and said goodbye, then called Hanrahan and asked for progress on the crime scene at Maysville. They were still digging, but cadaver dogs had shown a strong indication that there was another body in the clearing.

He hung up feeling lightheaded with fatigue. There wasn't much they could do here until the ME showed up, except protect the scene.

"Erica." He waved over a CSU and knew he'd been there too long when he was on first name terms with evidence techs. "Can you bag that phone? I want it couriered to Quantico ASAP."

The body had already been photographed. The CSU tech took care of his request with quiet efficiency. There were dark circles under her eyes that probably matched his own.

Parker had gleaned everything he could online, but it was possible the perp had left DNA on the cell phone, maybe inside the casing. It was also possible he'd brushed it against his own body, or a gloved hand had touched his body as he'd desecrated this poor young woman. And transferred that DNA onto the phone. Skins cells could have been shed, semen might have leaked. Frazer wasn't about to move slowly on this, or wait for anyone else to die.

Tyson approached him again. Randall was still going through Automatic License Plate Reader databases looking for vehicles leaving and returning to the island around the time of Elaine

Patterson's murder and Jessica Tuttle's abduction.

The chief spoke quietly. "My son's two girlfriends are now dead. Is this linked to him?"

Frazer blinked at the guy. It was a connection he hadn't thought of, which showed what level he was operating on—close to useless. "Did he receive any threats? Report any weird incidents?"

Tyson shook his head. "Honestly, the kid is like the golden child. Everyone seems to like him."

"Someone could resent that...he still has the guards on him, right?"

Tyson nodded.

"Your wife, Charlene. She know how to protect herself?" he asked, trying not to freak the guy out.

Tyson's eyes narrowed and his mouth hardened. "She does, but I'll call and warn her to be careful. This could be linked to someone I arrested."

Would a killer have followed Tyson to a place like this in order to torture him while helping Denker? Possibly. There were some twisted people out there.

"Can you think of any cases where a perp vowed revenge, or the victim's family members were pissed enough to threaten you personally?"

Tyson shrugged. "I've been a cop for a lot of years. Not everyone is happy with me arresting their loved ones, but generally I get on well with people. I try to do the right thing. I have a good rep." The smile in his eyes belied the way his hand rested near his holster. The guy was spooked.

"Put together a list. We'll see if anything pops." Frazer thought of all the people he'd locked up over the years, all the families he'd failed. His list was longer than he wanted it to be, but he never stopped working at it.

He looked at Jessica, at the increased level of violence the unsub had inflicted upon the poor girl. There was another connection apart from the police chief's son.

He pinched the bridge of his nose. He'd driven more than eleven hours that day and was operating on a few hours' sleep over the last four days. He needed to take a break. "Can I get a ride back to Rosetown?"

Tyson nodded. "I'll take you. Let me talk to a couple of guys to start them knocking on doors first." He indicated some of the big mansions facing the ocean. They were dark though. Probably unoccupied at this time of year. Just north lay the undeveloped spit of land that eventually turned into Virginia Beach. A quiet dumping ground. The guy knew these islands and had planned the location with enough exposure for the body to be found quickly, but not so fast he couldn't make his escape.

"I have someone getting a tent set up. Officers from Columbia Police are on their way, and they've taken charge of informing the parents."

Frazer's stomach tightened. He'd performed death notice duty too many times to count. As awful as it was to find an officer on your doorstep, witnessing someone you loved being murdered was worse. The helplessness. The impotent rage. The void that formed in your soul. Nothing could ever fix it.

He swayed on his feet. The memories of his parents' murder only resurfaced when he was exhausted. He could do without it.

This was why he'd taken up hypnosis. His

unconscious memories blindsided him when he least expected it, and he knew it was the same for others who'd locked away details of traumatic events. The mind protected itself from horror it couldn't deal with—another survival mechanism he leveraged for his own benefit.

Maybe he'd try some meditation techniques when he got back to the beach house, see if that would put him to sleep. First he wanted to check up on the Campbell women.

He went over to the chief's vehicle, pulling out the massive box of photographs Mildred Houch had given him. He turned on the dome light and started sorting through them, culling those private ones from images that could have been taken at the school.

He'd use every minute he had to try and catch this killer because one thing he did know for sure, this guy wouldn't stop of his own accord. Killing was his drug, and he was hooked.

CHAPTER EIGHTEEN

Izzy lay curled up beneath a thick woolen blanket on the wicker sofa on the deck of her house. Barney was sprawled across her with his cold nose pressed tight against her neck. They both listened to the crash of the ocean that was growing steadily louder as the storm built offshore. The Weather Channel didn't predict a direct hit, but Izzy knew enough to stock up on bottled water and cans of soup. The generator was fueled, and she had candles up the hoo-ha.

As promised, Kit had called when she left the restaurant and arrived home at ten minutes past ten. Her sister seemed subdued and had gone straight to bed. Izzy was worried about her. What else was new?

Izzy couldn't sleep. Nothing short of tranquilizers would put her out tonight, and no way was she knocking herself out with a murderer on the loose. She'd lain in bed for a couple of hours, staring at the ceiling, brain still whirling from Helena's murder and news of this missing girl from Roanoke—who also happened to be Jesse Tyson's ex-girlfriend. Was someone targeting the poor kid? Did he have some obsessed stalker after him? She tried to push the thoughts aside and despite what the girl had done to Kit, she hoped she was okay. She couldn't imagine what she and her parents were going through.

Her mind had kept returning to the Feds who'd been staying next door, wondering if ASAC Frazer would come back to the beach house tonight or if he was gone for good. The idea that she'd never see him again cut at her. Crazy. But thinking about the good-looking federal agent hadn't helped her nod off; instead she'd gotten up to feed her cocoa addiction.

She tensed beneath the blanket as the sound of a car engine grew closer and then slowed in front of the house. Then the quiet slam of a car door before the car drove away. Barney leapt off the couch before she could grab his collar, dragging the blanket with him and exposing her to a blast of frigid air. She stood and leaned over the edge of the railing to see who was there. The outside light was on between the properties, and she'd arranged to get motion sensor lights installed on both homes tomorrow, assuming the storm wasn't too fierce. No way was she letting someone ambush her from the shadows again.

A figure emerged from the road. ASAC Frazer, carrying a large cardboard box under one arm, a heavy bag in the other. Her pulse gave a little leap as she recognized his silhouette. Dammit. She pressed her hand to her belly and heard him laugh as Barney planted his front paws on his chest and tried to give him a kiss on the lips.

"Just my luck, I get the dog rather than the girl."

His words made her heart race, and she pulled back out of sight. God, what was wrong with her? The unsettled feeling inside her swelled and throbbed along her nerves. Her nipples tightened, and a tingle formed between her legs. It wasn't the recent attacks that had caused her insomnia—it was her attraction to this man.

She slipped quietly down the steps to the

beach. Her house was locked up. Her gun was holstered beneath her left arm. She called out, "Barney. Here boy."

Frazer came into sight and stopped. His eyes swept from the top of her messy hair to the bottom of her bare feet, taking in all the hotspots in-between. "Dr. Campbell." He cleared his throat. "Everything okay?"

She bit her lip. Was it? Not really. She shouldn't be here, but she didn't want to leave. There was something in his eyes—darkness, pain, and a searing heat, that matched what simmered inside her. She swallowed, trying to get some moisture back in her mouth.

"I heard you went to a lot of effort to make sure that image of Kit disappeared from the Internet. You don't know how grateful I am for that."

"There's no guarantee it won't reappear, and the last thing I want from you is gratitude." His voice was terse. Angry, even.

"Let me help you." She took the bag from his fingers. Tried not to react when she touched bare skin. He followed her silently up the stairs. She stopped at the door. Realizing she didn't have a key, she turned to him, nervous now, heart hammering.

He fished out the keys, unlocking the door and opening it wide. Barney rushed inside to check out the place. "Is this a booty call, Dr. Campbell?"

Her lips parted ever so slightly in shock. She knew he was direct, but she hadn't expected him to be quite so forthright. She looked away, annoyed with herself for not being able to meet his directness head-on. She didn't play games, but she knew she shouldn't get involved with this man. She folded her arms across her chest, realizing how pathetic she must appear, wanting him, but being too afraid to act upon it. "Maybe. I couldn't sleep."

He went inside, placing the cardboard box on the coffee table, dumping his bag on the floor and turning the murder board to face the wall.

"Come in." His eyes challenged her to be honest about her reasons for being here.

Her mouth went dry. Her body craved something that would take her mind off the bad things that were happening on the island, something that would wear her out enough to enable her to sleep. Sex was good stress relief. It didn't need to be anything more complicated than that.

She walked into the cottage with every nerve in her body feeling like it was raw and exposed. Holding his gaze, she closed the door softly behind her. "I could make you something to eat—"

"I don't want anything to eat, Dr. Campbell. Unless it's you."

Oh, God. She ached. Between her legs. Under her ribcage. In all the small places around her body that hadn't felt a man's touch in so long she couldn't even remember. Time to make a decision and either be honest about this or get the hell out.

"Then I'm thinking this is probably a booty call, ASAC Frazer." Her eyes met his. "But before we get naked, I do need to know your first name."

***

Frazer didn't do one night stands, or anonymous hook-ups. He didn't trust easily and sex involved a lot of trust—or, at least, it should. He'd seen so much unspeakable horror lately. He needed to bury the images, rein in the thoughts that constantly reeled around his head. Otherwise he was going to go insane. He'd had a few women friends in the past who'd wanted the same sort of no-strings relationship he did. But over the last six months, he'd let those relationships dissolve. He'd lost interest. They'd moved on. He hadn't cared.

Then he'd met Isadora Campbell.

Now every cell in his body exploded to life even though he stayed perfectly still. So much for exhaustion. And who the hell needed sleep?

"Where's Kit?" he asked.

"Asleep. The house is locked."

He could see nerves competing with desire in her expression. She was uncertain as to the wisdom of this decision. He got that. But they'd danced around this long enough, and he was ready to get Isadora Campbell out of his system. He took a step toward her, captured her face in his hands and kissed her, fiercely. Her soft lips parted in surprise. Her fingers gripped his biceps, and he wondered if she was going to force him away. She should. He was demanding and difficult. Distracted most of the time. Focused on death. The only thing that truly mattered to him was getting evil off the streets. He wasn't one for pretty words. Nor paying lip service to false images of romance.

Right now he was happy to spend a few hours paying lip service to Isadora Campbell's body.

It wasn't that he didn't believe in love. He did. His parents had loved one another until their last breath. But love and romance weren't always the same thing. Some women needed the imagery of roses and candlelight, whereas he preferred tangled limbs beneath plain white sheets.

She didn't push him away.

Instead she opened her mouth and kissed him back, pulling him toward her by his lapels. It was all the permission he needed, and he turned them around and walked her backward down the corridor. Her fingers began to undo his shirt buttons, and the desire he'd been fighting since he'd first seen her standing on that windswept beach, oblivious to the effect she had on men, burst free.

He needed a shower, but if he asked her to wait for him to get cleaned up, she might get cold feet and change her mind. He wasn't about to relinquish the advantage, so he maneuvered them both inside the bathroom, shutting the door behind them and locking it.

He left the room in darkness, alleviated by the outside light that shone through the window. He didn't want her to see the expression in his eyes—it was too grim, he was too wounded by death and failure. This was a selfish act, although he hoped to hell she enjoyed it. He needed her. He turned on the shower without letting go of her lips. She tasted of hot chocolate. He kissed her deeper, savoring her sweetness as she unhooked her gun holster before carefully laying it on the floor. He yanked her t-shirt out of her pants as her hands went back to his bare chest, her fingers skimming his body like she needed to touch every inch of him. He could get with that program. He shrugged out of his jacket, placing his SIG onto the floor beside her gun. He jerked his shirt off, throwing it aside. Her fingers were at his belt as he pulled her t-shirt up and over her head and then dragged her yoga pants and panties down her legs so she was completely naked in front of him. Her fingers shook trying to undo the button of his pants, but he was too busy looking at her body rimmed with silvery light to be in any rush to finish getting undressed.

"You are beautiful." He skimmed a gentle hand over her shoulder and down her arm. She had more curves than he'd anticipated. Her breasts were pale and soft and seemed to swell under his gaze. Small nipples beaded and hardened and he wanted to take them in his mouth. But, first, he wanted to look at her. The curve of her hips was subtle, the long slender legs and pretty feet with high arches and cute toes. Her hair tangled and twisted around her face. He ran a finger over a pale fine brow, down a high cheekbone and then smoothed it over the beauty mark that sat above her lips.

She brought her hand up to his. "I hate that mole."

He took her fingers in his, kissed them, kissed it. "I love it."

Her eyes flashed in the darkness.

It wasn't just her physical beauty that called to him. She had an integrity he admired. A sense of duty and service that spoke to his own. Depth. She had depth, and he'd never been good with shallow women even though he'd married one. And Isadora Campbell was enough of an enigma to keep his brain, as well as other parts of his body, interested.

It was rare to find both—or maybe that was just him.

She bit her lip, probably unsettled at the way he was staring at her like he was going to consume her. A rush of lust hit him. He took over undoing his pants before kicking everything aside. He tested the temperature of the water and adjusted it so it didn't freeze or scald them. Then he picked her up by the hips. She squeaked as he put her in the shower. He followed her, backing her up against the cold tiled wall. Her hair was tied up on top of her head, but loose tendrils clung to her damp skin and her teeth chattered.

But it wasn't cold.

He hesitated. "Changed your mind?"

"No."

"Scared?"

"No."

"Good." He took the shower gel off the shelf and poured a large amount in his palm. The scent of vanilla engulfed them both. He washed his body first, removing the grime and taint of death that seemed embedded in his pores. He shoved his head under the spray to wash away all trace of prison and crime scenes, murder and violence.

All he wanted was to forget. For a little while.

Isadora watched him carefully, those sage green eyes almost black in the darkness.

"You're beautiful, too." She raised her hands to touch him, but he moved out of reach, not because he didn't want her hands on him, but because he wanted his hands on her first.

He held up the shower gel. "Your turn."

Hot water steamed the small cubicle. He watched the ripple of her throat as he moved closer, and used both hands to smooth soap over her collarbones, tracing the delicate jut of bone that fascinated him. He washed down her arms, caressing her elbows, all the way to her fingers, which he squeezed slightly in reassurance.

Trust me, his fingers said.

She squeezed him back. They each seemed equally uncertain as to the steps they were taking. His hands moved to her hips and back up her body, cupping her breasts. He closed his eyes as he absorbed the sensation of peaked nipples and soft skin.

The pulse at the base of her neck throbbed against his lips. Her heart pounded against his palm. His erection ached, especially when she reached out, touching, molding, stroking. He gritted his teeth as those cool fingers wrapped around him and squeezed. He grazed his thumb over her nipple and she gasped. He moved on, washing her thighs and then turning her to face the wall while he ran his hands over the lean muscles of her back and the soft fullness of her ass, all the way down to the back of her knees. She shivered beneath his touch.

He trembled with desire, but he needed to take his time. Wanted her in a proper bed where he could languidly explore.

Sex was a ridiculously intimate act between two strangers and, although they'd spent time together over the last few days, he and Isadora Campbell were essentially strangers. The twist of biology that was lust meant they wanted each other anyway.

He turned off the water and grabbed a towel off a stack on the basket outside the stall. He wrapped her in it before picking her up and carrying her carefully into the bedroom he was using. She wrapped her arms around his neck and held on tight. He enjoyed the feel of her in his arms. The reality of her. The living warmth of her beauty.

The curtains were wide open and provided enough light to see her clearly as he laid her on the bed, leaving the towel in place for now. He held a finger across her lips when she went to say something. "Just a moment. I'll be right back."

He went back to the bathroom, grabbed their clothes, weapons, and a condom out of his wallet. Randall could come back any moment and although Frazer wasn't breaking any rules, this was his personal business. He liked his private life private. He dumped everything on the floral chair in the corner of the bedroom and then stared at Barney who now sat in the middle of the bed beside Isadora, giving him big puppy eyes.

"No way." He pointed at the door. "Out." Barney tucked his tail and jumped off the bed, slinking into the hall. Damn. "I love dogs, but there's no way he's watching this."

Isadora snorted and her eyes danced. "I have a horrible feeling he'd want to join in."

He closed the door on the forlorn looking mutt. "Does he usually..." Shit, he didn't generally worry about asking awkward questions—in fact he specialized in them. He needn't have worried.

"Does he usually watch me having sex?" Isadora grinned at him. "No. I've only had him since I got home last summer, and the issue hasn't come up."

He turned toward where she lay on his bed, covered only in a towel. "Why not?"

"I haven't wanted anyone, *ASAC* Frazer."

But she wanted him. His ego enjoyed that so he ignored it. "I like you, Dr. Campbell." He walked toward her and she eyed his naked body with avid interest.

"I like you too, *ASAC* Frazer, otherwise I wouldn't be here." She wasn't in the least bit shy about her body or his. No coy bashfulness or need for reassurance. He came down on top of her, stretched out, their limbs tangled, and he held her hands over their heads, their bodies separated only by the damp towel.

"I like you," he repeated, "but this is just sex." He needed to know she understood he wasn't the hearts and roses type.

She stretched her body languidly beneath his, her silky skin driving him out of his mind. "I know." Her voice was husky with desire.

"No strings."

Her smile was full of cool female wisdom that tugged at something inside his chest. "Sex between two single people of sound-*ish* mind, and legal age, who want one another. As to what I want and how I like it, I'm willing to explore the possibilities."

That's what he'd told Jesse Tyson during hypnosis. He nuzzled the soft skin beneath her ear. "God, I love your body, but I love that brain of yours even more. I want to eat you up, Dr. Campbell. Every inch."

Her head tipped back and her mouth opened. "What's stopping you?"

He took one of her hands and curled it, then the second, around the struts on the headboard. "You're going to need to hold on."

"No ties?" she said coolly. Her brow arched, and he knew she'd hate anyone trying to tie her up. He would, too.

"Don't let go of the bed unless you want me to stop."

Her eyes widened a fraction at the authority in his voice. Good. He intended to make her lose some of that laid-back cool and have her panting with pleasure. Pleasure seemed in small supply of late, probably for both of them.

He started at her shoulders, that collarbone that dipped so seductively, the place he'd wanted to taste from the very beginning. He ran his hand down her inner arm and she giggled.

"Ticklish?" He found her giggle disarmingly attractive. She was so not a giggler.

"Never," she denied.

He lay on one side of her as he trailed his hand from her little finger all the way down her arm. She laughed and jerked her arm free of the post.

He removed his hand with a heavy sigh. She bit her lip and grasped the wooden strut again. This time he trailed his finger harder against her sensitive skin, and although she squirmed beneath him she didn't let go. Her eyes never left his face. He traced the line of the towel across the swell of her breasts, then across the top of her thighs. "So pale, Dr. Campbell. I'm starting to think you're a figment of my imagination." Beautiful. Flawless except for the occasional freckle or mole, which he wouldn't call flaws—more punctuation marks. Like the one on the side of her mouth that he kissed again, tasting the edge of her lips.

"You're teasing me," she groaned.

"I *am* teasing you, but I intend to follow through on my promises. If we're going to break the rules we may as well do it properly."

"We're breaking rules?" she asked.

"My rules." His fingers found the edge of the towel and tugged it free. Unwrapping her like the sort of Christmas present that made grown men weep.

She smelled of sunshine and heat. Salt spray

and vanilla soap.

He trailed a finger along her breast and up over her nipple, watching it tighten and harden into a dark bead. He leaned down to capture the nearest one in his mouth, scraping his tongue over the sensitive flesh as his fingers caressed its mate. Isadora's hips jerked and her thighs parted an inch. He bit down a little harder and her hips arched up off the bed. His hand moved lower and traced the fine skin where her thighs met her body.

He let go of her nipple and nuzzled the skin beneath her ear again. Licked the hot beat of her pulse. "Open up," he whispered.

She complied, and he sank his fingers between folds and deep into wet heat. She came up off the bed but still she didn't let go of the bedposts. He pressed deeper, first one finger, then two, finding a rhythm that matched the roll of her hips, and he curled his fingers inside her and pressed the heel of his hand against her mound. Over and over again, slowly, patiently, as her hips increased in pace until finally her back bowed up off the bed, feet digging into the mattress as she cried out. The expression on her face was one of ecstasy, and he didn't think he'd ever seen anyone more beautiful.

Pure unadulterated pleasure.

Not twisted lust.

His own heart raced, and he tried to cool his raging lust by concentrating on her body. On the subtle curve of her stomach, the dip of her navel, the deep dusky pink of her nipples. Playing, stroking, easing her back down to earth.

After a few moments her breathing slowed, and she lowered her hand to grab a fistful of his hair, pulling him up to meet her lips. "My turn," she mumbled against his mouth. "On your back and assume the position, Frazer."

A deep laugh rumbled through his chest. "What if I don't want to?"

She raised a brow that told him how stupid that suggestion was, and he rolled over on top of her, pausing to press a kiss to her mouth before lying on his back and reaching up to grab the headboard.

"Fine." He used his "this better be good voice" but she laughed at him. Jesus, he liked that. Loved the fact his usually icy demeanor didn't offend her the way it did so many others.

She knelt beside him and ran her fingers over his chest. "I think I'm going to need to know your first name even if I have to torture it out of you."

"Do your worst, Isadora Jane Campbell."

She grinned and leaned down to kiss his mouth. "Is that a challenge?" She didn't wait for an answer. Her lips drifted over his unshaven chin and down the front line of his throat. He swallowed at the strangely intimate act, trying to remember if anyone had ever kissed him there before. Next her lips touched his shoulders, but he was distracted by the stroke of her hand across his stomach, and then lower. Her hands were warm, fingers strong and, shit, he gasped out loud as she brushed her thumb lightly over the top of his penis.

"Try to hold out a little longer," she whispered knowingly as she ran her tongue around the shell of his ear.

She knew exactly how to drive him crazy. She caressed and stroked him, and his eyes rolled in his head as she touched all of him with light, dancing fingers that made him want to pant for more. She started to slide down the bed, but he caught her arms and dragged her back up over him. There was no way he'd last if she used anything but her hands on him.

He brushed her hair off her forehead, holding her gaze. "Linc. Lincoln."

"Suits you." A dimple cut into her cheek. "No middle names I need to know about?"

"God, I wish." He didn't recognize the guttural voice that came out of his mouth.

She straddled him, and he handed her the condom because she seemed to need to be in charge, and right now he liked what she was doing. Who was he kidding? He was going to like anything she wanted to do to him as long as she did it naked.

She ripped open the condom and rolled it over him gently. He shook uncontrollably. He held her thighs in a firm grip and then she was lowering herself over him, and he was engulfed in the feeling of rightness.

He'd had sex too many times to count, but it had never felt like coming home before. He froze at the thought, but realized any woman would feel good after months of abstinence.

Probably.

She moved over him with grace and confidence, arching her back as she slid lower and lower before raising herself back up again. His hips followed hers, mindless as they sought her engulfing heat. Her breasts jiggled, and his mouth went dry watching her move so sensually above him.

"You feel amazing," she said.

Christ, how could she talk? He couldn't form a single coherent word let alone an entire sentence.

She rode him slow and then she rode him fast and he held onto his control by a whisper as her fingers bit into his chest and her face turned toward the ceiling and inner muscles contracted around him, driving him to the very edge. As she cried out again, he pulled her tight against him and carefully turned them over so he was on top. Then he began moving, harder and faster, until he was worried it was too fast and too hard. But she was right there with him, matching his rhythm, fingernails digging sharply into his back in a grip that felt gloriously uncontrolled. She wrapped her legs around his waist, digging her heels into his ass as she started to climax again. He held onto her hips as she writhed and twisted, smooth muscles and soft skin feeling like silk against his fingers.

His own release snapped at the base of his spine as her inner muscles milked him until finally his hips were bucking into her and he flew off that cliff, spinning over the edge into blinding light that made pleasure screech along every neuron.

Holy crap.

He lay panting on top of her, the pounding of his heart loud enough to block out the ever-present drum of the ocean. Slowly he opened his eyes. They were nose to nose and she grinned at him, a satisfied grin. Then she squeezed him again and ran her heels down the back of his legs, letting them rest on his calves as he stayed inside her.

He couldn't move.

"You're good at that."

He withdrew carefully and rolled onto his back, disposing of the condom. "My ex-wife said I was good at two things. That was one of them." Although, honestly, he hadn't done anything except let her have her way with him. It had felt good. It had felt incredible.

"What was the other thing?" she asked curiously. So Isadora Campbell was one of the few women on the planet not to be pissed off by the mention of another woman while in bed.

Was that why he'd said it? As a test? To drive her away? That was cold, only moments after red-hot sex.

He found himself grinning down at her because she never reacted exactly as he thought she would. He kissed her. Long, lingering. Exploring more of her mouth, which he didn't feel like he'd even begun to get enough of. He drew back. "The other thing she said I was good at was making her miserable."

"Ouch." She brushed his hair off his forehead. "You left her?"

"Officially, she left me." He shrugged. His marriage had died long ago. "We met in college. I was studying criminal justice. She was pre-law. I told her from the start what I wanted to do with my life, where I was going, but the moment I became a beat cop? Let's just say the offers from her daddy's firm kept getting higher and higher until one day she realized that I actually meant what I said, and wouldn't be swayed from my path." He blew out a huge guilt-laden sigh. "She called me 'emotionally derelict' and 'borderline sociopath'."

"Ouch. The worst I've ever been called by an ex was a cold bitch." Isadora pushed him off her, stretching her arms over her head.

He watched her breasts and wanted her again. "I guess no one wants to feel like they matter less than your job."

"Some careers aren't just jobs. It's not what defines us, it's literally a part of who we are—like hair color or how many fingers we have on our right hand."

He picked up her hand and kissed each finger.

She smiled. "It was her mistake for not seeing it."

"It was my mistake. She thought she knew me but she didn't." He'd been wrong to marry her. Because although he looked okay on the outside, inside he was a writhing mass of flawed humanity, trying to save his family and failing every single time. No one should have to cope with a career drive that came from a constant sense of failure. "I knew it wasn't going to work. I married her anyway."

He started nibbling her neck, surprised he was growing hard again. "What about you? Why aren't you married?" And why was he talking about marriage when he was in bed and had just had sex with a woman?

"You're not the only one with an important career, Lincoln Frazer." Her eyes shone with humor, but he knew she was hiding something. Some bad breakup? Unrequited love? Shit happened. Why should she tell him everything? They were simply spending a few hours having fun. God knew they both deserved a break from their never-ending workload.

"You don't let anyone close, do you?" he realized. Neither did he, but suddenly he wanted her closer, he wanted more than a few hours. His hands caught her hips and he captured one of her nipples with his mouth. He moved over her as she arched off the bed to meet him.

"This is as close as it gets, Frazer."

Not close enough. The voice in his head should have scared him, but for once being held at arm's length wasn't enough. Or maybe Isadora's own reluctance to get involved made him feel more secure. More able to be who he really was. Not pretending to be perfect. Not pretending they were gonna get married and raise rug-rats. The marriage thing hadn't worked for him, and he never wanted to feel that miserable or out of control ever again. Maybe he could manage a relationship, though. Definitely more than one night of fucking. The thought would have worried him if the woman he was contemplating it with hadn't been sliding down the bed doing something amazingly hot with her mouth.

He could definitely get used to more, if more included having this woman in his bed.

***

It was still dark when she slipped out of Lincoln Frazer's bed. She'd stayed far longer than she'd intended. He didn't strike her as the cuddling type, but they'd fallen asleep entangled and sated.

A strand of blond hair fell across his forehead as he lay on his back, sleeping. She dressed quietly, not wanting to wake him, not really wanting to leave, but knowing she had to. The sex had been fantastic and she ached in all the right places. But she wasn't hanging around for that awkward morning-after moment. And she wanted to get back to Kit.

Dammit, she shouldn't have let herself get distracted, and yet she'd needed this particular distraction more than she'd needed her next breath. Unfortunately having sex hadn't ended her fascination with the guy. He was direct, determined, demanding, and competitive. It didn't make for an easy personality, but it made for an interesting one, not to mention a hell of a partner in bed.

The fact she was reducing everything to sex told her more than she wanted to know about how she was trying to push her feelings for this guy into a box. He was gorgeous, built, and fought monsters for a living. She'd been halfway in love with him before he'd proven to be an attentive and generous lover, and to have an unexpected vulnerable side.

And he carried a badge.

Yeah, she was totally screwed.

She grabbed her Glock and held her keys in her pocket against her thigh so they didn't jingle as she walked. She eased open the door. The other bedroom door was open, and Barney leapt off the top of the blankets as someone turned over in bed.

Agent Randall. And from the way he moved he was awake. Her cheeks heated because it wouldn't take a rocket scientist to figure this out. She hoped Frazer didn't get in trouble, but she didn't know what the rules were regarding hook-ups during work time.

She snuck past the murder board and guilt crawled up her spine and expanded inside her brain until it forced her to blink hard against the pressure. She still wasn't convinced she knew anything about the current murders, but she knew who those bones belonged to. She knew how they'd come to be buried in the dunes. Without a word she opened the front door and let her dog out. She closed it softly behind her, hurrying down the wooden steps in her bare feet, aware of the intense chill in the air.

The waves still crashed against the shore, but the tide was out and the storm didn't seem so bad, yet.

As she went up the steps to her porch she noticed the blanket that Barney had dragged to the floor earlier was now neatly folded and placed on the wicker sofa. She looked across to the beach house and saw Frazer's silhouette at the window. Her heart beat a little harder, not only because he was watching her sneak away, but also because anyone standing here could have seen them earlier. God, had Agent Randall stood here? Or Kit? A wave of humiliation rolled over her at the thought.

What about the killer?

Cold dread spread over her nerves.

That was stupid. Paranoia. Just because someone had folded the blanket did not mean they'd spied on her and Frazer.

She let herself into the house, Barney racing to his chow bowl in the hopes of magical food regeneration. She took out her Glock and slowly worked her way around the building, room by room, until she reached Kit's bedroom. Izzy gently eased open the door, and there was her sister, curled up on her side, covers raised high under her chin as she snored softly.

Tenderness welled up. The kid was a brat and a pain in the ass and she loved her sister more than she loved life. She'd sacrificed so much for this incredible child already, even before she was born. Izzy silently backed out of the room.

She needed her sleep.

Barney was already there, taking up the middle

of the bed. She pushed him over and then slid beneath the sheets. Barney placed his head on her chest, his weight solidly reassuring. Izzy closed her eyes and images of Lincoln Frazer smiling, touching her, telling her about his ex, ran through her mind. But rather than keeping her awake, sleep crept over her as she pulled him tight and held him close.

CHAPTER NINETEEN

Next morning, Izzy called the garage but no one answered. It was early, but Seth Grundy usually started work around seven. She left Kit sleeping in and put Barney in Ted's truck, figuring she'd stop at the garage first and if her car wasn't ready yet, she'd go up to Currituck National Wildlife Refuge to check out the ponies and take some pictures of the sunrise. She missed seeing the horses roaming the beaches the way she had as a kid, but at least up there they weren't getting run-over in traffic.

It was still dark.

And, perhaps, she was hoping to avoid both of the federal agents staying in her beach house. Perhaps she wanted to pretend last night hadn't happened. Sex was one thing. Sex while hiding a secret as big as hers, with someone whose integrity meant everything to him? Whose career meant everything to him? She'd made a massive mistake.

The entire episode had been completely selfish because Lincoln Frazer wouldn't have touched her if he'd known the truth about her past. The fact he was attracted to her was irrelevant. She'd gone to him under false pretenses, and it was unforgivable.

Self-disgust rose up inside. She was going to have to tell him everything and trust he'd protect Kit from the worst of it.

After years of trying to outrun the grimmest episode of her life, she knew she had to stop and confront it. What was that saying? "The truth would set you free, but first it would piss you off." That was exactly how Lincoln Frazer was going to remember her.

Seth's garage was on the west side of Whalebone, tucked into some scrubland just before you hit all the outlet malls and mini golf emporiums.

Ted's truck bounced over ruts in the road as she got off the main highway. She'd been here many times in daylight, but it was a lot creepier in the darkness. Fog crept over the island and made it hard to see more than ten feet in any direction. The hairs on her nape stood taut, and even Barney whimpered.

She pulled up around the front of the garage, but there were no lights on that she could see. Seth lived in an apartment above the shop. In her headlights, she could make out her SUV inside the bay doors, glass intact, outside gleaming. He'd not only fixed it in record time, he'd obviously detailed her vehicle too, and that brought a little lump of gratefulness to her throat.

Barney whined again, and she realized belatedly he needed to go. Duh. She turned off the engine and opened the door and climbed out, stuffing her hands in her jacket as the cold wind buffeted her. Barney jumped out of the truck and went to sniff the nearest patch of grass. Fog crept close to him, and the eerie shadows made her flesh crawl. It felt like a million sets of eyes watched her just out of sight. The brunt of the latest storm had hit the mainland south of the Banks but was still creating high winds and blustery skies. She took her weapon from the holster and slipped it inside her coat pocket. She closed the cab door, quietly, not wanting to disturb Seth if he was sleeping, as the guy had obviously worked his balls off last night fixing her vehicle.

The thin shriek of a birdcall shot through the air and straight through Izzy's heart. Barney shot off into the darkness. Dammit.

"Barney!" she called softly. Nothing. *Crap.* She really needed to work on his obedience training. She sniffed cautiously. The scent of gasoline and burning rubber hung on the damp air. A rustle in the bushes had her swallowing nervously and backing up a step. "Barney," she called again.

Nothing except the sound of the sea. Not the whisper of the wind in the grass or the racing of paws. It made the pounding of her heart seem even louder. And then she heard it—the sharp whimper that told her her dog was in pain.

"Barney?" She edged into the marsh, taking a few steps off the narrow path and immediately becoming disorientated. He whimpered again, and she wondered if he'd chased a rabbit down its burrow. "Here, boy," she called out, trying to sound positive.

Nothing.

Damn.

Something slammed into her out of the mist and smacked her headlong into the ground. Pain exploded in her jaw, but whatever sound she made was smothered by a heavy leather glove that also cut off her air supply. She tried to bite, but was dragged to her feet against a lean body and lifted up into the air. She flailed wildly, kicking, trying to get to her gun, but her assailant wrapped his other arm so tight around her waist her arm was trapped and the Glock dug painfully into her abdomen.

Her brain was struggling to comprehend what

was happening, pain and lack of oxygen and plain old-fashioned shock making her thought process dull and blunt. Her kicks grew weaker as she was hauled across sandy paths into the scrubby dunes near the inlet. Barney barked again, and she managed to nail her attacker hard enough in the knee that he stumbled. But rather than releasing her he fell on top of her, his weight crushing. He pressed her face into the sand, punching the back of her head, pummeling her with thick meaty fists.

Oh, God.

She couldn't breathe.

Then the words began to penetrate. "Fucking whore. Fucking bitch. Worthless piece of shit." All hissed in a low voice, saturated in hatred.

The constant rain of punches made her head pound. She tried to protect her nose from a direct hit that might kill her outright, protect her airway, her eyes, her vital organs. She was already on her way to a possible concussion, and she had the feeling this guy had barely gotten started.

She raised her head enough to spit out the sand in her mouth, and forced a sound past her frozen vocal cords. Not a scream. A pathetic groan.

Remembering what had happened to Helena made her heart slow for a few seconds before furiously speeding up. The attacker stood, and the relief at the removal of his weight from her ribcage was tremendous. Then he drew back his foot and kicked her in the stomach. His boot caught her gun, and the combination made her head spin as she cried out and sprawled on her back.

Lincoln Frazer would not be happy to find her dead body here in the scrub. He'd wonder why she hadn't fought the man off, why she hadn't screamed louder. She tried to inhale but still no real sound wanted to come out of her body.

Peering up through the fog she saw a tall, thin man. He wore a balaclava that hid his features, but she could smell the pungent scent of sweat along with alcohol and the heat of his hatred. Words of hate spilled endlessly from his lips, but she couldn't make sense of them—maybe she wasn't supposed to. He kicked her again, and she almost vomited from the blow.

She couldn't believe she was armed and yet still lying here helpless. She tried to reach for her gun, but he stomped on her wrist, crushing the delicate bones there and making her scream in agony. At least she finally made some noise, so she screamed again at the top of her voice. The man smacked his fist into her chin and stars whirled around her mind. Then the asshole jerked at her shirt, ripping the front, buttons flying off in all directions. Ice crawled over her flesh. She didn't want to be raped. Didn't want to die. She forced her injured wrist to move, despite the fact she was pretty sure something was broken. White-hot agony screamed along her nerves, but she ignored it and finally got her finger on the grip of her pistol.

But suddenly someone else was there and her attacker was crying out and tumbling off her to land in a heap in the grass. Whoever had come out of the darkness to rescue her was punching her assailant in the face over and over again.

She lay there panting and then a cold tongue touched her face, kissing her, madly trying to revive her.

Barney.

He was safe. Him being there put her scattered

senses back together. She hugged him to her. Glad they were both okay.

Somewhere in the background she heard Seth Grundy speaking on his cell. "Hank. You need to get down here fast. I think I caught your serial killer attacking Izzy Campbell right here on my property."

Izzy turned her head to see the man lying on the ground beside her. Seth leaned down and yanked the balaclava off the man's head. Izzy flinched.

It was Duncan Cromwell.

***

Frazer sat on the couch, staring at the murder board. It was still dark outside, but he'd managed a few hours of sleep and was awaiting updates from the lab, the ME's office, Hanrahan, Columbia Police Department, Parker and Rooney, and Chief Tyson.

He was getting the silent treatment from Lucas Randall, but he shrugged it off. Memories from last night kept coming back to blast him, including the one where Isadora had crept out like a drunken college hook-up. What irritated him more is he'd let her—pretending to be asleep when what he'd really wanted to do was snag her hand and drag her back to bed.

Why hadn't he stopped her?

"You worked up a profile yet?" Randall asked finally, coming out of the kitchen munching on a bowl of cereal.

"Working on it," said Frazer. "Did you get anywhere with the traffic cams?"

"I sent a list of fifty possible vehicles to cops in Maysville, hoping we can get some sort of hit on their ALPR system, but nothing yet. The system flagged a few unreadable images that I need to go check out."

There were other ways for the unsub to travel too. Boat or even his own plane. But some of the photographs suggested Jessica might have been assaulted and murdered in the back of a van. Frazer found himself staring at all the names on the white board. He'd added Jessica Tuttle to the list of victims. The boy Jesse Tyson was a common connection, and the chief was working on that list of old cases that might have generated someone with a personal grudge against him. But it didn't feel right. It would mean that not only had Denker buried his victims here seventeen years ago, but also that Chief Tyson had subsequently happened to move to this area. It was one coincidence too many.

Jesse could still be the link but probably not because of his father's distant past. He made a note for Tyson to list any cases that had occurred on the Outer Banks itself. If the killer was from here that might make more sense.

Frazer glanced outside. The first glimmer of an orange dawn was lightening the horizon, but the weather was grim and the ocean stormy, which fit the simmering undercurrent of tension in the room. He decided to meet it head on. "She came to me." Technically.

Randall's lips curled. "Is that supposed to make me feel better?"

"I don't give a shit how you feel. I'm just telling you I didn't set out to seduce her. She came to me." He forced himself to push out the next words. "I like her."

"You *like* her? You sleep with a smart, courageous, hardworking, beautiful doctor who served her country in uniform, and you *like* her? Don't go overboard with the yucky stuff there, pal."

"You want me to declare undying love after knowing a woman for a few days?" Frazer asked dryly. "Not my style."

Randall stared at him stone-faced for a long moment, then nodded, apparently satisfied with whatever he saw. "She seems like a good person. Don't fuck her around."

Frazer eyed him. "You do remember I'm your superior, right?"

"Only in rank." A grin caught Randall's mouth. "And you owe me, especially considering you got to make out with a gorgeous woman last night and I got to sleep with her dog."

Randall was a good guy.

"I should have told you about Rooney." Frazer's voice became gruff. "I was pretending none of it was happening so I didn't have to worry about her or the baby." The woman had already risked everything once and deserved nothing but the best. But life didn't always keep its promises of happy-ever-after, as he'd witnessed firsthand when T.J. Knottes had walked into his family home in rural Wisconsin and shot his father dead, and fatally wounded his mother while she'd been making banana bread in their pretty cottage kitchen. To this day the smell of bananas made him want to puke.

"Caring about people sucks. I get it." Randall

sipped his coffee. "Anyway it was my fault. Mal pushed me away when I was critical of Alex. She loves him and he's a good guy. I've got to stop with the overprotective bullshit. She's having his baby for Christ's sake. The woman can handle herself."

Yes, she could. Isadora Campbell could handle herself, too. Was she awake yet? Did she regret what they'd done? Would he be able to persuade her to do it again?

He reminded himself he had a job to do. He cleared his throat. "The basic profile is simple. The unsub is physically strong enough to carry the dead bodies of his victims for short distances over rough terrain." He thought of poor Elaine Patterson. "He likely has above average intelligence, but underperformed academically. He's able to blend in with the community and is highly mobile. Despite the fact that only two bodies have been found on the Outer Banks, his familiarity with the locale suggests he either lives here or has spent considerable time here in the past. I'm betting this is his home territory." He picked up his own coffee, staring at the murder board, wishing there were fewer victims and knowing there were likely many more. "The ease with which he takes women tells me he's gregarious and socially competent. He's also manipulative and self-centered. He knows how to make people do what he wants them to do. He drives a van or truck that he uses for both the abduction and to transport the dead bodies, and probably to commit the murder. Also, he sometimes rides a dirt bike—you run those yet?"

"DMV sent through a list but also noted you don't need a license for a moped."

Frazer grunted. "He travels frequently to the mainland, as there are easier victim pickings over there. He has a violent temper and holds a grudge, but he's a damn good actor. He might be married with kids, or have a girlfriend. He was probably sexually abused as a child. Usually it's by a dominant female but for some reason I'm thinking in this case possibly by a male." Assuming his hunch that this unsub was a schoolmate of Ferris Denker's. He wasn't ready to share that theory yet. "I believe he takes shoes as trophies, but I'm not sure how far that piece of information will get us in catching him unless we actually find the guy with a cupboard full of shoes."

Frazer lifted the box Mildred Houch had given him and dumped it on the table. He removed the stack he'd already rejected.

"What are these?" asked Randall.

"Photographs from Ferris Denker's school—which happens to be the same place where the prostitute Elaine Patterson's body was dumped. I'm trying to find any photographs from when Denker attended the school." Mildred Houch had thankfully written the year on the back of most of the photos.

Randall picked up one that was obviously from a recent wedding, and he added it to the reject stack.

Frazer's cell phone buzzed. Tyson. He answered it.

"Duncan Cromwell attacked Izzy Campbell when she went to pick up her SUV in Whalebone Junction. He was wearing a mask and dragged her into the marsh," Tyson informed him. "He tried to kill her."

Frazer felt like someone had reached into his chest and squeezed his heart with a fist. "Is she all right?"

"Yeah. She's alive anyway. Seth Grundy heard her scream and rescued her."

Frazer's lungs expanded, but he wasn't sure he was breathing. "Where is she now?"

"She's been taken to the hospital. Cromwell is in custody, being processed. I'll see what I can get out of him before he lawyers up."

"I'll meet you there shortly." Frazer sat there stunned. She'd only left his bed a few hours ago, for Christ's sake. He hung up and released a long breath. "They caught Duncan Cromwell attacking Isadora Campbell."

Randall's eyebrows shot up in surprise.

"Tyson didn't say it, but he thinks Cromwell's our guy." Frazer grabbed his jacket. The idea a father would rape and murder his own daughter was repulsive, but it happened. And wait until the media got hold of that story. "I'm going to take Kit to the hospital, and I'll meet you at the police station in an hour. I want you to start preparing items for a search warrant. Include photographs, diaries, computers, DVDs, and shoes." He was dialing Parker as he walked out the door. "I need a detailed background check on Duncan Cromwell, Helena's father, going all the way back to when and where he was born. Any overlap with Denker you can find, even if they only bought a candy bar from the same store thirty years ago."

He hung up. Ran up the steps to the Campbell cottage and used the key he'd lifted a few nights ago to let himself in.

"Kit," he shouted.

He heard a groan, and he strode farther into the living room, noticing Barney was gone and hoping to hell the dog was okay. "Isadora's been hurt. She needs you."

That brought some cursing followed by the sound of feet stumbling around the bedroom. She appeared seventy-seconds later, dressed, hairbrush in one hand, coat in the other. "Is she okay?"

He held her gaze. "Let's go find out."

***

Izzy lay on the bed, staring at the ceiling, wanting to escape. They'd run chest X-rays and ruled out fractured ribs and pneumothorax. Liver, spleen, and kidney all looked good on the abdominal ultrasound, and her blood work—count, electrolytes, liver function, coagulation—had come back normal. They were insisting on a CT scan before they'd let her escape. Stupid. Except for her wrist, which had already been put in a small cast and X-rayed, she'd suffered more damage during hand-to-hand combat training—for all the good that had done her.

She couldn't believe how easily he'd overpowered her. Dammit. Aside from her wrist, nothing was broken but she hurt. She stuffed down the pain and the pity party. She remembered soldiers who ended up on her table—shot, blown up, concussed from bomb blasts. So she'd taken a few blows and had a fright. It would remind her to pay more attention to her surroundings in the future.

She checked a mirror she'd asked one of the nurses to give her. Both her pupils looked normal, not blown, so no coning, which was beyond excellent news. Then she made herself remember the name of every commanding officer she'd ever served under, to prove her brain was as intact as it had been when she woke up that morning. She was pretty sure she wasn't concussed. Basically, there was nothing wrong with her that strong narcotics wouldn't fix—except the humiliation, which she'd learn to live with. But her fellow physicians were being overzealous with her care—hence the CT scan even though she had no abdominal pain and all the other tests had come back normal.

God knew what would have happened if Seth hadn't turned up. She slid her legs over the edge of the bed, thinking escape might be a reasonable possibility. But the sound of footsteps down the corridor had her grimacing. She recognized Lincoln Frazer's purposeful stride even after their short acquaintance.

Long enough to screw his brains out.

Damn.

She got back under the covers and winced as a sharp pain shot from her neck to the middle of her skull. Dammit.

Then Frazer came into view, looking as handsome as ever, even if his shirt was a little creased from her throwing it on the bathroom floor last night. She avoided his eyes and looked at Kit instead. Her sister's pace was hurried, her face a vision of fear and uncertainty as she clung onto Frazer's arm like he was a close confidante. Izzy raised her brow at him, and he shrugged as if to say he didn't know how it had happened. That was Kit for you. She chose you, rather than you choosing her.

"Hey. There was no need to come down here. It's not that bad," she tried to reassure them, but Kit flew to her side and hugged her tightly. Izzy bit back a yelp and let her hold on. Her sister had already lost way too much in the last twelve months, she'd have been terrified at the idea of anything happening to Izzy, too. Her gaze locked on Frazer's over Kit's head, and she knew he could tell she was in pain.

Izzy hugged her sister tighter. She wanted to stroke the hair off Kit's cheek. She'd obviously just climbed out of bed and rushed down here because there were still sleep marks creased into her face.

"Who did this?" Kit wailed, taking in the cut at the side of her mouth where Duncan had landed a punch.

Izzy had barely believed her eyes when she'd seen Duncan Cromwell lying there on the ground. "Helena's dad."

"What?" Kit jerked away.

Izzy squeezed her eyes shut as her ribs were jostled. Ouch. Being brave sucked. She wanted to burst into tears and be done with it.

"Did he kill Helena?"

"Shush." Izzy glanced at the open door. "I don't know," she said quietly.

"Did he hurt you?" Kit's eyes were huge, looking at her properly, taking in her hospital gown.

"Chief Tyson bagged all my clothes as evidence. I'd appreciate someone going to my locker and grabbing the spare set I keep there." The sooner she got something to wear the sooner she could escape.

"As soon as the doctor releases you." Frazer's

blue eyes pinned hers.

Dammit. How'd he know her so well, so fast?

Her sister bit her lip. Izzy caught her hand and squeezed her fingers. "Look, he beat the crap out of me, but he didn't touch me sexually." She kept her voice down, glad she was in a separate room a couple down from where Jesse was holed up. He was supposed to be going home today. "I'm okay. I promise."

"Kit," Frazer said suddenly. "Why don't you go buy your sister a drink from the vendor stand? And get me a coffee while you're at it, will you? Black. No sugar." He handed her ten bucks and Kit gazed at him stupidly for a moment.

"Oh, you guys want to talk. Sure. Okay." She looked between them nervously. "I'll be back in five minutes. Be good."

"Too late," Frazer said under his breath as her sister ducked out of sight.

Izzy laughed, holding her side carefully. Frazer sat beside her on the bed, way too close. He eased the side of her hospital gown up and she felt ridiculously exposed, which was crazy considering he'd licked every inch of her body last night.

"It isn't pretty," she warned, rolling over enough to let him free the gown.

His hands stilled when he revealed a series of bruises. He indicated she roll over farther so he could see the rest of her back. She did, aware he could also see her bare butt, but she guessed that ship had sailed last night. But this was the hospital and fluorescents were not as kind as the gentle light of the moon.

"How bad was it?" His voice was cold and emotionless, but she heard the undercurrent of rage it concealed. Just because he controlled his emotions didn't mean he didn't feel them.

"Honestly?" She let out a noisy breath. "I thought I was going to die." She turned back so she was facing him, but sat up straighter, wincing at the sharp pains that attacked her body, and grateful for each and every one of them. "What was so frustrating was I had my gun in my front pocket, but he held my arms so tight I couldn't reach it, and then he started hitting me and calling me a whore." A wave of remembered revulsion rushed over her skin.

"It's okay, Isadora." Frazer captured her hand and brought it to his lips.

"You need to start calling me Izzy, like everyone else."

"You want me to treat you the same way everyone else treats you?" His blue eyes were so bright it hurt to stare into them, like looking directly at the sun.

"I don't know," she said honestly. How ironic she couldn't lie to the guy considering the huge fat secret she kept from him. "I think someone watched us in bed last night."

"What makes you say that?" His gaze sharpened, switching from lover to FBI agent in a split second.

"Someone folded a blanket that I'd left on the floor, and from that part of the deck you can see straight into your bedroom. The drapes were open," she reminded him.

"I remember." The spark of heat in his eyes made her tingle. Then his lips pressed together. "Doesn't mean anyone watched us. Agent Randall, or Kit could have folded the blanket?"

Izzy closed her eyes in horror. "I don't know who would be worse, but I'm never making love with the curtains open again."

"I'll bear that in mind." His gaze was bold and direct. He was clearly expecting a repeat of the night before.

There was a funny little flutter beneath her breastbone.

"Why'd you sneak away?" he asked.

"I needed to get back to Kit."

His eyes said he didn't believe her.

"It was just sex, remember? I didn't think you'd want the awkward morning-after scenario, especially with you bunking with another FBI agent."

"Remember when I said I like you, Isadora Campbell? I meant it." His eyes narrowed. "I would have liked to have woken up with you, but I understand your need to be with Kit." He looked away for a brief moment and then back. "I'd like to see what might happen if we let this thing between us become a little more than just sex."

Her heart beat violently and she felt sick. She'd screwed this up so badly. She'd love to have more with Lincoln Frazer. She'd give anything to go back seventeen years and tell the truth—or even a few days, to when Helena was killed. Now the ugly lies lay between them, and she didn't think he was the sort of man to forgive that kind of blatant omission.

He mistook her silence for something else. "I'm sorry I didn't follow up on the vandalism to your car yesterday. I didn't even think about it." He dragged his hand through his hair.

"You had more important things on your

mind." At his tortured expression she reached out and touched the back of his hand with her uninjured one. "It's okay, Linc. I'm not one of your victims, don't add me to that list."

He blinked in surprise.

"I have them, too," she explained. "The people we fail. The people we can't save."

Her boyfriend Shane had been the first. Her father the second, but she still didn't know if he'd deserved to be saved or not.

She drew in a breath and opened her mouth to tell him what had really happened all those years ago and why they could never be together, but Kit came strolling into the room with a look of intense concentration as she tried not to spill the drinks.

"They provide lids, you know."

Kit's eyes flashed with hurt and Izzy immediately realized she'd said the wrong thing. Again. Damn. "Sorry."

Frazer stood and took the cups from Kit. Put them on the side table. Then he leaned down, cupped the back of Izzy's head, and kissed her straight on the mouth. Izzy resisted for a split-second and then ignored the shafts of pain to wrap her arms around his neck and kiss him back, silently telling him all the things she didn't have the nerve to say out loud. He pulled away, his blue eyes taking in her expression. "I'll see you later, Dr. Campbell."

Kit stood there, open-mouthed.

"Later." It came out in a breathy whisper. Damn. What the hell was she going to do now?

CHAPTER TWENTY

Frazer arrived at the police station in a taxicab amid a swarm of media vans. He'd already requested the rental car company drop off another vehicle for him ASAP. He braved the scrum of reporters, fielding questions from some of the network people who recognized him.

"ASAC Frazer, what can you tell us about the rumor there's a serial killer operating on the Outer Banks?"

"ASAC Frazer. Can you confirm that one of the bodies recovered here was that of a Ferris Denker victim?"

"Can you tell us who you've arrested?"

"Why are the BAU involved?"

The noise turned into a gray buzz that sawed at his ears.

"No comment." He elbowed his way through the thick tangle of reporters and cameramen, hoping he could leave via a back door.

A uniformed officer guarded the entrance and prevented the press gathering inside. It was the waste of another resource they could better use on the case. Once inside, Frazer was waved through to the back. He found Randall in Tyson's office, the two men hunched over a bunch of documents. "You have the search warrant?"

Tyson pulled a piece of paper off the fax machine. "Just. How's Izzy?" The guileless way Tyson asked made Frazer roll his eyes.

He turned to Randall. "You told him? What are you, in high school?"

"We were Army buddies." Randall grimaced. "Anyway, I had to tell him why you weren't here yet, when we'd just pulled in a suspected serial killer."

Frazer shook his head. Shit. This wasn't his usual MO. There were rarely things in his personal life that allowed teasing.

"How do you want to do this?" Tyson got down to business.

"Randall, you go with police officers to the Cromwell home to execute the warrant. Make sure everything is seized and handled appropriately. We want no mistakes. If he's our guy I want an airtight case against him. I also want you to interview the wife and figure out what she knows. And if you can access the kids—do it."

"Does Cromwell fit the profile?" asked Randall.

"Some of it. White, male, strong, mobile. Drives a truck, has access to work vans. Above average intelligence. Wears a uniform, but doesn't carry a weapon—could be a wannabe cop who didn't have what it takes. Frankly I haven't had time to work up much more than that."

Tyson looked less than impressed. Frazer didn't blame him. He was less than impressed himself, but it wasn't profiles that caught killers, it was basic investigative police work. They had a number of leads they were following now. It was a matter of time. Was Cromwell their guy? Were people now safe from this killer? He didn't know. Felicia Barton was working on geographical profiling along with Bradley Tate of the Highway Serial Killings Initiative. Because of limited access to the islands some of the normal principles of geographical profiling didn't apply. However, limited access meant they might be able to spot his means of transport more easily.

"We need to graph out Cromwell's movements every day, starting with New Year's Eve. I have someone working on his past to see if or when he and Denker crossed paths."

"You really think he killed his own kid?" Tyson asked uneasily.

"It's possible. I want to talk to him."

Tyson nodded. "We'll do it together."

"Someone gave the press the Denker connection," Frazer said bitterly.

They all grimaced because conducting an investigation under a media spotlight was like trying to get dressed wearing a blindfold and hoping no one saw you. But there was nowhere to hide in a community this small. Any mistakes would be amplified. Any errors jumped upon gleefully.

"Let's move. If Cromwell is our guy I want him nailed to the wall," Tyson grabbed his jacket.

"And if he isn't, I want the community to know not to drop their guard," said Frazer.

"You have doubts?" Tyson frowned.

Frazer smiled grimly. "I always have doubts. Cromwell exhibited a lot of antagonism toward Dr. Campbell when I interviewed him." He met Tyson's eyes. "It could be a personal attack stemming from grief at the loss of his daughter."

Tyson and Randall both looked doubtful. "It shared a lot of similarities with the other attacks."

"So let's go talk to the guy. See what he's ready to spill."

***

Frazer walked into the room, followed by Tyson. That Cromwell had attacked Isadora made him feel physically ill, but he was professional enough to be able to dissociate his feelings for the woman from those for the suspect in front of him. He brought Cromwell a cup of herbal tea, which smelled disgusting but, according to the officer who was a friend of the Cromwell family, was all he ever really drank.

"How are you feeling, Duncan?" he asked. The guy looked like shit. The skin around his eyes was swollen and angry red. Both eyes would be blackened by tonight. Blood rimmed the inside of his nose that had also possibly been broken. Seth Grundy had done quite the number on the man. Frazer stilled the rage that wanted to rise inside him. Someone had beaten him to it—literally.

"I feel like horseshit. How do you think I'd feel? My daughter is dead, and you're doing nothing to catch her killer."

Frazer ignored the complaints. "Can you tell us what happened this morning?"

Cromwell pressed his lips together and glared.

"I know you're going through a tough time, Duncan. I know you're hurting." Assuming he wasn't a full-blown psychopath. "Helena's death must have hit hard."

Tears streamed down the man's face. It was possible he'd killed Helena in a rage and the remorse he exhibited was genuine. Frazer put the tea down and pushed it in Cromwell's direction. "I need to ask you about your movements last night."

Something sparked in Cromwell's eyes.

"Really."

"Can you walk me through your day?"

Cromwell shrugged. "I went into the office yesterday morning. I needed to get away from Lannie and the kids for a few hours. To try and forget."

Just a couple of days after his daughter was murdered. "Sure. I understand." Oddly enough, Frazer did, but he wasn't a married man with a wife and kids who'd also suffered unbearable loss.

"You married, ASAC Frazer?" There was something snide in Cromwell's tone. Something unkind.

"Divorced."

Cromwell nodded, but he looked disappointed for some reason.

"How long did you stay at the office?"

Cromwell shrugged. "An hour. Maybe two."

"Where did you go after that?"

"I drove around for a while."

"Why?"

"Because I wanted to think," he snapped.

"Did you go by the hospital and take your baseball bat to Dr. Campbell's car windows?"

Cromwell stared at him sullenly. Nothing.

"Do you remember anywhere you went?"

"I drove up to Currituck. Checked out some of the Wildlife Refuge. We've had problems with illegal hog hunting up there."

Frazer felt his pulse speed up. He wanted to pursue the question of Jessica Tuttle but had to ease his way into it. "How long did you spend there?"

"About an hour or so. I wasn't timing myself." Cromwell frowned and looked up and left. The guy was right-handed so he was either a superlative liar, or telling the truth.

"Anyone see you?"

He shook his head. "I didn't talk to anyone I knew, if that's what you're asking. There were a couple of people out walking, but I wasn't exactly looking for company."

News of Jessica's death had been kept quiet overnight. It had hit the news channels in time for the breakfast news. If Duncan was going to pretend he wasn't the person who'd murdered Jessica, he was setting up an alibi that might explain why anyone had spotted him there.

"Did you go home for dinner?"

Empty eyes drifted to stare at the wall. "I wasn't hungry."

"Where'd you go next?"

Cromwell shrugged and clammed up.

Tyson interjected. "I know you bought a bottle of rye at the liquor store. You go get drunk?"

Cromwell's gaze hit the floor. "Yes. I got drunk." He sounded ashamed. "Then I got behind the wheel of the truck and I drove to Isadora Campbell's home. I was going to make her pay for not looking after my daughter the way she'd promised. Do you know what I saw?" Duncan's eyes contained hellfire as they met Frazer's, talking loudly now. "You, fucking her. My daughter's murderer is out there, slaughtering girls, and you're busy nailing that fucking bitch. You should be ashamed."

"Hardly." The hatred was palpable, and the fact that Frazer had stoked those flames sat badly, but he wasn't going along on that guilt trip. He had enough real sins on his conscience that actually having a sex life barely registered. He hadn't officially been on duty, although he'd find it difficult to define exactly when he was off duty. "Did you get off watching a private moment between lovers? Did it turn you on?"

Cromwell looked horrified by the idea. "No."

He watched the man carefully and didn't see any signs of deception. Most sexual sadists would have probably jerked off to the show. Hell, a lot of normal guys would have, too. Next time he was definitely closing the drapes—assuming there was a next time. Isadora hadn't exactly been enthusiastic when he'd suggested the idea earlier. But then she had just been attacked by this guy. Christ. His timing needed work.

"How long did you watch for?"

"Not long," Cromwell turned away from him now.

"Do you and your wife still have sex, Duncan?"

Cromwell's mouth dropped open as he faced him again. "That's none of your damn business."

"Why not? You now know the sum total of my sex life for the past twelve months. I think I'm entitled to a bit of turnaround, don't you?"

"No. What happens between my wife and me is private. I'm not talking about it here, with you."

"She satisfy all your needs, Duncan? She's a beautiful woman, but it doesn't always translate into being good in the sack."

Tyson sat stoically beside him, letting him ask the shitty questions.

"Sometimes a guy needs more, you know? Or maybe something a little extra. I certainly wouldn't blame a guy for helping himself to a little extra if he wasn't getting what he needed at home."

Cromwell crossed and uncrossed his legs. "I love my wife. I don't cheat on her, ever."

"Then why were you trying to rip Isadora Campbell's shirt off in the marsh this morning? You saw the goods and figured you wanted some of that? I know I did. She's hot."

Cromwell's mouth moved uncertainly. "I-I didn't want to have sex with Dr. Campbell."

Interesting he said *sex*, not *rape*, as if it would have been consensual.

"You wanted to beat her and leave her out there, like Helena?"

"Yes." Cromwell nodded and then backtracked. "I wasn't going to touch her that way."

"Were you going to take off her clothes?" asked Frazer.

Cromwell closed his sore-looking eyes.

"You can't tell me that you didn't get a boner watching me fuck Izzy last night." The language was coarse, but it was the sort of conversation a sexual sadist could relate to. Not love or cherish, but fuck and nail.

Finally the guy nodded.

"Did you get a boner again when you started taking her clothes off?" Ripping her shirt open after she'd been beaten almost unconscious. That was in the report he'd read. "She's a beautiful woman." Not that it mattered. For most rapists it was about fear and domination, not attraction or beauty. "Did the attack arouse you?"

Cromwell swallowed and nodded slowly.

"But you weren't going to have sex with her?" Frazer wanted to smack the guy, but kept his voice neutral, which the man seemed to respond to.

"I was going to strip her bare and leave her

323

unconscious alone in the darkness."

"Like Helena," said Frazer.

Cromwell nodded.

"Helena died. Did you want Dr. Campbell dead too? Naked and dead in the dunes like your daughter?"

"Alone in the darkness," Cromwell repeated in a detached voice.

"Helena wasn't alone." Tyson said quietly. "My son was with her."

Cromwell's eyes opened and narrowed. "Some good he did her."

"So you attacked Isadora Campbell as a punishment?" said Frazer.

Cromwell nodded.

"The same way you punished Helena?" Frazer pushed gently.

"What?" Cromwell looked genuinely shocked. Both his feet hit the floor. "You think I..." Horror stole over his features, and he spoke very slowly. "You think I raped and killed my own daughter?"

But Frazer wasn't hearing any real denials. So he changed the subject. "You ever heard of St. Joseph's School for Boys?"

***

Izzy was sprung at lunchtime. She'd sucked down some Tylenol 3, so the pain was manageable. The only real injury was her broken wrist, which pissed her off more than hurt, as it meant she wasn't supposed to drive for the next couple of weeks. She had an appointment back at the fracture clinic in two weeks. It could have been so much worse.

She needed to thank Seth for everything. The

man had saved her life today.

Kit had spent some time with Jesse before he'd been discharged. The kid was messed up. He'd been told about his ex-girlfriend, Jessica, and even though he hadn't really liked the girl anymore, he was suffering from shocked disbelief and a strong dose of survivor's guilt. Charlene had popped in and told her she was taking Jesse and his little brother off the island for a few weeks. She didn't mention where they were going, and Izzy didn't ask. The bodyguards whisked them away without the press sniffing them out, which seemed like a smart plan.

According to the charge nurse there were fifteen-to-twenty news vans in the parking lot. The last thing Izzy wanted was to end up on TV.

So Kit had driven away from the hospital alone and then one of the ambulance crews had secreted Izzy into the back before meeting up with Kit along Cape Hatteras National Seashore. Izzy wore a woolen hat that completely covered her hair, and some dark glasses one of the nurses had lent her. Black fingerless gloves hid the small cast and she refused to wear the sling, yet. Instead she'd stuffed it in her bag. She'd wear it later if her wrist started to hurt more.

She wanted her gun back. She'd texted both Chief Tyson and Lincoln Frazer to see if one of them could swing that for her, but neither had replied yet. The orthopedic surgeon had lent her a pale beige trench coat that was a hell of a lot more sophisticated than her usual Gortex or down jackets. The effect was rather stunning, and rather than looking like she was in hiding, she looked like a stylish confident woman.

Getting out of the rig, she thanked the ambulance crew, suddenly aware how limiting a broken wrist was when she tried to shut the back door with her right hand. Ouch.

Kit leaned over and opened the passenger door of her Beetle. Izzy eased carefully inside. Her ribs were only bruised, but any sudden movement gave her a nasty reminder of her morning's workout. She'd much rather remember the mad crazy lovemaking session with the buttoned up Fed than getting the shit kicked out of her.

Kit checked her phone. "Ted texted me from the diner. He wants us to drop in on our way past." Izzy opened her mouth to argue, but Kit cut her off. "The press isn't there right now. He figures you have time for a coffee. He has Barney."

Her poor dog. Ted had taken him to the vet for a thorough check up, but he seemed to be okay. It looked like Cromwell had simply lured him away with a treat and tied him to a bush with a bit of rope. Everyone carried rope, right? She shuddered. "Is Seth there?"

"Yeah."

Izzy nodded. "Okay."

Kit grinned at her easy capitulation, but there was a glint in her eye. So far she hadn't asked why a senior federal agent had kissed the hell out of her earlier. Izzy didn't know how long the reprieve would last, but she was going to ride it as long as possible.

"I'm going to go visit Damien later." Kit watched the road ahead, but Izzy knew she was feeling out her reaction.

Izzy squeezed her thigh with her good hand. She needed to start dealing with Kit as an equal.

"He could come over to the house later," Izzy offered. Although wasn't that going to be awkward?

"Yeah," Kit laughed. "I don't think so. He says his mom wants to meet me, which is probably going to head south fast, but he needs a friend and high school has turned into a cesspool recently." She turned her head and gave Izzy one of her wise smiles. "We're not going to smoke pot or pretend to have sex. Promise."

Izzy held her ribs and groaned. "You're not going to 'pretend' to have sex. Shoot me now."

Kit grinned, because she was a smart young woman who was old enough to make her own choices. Pity Izzy needed to be assaulted to figure that out. She needed to let go of her past suspicions, give Kit's friends a chance. She didn't have many now that Helena was dead. "Keep your phone on and answer if I call you. We don't know for sure Duncan Cromwell is the guy who killed those girls."

Kit gave a disbelieving snort. "How many maniacs do you think live out here, Iz?"

"More than you know." Izzy pressed her lips together and thought of their father. Her sister seemed to have turned the corner in maturity. She seemed to have screwed her head back on straight. How would the news that their father had been responsible for the murder of at least one young woman go down? Or that when their mom had found him hunched over a naked body in the trunk of his car, she'd stabbed him with a screwdriver, and pleaded with Izzy to help her hide all the evidence?

How did anyone deal with that?

Izzy should have refused, should have gone straight into the police station the way she wanted to. But her mom had been nine months pregnant and threatening to kill herself if anyone found out the truth. The emotions felt so vivid, memories so alive in her mind that bile rose up inside her throat. Grief, horror, and fear all churned inside her— emotions she'd never been able to share with anyone. Her nails bit into the soft flesh of her palms. She was so sick of the secrets. So sick of the guilt. Izzy knew what she had to do—she just didn't think Kit would ever forgive her for ripping away her ignorance.

Kit swung into a parking space in front of the diner, and the seatbelt pressing against her bruised ribs snapped Izzy out of the past. Kit jumped out of the car and came around to open Izzy's door. Izzy swung her legs around and used her left hand to haul herself up and out of the bucket seat. She rolled her shoulders, scanned the surroundings for media types, and headed inside.

Heat. Coffee. Bacon. The smells were old, familiar, and comforting.

Sal stuck his head through the service window and caught her sister's eye. "I'll be right back," said Kit. "I'll grab you a drink. Want anything to eat?"

Not even the smell of bacon made her hungry. "Just coffee, thanks."

She went over to the booth where all the usual suspects were ensconced, except Hank, who was probably either working or sleeping. Ted stood up and wrapped a beefy arm carefully around her shoulder. Seth stood next. She took a step toward him, rose on her tiptoes, and pressed a kiss to his cheek. "You saved my life."

Seth grinned at his buddies. "See?"

Izzy laughed and stole Ted's seat, sliding in next to the pastor who gave her a solemn nod. "Glad you're still amongst the living, Miss Isadora."

"Me, too, Pastor. Me, too." Kit came back with her coffee. Izzy took a mouthful and the acrid taste burned all the way down her throat. "I also owe you for the work you did on my SUV, Seth."

"I'll stick the bill in your mailbox when I drop off your car," Seth told her.

His buddies moaned and guffawed. Izzy held his gaze. "I appreciate it. For the work on the car *and* for finding me in the marsh and beating the crap out of Duncan Cromwell."

He looked away, but she noted a slight reddening of his cheeks. She'd embarrassed the guy, however he was obviously enjoying hero status. She turned to Mr. Kent. She wanted to talk about something other than her brush with death. "How did your date with Mary go last night?"

He laughed a little self-consciously. "Fine, I think."

Izzy grinned until Kit broke in, "I hope you didn't eat the same thing Mary did. She sent Sal a message earlier saying she had food poisoning. He wants me to cover her shift for a few hours this afternoon."

"Darn. She seemed fine last night." Mr. Kent pulled out his cell phone and looked disappointed by the radio silence.

"Poor Mary," said the pastor.

"That'll teach you to skimp on the restaurant." Seth snorted. "Now you'll never get laid."

"Unlike Izzy," Kit said slyly, "who had a late

night hook-up with the hot federal agent next door."

Every drop of blood drained from Izzy's face. She opened her mouth to deny it, but it was too late. Her shock and embarrassment were obvious. She'd already given herself away.

"Which Fed?" Ted asked Kit.

"The tall blond one who's all business."

"*Really?*" His brows rose. "ASAC Frazer. I figured she'd go for the rugged dark-eyed one because he obviously has the hots for her."

"Lucas is cute," Kit conceded.

Lucas?

"But if you think Frazer hasn't got the hots for our Izzy, you haven't seen them trapped in a room together, pretending not to imagine each other naked."

"Kit!" Izzy was mortified her personal business was being gossiped about—in front of her. This was why she didn't like small towns.

"Perhaps this is where your porn queen fantasies originate?" The pastor cut in. "What?" he said when everyone stared at him in silent shock. He frowned. "You all know she was pretending, right—didn't you see the other image?"

Seth and Mr. Kent shook their heads and the pastor pulled out his cell phone and showed them the second photograph taken from the side. "Mrs. Ridgeway, this young man's mother, forwarded it to me, because she didn't want me tossing her out of the home she so desperately needs because of her son's rumored debauchery."

"I guess my dirty secret is out." Kit's expression morphed into a reluctant smirk.

"*I* told Mrs. Ridgeway it was a classic case of

jumping to the worst possible conclusion and 'let those who cast the first stone' yada yada yada. I used it in my sermon this morning. Not the image." He reassured Kit when he saw her eyes widen. "I pointed out that judging people without knowing the full facts didn't exactly reflect a Christian spirit."

"I'm sure it was a wonderful sermon," Izzy said, gamely trying to get them off the subject of a photograph she'd hoped everyone had forgotten about. "I'm sorry I missed it."

"Damn glad I missed it," Seth murmured fervently.

"Me, too," whispered Ted in her ear.

She kissed her uncle on the cheek. She wasn't generally affectionate, and she was going to miss him when she moved away. "Where's my dog?" she asked.

"In the van. I took him for a big long walk earlier so you don't need to go out later unless you want to."

She nodded, finishing her coffee, then stood to leave.

"What did they say about Cromwell?" Seth asked.

"I didn't hear anything, yet."

His mustache twitched. "I should have beaten him some more."

A big ball of emotion wedged itself inside her throat and she couldn't speak. She put her good hand over his fist and squeezed. He'd saved her life today, and she didn't know how to properly convey her gratitude.

"Okay, I'm taking her home as per doctor's orders." Kit clapped her hands together. "She looks like she might vomit otherwise."

"Kit..." Izzy complained.

"Then I have to come back and wait tables for a couple of hours. See ya'll later."

Izzy eased out of the booth, said bye to Ted's cronies, and headed outside. Ted's van door was unlocked, windows cracked for Barney. The little silver disco ball that hung from the rearview glittered with reflected light.

It was a cold blustery day and the sea still had that look of potential fury. She tugged one-handed on the side-door that slid open automatically. Barney went wild, giving her cold wet kisses. She grabbed his leash before he could jump down and run into traffic. The dog bent down and gathered something in his mouth. Izzy gently pulled out the offending mess. Holy shit. It was a pair of panties covered in dog slobber. Ew. Looked like she wasn't the only one getting a little action, although her Uncle Ted hadn't mentioned he was seeing anyone. Not that it was any of her business. Just like what she did with Lincoln Frazer wasn't anyone else's business, either. She tossed the panties in the back of the van. "Come on, Barney. Let's go home."

CHAPTER TWENTY-ONE

Despite Jessica's online super-bitch attitude, she'd proven surprisingly unadventurous when it came to the hard stuff. Less "Fuck you" and more "I'll do anything you say and I won't tell anyone what happened just don't hurt me." So he'd tested her. Made her do a lot of shit that had felt so good he was aroused again just thinking about it. And then he'd squeezed her slender throat until he'd not only watched, but actually *felt* the moment life released its tenuous grip on her young body. He'd seen the flicker in her eyes when she'd gone from terrified to realizing there really was something on the other side. Something wonderful. Something beautiful.

And he'd felt like God.

He replayed the video on his cell phone, touching himself, wishing he could stay here and enjoy it.

Instead the real world crept closer.

He'd had to get rid of his shoe collection. It was necessary but, damn, that had hurt. As he re-watched Jessica bend her creamy-white ass in the air he pumped his hand, reliving the things he'd done to her.

He'd never understood Denker's need to torture and mutilate but the effect of a woman's scream on his dick?—better than a blow job. Maybe it was as simple as that. Denker needed a specific type of scream to get him off—which meant prison had been seventeen years of torture for the poor bastard, while he'd been getting his jollies.

He grinned.

He felt sorry for the guy, really, but even though the hunger was growing again he couldn't risk another murder, not here. Not yet. Cromwell was taking the fall for the latest round, like someone else had taken the fall years ago for the others. If he didn't want to end up in a cell himself, he had to cool it for a while.

People had always said he was a lucky sonofagun, but after being dragged back from death while sighting heaven, he hadn't believed them. Now he was starting to understand.

His finger flicked through the images and paused over the one of Kit Campbell pretending to blow that little prick. She'd been pretending, which amused him. For all her sass and confidence he figured she was still a virgin.

Would she scream as loud as Jessica had? Or be silent like Helena? He rubbed himself but nothing was happening, just that growing need for arousal cruising his veins like an animal trying to get out with no exit in sight.

He flicked to another image. Izzy.

The fact she was screwing a Fed was like a kick in the teeth. But maybe she was doing it to get access to a source of information, to figure out if they were getting any closer to discovering her secrets.

Could he blackmail her into working with him? No. Despite her actions she was too "principled" to allow herself to be compromised like that. It was another reason he liked her—all that moral backbone strapped over a dark ugly secret…beautiful juxtaposition. And now he was stiff again as he looked at the image of Izzy smiling.

He found the video of Jessica and played the audio, all the while he looked at Izzy's smiling face. He didn't cry out his release. He roared.

***

Frazer watched the lunchtime news report at the police station with growing trepidation. Ferris Denker's lawyer was making a statement to the media from the imposing steps of the State Capitol building in Columbia.

All the cops stopped what they were doing to watch as someone turned up the volume.

"After seeing this new spate of murders on the Outer Banks, my client is horrified by what some people have labeled a copycat murderer of Mr. Denker's, just weeks before he is sentenced to die. He has been hit by a huge feeling of remorse—not only for the women whom he attacked and robbed of their lives, but also for the families of the victims. Mr. Denker knows he can't atone for his past sins, but he's desperate to at least ease the burden on families of the victims whose bodies were never recovered. Knowing that his recent offer to the Governor's Office was rejected when he asked for his sentence to be commuted to life with no chance of parole, he is renewing his offer, but this time without stipulations. He wants to meet God with a clear conscience. I'm here to petition the governor to allow Mr. Denker to help authorities locate the bodies of his victims while there is still time. God rest their souls."

The lawyer slid the crib note into his pocket and turned and jogged up the steps.

Shit.

What was Denker's end game? Screwing with the families one last time? Dangling that carrot to people desperate for information? Bastard.

He wasn't fooled by the sudden talk of remorse. Psychopaths didn't feel remorse. The dominant personality traits of organized serial killers were fantasy, control, and domination. The only thing that mattered to these predators was finding a way to carry out their fantasies, of making them real.

But Frazer knew Denker did not want to die.

Had Cromwell been involved with Denker, or had the recent murders acted as a catalyst and a smokescreen for Izzy's attack? Was the real killer still out there?

The news article ended with shots of this very building and him pushing his way through the melee of reporters with a terse "No comment" earlier. Some of the other police officers gave him a look before they went back to work. He headed into Tyson's office where the other man was on the phone.

"It's only for a few days, honey." One hand was pulling his hair. "Go enjoy yourself while I sort out this mess." His eyes met Frazer's and then he turned his back. "I have to go. Talk to you later. I love you, babe." He hung up.

Randall walked in behind him. Hair disheveled, suit jacket creased, tie askew. He dropped into the visitor chair in Tyson's office and cradled his head in his hands. "Well, that sucked."

"Anything at the house or workplace? Forensics find any sign of blood or semen with the black lights?" asked Frazer.

"Nothing." Randall leaned back in the chair and stared up at the ceiling. "We did find a metal detector."

That was something. Lack of trace was a worry though. Maybe he hadn't killed Jessica in that van. "Can we check any of the other vehicles Cromwell had access to at work?"

Randall nodded. "CSU techs are on it. DNR office is cooperating fully with the investigation."

How did they prove a connection to Denker? Maybe Cromwell had come across the bracelet in the dunes—dunes he was one of the few officially allowed to enter? Maybe he'd somehow figured out who the bracelet belonged to and contacted Denker... It didn't feel right, but it was vaguely plausible. Frazer's instincts had been way off on this case—so much for years of experience.

"Do you have that vehicle anywhere near Jessica Tuttle's home?" asked Frazer.

Randall shook his head. "Not yet but I sent specifics and they're running it through the ALPR system as we speak. Did he confess?"

"To attacking Dr. Campbell? Yes."

"You're still calling her Dr. Campbell?" Randall laughed tiredly.

Frazer eyed him narrowly. "In here? Yes. But Cromwell isn't admitting anything regarding the other murders, nor to being in contact with Ferris Denker." He checked his watch. "I'm going back to the beach house and through that box of photographs in the hopes of finding some images of Denker."

His cell rang. Parker. "I have to take this." He stepped into the corridor. "What do you have for me?"

"Cell phones are regularly smuggled inside or thrown over the outer walls of the prison. Once inside they're available for a price. I'm pretty sure I saw one of the guards overlook a phone in Denker's cell but the camera angle wasn't great so I can't be sure."

Parker had hacked into the surveillance system, obviously. "I don't want to know," said Frazer.

"Know what?" Parker asked. "I can't get the number off the SIM or a lock onto the device until he turns it on and so far he hasn't."

"The guard might know the number," said Frazer.

"Want me to go ask him?" The calm in Parker's voice told him the man had lost none of his knack for getting in and out of places without anyone knowing he was there.

"I take it Rooney's feeling better?"

"Much." Frazer heard the relief in the other man's voice. "But she says I'm driving her crazy so a little field trip wouldn't be a problem."

It was tempting.

"I don't want him spooked and then warning Denker. Did you see the news?"

"That smarmy sleaze-ball lawyer? Yeah, I saw him. You think he's going to try and play on the governor's sympathies?" asked Parker.

"On the families' sympathies. They'll work on the governor for him, and it'll be a hell of a lot more effective." Frazer pinched the bridge of his nose. A sure sign he needed a break, and he knew who he wanted to see when he took one. It wasn't Randall, and it wasn't Tyson.

"The governor wouldn't let him out to find the bodies, would he?"

Frazer pressed his lips together. "He might if he thought Denker would follow through on his promise and not make him look like an ass."

"Yeah, God forbid a politician ever looks like an ass," Parker said dryly. "Those families need closure, Linc."

The same way Rooney and her parents had needed it only a short time ago. Hell.

"Keep your eyes on that cell phone. I want to know who he's phoning. I want to know if Duncan Cromwell is our guy or not."

"Cromwell and Denker both attended NC State."

"Same time?"

"They crossed over by one year."

"Good. Keep checking. There has to be something solid we can pin down."

"I'm on it."

Frazer hung up and headed out, through the thankfully thinning crowd of press. He ignored their questions and drove straight to Isadora's house.

***

"What are we supposed to be looking for?" Izzy was stretched out on the couch, her head resting on Frazer's thigh. He'd brought over the cardboard box he'd carried home last night. Made them both coffee and told her he needed her help. As she was bored out of her skull with not even the view to look at thanks to the storm shutters, she was grateful for the distraction. She was wearing a knee-length button-up stripy pale blue and white nightshirt, panties, and thick woolen socks. Not exactly seductive. Not even cute. She hadn't thought she'd be having visitors, much less this particular visitor.

Sexy she wasn't. Happy to see him she was.

"Any photographs dated from the late seventies or early eighties, with boys in the shot. Thankfully, Mrs. Mildred Houch wrote the dates on the back."

She frowned. "Is this to do with the current case? Does this mean Cromwell isn't the murderer? Even though he attacked me?" She didn't know why that idea upset her so much. Maybe because she'd been no more to blame for Helena and Kit's deception than he'd been.

Frazer smoothed his hand over her hair. "I have many current cases." His beautiful blue eyes darkened and he bent down to kiss her lips.

"Shouldn't you be at work?" She mumbled, catching him with her good hand and keeping him there when he tried to pull back.

"I'm always working." There was such bleakness in his eyes when he said that, she kissed him deeper.

All the terror from the morning meshed with all the burning need from last night.

"What time is Kit coming home?" he asked roughly.

"She's working until five and then visiting Damien for a couple of hours. Said she'd be back in time for supper."

"Good." He placed the box on the floor and the stack of photographs in his hand on the coffee table. Then he stood and lifted her into his arms. He was gentle, but her ribs were still sore, and she winced. She'd taken another dose of painkillers, but they hadn't taken effect yet.

"Don't worry," he kissed her forehead. "I'm not going to hurt you."

"I think we might end up hurting each other."

Rather than explore that terrible truth, Frazer fused his mouth to hers and walked to her bedroom. He closed the door on Barney who whined at being shut out.

"My poor dog." Izzy chuckled.

"He sleeps with you every night, I only—" He cut himself off.

They both knew this couldn't go anywhere. They'd just met. They both had important work to do. And even if the little voice inside her head insisted she could work anywhere, the sensible, practical Isadora knew it was foolish to follow a man anywhere. But it took the soft vulnerable part of her heart to remind her that he hadn't asked her for anything more than this.

He stood her next to her bed and strode over to make sure the drapes were tightly closed over the shutters. Neither of them wanted their sex life on the NBC evening news, although why anyone would be interested was beyond Izzy.

He came back to stand in front of her, crouching down to undo her nightshirt one button at a time, revealing a pale, vertical strip of flesh. He ran his finger gently down her middle, all the way to her bright pink panties. His finger skimmed the edge of lace and she jolted. He leaned in to nuzzle her neck and gently eased the brushed cotton from her shoulders.

His eyes took in her bruises and uncertainty creased his brow. "We probably shouldn't be doing this." But they didn't have much time left. He'd be leaving soon. They both knew it.

She took his hand in hers and bit the fleshy part of his palm, then licked it better. "We'll figure it out."

She toed off her socks and then realized she was naked except for her panties and her cast. "As much as I'd like to strip you with my teeth, it's going to be a little tricky."

A smile tugged a corner of that beautiful mouth. But he looked serious as he removed his holster and gun and laid them on the dresser. He'd returned her Glock, which was back in the bedside table, much good it had done her earlier. Still, carrying a deadly weapon did bolster her courage although she was going to have to go to the gun range and practice with her weaker hand now.

She watched him undo the buttons on his shirt and then realized he was going slowly, very slowly, enjoying the way her eyes followed every move with avid hunger.

She licked her bottom lip and he paused. Two could play at that game.

He wasn't bulky, which was why he looked so good in a suit. But he was muscled and lean, golden hair sprinkled sparingly over his chest. He shucked his pants and hung them over the back of the chair—ever the federal agent. His legs were solid and strong, an impressive erection tenting the front of his boxers in a way that made her insides clench. The image of him, pinning her to the wall and fucking her blind flashed through her brain.

"What were you thinking about?" he asked carefully.

She smiled. "Sex. Against the wall."

"Put it on the wish list."

"Wish list?"

"Your wish list. Today we're working on my wish list."

It sounded like he thought they had a chance of a future, which they didn't. But Izzy didn't have the heart or the courage right now to tell him the truth.

He made her lie down on the mattress with her feet still touching the floor. He lay down beside her.

"Close your eyes," he ordered.

She did as he asked. It was easier when she didn't have to look at his face, knowing that she wanted this man more than was sensible. He traced his fingers carefully over her body, starting at her brow, over her eyelids, her nose, her mouth. She caught his finger with her lips and sucked. He tasted of paper and ink. She felt his lips touch the corner of her mouth, the stupid mole he seemed to like. Then his hands drifted lower while his lips lingered on hers. He caressed and stroked her breasts, teasing her nipples until they were tight and aching. Only then did his mouth move lower, following his clever hands.

His fingers skimmed her stomach, around her navel, down the crease of her leg, brushing over her labia as he moved to the crease of the other leg. Round and round, brushing her sensitive flesh fleetingly on each pass by. His mouth sucked on her breasts, making the sharp pleasure shoot down to her sex. Her hips started to move, rotate, following his hand, those fingers, her thighs parting, practically begging for him to touch her there.

Finally, he did. He slid his hand over her panties, rubbing the smooth material against her flesh until it was damp with desire.

She reached out to touch him but the angle was wrong for her good arm. She growled in frustration. He kissed her mouth again. Smoothed her hair off her forehead, staring deep into her eyes. "This is about you." Then he sank three fingers inside her all at once and she came on a shuddering breath.

He kissed her again and smiled, dropping off the bed, moving between her legs, shouldering her knees wider apart as his breath blew over the damp fabric of her lingerie. His tongue touched her through the material and her knees started to shake. He rubbed the flat of his tongue over and over her until she couldn't bear it any longer.

"Please," she begged. "I want you inside me."

"I'm *not* going to hurt you."

"The narcotics just kicked in. You're hurting me by not being inside me."

"So now you're high? No."

"Not high. Happy." She gripped his shoulder. "Trust me, the only pain I'm feeling is unsatisfied lust for your exceptional body."

He planted his hands on either side of her head. "Unsatisfied?" he queried.

"Unsatisfied-ish," she qualified before pulling him down for a kiss and tasting herself on his lips.

He pulled back, and one side of his mouth quirked. "Exceptional, huh?"

She traced his features with a fingertip. "Magnificent."

He smoothed her hair back with one hand, his expression uncertain. "I really don't want to hurt you."

She reached out to the bedside table and opened the drawer so he could grab the box of condoms. "I want you, Linc. Inside me. While we still have the chance..." Her voice cracked. "Don't make me beg."

His cold eyes sparked with molten heat. "My terms."

The rustle of a wrapper made her sigh with relief. Then he dragged her panties down her legs and positioned himself at her core, but nothing happened. She opened her eyes to find him staring at her with an odd expression on his face. "What is it?"

He moved forward an inch.

"Oh, God. More." Her back wanted to arch, but her ribs were too sore.

His smile got bigger. "Only if you promise not to move."

"What?"

"I'll do all the work. You just lie back and think happy thoughts."

"I can do that." Her eyes crossed as he pushed inside a fraction more. Her hand grasped the bedspread and gripped tight. "I will get my revenge on you, you know."

"I hope so." The smile reached his eyes when he grinned this time. He leaned back, holding her hips gently as he slowly and inexorably pushed inside her. Her inner muscles gave in to his invasion, stretching, clenching, wanting. Izzy lay there, burning up with sensation when he started to move, his hands keeping her absolutely steady as he moved relentlessly inside her. The wonderful sensation of him slowly, carefully, sliding in and out of her slick wetness made her feel like she could do this all day. Just lie here with him filling her so deliciously. Her orgasm felt as if it was a million miles away, but then it hit her like a hurricane that blew up out of nowhere and she was panting and crying out with desperate little sobs. He kissed her on the mouth as she spun into the stratosphere.

"Think you can lie on your front?" he asked when she returned to Earth.

He helped her roll over and moved her gently down the bed.

"I feel like a geriatric sex fiend," she complained.

"You any less unsatisfied?" he asked, sounding unaffected, but she wasn't fooled.

"Three orgasms or go home, that's what I always say." She laughed, but inside a little piece of her wept. He would go home, and she wasn't sure why the idea left her so bereft.

She felt him behind her then and for a moment remembered Duncan Cromwell beating her as she lay cowering on the ground. But Frazer's touch was feather light, barely grazing her skin as he smoothed the blackening bruises on her torso. With no warning he slid inside her, curling his body protectively over her back, but giving her none of his weight.

It felt amazing. She felt wrapped up in him, filled by him, mesmerized by his strong body, his clean fresh scent, his healing heat.

Then he held her hips again, moving slowly, gently, but going deep, touching her just there and that feeling of wonder spiraled tighter and tighter inside her, contracting down until all that mattered was the friction of his flesh dragging against hers. His hand slipped down between her folds to touch her and she was spinning again, out of control, extraterrestrial, outer space, flying and cartwheeling all the way to Mars. He joined her, shuddered, and cried out.

She pressed her face into the pillow as he withdrew, and he shifted her on the bed and then cradled her to him.

As battered and sore as she was, she'd never had sex that good before. She doubted she'd ever have sex that good again, because it wasn't just about technique or size of the equipment. It was about the human connection. The person you were with. About how you felt about them. What they meant to you. And Izzy had the horrible feeling that Lincoln Frazer could mean everything to her.

His phone rang, and he rolled over to answer it. "Frazer. Yes. In the clearing? You mean *directly* beneath the other body? This is no copycat. It has to be an accomplice." Frazer's voice faded as he left the room and headed into the bathroom. She heard the shower turn on and the words were lost, but not the level of urgency. She rolled onto her side and slowly eased into a sitting position. She found some fresh underwear and loose sweats and pulled them on, one-handed. Forgoing a bra, she dug out a large t-shirt from her drawer, and then a fleece-lined zipped hoodie.

She didn't know what had Frazer all riled up, but she feared the murder investigation wasn't over yet. She went into the living room and sat on the couch, dragging the box toward her. She quickly sorted the photographs into stacks of different years. What had been an unmanageable mess was turning into something much more doable. Organizing was one of the things she did best. Keeping busy kept her sane. Especially when she realized she'd fallen in love with a man who was going to hate her, just as soon as she worked up the courage to tell him the truth about her past.

CHAPTER TWENTY-TWO

Frazer never usually spent more than a couple of nights away from the office. The work was piling up, his agents needed his attention, and yet he wasn't done here. He had a horrible feeling he'd never be done.

He went to check on Isadora sorting the photographs into piles with military efficiency. All composed on the outside, battered and bruised beneath. He went back to the bedroom to get dressed. She'd withdrawn a little—she knew he was leaving soon. Even though they'd agreed it was just sex, neither of them actually believed it. And neither believed they had a future.

She still had secrets he wanted to delve into. Hell, he had secrets, darker than anyone would ever imagine. As much as he wanted to know what made her tick, he couldn't afford that level of honesty.

The phone call he'd received had been Hanrahan. They'd found the body Denker had told them about, not just in the clearing but buried directly below where Elaine Patterson had been found. Not only that, Elaine had been placed in the exact same orientation as the skeleton. It was extremely unlikely this was the work of a copycat or a disciple. The killer had to be someone who'd actually seen the first woman buried. Participated. Ferris Denker had had a partner.

Hanrahan was furious with himself for missing it, but how could he have known? They hadn't even heard about this victim until Denker told them.

How many other women were out there somewhere? Lying in unmarked graves; some serial killer's twisted little secret?

It tied his gut in knots that no matter how hard he worked, how diligently he fought them, there was always another predator out there, biding his time.

Frazer didn't think Denker had always worked with someone, but Denker said this victim was his first kill, the first victim probably for both killers— so they could easily have messed up and left some damning evidence at the scene. Frazer felt certain both killers had attended the school where they'd buried the body.

Was Duncan Cromwell the man who'd honed his killing skills with a young Ferris Denker? Frazer didn't know, but he intended to find out.

Dressed, he headed back into the living room. While he'd been brooding, Isadora had stacked the entire box worth of photographs into about twenty different piles and was now sub-sorting the years he'd mentioned into those images with boys' faces, and those without.

Her efficiency snapped him out of his lethargy.

"What are you looking for?" she asked, sitting back on her heels. She'd put her sling on, so her wrist must be hurting. He hoped that wasn't his fault. If it was, he hoped it had been worth it.

"I'm hoping to find a photograph of a young Duncan Cromwell."

"Really?" She looked surprised.

She pulled out a series of photographs of boys. Then hit the jackpot with a photograph of several hundred kids in the official school portrait for 1979. The problem was he didn't have time to get everyone in the picture age-progressed and he didn't recognize Denker or Cromwell straight off.

"Do you have a scanner?" he asked.

She nodded. "In the office. Go ahead and help yourself." She pointed down the hallway.

"Thanks." He hesitated, trying to remember the manners his mother had tried so hard to instill. "I really appreciate your help."

Isadora smiled but there was a distance there now, one he didn't have time to breach. Later. Later he'd make time. When the case was over and they managed to talk about something other than murder.

Sure. When hell froze over.

God, he needed a life.

The office contained a stack of packing boxes. He flipped open the top of one and realized they were Isadora's belongings, as if she hadn't quite convinced herself she was staying. Did she love it here? Was this where she intended to spend the rest of her life? Or did she resent being forced to stay here and look after a teen who was more than a handful?

Did they have any chance of a relationship? He was a man defined by his job, but she was a doctor and seemed to feel the same way about hers. A couple of days ago, these sorts of musings would have sent him straight out the door, but now he wanted to figure her out—and figure out a way to keep seeing her. To maybe have a future together.

He shook his head at himself. After avoiding any entanglement for the last two decades, he'd gone and fallen for a woman who was guardian to a seventeen-year-old female with an uncanny ability to raise hell. Still, Kit Campbell was a good kid.

Probably.

It didn't take a psychology degree to figure out some of his "issues" stemmed from the fear of being rejected. Most kids who lost a parent had abandonment issues, even when the parent had no choice as to whether or not they left. Fear of rejection led to emotional distancing, which had contributed to the breakup of his disastrous, short-lived marriage. He was scared to let anyone close, scared to reveal that the real him was less than the perfect shell he showed the world.

He rubbed his beard-roughened jaw and knew he really needed to duck next-door to shave. He stayed where he was, booting up the old PC, figuring out how to hook up the scanner.

He heard the TV go on in the living room. Isadora was watching the news. He called Hanrahan and told him what he wanted him to do. It involved a trip to Mildred Houch's house and a truckload of patience as she looked at the school photo. He scanned the image to maintain resolution. Hopefully, Mildred could ID Denker and his friends. And perhaps she'd remember the name Duncan Cromwell, but he didn't want Hanrahan to give her that name upfront. See if the lady came out with it on her own. His old mentor was good at that sort of thing. Good at eking out information. The key was to get people talking without even knowing they were doing it, and then learning how to listen. Frazer's forte was more prodding and poking until he got a reaction. Different things worked on different people.

He emailed the file and then heard a sound from the living room, as if Isadora was in pain. His hand reached for his SIG as he raced out the door.

Isadora's eyes were huge as she stared at the news screen. "The reporter said there is evidence to suggest Ferris Denker didn't kill any of those women. The press is starting to speculate the state might be about to execute an innocent man."

He put his gun away and walked towards her. "Ferris Denker is trying to stir up trouble to get himself out of the hot seat at the end of the month. He's guilty as hell."

She hugged herself with her uninjured arm. The pain in those sage green eyes did something to his insides. "One of the women he was convicted of murdering was the one you found on the beach. Beverley Sandal, right?"

He nodded. The information had been released to the media, but they hadn't IDed the unknown male found with her yet.

"And because of that fact you're now trying to link Duncan Cromwell to Ferris Denker—you're trying to link the new crimes to the old ones." Her knees seemed to give out as she collapsed to the sofa. She pointed at the box of photographs. She'd placed all the ones they hadn't used back into the box. "That's what this is all about, isn't it?"

He nodded, but suddenly the feeling in his gut wasn't admiration or something unnamable. It was dread. Because those eyes told him she knew something he didn't. Something important to this investigation.

She massaged the fingers at the end of her casted wrist. "What if Denker didn't kill Beverley Sandal. Would that change anything?"

The wash of the waves was growing stronger on the beach. The rise of the wind was starting to howl. Everything grew louder inside his head. His own personal storm. "Denker named Beverley as one of his victims."

"But what if he lied?" she insisted. "What if he really is innocent and spent all those years in prison…" She looked as if she was about to throw up.

"That's what he wants us to believe. If he can create doubt about his conviction he might get a stay of execution from a governor notoriously unsympathetic when it comes to condemned killers."

Isadora shook her head and he noted the expression in her eyes. Absolute devastation. "But I know he didn't kill her," she whispered.

Ice spread over his body. "How do you know?"

"Because my father did."

Frazer felt like someone had slammed him into a brick wall. "What do you mean?"

"I have something to tell you." Her voice was fluttery and weak. "I meant to tell you before, but I was worried about Kit, and I honestly didn't know how to bring it up. I didn't plan everything else that happened between us." She bit her lip, and he felt himself shrinking inside, withdrawing, moving further away from the lover and becoming the federal agent he was supposed to be.

He sat beside her, but didn't touch. "Tell me."

She glanced at him, and he knew whatever she said was going to rip him to shreds. He sat there, waiting for it.

"A little over seventeen years ago, I came home late from a party and found my parents in the driveway of the beach house." She pointed outside. "Dad had been away on a business trip and was back early. I saw the light on and ran down to say hi."

The murmur of the storm, the tick of a clock, the muted buzz of the TV, all formed background noise, but only Izzy's words mattered. "I found them sitting on the ground. Mom was holding Dad in her arms, and at first I didn't understand what was going on. I thought he'd had a heart attack or something."

Frazer felt cold all over. Detached. Desolate. But he had a job to do and the job *always* came first—something she'd made him forget for a brief period of time. "Okay, hold on for a moment. I'm going to take you back to that night, Isadora. I want you to lie on the couch and I'm going to hypnotize you and you are going to tell me *everything*." This way she'd be less likely to lie or forget some small relevant detail. "Are you okay with that? If you need a lawyer, say so now."

"No. No lawyer. I want to get this over with." Her eyes met his, swimming with tears, but they didn't affect this version of Lincoln Frazer. This version hunted monsters.

He smiled. "You're in safe hands. Trust me."

***

The distance between them yawned to a gulf as big as the Atlantic stirring up outside. This was what she'd known would happen, what she deserved. The feeling of cold rushed over her with a blast of grief. Whatever they might have had was lost now. Gone. Dead. Destroyed. And she'd been the one to do it.

"Take a few deep breaths..." His voice sounded like an icicle being dragged down her spine.

What did it even matter anymore? Just give him this. Get it over with.

He entranced her with the calm quiet voice she recognized from when he'd hypnotized Jesse. Impersonal. Kind. She hated it, because it hid the real him beneath a cool perfect facade, rather than the flesh and blood man who'd made love to her as if she meant something.

"Let go, Isadora."

The words made her eyelids heavy, and they drifted shut even though she tried to keep them open. Suddenly she was reliving that awful night seventeen years ago...

The first thing she noticed was a light on, down at the beach house. She sure as heck hoped her mother wasn't down there cleaning for any last-minute guests. That was the service industry for you, hard work, constant interruptions, and snarky members of the public thinking you were their slave. Izzy turned off the engine and listened to the hot metal ping as it cooled.

Her mother was pregnant with her fourth child—unfortunately her mom had miscarried the two she'd conceived after Izzy and, after all these years, this was a miracle baby. Now in her ninth month of pregnancy everything looked good, but no one was taking any chances. Izzy got out and dumped her purse on the front step, heading around the side of the house to see what was going on. She followed the path that linked the two properties, hidden behind a row of sage bushes that rustled softly in the breeze.

She smiled when she saw her father's SUV

parked down beneath the rental cottage. He'd been away on a sales trip, but must have come home early. She frowned when she heard raised voices. Her father saying something like "*it isn't what you think.*" And her mother was screaming at him. Words that didn't make any sense. *Murderer. Evil. Monster.* Izzy's heart banged in a nervous staccato.

What was going on? Her parents never argued. They were perfect together, but this was a humdinger. They didn't know she was there. She was torn between giving them privacy and stopping them before someone said something unforgivable or her mother got upset and went into premature labor.

Izzy started to jog forward when an ear-shattering scream pierced the night, followed by an indescribable gurgling sound. She stopped dead for a moment and almost backed up in fear before realizing something terrible had happened to one of her parents.

Running, she rounded the corner and found her mother kneeling on the ground with her father's head propped against her distended stomach, rocking him back and forth.

"Oh, Will. Will. I'm so sorry…" Tears streamed down her mother's cheeks, glistening in the reflection of the porch light.

"Mom?" But her mother didn't hear her.

What on Earth is going on?

Izzy watched in horror as a dark stain spread over her dad's shirt. He wasn't moving. He wasn't breathing. A horrible chill started in her core and expanded outwards until it pushed against the inside of her skin, panic threatening to burst out.

"Mom!" It felt like her voice was coming from

far away. "What happened? What's wrong with Dad?" She wanted to run and call the ambulance but her feet wouldn't move.

"Izzy?" Her mother blinked, coming out of her fugue state with a snap.

"What did you do, Mom?" Izzy asked.

Her mother looked at the man on the ground. Her husband. Izzy's father. Then she blinked and started crying. "It was an accident. I didn't mean to hurt him. I was scared...I thought he was going to kill me."

Her dad wasn't a violent man. This didn't make any sense.

"I'm going to run up to the house and call 911, okay? You stay put and see if you can stop the bleeding."

"You can't do that. You mustn't!" Her mother's eyes grew huge, and she started rocking back and forth.

"He's going to die if I don't," Izzy said sharply. But somehow she knew it was already too late. There was too much blood for her dad to still be alive. She was rooted to the spot in shock and horror. Her mother had just murdered her father. Tears filled her eyes, and she had to concentrate with all her might not to start screaming. If she did she might never stop.

"You don't understand what he's done." Her mother pointed at the car beside her.

Slowly, Izzy walked around. The rear door of the SUV was raised and inside, a naked girl lay curled up on a sheet of plastic, partly hidden by a blanket. Izzy blinked. It was like she'd been thrown into the middle of a horror movie with no idea as to what her lines were. The girl's hands and feet were bound with duct tape. Tape also covered her mouth. She was obviously dead.

Izzy's legs started to shake. "I-I don't understand, Mom."

"He came home half an hour ago. I was asleep at the house, but I heard his car, and I saw him come down here to the beach house. He'd mentioned he was going to fix the pilot light on the gas boiler in case we got any last minute bookings. My back was sore so I thought I'd take a walk." She sniffed, tears flowing down her cheeks and dripping onto Izzy's father's hair.

"I found him bending over that poor woman in the trunk." Her mother's breath rattled in her chest. Izzy felt the echo inside her own. "He tried to deny it, but how could he deny anything?" Her mom's voice grew strident, but her eyes lost focus. "I accused him of being the serial killer the police are looking for on the mainland and he *laughed* at me! Then he lunged toward me." She finally focused on Izzy again. "I stabbed him with this." Her left hand groped in the sand before raising a long screwdriver. Crimson blood coated the shaft and handle.

Izzy's thoughts crackled inside her head like there was interference in the atmosphere and she couldn't understand the conversation. But she could. She knew exactly what had happened. Her mother had murdered her father with a screwdriver because she thought her father was a serial killer. She looked back at the pale glimmering corpse of the woman in the trunk. A thick silver chain encircled her wrist. A medical alert bracelet.

Gore rose up inside Izzy's throat, burning the soft tissue of her gullet. Every nightmare she'd ever had paled next to this new grim reality. She went over and felt for the pulse in her father's neck. Searched frantically for a few long seconds before recognizing the vacant eyes for what they really were. Dead.

A wave of absolute dread hit her. "We need to call the cops, Mom."

"No." Her mother climbed awkwardly to her feet, holding her baby bump with her right hand. "No."

"Mom, we have to tell the cops." Revulsion and grief raced through her as she looked at her beloved father. "They'll know you did this in self-defense. It was an accident."

"No. They'll take away my baby!" Her mother backed up a step, shaking her head. "Do you know what will happen when they find out your father was a killer? Do you think they'll believe we didn't know about it? We'll be pariahs, shunned." She rubbed the hand holding the screwdriver over her belly in a way that disturbed Izzy.

"How could I not know I was married to a monster? *Oh, God*, I *loved* a monster. A monster who slept in my bed every night and fathered my children."

Izzy's father was a murderer...she couldn't believe it. There had to be some mistake but the girl in the trunk said otherwise.

"We *have* to tell the cops, Mom," Izzy insisted. She pointed to the bodies. "What else are we going to do? Bury them in the sand dunes?" She was being sarcastic, but her mother started nodding.

"Yes. That's exactly what we're going to do."

"Err, no. That's nuts." Izzy flinched when her mother grabbed her arm, short fingernails digging into her flesh. She waved the bloody screwdriver. "Do you know what he did to those girls? Look at her." Her mom spun her around and pointed at the bound naked girl. "He kidnapped her. Raped her. And then he killed her. Do you think she's the only one? Do you know what will happen to us? I'll be arrested and questioned. I'll probably lose this baby or she'll be born in prison. You'll have to take care of her. Is that what you want?"

Izzy scrubbed her shaking hands over her face. She didn't want any of this. Her mother was verging on hysteria and no wonder. The community of Rosetown was close-knit and superstitious. Gossip and speculation about everyone's private business was a way of life here, but they'd deal with it.

"We still have to go to the cops, Mom. They'll know what to do."

Her mother backed up, cradling her stomach. "If you do that, Izzy, if you tell anyone, I'll kill myself." The screwdriver rose to hover near the tender skin of her neck. "I can't live with the idea that your father…that he lied to me and I was foolish enough to believe him." Her eyes bulged.

"You're not thinking straight, Mom."

Her mother placed the screwdriver against her throat. "I'm not kidding, Izzy. I can't live with the idea other people will find out what he did. What I did." Her eyes flashed to the dead man on the ground.

Izzy's hands clenched and unclenched. She couldn't believe this was happening. She'd gone from being a normal teen sneaking out to a party to being on the verge of losing everyone she loved, and she hadn't even gotten over losing Shane yet.

Her mother was clinging to the narrowest edge of sanity. She was all Izzy had left, and she carried an innocent baby inside her who needed protecting.

Her mother's hand tightened on the handle of the screwdriver.

"Stop," said Izzy, swallowing down hard. "We'll do it your way. I'll move the car a bit so we don't have to carry him—" Her voice stumbled over the distant pronoun. "*Him,*" not dad or daddy. "*Him*" said with an inflection of hatred, of abhorrence. "We don't want to drag him so far. Don't strain yourself," she warned, thinking of the baby.

Izzy hauled her father sideways and then pushed him up on top of the dead girl.

"We'll need to get rid of this car after we get rid of the body," her mother told her.

God. Izzy wanted to vomit as her father's blood soaked into her t-shirt. She couldn't believe she was doing this. Izzy eyed her mother's bloodstained nightgown. "I'll go get us a change of clothes from the house, and some rubber boots. You get a shovel from the shed. I'll fetch your coat. You follow me in the van and we'll go out to Parson's Point." They were about to slap a protection order on the dunes, which meant the chances of the bodies being discovered would be reduced. She needed to get her mom through the next couple of weeks. Keep her healthy enough to have her baby. Then she'd persuade her to go to the cops and tell the truth.

Izzy ran into the main house. She knew nothing would ever be the same again. Hopefully God could forgive her for what she was about to do, because she sure as hell would never be able to forgive herself.

***

Frazer carefully brought Isadora back into the present, trying to figure out how this affected things. The case. Not them. There was no them. Had he really considered a relationship? Stick to sex—apparently, it really was the only non-job related thing he was good at.

She blinked awake, quickly going from seventeen-year-old girl in a panic, to mature woman with years of life experience. Her green eyes went to him as she shifted herself carefully into a sitting position. Even though she looked awkward and uncomfortable, he didn't offer to help.

"I should have told you this as soon as they found Helena." Her voice was croaky.

"Yes."

She flinched.

What the hell did she expect?

"Will you promise me one thing?"

Seriously? She was asking for promises?

"Talk to Kit for me. Explain it isn't her fault."

Frazer hardened his heart. Had she seduced him on purpose? Had she been snooping to see what they discovered? "You should have told the police years ago."

She nodded. "I know. I ran away instead." She looked remarkably composed now. As if unburdening herself had lifted her guilt. Well, lucky fucking her.

"You left a mentally unstable killer in charge of an infant?"

Isadora's mouth tightened. "My mother wasn't unstable, she was overwrought that night. I watched her with Kit after she was born, and she was a great mom. I would never have gone away if I thought she'd hurt a baby."

He raised a skeptical brow. "How did you explain your father's absence?"

"She told people Dad left her. After a year or so she told them she'd heard he died."

"People accepted it?"

"She was the local here. Yes," she rubbed her arms, "people accepted it."

"Did Ted know?"

He stared at her and realized that although she looked calm on the outside she was actually trembling. She hid her feelings well. So did he.

She shook her head. "I don't think so."

Someone knew. His eyes narrowed.

"Are you going to arrest me?" she asked in a very small voice.

"I don't know yet. I need you to keep this information to yourself for now—"

"But Ferris Denker might be innocent."

"He was never innocent!" Frazer lost it then. This was one of the things Denker had kept up his sleeve, and he wasn't about to let him use it to save his sorry ass. "You know when they caught him, Denker? He had a woman in his trunk?"

She nodded, probably remembering the woman in her father's trunk—Beverley Sandal.

"Was the woman in your father's car mutilated in any way?"

Her eyes flashed in surprise. "What? No."

"Then you're right, Ferris Denker probably didn't kill Beverley Sandal." He drew in a long breath to steady himself. "When the highway patrol pulled Ferris Denker over with a broken taillight they noticed he had blood on his jacket. That's because Denker's sexual proclivities included cutting off women's breasts. The woman in the trunk? He cut off her breasts while she was still alive."

Isadora's throat worked convulsively, but he was done with hiding the exact shape of Ferris Denker's monster.

"He had one breast in each of his jacket pockets, placed in freezer bags. When the officers searched his house they found a freezer full. When he confessed, he told detectives he liked to suck on women's tits. He'd take his victims' breasts out of the freezer, and he'd suck on the nipples while he jacked off to the memories of torturing them. He. Was. Never. Innocent!" His voice shook the room and he realized he was shouting and Isadora was crying with Barney pressed against her.

Christ. He dragged his hands over his face and drew in another breath because what he was about to say would probably hurt her even more. "But I think your father may have been innocent."

Her chin came up. "What?"

"In case you hadn't noticed, there's another serial killer operating right here on the Outer Banks."

Her eyes flashed. Smart women hated their intellect questioned.

"The killer knew where you buried Beverley Sandal because they probably followed you that night. They knew Beverley was wearing that bracelet because she was wearing it when they killed her. A few days ago they dug it up and put it on a fresh victim."

Realization dawned on Isadora's face. One of her hands rose to cover her mouth. The look in her eyes was one of complete and utter devastation.

He didn't care. "You said your dad was trying to tell your mom that the dead girl wasn't what she thought?"

She jerked her head in a sharp nod.

"She should have listened to him."

Isadora said nothing. Just looked at him with a shattered gaze.

"Did someone else have access to his car?"

"I have no idea." She searched his face. "You really think he might not have done it?" Her voice was an anguished whisper that sliced him open. But she didn't weep. No tears fell.

He ran his hand through his hair. Her self-contained torment got to him, but he couldn't afford to let her distract him any more than he'd already been distracted. He had work to do. Isadora Campbell had slowed him down.

"There may be way too many serial killers in this world, Dr. Campbell—trust me, I know—but to have two, right here in Rosetown? Killing women in exactly the same manner? It's the same guy, which is something you could have confirmed for me days ago if only you'd told me the truth."

She seemed to shrivel in front of him, but it pushed her away from him, and he needed her far, far away from him now.

His phone rang. He listened for a moment and then hung up. "Another woman was reported missing." *And it's your fault* seemed to reverberate unspoken around the room.

He let it.

He grabbed his jacket, shoes, and left without reminding her to lock up or saying goodbye. It was too late for goodbye.

CHAPTER TWENTY-THREE

Izzy sat on the couch, stunned. The shaking in her limbs was so bad she couldn't stand without falling over. Her father might be innocent. Her dad might not have killed the poor woman who'd been in the trunk of his car.

The knowledge took a moment to settle in. Her father had been innocent, and she and her mother were the criminals—along with some insidious murderer who, if Linc was correct, was still plying his evil trade. It was insanity, and yet a weight lifted off with that knowledge, only to be replaced by grief and remorse at how they'd desecrated a good man's memory.

The trembling in her limbs eased as she took a few deep breaths. She had no idea what would happen next, but at some point, when Lincoln Frazer could be bothered, he'd have her arrested and sent to jail. Which was fine. She blinked away the tears that wanted to form.

Maybe it wasn't fine, but it was okay. She was a strong person, she'd get through it. Move on.

Would the medical board take away her license? Would anyone hire someone who'd done what she had done? Would the Army take her back? She didn't know. All her knowledge and training might go to waste. She could help people, but she might never be allowed to again.

God, she felt cold. Her teeth actually chattered, and she went into the bedroom to chase down her socks. She ignored the messy bed where Lincoln Frazer had made love to her for long enough to convince her he might have feelings for her, before he'd booted her to the curb.

She'd told him she'd helped her mom hide two murders. What had she expected?

Exactly what she'd got.

What she hadn't expected was that it would hurt quite so much. That his coldness would rip into her flesh and tear out what was left of her heart. His reaction had reaffirmed all the reasons she'd kept quiet all these years. But that was cowardice, what she'd done was wrong, and he so obviously tried to do the right thing all the time. She hoped he sent someone else to arrest her. The thought of him taking her in, maybe having to listen to him confess the awful error of screwing her senseless a couple times before he found out the despicable truth. Nausea churned in her stomach.

Whatever happened she hoped he'd sit down and talk to Kit. Explain the situation.

Dammit, she needed to tell Kit herself.

It wasn't Frazer's problem—he was here investigating a murder and they'd had a fling, it didn't mean he was suddenly responsible for the emotional wellbeing of a young woman he barely knew. As awful as the truth was, it was better coming from her, especially with Frazer's small crumb of comfort that her father might not have been a killer.

Crap. That knowledge would have driven her mother over the edge. She hadn't believed him when he'd denied it. Love hadn't been enough to earn her mother's blind trust even after years of marriage.

Izzy finished pulling on her woolen socks using her good hand and grabbed her cell phone. She dialed Kit but got voicemail. She checked her watch. It was only 4.45 PM so she was probably still on duty at the diner. She checked the tracker app only to discover she couldn't see Kit's phone. Dammit.

Unable to settle, she called the diner. Sal answered.

"Can I talk to Kit, Sal? It's important."

"I let her go early. Did you hear? Mary Neville is missing so I closed the place down. I swear to God, if anything bad happens to Mary, I'm gonna—"

She cut in. "Did Kit say where she was going?" Sal was from New York and once he started talking he wouldn't stop, especially when it came to issuing threats.

"Nah. She just took off in her little car."

Izzy said goodbye to Sal and put the phone down, collapsing onto the sofa.

If Mary Neville had been abducted, then Duncan Cromwell wasn't the killer. His attack on her had been personal, because of Helena. Did that make her feel better about having the shit kicked out of her?

Not really.

Frustrated, she didn't know what to do with herself. She didn't even have a car, not that she could drive anywhere if she did. Maybe that's why Frazer had left her here like this. He knew she was stranded. At least she had her Glock. She went into the bedroom and brought it back into the living room, setting it on the coffee table beside Frazer's box of photographs.

She needed to get hold of Kit ASAP. She didn't have Damien Ridgeway's number, but she had Pastor Rice's. She called him.

"Izzy! What can I do for you?"

"I know this is probably a weird question, but can you see Kit's car outside on the street?" she asked.

"Hang on, I'll go look." It only took him a moment. "Nope."

"Darn."

"Can I do anything to help?" The pastor must have heard her distress along the phone lines.

"Would you call me if she turns up?"

"Of course. Nothing I like more than twitching the drapes." The man laughed and she tried to respond.

"Thanks, Pastor, I appreciate it." There was a sharp knock at her door. Her mouth went dry and her hands grew clammy. "Sorry, I have to go."

***

Frazer didn't remember the last time he'd been this angry. Maybe the day in the West Virginian woods when he'd learned not to trust the people giving orders. The anger felt good. It felt righteous. It burned away every scrap of sympathy he felt for Isadora Campbell.

Another woman was missing, and she'd withheld information that could have helped him nail down his profile and find the killer.

He needed to keep telling himself this.

Randall answered on the fifth ring.

"Who's missing?" Frazer asked.

"Mary Neville. She's a waitress at the diner in Rosetown." Where Kit worked. Another goddamn connection to the Campbells. "Hasn't been seen since she was dropped off at home by a Carl Kent last night. He swears he watched her go into the house and then left."

"Any witnesses?"

"Are there ever?"

"How do we know she's missing?"

"She was supposed to visit her sister but didn't show. Sister went to the house and found signs of a struggle. She called the police straightaway."

Frazer grimaced. Different MO, but what were the chances of it being unrelated to the current spate of abductions and murders?

"I think I've got something." Frazer heard excitement rising in Randall's voice. "I checked out all the vehicles that the ALPR couldn't read the license plates of and I think I found our van."

"Was it Cromwell's work van?"

"No. It was a big white panel van. No markings. Someone sprayed the plate with a reflective coating to stop the image analysis program being able to distinguish the numbers from the background."

"And?" Frazer knew how the spray worked.

"Same van was picked up on cameras in Greenville and in Maysville on the day of Elaine Patterson's murder."

"Any ID on the driver?"

"No. He wore a ball cap and dark glasses."

"So how does this help?" Frazer asked, maneuvering around TV vans that stretched down the main street of Rosetown.

"I recognized the vehicle from a little disco ball that hangs from the rearview mirror. It belongs to Ted Brubaker. Izzy and Kit Campbell's uncle."

Who'd had access to Isadora's father's vehicle

and could easily have watched them bury the bodies all those years ago. Shit. The bell in his head rang—ding, ding, ding.

"We got a signed warrant to go search his property and vehicles. Where are you?"

"Pulling into the parking lot of the police station."

"Don't. Keep going north and take the first left after you cross the bridge. Chief Tyson organized a news conference in about twenty minutes to keep our media pals otherwise occupied."

Frazer turned the wheel of his sedan, heading out slowly as reporters eyed him like crocodiles eyed prey. Crossing the bridge, he passed Seth Grundy driving Isadora's Subaru. The guy raised his hand in greeting. Frazer drove on.

Waves crashed against the bridge's pillars and sprayed sea foam across his windshield. Frazer turned on the wipers, salt smearing across the glass until the wiper fluid cleared it.

If the killer was Isadora's uncle, this was going to hit her hard. He remembered that the only thing she'd asked of him was to protect her sister, who was the exact same age she'd been when her mother had put her in an untenable position.

Had Isadora ever had anyone look out for her—ever? The thought punched against his throat, but he didn't have time to think about it. He was turning down a rutted side road and pulling up behind five squad cars surrounded by officers all wearing bulletproof vests. Randall waved him over, and Frazer got out, retrieving his own vest from his bag and checking his sidearm.

The wind howled through the trees that were bent over from the oncoming storm.

"Feels like a hurricane," Frazer said to Tyson—who was going to be late for his own press conference.

"This is nothing like a hurricane. We can still stand up." The man grinned. "This is just a tempest."

Frazer looked at him from under his brow. Sure. They all crowded together near one of the vehicles. Hank Wright was conspicuously absent. "Two officers around the back, one covering the storm cellar doors. Four more officers on the barn, in case he's in there with our missing woman."

That left one officer with the vehicles—in case Brubaker got past all of them, and to stop anyone entering the scene—and four of them, him, Randall, Tyson and a female officer knocking on the front door.

Everyone had their weapons in double-handed grips and pointed at the ground. The female officer carried the breacher in case Brubaker didn't want to open up.

They jogged over to the porch steps. There were a couple of loose boards and the place needed a fresh coat of paint but it was by no means dilapidated. Storm shutters were on all the windows. Tyson knocked hard and yelled, "Rosetown Police Department. Open up, now!"

Frazer strained to hear anything over the violently lashing trees but couldn't. He flashed to Isadora's green eyes as she'd told him her secret.

They'd been full of loneliness.

His throat felt like he'd swallowed thorns. If anyone understood all-encompassing loneliness, it was him.

Why the fuck was he thinking about a woman

who'd blatantly lied to him about a murder when he was in the middle of a takedown? He needed to push Isadora out of his head and forget about her. She'd lied to him. She hadn't trusted him because when it came down to it, she didn't trust anyone.

And if the word hypocrite reverberated around his skull, that was his problem.

***

Izzy peeked through the office window to see who was knocking at her door. A bolt of relief shot through her when she saw it wasn't a police officer there to arrest her. God, what would she do when it was? Run away? Pee her pants?

She shoved her cell phone into her back pocket, went to the door, and opened it.

"Hi, Seth." He held the keys out to her, and she took them with a grateful smile. "You didn't have to bring it over, but I appreciate it." She bit her lip. "How are you going to get home though? I'm not supposed to drive yet." She held up her cast with a self-pitying grimace.

"I threw a bike in the back. Hope I didn't get any marks on your upholstery."

She waved him inside. "It won't be any worse than wet stinky dog. I really appreciate it. Come on in while I write you a check."

He hesitated on the threshold and then came inside, wiping his feet on the front mat, bending to take off his shoes.

"Don't worry about those. I'm going to mop the floors later." *Assuming I haven't been arrested for interfering with a police investigation and illegally disposing of dead bodies.* Seriously, how had she ever thought that was okay? No wonder she'd run away to join the Army Medical Corps.

She decided to ignore the fact he was wearing the same black jacket Ted had worn last night.

"You heard anything about that cocksucker, Cromwell?" asked Seth.

"Nothing." She wasn't offended by his language. She'd been a captain in the Army. She dug deep in the recesses of her purse for her checkbook. She clicked on her pen and started writing awkwardly with her casted hand. "What do I owe you?"

He gave her a very reasonable figure, and she wrote out the check. She was still anxious to track down Kit, but this guy had saved her life today. She couldn't blow him off. "Would you like a coffee or a beer or anything?"

He ambled around the room, looking at the framed photos on the mantel. He pulled out the one of her mother and father's wedding and put it at the front. She flinched.

"He was a good guy, your daddy. I used to enjoy the barbecues he and your mother threw."

Izzy wrapped her good arm tight around her middle. She'd forgotten all about their annual July 4th celebrations.

Hands in his pockets, he ambled over to look inside the box of photos that sat on the table. "You going through some old stuff?" Something caught his eye. He leaned down and picked up the photograph of the entire school. "Where did this come from?"

She signed the check with a wobbly flourish, struggling to tear the perforation with only one good hand. "Some old lady called Mildred Houch,

376

apparently."

"That old boot still alive?"

She paused in the act of walking around the kitchen counter to hand him the check. "You went to that school?" Her voice cracked nervously.

He looked up and smiled as he seemed to realize his mistake. The smile never reached his eyes. The calculating coldness she saw there made alarm streak over her flesh. Her eyes darted to her gun, lying so far away on the coffee table.

Seth saw it, too. As his fingers reached for it, Izzy bolted. Footsteps rang out behind her, but she was fit and fast. She could get out before he got off a shot. She skidded in her socks, but hit the front door and thought she'd made it, only to be slammed by what felt like a rhino landing on her back and dragging her to the floor. The air was squeezed out of her lungs and her damaged ribs felt like they'd shattered. The agony was all-consuming. She couldn't breathe, couldn't scream, couldn't think.

Seth panted heavily, holding her down as he caught his breath. Horror crawled around inside her skin and threatened to erupt into hysteria. Somehow she held her panic at bay. Seth had saved her life earlier. He couldn't be the killer...but he was. She knew it as surely as she knew the color of her own eyes.

She shifted slightly, testing her range of motion. He grabbed her good arm and twisted it high and tight behind her back. Pain shot from her elbow to her shoulder and she cried out. The way he paused at her scream made a chill run along her spine. As if it excited his prey drive and made him forget they were supposed to be friends. He rolled her onto her back, rough fingers biting deep into her skin. It hurt, but she wasn't about to show him any more pain or fear. Barney danced around them as if wondering why they were on the floor and could he play, too? Her dog knew Seth. Liked him. He was obviously no better judge of character than she was.

She lay quietly, knowing that in her weakened state she was going to have to wait for the right opportunity to either grab her gun or escape. The good news was her cell was in her pocket, and he didn't seem inclined to search her.

A thought occurred to her. "Where's Kit? What did you do with her?"

Something ran through the man's eyes but she couldn't read him. Dammit.

"Come quietly and I'll take you to her." The rigid metal of her gun pressed against her temple.

Izzy swallowed to wet her suddenly dry mouth. Like she had a choice. "Is she alive?"

"I'd never hurt, Kit, Izzy." Seth whispered in her ear and 'tut-tutted' at her. "I've watched over her since the day she was born. She's the closest thing I've got to a daughter."

A wave of horror washed over her at the idea he'd taken a special interest in her sister. "What about Mary Neville? You were jealous of Carl getting a date with her, weren't you?"

"Mary's fine. Just a bit tied up right now, is all."

She flashed back to that girl in her father's trunk all those years ago. She didn't believe him. He let go of her arm and stood back far enough away that she couldn't attack him without him shooting her first. Although she'd rather be shot than endure what he had in mind.

"It was you who attacked me under the deck." She nodded to below the house. She thought about what he'd done to a girl as sweet as Helena. The idea made her stomach roil.

"You had to interfere. Couldn't leave it alone."

As if it was all her fault. Hell, in the mind of a serial killer, it probably was. She rolled slowly to her knees, not having to pretend her wooziness as she held onto the wall. She needed to stall, but Frazer could be gone for hours. Realistically, he might never come back.

It hurt, she finally allowed herself to acknowledge. The fact he'd walked out of here pissed. She got it—she'd gotten close and he probably felt as if she'd betrayed him. Between her and the ex-wife, she doubted any woman would ever get close again. She'd been the wrong woman to take that leap of faith with, as he'd figured out pretty damn quick. At least he wouldn't have a broken heart. That was just her. Although she doubted Seth would let her suffer for long.

She brought one foot up, bracing to stand. "Why'd you take my shovel? Why not use your own?"

"You *know* why I took your shovel." His mustache twitched, but his eyes didn't change expression. Had they ever been anything except dark and beady? "I've been watching you ever since you hauled your old man out of the back of that SUV and shoved him in that pit."

The knot in her stomach tightened. He thought she was like him.

"How'd that feel, Izzy? Burying your old man before you even knew for sure he was really dead?"

"He was dead," she said.

"He could have been saved—with your training you must know that now."

Did she? Could she have saved her father's life if she'd called an ambulance rather than given in to her mother's hysteria?

Maybe. The knowledge was another nail in her soul.

"I always reckoned that's why you went into medicine. To try and figure out how many ways you let him down. You wanna know the best thing?"

Her eyes filled with tears, but she blinked them away. She wasn't about to let them fall.

Seth laughed. "He wasn't even the killer. He got a flat as he was leaving town on that business trip and I lent him one of my cars. Your daddy came back a day early and I hadn't had time to get rid of the body outta the trunk yet." He laughed. "He drove away without knowing she was in there. Until your momma stabbed him, that is. Poor bastard."

Frazer had been right. Her father was innocent.

Thank God.

She brought herself to her feet, swaying slightly from the pain that sliced through her chest.

"I'd been out on another job and got back to the garage and found his car gone, body along with it. I about shit myself. Raced off down here, figuring I was either going to have to kill him or run, depending on whether or not he'd called the cops."

"Instead you saw my mom kill her own husband in what she thought was self-defense."

He scratched his forehead. "That was

unexpected. Not as unexpected as you helping her get rid of the bodies though. That made me see you in an entirely different light. I always liked you, Izzy." His gaze ran down her body in a way that made her stomach twist.

"What made you stop killing?" Stall, stall, stall.

His brows bobbed. "What makes you think I stopped? I just traveled elsewhere." One side of his lips twitched. "Way I see it, you've got no choice but to do what I say. If you don't I'll tell the FBI all about you."

"Too late. I already told them."

Something flashed through his eyes, something dark and wily. He grabbed Barney's collar, pointed the Glock at the retriever's silky head. "Get in the car without any fuss, Izzy. Else I'll shoot your stupid dog."

CHAPTER TWENTY-FOUR

Seth forced her to get behind the wheel, despite her damaged wrist. The moment he put the gun to Barney's head she knew she was probably dead. She'd do whatever he wanted to save her dog or her sister.

Seth climbed in beside her, Barney held firmly at his feet. The barrel of her gun pointed squarely at her chest. She tried not to think about the damage a bullet could do at close range. She'd seen the results and didn't want to experience them firsthand.

She glanced into the back of her car. The seat was down, and a bike was wedged inside just as he'd said. At least it wasn't a body. As she reversed out of her driveway, her eyes caught the shovel she and all islanders carried in their trunks.

"Where to?" she asked.

"South."

"Where are we going?"

He jerked on Barney's collar, forcing the dog's head up at a sharp angle. "Quiet."

She headed south, sea oats lashing along the margins of the highway. Her headlights cut through darkness and made her feel like she was trapped in a tunnel. She tried to think what the hell to do. They were headed toward a more deserted part of the islands. "Does Ted know about any of this?"

Seth gave an ugly snort. "That pussy? His idea of excitement is sneaking a look down some waitress's blouse."

She didn't want to know what his idea of

excitement was, but he told her anyway. "He has no clue what it feels like to hold someone's life in your hands. You do, though." He eyed her speculatively, then turned away. "I'm pretty sure if Teddy boy gets to have sex again, he's gonna die of a fucking heart attack."

Izzy's mind flashed to the panties in Ted's van. The van had been at Seth's garage the day before. She had the horrible suspicion that part of Seth's MO was to use other people's vehicles to commit his crimes. The idea made her shudder.

"You ever killed anyone on purpose?" he asked suddenly.

"What? No."

"You ever brought anyone back to life?"

She didn't know where he was going with this. "I've resuscitated people after their heart has stopped, yes."

"Did they ever see anything?"

The guy had lost his ever-loving mind. "Like what?"

He glanced at her, shifting in his seat. "The lights, the woman who comes for you."

Izzy was sore from ribs to wrist. Her head throbbed from a headache and fear. And he was talking near-death experiences? She'd be happy to provide him with one.

Stall.

She frowned, trying to remember what people she'd revived had said. "Some of them claimed to see bright lights. One guy said he'd found himself in a field, stroking a massive tiger." She'd put it down to the drugs he'd had an allergic reaction to.

Seth was eating up the words.

"Did you have an experience like that, Seth?"

she guessed.

He nodded. "When I was fourteen I went swimming in a quarry with Ferris and a boy called Sidney. There was a car down there and we were all trying to swim through it. Sidney got caught up on the steering column and couldn't get out in time. Me and Ferris tried to save him but he swallowed water and panicked. We couldn't get him out."

He was so deep in memory Izzy contemplated jumping out of the car and making a run for it, but he still had Barney and he'd probably catch her on this open stretch of the island. She not only had to survive the fall with her broken wrist and battered ribs, she also had to outrun a madman with a gun.

"You said you almost died?" she prodded.

He gave her a curt nod and his eyes seemed to tear up. "It was beautiful. I never felt so much love or peace as I did in those few seconds."

"What happened?"

He shot out an angry snort. "Some fucking bitch 'saved' me. Jesus, I wanted to hit her and dive back into the water but they pinned me down. They dragged Sidney out too and kept trying to revive him. I told them to leave him alone, but no one listened. Anyway, he was lucky."

"But he drowned?" she queried.

"Exactly." He looked out the window. "Pull over on the side of the road, right here."

Izzy looked outside and dread settled into her bones. She put on her blinker and pulled over—talk about a rule follower. She spotted the lighthouse up ahead. He grabbed the keys and opened the door, dragging Barney with him. Quickly, she pulled out her phone, hit 911 and thrust it under the seat, praying he didn't notice. He opened the trunk and took out the shovel.

They were at Parson's Point. And if she followed him into the dunes, she was a dead woman.

***

Tyson knocked on Brubaker's door, harder this time. Still there was no noise from inside. He was about to motion the breacher forward when the door swung open. Ted Brubaker stood there openmouthed, obviously about to leave as two officers rushed past him. Tyson patted the guy down and then cuffed him, reading him his rights.

"What the hell is going on?" he shouted.

Frazer ignored the question as he helped clear rooms. It was dark and creepy inside, but there wasn't anyone else immediately visible.

"I'm going to check the van." Frazer pulled latex gloves from a box in the closest squad car. He approached the vehicle with Randall at his side. He rolled open the door and cautiously climbed inside. No female hostage. Shit. He had a horrible feeling they might be too late for Mary Neville.

It certainly looked like the same van from the photographs on Jessica Tuttle's cell phone. A piece of balled up material caught his eye. He reached out and carefully picked it up. A woman's thong unraveled.

"Pretty sure I wouldn't want to see Ted Brubaker wearing that," said Randall.

Frazer bagged it and noted it in the evidence log. This was definitely their guy.

He went over to where the chief was questioning him. Brubaker started giving him the usual denials. Frazer stopped listening. "We've got evidence placing you in Maysville day before yesterday. If you tell us where Mary Neville is, I'll make sure the judge knows you cooperated with authorities."

"Mary? Why the hell would I know where Mary is?"

Frazer tried to hide his disgust, not just at the guy's denials, but also the fact he'd murdered his niece's best friend in cold blood, causing someone he claimed to care about extreme distress.

Brubaker shook his head. "Look, buddy, I wasn't in Maysville day before yesterday. I was right here."

"We have photographic evidence placing your van in Maysville," Frazer told him.

Brubaker snorted. "Which proves how full of shit this whole thing is. My van was in the shop until this morning because it needed a new alternator. It didn't go anywhere."

Frazer's whole body snapped to attention. "Which shop?"

"Seth Grundy's place."

Frazer staggered back as if he'd been shot. Tyson put Brubaker none too gently in the back of a squad car.

The clock was ticking in his head as the image of Seth driving Isadora's SUV flashed through his mind, but he didn't rush. Headless chickens didn't make good law enforcement officers. Frazer made a quick call to Hanrahan. The man was in Mildred Houch's living room. "Ask her if the name Ted Brubaker means anything to her."

"Mildred says no."

"Now ask her about Seth Grundy."

Hanrahan repeated the name and Frazer heard the "Oh, yes! That's the name I was trying to remember," in the background.

Then Hanrahan came back on the line. "Mildred says he was one of Denker's best friends. He almost drowned, but a teacher rescued him. One of his friends died though. This help?"

"I think we just found Denker's accomplice." Frazer hung up. "You can let Brubaker go. Get a new warrant for Seth Grundy's workplace." He pointed at the white van. "That is evidence. Impound it. Grundy is our man."

Chief Tyson pulled out his cell. "I'll call dispatch to put out an APB."

Frazer's heart pounded as he shook his head. "I know where he is. I saw him headed south on Highway 12 ten minutes ago, driving Dr. Campbell's SUV." His brain flashed to the image and he swallowed his frustration. He'd missed the obvious. "Put up road blocks, north and south. Let's pin this bastard down."

He started running, Randall on his heels as they scrambled to go after this new suspect. And suddenly Frazer realized he'd screwed everything up. He got in the car and wished he had sirens. Didn't matter. He floored it, driving backwards along the pitted lane as Randall battled with his seat belt.

He sped out onto the highway screeching across the road, narrowly missing another vehicle. Then he put it in drive and prayed that he was in time, or that Grundy was just using Isadora's car the way he used other people's. To throw cops off the scent. To get rid of evidence. He dialed Isadora's cell number, but it came back busy.

"Try Kit," he told Randall as he concentrated on not crashing into the bridge barricades.

The thing that mattered most to him right now was a woman who had more courage than he had ever owned. She'd admitted her past mistakes, and he'd despised her. But Frazer didn't dare risk exposing his faults or past mistakes. He had to be perfect. He'd had to be perfect since the moment he was rescued from that fleapit motel in fucking Ohio.

Perfect. Worthy. Important.

Because that's how he'd survived those five horrific days and somewhere, deep inside, he'd associated perfection with the hope of being loved, the way a serial killer associated someone else's pain with their own sexual arousal. Same mechanism. Different character flaw.

Isadora Campbell wasn't perfect. What the hell would he do with anyone who was? If they didn't bore him to death, they'd reflect his own glaring flaws so boldly a relationship wouldn't last a week. What the hell was perfection anyway? Even the concept made no sense.

What did he really want out of life? To chase killers? To save people?

That was important, but was it enough?

And what did being *saved* matter if you didn't live your life to the fullest extent afterwards? And what good was being "perfect" when you were too much of a coward to risk the one thing that truly mattered—your heart.

He got to the Campbell house in record time. No vehicle in the drive. Good news? Or bad? Weapon drawn, he dashed up the steps and burst through the door. But the house was empty. There was just the box of photographs on the table. If Grundy had seen them he'd realize it was only a matter of time before they tracked him down.

"Did you reach Kit?" he asked.

Randall nodded. "Yes. Izzy tried to call her, but she'd turned her phone off. She doesn't know where she is."

There was a slip of paper on the floor. Frazer crouched down and saw it was a check made out to Seth Grundy. He climbed back to his feet.

"Grundy was here," he told Randall. "I'm going to get Parker looking for her phone, and we'll block all exits off the islands. He won't get away." Frazer tried to swallow before his too dry throat strangled him. He'd find Isadora. The question was whether or not she'd still be alive when he did.

He was about to dial Parker when his cell rang.

"We have a 911 from Dr. Campbell's cell phone." Terror gripped him as he walked back out into the blustery night. The chief continued. "Can't make out voices but it's all being recorded in case we can digitally enhance it later."

"Did you track the signal?"

"We have a call in to the service provider—"

"I'll call you back." Frazer hung up and called Parker. "911 call coming from Isadora Campbell's cell phone. I need to know exactly where that phone is, right now." Frazer waited for what seemed like forever.

Thirty seconds later. "Phone's at Parson's Point. Not sure exactly where but—"

"That's okay. I know where he'll be." It was the only place that made any sense. Grundy didn't know they were on to him. He thought he had plenty of time. Frazer got in the car, Randall throwing himself into the passenger side as Frazer drove away. "Call Tyson. Parson's Point. Fill him in."

His cell phone rang again, and he checked the number. Patrick Killion—the spook who was helping him hunt the Vice President's assassin. He owed the guy too much to ignore the call.

"What is it?" he bit out.

"I think I found her."

Shit. They'd been hunting this woman for weeks. "I'm in a situation here."

"She might be gone in an hour. You want her, you need to make some calls now."

Dammit. He didn't have time, and as far as he knew, she was only a threat to the bad guys. Shit, he needed to stop being such a hypocrite. He'd made choices that should have him in prison serving life for murder. It made Isadora Campbell's misdeeds positively tame in comparison.

"Leave her, Killion."

"You sure?"

"We'll figure it out later. I've got something more important to deal with." Much more important—like trying to save the only woman ever to sneak past his guard and into his heart from a vicious serial offender who'd been getting away with murder for decades. He hung up. He could only assume Seth Grundy didn't know Isadora had activated her cell phone. The guy hadn't planned to take her. Just like he hadn't planned to kill Helena. But Grundy sure as hell knew how to improvise.

***

Yellow police tape surrounded the entire dune system, but the place was unguarded. The tape was fighting a losing battle against the wind and more than one length had ripped free to dance above the lashing grass. Seth had Barney on a tight leash, the gun pointed very steadily at her poor dog as he motioned her ahead of him. There was no way he had Kit—or if he did, there was no way her sister was alive.

Izzy climbed carefully over the wooden fence, carrying the shovel. She'd been thrust back in time and was finally paying the price for her sins. Sand filled her socks, and her feet were freezing. For some reason, that felt like the most surreal thing of all—practical Izzy Campbell, walking in the sand dunes in winter without her shoes. The feeling of gritty particles between her toes made her teeth ache. She had no idea if anyone was coming to help her, or if she'd even successfully called 911.

"Where's Mary?" she asked.

"She's up ahead."

"Is she alive?"

"Of course she's alive. I tied her up is all."

Tied Mary up and then returned Izzy's car? Actually, she wouldn't put it past him, but she doubted that meant the woman was alive.

Every stride brought Izzy closer to the end. She wasn't going to just give up, but how could she get Seth to drop the gun? Her fingers tightened on the shovel.

The wind almost pushed her over when she reached the top of the foredune. A strong hand pushed her, and she stumbled down the steep slope on the other side, sprawling to the ground and drawing in a sharp breath as pain slashed her ribs.

She drew herself up, using the shovel as a brace.

"Get up," Seth shouted over the wind. "Keep moving." He waved the gun in her direction, and she staggered to her feet.

He was taking her back to where she'd buried her father all those years ago.

Before they'd fenced this area off, there had been a small access road that had cut through the sandy peaks. The Department of Natural Resources had torn up the asphalt and let the land take over. There was no sign of the road now.

She remembered the look on Frazer's face when she'd told him about that awful day—betrayal, bitter disappointment. She'd let him down. Pretended to be something she wasn't. Worse, she'd hurt him. So what if he didn't show it? She knew the truth. He'd opened up to her, and she'd committed a cardinal sin—she'd interfered with his investigation.

She started climbing the next dune but stopped after a few feet and turned around, clutching her side as if she was hurting. If she ever got the chance she was going to tell Frazer she loved him. The emotion had snuck up on her, taken her by surprise, and he deserved to know that what she felt for him was real. He deserved to know he mattered, not just as an FBI agent, but as a man. It wouldn't change the outcome—even if she lived through today, they had no chance of ever being a couple. But it would be closure. It would be the sort of brutal honesty Frazer could appreciate.

For now her only hope was to keep Seth talking. Make him forget she was supposed to be his next victim. "How did you know where to find the bodies, after all these years?"

"I staked a piece of wood near where I saw you digging that night, which was fine until that asshole Cromwell pulled it out a few years ago. Pastor gave me the idea of the metal detector with all the crazy treasure hunting he does. Knew more or less where to start." He shrugged. "Didn't take long."

"Why? Why dig up that poor woman's bracelet? Wasn't it enough to kill her?"

It was almost full dark, but she saw the flash of teeth when he smiled. "A friend of mine needed a little help in prison, and I wanted to claim what was rightfully mine."

Ferris Denker. Frazer's revelations about the man's crimes had shocked her. "She wasn't yours," she argued. "People aren't defined by how they die."

Seth moved closer. "She was mine when I put my hand around her throat and sent her to a better place."

The absolute certainty in his voice made her feel ill.

They got to the place where she'd buried her father, and Seth let go of Barney's leash. Thankfully the dog ran off to sniff grass. *Run, Barney.* Seth grabbed her shoulder and stuck the gun in her face before she could escape.

"I wish I could do the same to you, Izzy." His fingers squeezed painfully into her flesh, as if he were imagining them around her neck. "You'd know exactly how to come back and tell me if they're still there, waiting for me."

"Why didn't you just kill yourself?" she asked. He'd have done them all a favor.

He shook her roughly. "It's a mortal sin."

But serial rape and murder wasn't? She didn't say it. The guy wasn't sane. Then she registered what he said. "Why can't you do the same to me?" Not that she wanted that, but she wanted to know what the hell was going to happen to her.

His fingers squeezed harder, with bruising force. "It's got to look like a suicide. Poor Izzy. Tells the Feds about the terrible things she's done and can't live with herself. I'll be sure to comfort Kit for you." His fingers started squeezing the trigger. Fuck. She used every ounce of force she could muster and hit him in the temple with her plastercast.

He went down hard, but he wasn't unconscious. Izzy took off, dropping the shovel when it slowed her down. Running with battered ribs and a broken wrist was difficult enough. She heard a shot in the darkness, but ignored it. She wasn't going to sit around while Seth staged her suicide. *Asshole*. There was another shot and a warm sensation on one side of her calf where a bullet skimmed her skin.

She dove right and kept running.

***

Frazer had a reputation for being cool under pressure, but the truth was, underneath the facade, he was a raving lunatic with fantastic acting skills.

They pulled up behind Isadora's SUV. A pushbike was in the back.

Seth Grundy didn't know they were onto him. Frazer called Tyson. "Dr. Campbell's car is at Parson's Point. I don't think Grundy knows she's activated her cell or that we're actively looking for him yet. He knows Cromwell and Brubaker are both in the frame for the murders and probably figures that'll keep us busy while he has time to slip away."

"An officer found Mary Neville in the trunk of one of the cars at the garage. I have a horrible feeling she was there the whole time we were patting him on the back this morning. Getting his rocks off."

"Dead?" Frazer asked.

"Not yet."

Thank God for small mercies.

"I'll tell all units to come in dark with sirens off."

"Good. Me and Randall are going in now."

"My guys are five minutes out. Wait for back up."

Frazer cut the connection. No way was he waiting. "Ready?" he asked Randall.

The other agent nodded. "Let's do it."

They headed into the dunes, unable to use flashlights, because it would give away their presence, unable to hear any screams or conversation because of the howling wind. The sound of a gunshot did register, then another. Adrenaline raced through his bloodstream as he and Randall ran toward where it came from.

It was tough to see anything with the cloudy sky and no moon. "Go right," he said to Randall as he split left. A minute later a dark shadow ahead made him slow down as he tried to figure out whether or not it was Grundy.

He shouted, "FBI, put the weapon on the ground, hands on your head." But the shadow rabbited over the far side of the dune. Dammit.

Frazer leapt after the guy, approaching from the side. When he crested the top of the dune, a shot whizzed past his head. He threw himself to the ground, felt the horrifying snap as something went in his ankle. He rolled several times. Shit. His Achilles tendon had either torn or snapped. He heard another gunshot, and a grunt. Then he heard a woman scream, and his whole body froze. He tried to take a step, but he couldn't push off on his right foot.

This was not happening. He wasn't about to lose the one woman in his life he'd truly come to care for—shit, *love*—because he'd injured his ankle. It was too soon to know if they'd have a future together, but he intended to make sure she lived long enough to get to make a choice.

He dropped to his hands and knees and started to crawl.

***

Izzy's head whipped up when she heard Frazer's voice snatched away on the blustery wind. She heard a shot and yelled out instinctively. Damn. Had they caught Seth? Was she safe? Or had Seth shot Frazer?

That thought had her pausing in her headlong flight. Where was everyone? She turned back toward where she'd last seen Seth, surreptitiously peering through the grass. Below her, a shadow moved and she froze, not knowing if it was Seth, or someone trying to help her.

She caught a glint of what looked like FBI initials on the back of a black jacket and opened her mouth to cry for help, only to feel strong fingers manacling her ankle and hauling her roughly down the slope. She screamed and kicked with her free leg, catching the gun and knocking it out of his hand. The connection hurt, but it was worth the pain.

Seth swore, but rather than searching for the weapon, he threw himself down on top of her, jamming her cast against her battered ribs, causing so much pain she almost blacked out. He clamped one hand over her mouth to silence her, and the other squeezed her throat, cutting off her air.

Oh, God. She panicked, bucking and flailing beneath him. She could feel his arousal against her stomach and had enough presence of mind to be grateful he wasn't raping her.

"Do you see it, Izzy?" Seth whispered urgently in her ear.

She gave a nod, and he paused as if shocked, easing the pressure on her throat enough for her to draw in a tiny breath.

"What? What do you see?" His hot breath brushed her cheek and turned her stomach.

He ground his dick against her, and it made her want to throw up, but he was obviously obsessed with near-death experiences so she made something up.

"There's a woman, and she's beckoning me." It seemed to be what he needed to hear. "I feel as if I know her."

He pressed his fingers tighter around her throat again, dry humping her, because apparently this stuff got the guy off. "Tell her to wait for me, Izzy."

"Tell her yourself, asshole," came a voice from the sidelines. Frazer tackled Seth and took him flying down the dune, sand cascading around them as both men rolled on the ground.

Her gun. Izzy scrambled through the sand, hands searching as she sucked in oxygen and prayed her vision would realign sooner rather than later. Her fingers hit pay dirt, and she snatched up her Glock. *Don't let the firing mechanism be clogged.*

She tried to scream for help but nothing came out except a gravelly croak. She went down the steep side of the dune on her backside. Then she hesitated as one of the shadows leaned over the other and punched whoever was on the ground over and over in the face—just like Seth had done to Duncan Cromwell that morning.

"Stop." The word shuddered out of her mouth. Was it Frazer being beaten? Her finger eased onto the trigger, but she was unable to see clearly in the darkness. "Stop!"

"It's okay. It's me."

Frazer stood and stumbled toward her, and she realized he was okay. It was Seth knocked out cold. She ran toward Frazer. She wanted to throw her arms around him, but he got out his cuffs.

She froze.

He gave her a tired-sounding laugh. "Help me get him on his stomach so we can secure and arrest him."

She approached Seth with caution, and noticed Frazer was limping heavily. "What's wrong with your leg?"

"You hold the pistol on him, and I'll turn him over. Shoot him if he tries to escape, okay?"

She nodded, awed at the trust he was placing in her. Frazer rolled the unconscious man onto his front and then grabbed both wrists behind his back. The ratchet of metal against metal was the best sound she'd ever heard. Then the next best thing filtered through the night. The sound of other officers arriving, and Lucas Randall rushing toward them.

"Are you all right?" Randall asked.

"We are now. But we both need to go to the hospital." Frazer removed her Glock from her numb fingers and put it in his pocket. Took her good hand and kissed her knuckles. His were dark with blood.

She grabbed him when he collapsed to the ground. Her hands raced over him, looking for wounds.

He caught her hand, kissed it again. "I think I tore my Achilles. I feel like a lame frickin' idiot."

Izzy winced.

He handed her his flashlight. She gave his ankle a cursory examination to test the range of motion and make sure there was no bleeding, or obvious broken bones. There wasn't.

"Seth said he had Kit."

Frazer brushed her hair off her forehead. "Kit's fine." She opened her mouth to ask another question, but he preempted her. "Mary Neville is in the hospital." He dragged her close to his chest. "Come here." And kissed her full on the mouth.

She sank deep into it, unable to believe he was here, that he'd helped save her life, and he didn't hate her. The way he kissed her was both reverent and domineering, and a total turn-on despite the circumstances—until her beautiful retriever joined in.

She hugged Barney against her face, absorbing

the silky softness of his coat. She kissed him, too. "I'm so glad you're okay, boy."

"This is going to be a problem, isn't it?" Frazer spoke sternly to her dog and got a wet lick on the lips for his trouble. He laughed, and that's when Izzy knew how completely she had fallen in love with this guy. "I know I was angry earlier. I was furious with you for holding back information so important to the case. Mad as hell you hadn't trusted me enough to confide, which was stupid because why would you? As soon as I realized you were in danger it didn't seem to matter anymore." He kissed the corner of her lips. "I want a real relationship with you, Isadora Campbell. I'm done with this half measure shit."

She drew back, blinking away the emotion that wanted to overwhelm her. "You know that won't be possible." She kissed him anyway because soon she'd have to tell everyone the truth about what she'd done, and she didn't want to leave him. She didn't want this to end.

His arm wrapped around her, and she leaned against him as Randall orchestrated the arrest of a man she'd known almost her entire life.

"Don't tell them," Frazer whispered in her ear.

She closed her eyes. It was so tempting. "I have to."

His voice got lower. "I once shot a man like Seth Grundy in cold blood because he could have brought down the entire BAU. Should I turn myself in?"

Izzy looked at him open-mouthed, surprised he'd confessed that to her. Surprised he trusted her that much. She touched his stubbled jaw. "No, you shouldn't. People like that aren't like the rest of us.

If you killed him, he deserved to die."

Something in his eyes changed. Relaxed a fraction.

"But I've lived with this secret so long, I think it will destroy me if I don't tell the truth now."

He kissed the top of her head. "I still want a relationship with you."

She pulled away and shook her head. "It could damage your career. I might not be allowed to practice medicine—"

"I don't care."

The stark simplicity of his words made her want to believe him. "I'm also the guardian of a seventeen-year-old girl," she reminded him.

"Who is going to *love* Virginia."

She blinked at him. Touched his forehead. "Do you have a head injury?"

"Ha." He caught her hand and had a very serious expression on his face when he answered. "I've been fighting monsters since my parents died, Izzy." She swallowed as he finally called her that. Like he'd stopped holding her at arm's length. "But the one thing I never let myself search for was a way of moving on. I guess I figured if I kept hold of the anger and the pain I'd always have them with me. But I'm tired of doing nothing but hunt killers. I'm tired of being lonely. I want what they had. I think we might have a shot of that. What do you think?"

Paramedics placed Grundy on a stretcher and were carting him off with two armed officers flanking him.

She wiped away the tears that now were dripping off her chin. "You really want that with me? Because I'm already completely in love with you—"

He kissed her again, oblivious to the flashlights and law enforcement personnel milling around them. She let herself sink into the texture and taste of him. The hard planes and no bullshit attitude.

"What about Kit?" she asked, breaking away.

"We'll see what the DA decides to do about you before we talk to her. I don't want to rush you, but I think Kit would benefit from a change of scenery. There's a good school in walking distance from where I live."

She was unable to believe they were discussing this as the investigation whirled on around them. He mistook her silence for reluctance. "There are major trauma centers nearby, or if you want to go elsewhere or stay here, we can do the long distance thing for a while. Or I can get a transfer. Figure something out with work—hell, I can retire in a few years if I want."

She frowned up at him. "You'd go insane. You can't be serious."

"Of course I'm serious. Aren't you listening?"

"Chasing killers is what you were meant to do—"

"No. It's what a killer made me want to do, and for a long time it was all I had. For the first time ever I want something else. I want more."

How could she believe that? "But it's why you got divorced!"

"I got divorced because my wife was a bitch, and I'm done letting her destroy any chance I have of future happiness. Listen to me, Isadora Jane Campbell. All these years I've chased a thousand bad guys. For the first time, the thing that mattered most was not stopping him, but making sure you were safe. I don't let people in." His fingers squeezed her gently. "Ever. You have to know this is real."

She touched his face. "You don't let people in because they hurt you. I hurt you. I'm so sorry."

His smile was pure male arrogance. "Is that a yes to us being together?"

She shook her head. "You're incorrigible. And way too bossy."

"So I've been told." He caught her hand and kissed it. "I am not an easy man."

She swallowed. She'd been looking for someone her whole life, and she was terrified she was going to ruin it by not being brave enough to move forward. She rested her head against his shoulder, needing to be practical even though what she really wanted was to dance in a circle with happiness. "Let's take it one day at a time, okay?"

He kissed the top of her head as the paramedics finally arrived to check them out. "One day at a time for as long as it takes. You've got it."

***

The sound of keys in the main lock jerked him upright in his bunk. Footsteps moved down quiet corridors, and Ferris's heart pounded against his ribs. The footsteps stopped in front of his door, and there stood the warden.

"You want your chance to help people?" Her gaze raked his stained sweaty garb as if it were his fault he wasn't properly dressed. Ten minutes alone, and he'd have her stripped and bloody and begging. "I suggest you get dressed." She tapped something against her other hand. Maps. *Shit*.

They were going to let him show them where he buried the bodies. He shook with excitement. He'd draw out the process, give them a snippet of information on every outing—another name, another shallow grave. He'd prove his worth to the system and the families, delay his execution, and look for the chance to escape. He stood and dropped his pants, giving her a full view of his nakedness. She didn't look away, just stared into his eyes until he figured he better hurry up before she changed her mind.

The phone. Shit. He needed the phone.

"Would you mind giving me a moment of privacy, Warden, please?"

She stood farther back, between two hulking guards. The others stirred and shouted out questions from their cells.

"Where you taking him?"

"Mr. Denker wants to help us find the bodies of some of his victims," the warden said.

"Why you moving him in the middle of the night like a..." Billy Painter trailed off.

"Like a thief?" Warden Jones arched a sharp thin brow. She was a little harsh compared to the last guy. Denker knew women often compensated for lack of a penis with increased bitchery. "We're trying to avoid having a cavalcade of press on the road."

Nighttime suited him just fine.

"I don't trust her, Ferris," Billy complained.

Ferris palmed the phone, put the battery in real fast, and placed it under his dick as he pulled up his underwear. He pulled his prison-issue cotton shirt over his head, slipping the SIM card into a tiny hole he'd picked in the hem. He dragged on threadbare socks and the shit canvas shoes they were forced to wear. "It's okay, Billy. My lawyer told the press that I'd try and help those families get some closure. Governor must've agreed."

"I don't trust her, Ferris." Billy looked genuinely perplexed that he was using any way possible to get out of here.

"Hey, don't worry. I'll be back later. I'll tell you what color the leaves are and how sweet the grass smells." He hoped to hell he escaped. He put his arms through the slit in the bars and the biggest guard, a guy called Henry, attached shackles around his wrists. He stood back while they opened the door. Then they fettered his ankles and connected the restraints to his bound hands so he couldn't bring them high enough to wrap the chain around someone's neck and squeeze.

Spoilsports.

"See you later, guys." Hopefully not. The idea he might find some opportunity to escape ate at him.

He walked through corridor after corridor. Endless locks and checkpoints. Guards in their little fortified electronic cubicles, playing God with men's lives. The thought of hunting down the female guards, one at a time, held a satisfying sort of appeal. And then finishing off with the warden herself. He watched her walk in front of him. Plain black skirt suit with low heels. Nothing sexy on the outside, but when you hadn't made a woman scream in seventeen years you tended to readjust your criteria in a partner.

Finally they got to an outside door, and the cold damp air blew over his face like a benediction. He raised his face to the sky. Stars shone in a cool silvery light. Beautiful. His throat ached at the sight.

A guard opened the back door of a white prison van. Stood back for him to climb inside. Denker got in, and then the guy fastened him to the bars inside the van. All secure, Denker held out his hands for the maps.

The warden smiled. "This is your transport to Columbia, Mr. Denker."

A twinge of pain stabbed his heart. "But what about the governor? What about the bodies…"

The warden smiled, showing sharp teeth. "The governor refused your request. The families all agreed they would rather you pay for the murders of their loved ones than jerk them around in a fruitless search for their remains. The young women are with God, Mr. Denker. I doubt you'll be joining them any time soon."

She nodded her head, and the guard closed the door, and the van edged forward through the first gate. The full horror of his situation rammed home. He started pounding the crap out of his shackles and pulling and twisting, trying to get out of his chains. The two guards behind the wheel didn't even turn around.

They passed the spot where the death penalty protesters were camped, and there wasn't a single cocksucker awake. Useless bastards.

He started saying names, but the guards didn't react. He started giving detailed descriptions of where some of his victims were buried. He shouted until his throat was too sore to make more than a croak. Nothing. No reaction at all.

He remembered his phone and dug it out, along with the SIM card. The phone sprang to life, but the image on the screen showed a picture of Jesus, which was not his screensaver. *Shit*. He searched for the image his buddy, Seth, had sent him but there was nothing. He tried dialing 911 and sweat broke out over his forehead when someone picked up, but instead of a voice on the other end, he heard AC/DC's Highway to Hell.

His heart pounded as he realized this was really happening. All his plans and schemes, and they were too dumb to fall for them.

It took a couple of hours, but seemed like mere minutes before they were rolling along the long straight road to the prison.

The guard finally turned around. He waved a small digital recorder at him. "Prepared to meet your maker, Mr. Denker?"

Ferris shook his head, trembling and sweating at the idea that they were actually going to do this to him. "I want to see my lawyer."

The guard nodded slowly. Despite his bravado, they knew he was scared shitless.

They drove inside the prison gates. Stopped. Waited for the one door to close before the next one opened. Ferris looked behind him and watched his last chance of freedom disappear forever.

EPILOGUE

One Month Later...

Frazer hobbled down the steps onto the beach holding his cane. He'd had his Achilles tendon surgically repaired the day they'd arrested Grundy. He'd made Izzy tell Chief Tyson what she'd done while he was in pre-op, so the guy hopefully wouldn't haul her off to jail before Frazer spoke to the DA. Tyson had agreed, and Frazer had been carted off unconscious. He'd taken two weeks off work, citing injury, but really needing to spend quality time with the woman he'd so unexpectedly fallen for.

In those two weeks he hadn't discovered anything about her to make him change his mind.

He'd been back at the BAU for the last two weeks because his agents needed him. Even though he'd spoken to Izzy on the phone every day, he'd still gone crazy from being unable to touch her.

"Hey, stranger!" Kit ran over and hugged him when he reached the sand. "Miss me?" She rose up and gave him a kiss on the cheek.

"Depends." He eyed her narrowly. "Done anything I need to know about in a professional capacity?"

A dimple formed in her cheek, and she shook her head. "I did get a ninety-five on my math midterm."

"What happened to the other five percent?" he asked. Inside he smiled. She was a smart kid. A smart kid who did well when she applied herself.

She punched his arm. "For that, I won't tell you where your one true love is."

He rolled his eyes. She used that term to rile them both, but inside...inside he knew it was true. Isadora Campbell was his one true love, and he had some news for her.

He raised a bored brow at Kit and then pulled out his phone and checked the tracker app he'd installed on Izzy's cell.

He looked south where the beach curved, and there she was, running towards him, Barney loping at her side.

Her face didn't alter, but he knew the moment she spotted him. Her stride lengthened and, even though she was bright red from exertion, she ran faster.

She got to within a few feet and stopped dead, bending over as her lungs pumped oxygen. Kit handed her a bottle of water, and he watched her take a big gulp, liquid running down her throat in rivulets he wanted to lick off her skin.

She wiped her mouth. "Hello, you." She seemed nervous, unsure. She was always like that after a short absence, as if worried the time apart might have changed his mind about her, about them. It hadn't. "You're early."

"I couldn't wait any longer." He took a step, irritated by the cane he still needed to use to get about. He wrapped his free hand around her and pulled her to him. She rested her palms on his chest, her wrist in a light cast now, almost healed.

He kissed her just as she was about to start telling him that she was all hot and sweaty. Like he cared. He'd spent thirteen days without her in his arms, and the gap in his life felt like a black hole.

She sank into him, tasting sweet as a sea breeze. Heat invaded his cells—not just lust, although lust was definitely a big part of it. But love too. A deep abiding love he wanted to nurture and cherish. He needed to tell her. Needed to give her the words.

Someone cleared their throat, and he remembered they had an audience.

Kit.

Barney jumped against them and Frazer leaned down to give the dog a hug.

Izzy stepped back. "How's the ankle?"

"Driving me crazy."

"More crazy," muttered Kit.

He ignored her.

"Does it hurt?" Izzy asked him.

"Only when the physio tries to maim me during so-called therapy and looks happy doing it."

She grinned, a sparkle lighting those gorgeous green eyes. "I'll massage it later."

"Okay, that's it. I'm outta here," Kit raised her hands in grossed out self-defense. She winked and headed up the steps. "See you later, G-man."

"She has a shift at the diner so she's just being dramatic."

"Kit, dramatic? Never." He'd held the girl's hand when they'd buried her best friend. Izzy hadn't attended the funeral in deference to Duncan Cromwell. Kit had held up surprisingly well, and she and Jesse Tyson had supported each other through the ordeal.

Frazer eased Izzy back into his arms. She wasn't getting away from him that easily. She'd been on leave from the hospital ever since Seth Grundy had been arrested. He knew the enforced vacation was driving her nuts, but she'd put the time to good use, getting Kit on track.

"I've got some news for you," he told her, holding her steady in his arms. This was the thing she feared the most. Being sent to prison and maybe stripped of her license, unable to practice medicine ever again. "The DA's office has decided not to press charges." She sank her head against his chest, and her warm breath touched him through his shirt. "They still want you to maybe testify against Grundy so the truth might come out at trial."

Her grip on his shirt tightened. "I'll do anything as long as that bastard gets convicted."

Frazer stroked her hair. "Honestly, I doubt they'll even call you as a witness. The prosecution has got Mary Neville, and your Uncle Ted's van. There's forensic evidence from the oilcan where he tried to burn the shoes of his victims—some were still identifiable. There are images on his phone, and there's his connection to the now dearly departed Ferris Denker."

"I'm glad Denker's dead. Those poor women."

Frazer nodded. He didn't tell her he'd been in the viewing gallery during the execution. Him, Art Hanrahan, and a dozen of the family members of some of Denker's victims. It hadn't been pretty, but justice had been served.

"How's Duncan Cromwell doing?" Izzy tugged him up the stairs. They were the walking wounded. Her with her fractured wrist, him with his stupid cane.

"He's going to get probation." He watched her face for a reaction. She crossed her arms but nodded.

"I'm glad. I know he hurt me, but I don't think he was really sane at the time. Kind of reminded me of my mother when she killed Dad."

"Kit still dealing with the information okay?" They'd agreed to wait until after Helena's funeral before they'd told her the truth. It was a lot to handle.

Izzy shrugged. "She took it remarkably well. The main thing she wants is for Dad to be buried with Mom. I think it would probably be apt"—she pulled a face—"under the circumstances." She checked her watch and rather than drag him into the bathroom for a save-water shower, she led him to the front door. And opened it wide.

"Are you throwing me out? I just got here." He grinned as he said it. The sound of hammering had him frowning. Up on the roadside he noticed a man installing two white posts. "What's going—?"

"Shush." She placed two fingers over his lips, and he kissed them. "Watch."

The workman hung a large real estate sign, first on the beach house, and then on this property.

He told himself it was the wind that made his eyes water. "Really?"

"I was always going to sell up. I needed a fresh start." She paused for a moment, looking at him from out of the corner of her eye. "Interestingly, I got a call from a hospital in Aquia this week, offering me a job. I don't suppose you know anything about that, do you?"

He figured it might be wiser not to confess to everything just yet. He opened his mouth to deflect, but she smiled at him.

"I told them I had to think about it." She reached for his hand. "With this news from the DA, I'm finally free to move on with my life. I want to do that with you. I love you, Linc."

She'd said it to him several times, but he hadn't had the nerve to say it back. Until now. He cupped her face. "I love you, Dr. Campbell. Thank you for trusting me with your heart."

Joy shone from her eyes. "I didn't seem to have a choice."

"I know the feeling." He grinned and then winced as a pain shot from his ankle to his hip.

She frowned down at his foot. "I promised you a massage."

"Is it going to hurt?" he asked, carefully, because he'd been ready to put a bullet in the physio earlier.

"Only if you want it to." She leaned into his chest and whispered huskily, "But you are going to need to hold on for this, Linc."

He laughed and kissed her. "I won't let go."

"I'll make it worth your while." Her eyes danced, and at that moment he knew that no matter how much darkness he dealt with, he'd always come home to the light. He'd come home to Izzy.

COLD JUSTICE SERIES OVERVIEW

A Cold Dark Place (Book #1)
Cold Pursuit (Book #2)
Cold Light of Day (Book #3)
Cold Fear (Book #4)

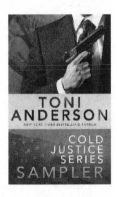

Free Sampler

Want to try the books without buying? Or share with friends who might also enjoy the stories? The first three chapters of each book are available online in a free ebook sampler.

Cold Justice Series Books 1-3 are also available as audiobooks from Amazon, Audible and iTunes.

A COLD DARK PLACE
Cold Justice Series Book 1

Justice isn't always black or white.

Former CIA assassin Alex Parker works for The Gateway Project, a clandestine government organization hell-bent on taking out serial killers and pedophiles before they enter the justice system. Alex doesn't enjoy killing, but he's damn good at it. He's good at dodging the law, too--until a beautiful rookie agent has him wondering what it might be like to get caught.

FBI Special Agent Mallory Rooney has spent years hunting the lowlife who abducted her identical twin sister eighteen years ago. Now, during an on-going serial killer investigation, Mallory begins to suspect there's a vigilante operating outside the law. She has no choice but to take him down, because murder isn't justice. Is it?

Sometimes it's cold and dark.

When Mallory starts asking questions, The Gateway Project management starts to sweat, and orders Alex to watch her. As soon as they meet, the two begin to fall in love. But the lies and betrayals that define Alex's life threaten to destroy them both--especially when the man who stole her sister all those years ago makes Mallory his next target, and Alex must reveal his true identity to save the woman he loves.

COLD PURSUIT
Cold Justice Series Book 2

Single mom Vivi Vincent is thrust into her worst nightmare when she's trapped inside a mall during a terror attack along with her eight-year-old son. With the help of Jed Brennan, an FBI special agent on enforced leave, Vivi and her son survive the assault. But the danger is far from over.

Vivi's son may have witnessed critical details of the terrorists' future plans and is targeted for death, but he's mute, and he's traumatized. Still someone launches a strike against the FBI's safe house, and Jed fears the bad guys have an inside man. No longer knowing who to trust, he hides mother and son in a log cabin deep in the heart of the Wisconsin Northwoods. There Jed and Vivi try to figure out how to unlock the information inside her son's head. What they don't bargain for is the red-hot attraction that flares between them, or the extent of the sinister plot that threatens to rip apart not only any chance of happiness they might have together, but also the very fabric of American society.

COLD LIGHT OF DAY
Cold Justice Series Book 3

Physicist Scarlett Stone is the daughter of the man considered to be the most notorious Russian agent in FBI history. With her father dying in prison she's determined to prove he's innocent, but time is running out. Using a false identity, she gains access to the Russian ambassador's Christmas party, searching for evidence of a set-up.

Former Navy SEAL, now FBI Special Agent, Matt Lazlo, is instantly attracted to Scarlett but life is too complicated to pursue a politician's daughter. When he discovers she lied to him about her identity, he hunts her down with the ruthless efficiency he usually reserves for serial killers.

Not only does Scarlett's scheme fail, it puts her in the sights of powerful people who reward unwanted curiosity with brutality. The FBI—and Matt— aren't thrilled with her, either. But as agents involved in her father's investigation start dying, and the attempts to stop Scarlett intensify, Matt and his colleagues begin to wonder. Could they have a traitor in their midst?

As Scarlett and Matt dig for the truth they begin to fall passionately for one another. But the real spy isn't about to let anyone uncover their secrets, and resolves to remain firmly in the shadows—and for that to happen, Matt and Scarlett have to die.

DEAR READER

Thank you for reading *Cold Fear*. I hope you enjoyed it. If you did, please help other readers find this book:

1. If you have time to leave a review, I appreciate it. Thanks.

2. To keep up-to-date with releases and find out about exclusive offers check out my website (http://www.toniandersonauthor.com) and sign up for my Newsletter/Mailing List.

3. Come "like" my Facebook Page: https://www.facebook.com/pages/Toni-Anderson-Author-Page/153356538022559?ref=hl

4. Interested in a writer's life? All my web links are on my website www.toniandersonauthor.com. I love chatting to readers!

Thanks again!

ACKNOWLEDGMENTS

For this book, I spent a lot of time researching North Carolina's Outer Banks. I took a few liberties with the landscape and decided to create my own fictional town for the setting. It's a truly fascinating region with a rich history that needs exploring—preferably from one of those gorgeous beach houses ☺.

I'd like to send an extra-special "thank you" to Sandra Buckenham who walked me through some of the medical aspects of the story. Needless to say, I used artistic license with all information gleaned, and any errors in the story are mine.

As always, biggest thanks go to my amazing critique partner Kathy Altman—she rocks! Also editors, Alicia Dean, and Joan at JRT Editing, who helped get this manuscript into shape, and my *beta* readers! I'm very grateful to Syd Gill for interpreting my vision and creating the awesome covers for the *Cold Justice Series*.

Thanks to my fabulous husband and children who put up with my insanity. It wouldn't be worth it without you!

ABOUT THE AUTHOR

New York Times and *USA Today* international bestselling author, Toni Anderson, writes dark, gritty Romantic Suspense. Her novels have been nominated for the prestigious Romance Writers of America® RITA® Award, Gayle Wilson Award of Excellence, Holt Medallion, Daphne du Maurier Awards for Excellence, and National Readers' Choice Awards in Romantic Suspense. *A Cold Dark Place* won the 2014 New England Readers' Choice Award for Romantic Suspense.

A graduate of Marine Biology from the University of Liverpool, and the University of St. Andrews, Toni was a Post-doctoral Research Scientist for several years, and travelled the world with her work. After living in seven different countries, she finally settled in the Canadian prairies with her Irish husband and two children. Now she spends her time talking to the voices in her head and making things up. Toni has no explanation for her oft-times dark imagination, and only hopes the romance makes up for it. She's addicted to reading, dogs, tea (never travels without it), and chocolate. She loves to hear from readers.

Toni donates 15% of her royalties from *Edge of Survival* to diabetes research.

Find out more on her website and sign up for her newsletter to keep up-to-date with releases.

www.toniandersonauthor.com

REVIEWS

COLD LIGHT OF DAY
(Cold Justice Book #3)
(2015 Holt Medallion Finalist)

"This has easily cruised into my top ten romances … in the history of EVER."—Heroes and Heartbreakers.

TOP PICK "*Cold Light of Day* has all the elements of a great romantic suspense…danger, romance, action, and intrigue. I'd recommend *Cold Light of Day* to any romantic suspense reader looking for a thrilling adventure!"—Harlequin Junkie

COLD PURSUIT
(Cold Justice Book #2)
(2015 The Gayle Wilson Award of Excellence Romantic Suspense Finalist)

"I'd highly recommend *Cold Pursuit* to any romantic suspense reader." —Harlequin Junkie

"Toni Anderson's new Cold Justice series is sizzling suspense and hot romance – the perfect summer read!" —Mom's the Word.

A COLD DARK PLACE
(Cold Justice Book #1)
(Winner 2014 New England Readers' Choice in Romantic Suspense. 2015 Holt Medallion Finalist)

"Toni magically blends sizzling chemistry between Alex and Mallory with lots of suspenseful action in

A Cold Dark Place. At times I wanted to hide my eyes, not knowing if I could face what might or might not happen! The edge of your seat suspense is riveting!" —Harlequin Junkies.

"Recommended for fans of Toni Anderson and fans of dark romantic suspense. You'd definitely love this one!" —Maldivian Book Reviewer's Realm of Romance.

THE KILLING GAME
(2014 RITA® Finalist, and National Readers Choice Awards Finalist)

"I'd recommend this to any romantic suspense reader looking for a unique, intricately woven story that will really touch you." —Peaces of Me (5 Stars)

"This is a smart story. This is a sexy story. This is a well written story. This is one of my favorite romantic suspense stories I've read all year. I wish there was more!" —Love Affair With An e-Reader (5 Stars)

DARK WATERS
(International bestseller. National Readers Choice
Awards Finalist)

"In this action-packed contemporary, Anderson (*Dangerous Waters*) weaves together a tapestry of powerful suspense and sizzling romance." — *Publishers Weekly*.

"The pacing in this book is superb. The tension really never lets up … I never felt there was a good 'stopping point' in this book, which is probably why I was reading all night." —Smart Bitches, Trashy Books.

DANGEROUS WATERS
(International bestseller. 2013 Daphne du Maurier
Award Finalist)

"With a haunting setting and a captivating cast of characters, Anderson has crafted a multifaceted mystery rife with secrets. Readers will have to focus, as red herrings abound, but the result is a compulsively engrossing page-turner." —*Romantic Times* (4 Stars)

"A captivating mix of suspense and romance, *Dangerous Waters* will pull you under." —Laura Griffin, *New York Times* and *USA Today* best-selling author

EDGE OF SURVIVAL

"Anderson writes with a gritty, fast-paced style, and her narrative is tense and evocative." —HEA *USA Today*

"... more substance than one would expect from a romantic thriller." —*Library Journal Reviews*

"*Edge of Survival* is without a doubt, one of the most exciting, romantic, sexy stories I've had the pleasure of reading this year and I will definitely be looking for more by Toni Anderson." —Blithely Bookish (5 Stars)

"Sensual, different; romance with a bit of angst, just how I like them; *Edge of Survival* is a romantic suspense not to be missed." —Maldivian Book Reviewer's Realm of Romance (5 Stars)

STORM WARNING
(Best Book of 2010 Nominee —The Romance Reviews)

"*Storm Warning* is an intense, provocative paranormal romance with a suspenseful twist...This is a book that I am unquestionably adding to my keeper collection." —Night Owl Reviews (TOP PICK)

"It is exactly the way I like my romantic suspense novels to be." —The Romance Reviews

"The plot is full of suspense and some pretty incredible plot twists. ... will have you on the edge of your seat." —Coffee Time Romance & More

SEA OF SUSPICION
(Best Book of 2010 Nominee —The Romance Reviews. National bestseller.)

"Deeply atmospheric and filled with twists and turns, *Sea of Suspicion* kept me flying eagerly through the pages." —All About Romance

"*Sea of Suspicion* is one heck of a book! The twists, turns, passion, and many colorful characters give Ms. Anderson's novel a delightful edge." —Coffee Time Romance

"Set along the coast of Scotland, *Sea of Suspicion* is a riveting story of suspense and the depths and heights of human character." —The Romance Reviews

HER LAST CHANCE
(2014 Daphne du Maurier finalist)

"A high intensity story, with action from the first page on, an intricate suspense tale with twists and turns that are surprising and a conclusion that is as near to closure as is possible to come. The characters are deep and rather brooding, but manage to lose themselves in each other. And the writing is clever, hot and altogether fabulous!" — Ripe for Reader

"From the opening scene I was turning the pages totally entranced in the story. I've loved all this authors books but at this moment this has to be my favorite." —SnS Reviews

HER SANCTUARY
(National bestseller)

"*Her Sanctuary* is a riveting fast-paced suspense story, filled with twists, turns, and danger. As the story flows seamlessly between the protagonists and antagonists, the tension rises to fever pitch. Just when you think you know the good guys from the bad, Anderson provides a surprising twist, or two." —Night Owl Romance (TOP PICK)

"Suspenseful, riveting and explosive, this reader absolutely loved this story." —Fallen Angel Reviews (5 Angels)

"Ms. Anderson presents us with one fantastic story that has me wanting more." —Romance Junkies (4.5 Blue Ribbons)

Made in the USA
Charleston, SC
13 May 2015